FAME FARM

For Robin,

All The Best!

Bruce Cook

3 - XI - 24

BRUCE COOK

ISBN: 978-1-7344168-0-0

Grateful appreciation for the editing talents of Shauna Zurbrug and Laurie Veitch.

Special thanks to Jeff Pfeifer for encouraging me to abandon tradition and pursue the electronic path to publication.

Book design by ebooklaunch.com

"To hell with the truth! As the history of the world proves, the truth has no bearing on anything. It's irrelevant and immaterial... The lie of a pipe dream is what gives life to the whole misbegotten mad lot of us, drunk or sober."

— Eugene O' Neil
The Iceman Cometh
1956

In memory of Susan Cook Behring
whose writing talent the world will never know

THE PROLOGUE

Somewhere in the hills north of Los Angeles.
May 1974

B ill Parker had run out of time. The money had run out weeks
before. All that remained was his determination to finish his
senior film. A Technicolor term paper that would demonstrate to peer
and professor at the U.S.C. School of Cinema that Orson Welles The
Second was about to premiere a world awakening Hollywood career.

God granted perfectly even grey skies over the Los Angeles Basin
for Parker's final day of filming as a student. The heavenly haze came
not from the exhaust fumes of several million automobiles crossing the
asphalt terrain, but rather from a fearsome firestorm whipped into a
frenzy by unexpected, late springtime Santa Ana winds. The crackling
dry air had ignited the brush-covered hillsides of the northern San
Fernando Valley. While it was barely six o'clock in the morning, the
sun was all but lost in the soot billowing over the city.

Word of the growing inferno spread over the radio air waves
catching Parker's attention as he sped out of downtown Los Angeles
with his film crew. He had planned to avoid the morning rush hour
traffic in order to have the camera roll by eight a.m. on the ranch
property secured by his collaborator, fellow film student, Randy Stein.
They had no idea that the ranch was in the direct path of the flames.

"I thought the fire season in L.A. was during the late summer
months," Parker said, turning his head momentarily away from the
road to see if Randy was awake and listening to the radio reports.

The only response from Stein was a grunt, confirming Bill's
original suspicion that the producer was asleep.

"How can you sleep?" Bill demanded in the excited tone of a boy
facing his Little League Championship game. "Wake up, Stein. We have

1

to plan. If this film is as good as I think it is, we can use it after graduation as our passport to Hollywood. It might open a few doors at the networks or studios."

Parker's challenge to rouse Stein was of no use. Instead, Randy turned away from him, resting his head against the back of the seat in the truck, positioning himself facing the passenger door. "Yeah, yeah, wake me when we get to the ranch," was all he said, pulling the collar of his jacket up over his ears to reinforce his private territory in the cab of the truck.

Parker's mind raced, as the early morning freeway slowed over the Cahuenga Pass in to the San Fernando Valley. His cast and crew bumped up and down on the hard metal of the rear flatbed of the truck with every depression of the brake pedal in traffic. The star of the film was Parker's roommate, Chris Reynolds, a blonde, extremely handsome Midwestern boy who held the precious, loaded 35 millimeter camera in his lap, and was surrounded on either side by the sorority co-eds that Randy Stein had lassoed to help out under the promise of some Hollywood magic.

Charmed by the devastating masculinity of the star, the two blondes clung tightly to each of Chris's arms, nuzzling against his big frame for warmth, for protection, and for the magic of Hollywood they wanted to experience.

Randy Stein lived the life of Hollywood magic. His father was Benton Stein. Rich, powerful and omnipresent, the elder Stein had his formidable hands in every piece of the L.A. power pie. Randy knew, from a very early age, that all he had to do was breathe, and the glitter and glory of Hollywood would be his own. So he slept in the truck, borrowed from one of his dad's warehouses, as his buddy Bill Parker drove like a maniac into the valley. Randy Stein did not require a passport to Hollywood. He held a gilded invitation.

The closer the Cecil B. DeMille reincarnate, his sleeping producer, cast and crew in the rear flatbed, got to their valley ranch location, the darker the morning horizon became. Bill Parker could now see the flames of the fire he had been warned of. The perimeter edge of the foothills glowed red-orange from the approaching devastation.

"Wake up, Stein. Look what's ahead." Parker jabbed his snoozing cohort with his free hand.

"Jesus! What's that?" Randy yelled out, witnessing the burning hillsides all around them.

"It's still miles away. We'll be okay." Parker was the eternal optimist. He had no choice. The film would be shot today. "You know, the billowing clouds of smoke will enhance this film. I may even start the shot on a long, slow pull-back from the flames on the hills, panning the camera over to Chris mounted on the gas-pump crucifix. This fire is really lucky for me," proclaimed Parker, offering his cinematic vision to a still half-asleep producer horrified by Dante's Inferno, L.A. style.

"You know, we may be SOL here, man," offered a rapidly sobering Stein, sitting up ram-rod straight in the seat to get a better view of the fire.

"No way," countered Bill Parker. "We're almost at the ranch. The fire is still miles away."

"Get a grip on reality. We're going to need hours to set up and film. By the time we're ready, the flames could be on top of us. Besides, are you forgetting the most important part?" Randy asked accusingly.

"No, I haven't forgotten," replied Parker in a tone that began to display his fear of not getting his movie finished in time.

"How the hell are we going to convince the ranch crew to let us start a controlled fire on their property when the entire goddamned Valley is burning all around us?" Stein was shouting.

But, there was a kind of devil-may-care, "are we absolutely, brilliantly insane," quality to his scream of protest. It was a "just dare me to do it" attitude. Actually, it was the kind of impossible problem Randy loved the most.

"We set this all up in advance. The ranch approved the plan, out in the middle of that dirt field. Even the fire department gave us authorization. I've got the permit and the water truck is set to be there," offered Parker as he turned down the final road to the end of the property they had scouted weeks before.

"You don't actually think that the ranch or the fire department will honor that permit, do you?"

"We're going to finish the movie today," answered Parker.

The student film was called, "American Dreamer." Randy Stein was certain that his ambitious partner was the real American dreamer. The star of the film, Chris Reynolds, was now pounding on the rear window of the truck cab, demanding to know what was up. The two co-ed assistants had evidently had enough of all the Hollywood magic. Soot and ash from the fire had dusted their pony-tail-tied hair, and the bump and thump of the ride down the final mile of unpaved road was more than they had signed up to handle.

"Stop the truck!" Chris demanded. "Hey, Bill, can you hear me? Stop the truck!"

It was no use. Bill actually stepped on the gas pedal, and the truck lunged forward over a particularly big pot-hole in the road. Chris flew back, still holding the camera in his arms, landing on the metal flatbed with a rather loud thump. Then, Bill made a sharp right and the Hollywood cargo slid to the far left of the truck. Chris held the camera close to his chest, clutching it with his arms crossed around the metal, as if he were holding an infant. The girls let out a major scream, begging Bill to stop. He did. They had arrived at the main gate of the ranch.

• • •

"Watch out for the jagged metal edge on top of the pump," yelled Bill Parker from across the dirt field. Chris Reynolds was climbing up on top of a rusting gas pump. The relic from the 1930's once served a ranch that spanned thousands of acres, now growing post-war babies in row after row of tract houses.

Perched on top of the old gas pump was a ten-foot tall cross, erected by Bill and Randy for the final shot of "American Dreamer." It was pure poetry for these post-teenage future Hollywood moguls.

Bill left the camera across the field to help Randy put Chris on top of the cross, mounted on the metal symbol of the industrialized Twentieth Century.

Blonde, muscular, macho Chris Reynolds was a perfect modern day Jesus, again crucified by an abusive society consumed by greed.

Actually, Jesus looked more like a surfer in a loin cloth. Bill Parker called for "Places." He was about to roll the camera.

"What the hell do you think you're doing? Are you crazy! Cut that out right now!" yelled a ranch hand running full speed across the dirt field into Chris's shot. The man waved his arms in all directions to get their attention, arriving out of breath, and spitting his final words, "You're not supposed to be here doing this. The whole area has been evacuated. Now, pack up and get the heck out of here before you get toasted."

"We've got a permit. We even got permission from the fire department," Parker waved his papers in the man's face.

"Do you think those papers mean jack when the entire ranch is going up in flames?" The ranch hand yanked the papers out of Parker's hand and threw them on the ground, stomping them into the dirt. "Now, get the hell out of here — and get out of here now. What the blazes is he doing up there on that pump in his underwear?" The rancher rolled his eyes in disbelief and took off in the direction of the main ranch house nearby.

"We don't have much time. Everybody get ready. We'll take this as fast as possible. Randy, start the fire around the pump." Parker ordered Chris to prepare for his delivery. The co-eds were sent back to the pickup truck. Randy then struck a match and lit a bale of hay set in the foreground dirt near the crucifix crowned gas pump.

"Action," called out Parker from behind the camera, across the open field. The fire was now all around them, burning the grass hillsides right down to the edge of the dirt. Parker started his shot on the perimeter flames, panning up into the grey, smoke-filled sky, then down on to Jesus. Sparks from the bale of hay below floated up into the frame of his lens. He was in cinematic bliss. Parker yelled out for Chris to deliver the final speech of the movie.

Chris delivered right on the money. He was a cool kind of Jesus, despite the holocaust of fire around him. On the third take, Parker got his scene and screamed out, "Print it, and let's get the hell out of here!"

Jesus leapt down from the crucifix, joining Bill and Randy who were attempting to put out the fire that had nearly consumed the bale of hay. "What are we doing," asked Chris, staring at the now smoldering bale. He could hardly see his fellow filmmaker-cum-firemen pals for all the thick smoke from the bigger fire choking the air. "Do we really need to be sure this bale of hay isn't burning — what's it going to do, start a bigger fire! Let's get out of here!"

With that, the three musketeers made a dash for the pickup. The two co-eds Randy had brought along for some fun trembled inside the cab. All five of them huddled together as Randy took the wheel of his father's truck and floored the gas pedal. "American Dreamer" was "in the can." Bill Parker clutched his precious film as the truck bounded over the rough road, away from the flames, heading back downtown to U.S.C.

"So, where do we go from here?" asked Randy as he looked over at Bill Parker holding the can of film.

"Hollywood, here we come!" answered Parker.

The rest of the truck was consumed in coughing, attempting to expel the noxious fumes from their lungs.

CHAPTER 1

High in the hills of Beverly Hills
Five Years Later
August 1980

"I don't want you to worry, but we do have a small problem." The voice on the other end of Bill's phone was very cool. Bill sat in his bed and listened. "I'll do everything possible to back you up, Bill. I always backed you on 'The Reilly's', didn't I?" The voice was still very cool, but oh-so-sincere, so secure. Bill couldn't remember ever being backed up by this guy.

John Moran, the studio senior executive vice president, took unfathomable delight in having some control over Bill Parker's destiny. Never mind that it was Parker's success as producer of "The Reilly's of San Marino" that added the "executive," and then the "senior" to Moran's ever enlarging title. Moran resented Bill's talent. He was simply, plainly jealous.

"I thought you said the deal was practically a commitment?" Bill asked directly.

"Practically is not the same as for sure, now is it?" said Moran.

"And success does not necessarily correspond with ability." Bill was losing his temper.

"What was that?" Moran snapped back.

"Nothing. Look, what do you want me to do?" Bill changed his tone half-heartedly. This new job meant everything to him. His life was on the line. Work was his life.

"Before I can help you, we need to overcome a hurdle the studio just threw in my face." Moran continued, holding onto his secret hurdle. He wanted Bill to beg for the information. "Apparently, somebody is out to get you. You know, Jim Underberg, my new boss

7

that the studio brought over from the network? Somebody told him to stay away from you. I quote, 'Bill Parker is manipulative, political, and ambitious.' That's what he told me."

Under the pretense of helping Bill land the top spot on a new show the studio was producing, Moran stabbed him with his insider information.

Bill went nuts. Some unknown enemy, possibly someone he considered a friend, was calling him "manipulative, political, and ambitious" and hurting his shot at a new series, a new life in Hollywood. "You're damned right I'm manipulative….What were the other words?" Bill asked Moran incredulously.

"Political and ambitious," Moran replied, laughing slightly.

The laugh did Bill in. "You're damned right, Moran, and you can tell Underberg as well — I'm all that and a whole hell of a lot more. And so the fuck is anyone else worth anything in this fucking dream town!"

A thousand disjointed thoughts raced through Bill's brain. How long would it take to put together another deal if this was lost? Who was his enemy? Why had he lost his cool with Moran, let him get the better of him?

"Bill, get me some names, heavy-hitters that will vouch for you, say you're okay — balance the shit." Moran was generous. Bill wanted to believe that he meant to help.

"John, I worked at your studio for almost five years. I know every employee from the mail room kid to the Chairman, Benton Stein. Are you kidding me about this list?"

"Call me back in a half hour, when you calm down. Make a list, an "A" list of the biggest names in the business who know you, and like you. Don't worry, I'll take care of it. It will all be fine," Moran reassured him.

How many times had Bill heard, "Don't worry, I'll take care of it." Five minutes, five days, five years later, the same person would say, "Sorry, friend, I just couldn't save it. Out of my hands. Tried. Did my best. Really."

"Moran, what if this list isn't enough?"

"Then you better win the Emmy next week, Parker, or you're in for a very long winter." Moran hung up.

Bill lay absolutely still in his California king-size mattress that sat on the floor of his otherwise empty master suite.

For the previous four years Bill had slept in a one bedroom apartment in nearby Westwood, paying top dollar rent of three hundred a month. Now he lived in Trousdale, a contemporary hillside enclave on the north slopes of Beverly Hills, studded with enormous white marble houses replete with swimming pools suitable for expensive and elegant hotels.

His business manager had made him buy it. After all, Bill had made over a million dollars the previous season as the head writer-producer of the network television hit, "The Reilly's of San Marino." He was in the big time, he needed to live like a success, he needed the tax write-off, he had to have a house, advised the business manager. Besides, the manager's wife was a real estate agent in Beverly Hills. She had found him a fabulous house, at a fabulous price.

At 5:11 a.m., Bill Parker gave up pretending to sleep, bolting from his bed. Sliding open a massive ten-foot-tall wall of moveable glass, he headed for his new swimming pool. The Olympic-sized tank of water protruded out from the house, over to the very edge of the property. A cliff dropped dozens of feet down to the next marble palace carved into the hillside below. The pool seemed to span infinity, magically stretching out over the cliff and meeting the horizon. Tall, symmetrical palm trees, a half dozen of them, lined the pool to one side. A living Hockney painting.

Bill dove in. Instantly relieved by the velvet chill of the early morning water temperature, he moved his tall, athletic naked frame through the glorious liquid, all thoughts of Moran and the studio drowning in the water around him.

Stroking the pool harder and faster, Bill Parker completed his ritual one hundred lengths in the allotted twenty minutes he now dedicated to aquatic exercise. It was just part of the mental justification for the extravagant house. Tapping the tiled edge of the fifty foot long hole in his yard, Bill ended his swim and propelled his muscular torso out of the water, and up onto land with Olympic grace.

Alone, out of work, and living in a grand but empty Beverly Hills home, Bill Parker stood naked, semi-erect from his swim, surveying his fate and the City of Angels spread out at dawn before him beyond the edge of his property. At twenty-nine, he was a millionaire, at least on paper. He was a nationally recognized television writer-producer nominated for an Emmy Award. He was fighting for his life.

CHAPTER 2

Early 1975
Downtown Beverly Hills

"It's ten minutes of noon and that asshole Stein still isn't here. What the fuck does he think this is, a resort?"

Bob Davidson was looking for blood. Most mornings, most afternoons, and probably most evenings, he was angry. If he didn't have someone in particular to be angry with, he had the entire world to despise. Davidson was the perfect boss for the upstarts in the mail room at the William Morris Agency in Beverly Hills.

Randy Stein deserved the wrath of Bob Davidson. He was a smart-ass, full of himself, or, as Davidson was fond of saying, the perfect young-asshole-agent-in-training. Stein was also a fast talker, bright, a real manipulator, a complete lady killer, and, in general, he was totally wild. "Fuck" was a word he used often, and did often. As often as possible.

Six-foot-four-inches, his body was the perfect male "A" frame. Broad shoulders, tapering to a small waist, with long, muscular legs, Randy Stein had grown up on the swim team. If show business had not been such an attractive calling, he might have easily ended up a lifeguard at the Santa Monica beach. He had very dark, wavy hair, and blue eyes. Incredible blue eyes with long, dark lashes.

Randy Stein still lived his life as an untouchable. His self-assurance continued, in part, due to the safety net established by his father, Benton Stein, who had accomplished the impossible in his lifetime. His rise to the top of the show business strata was legendary. At the same time, he had made millions in real estate, oil, and other mainstream lines of business and was one of the handful of Jews with show business ties to be accepted into the conservative WASP society

11

controlling the uppermost echelon of Los Angeles life. This entre into society came courtesy of his wife, Jennifer, who was the fifth-generation daughter of one of the old-line publishing and banking families. More significantly, Jennifer Shields Hartman was the heiress to a vast fortune. Her life contained only open doors. Wide open doors held by black porters wearing white cotton gloves at the Los Angeles Country Club. Even her marriage to an outsider like Benton Stein didn't matter. She was the real untouchable, and in truth, Randy Stein inherited much of his own form of fearlessness from his quietly powerful mother.

"Hey, it's about fucking time you showed up," screamed Bob Davidson, as Randy Stein strutted in through the doors of the William Morris mail room. He turned back and glanced at the functional clock over the double swinging doors he had just bolted through. Twelve-ten, the sweeping second hand looked for a vanishing moment as if it was speeding around the clock in circles like in a cartoon. Randy blinked, then pushed his hair out of his face. He tucked in his white dress shirt, and finished the Windsor knot on the blue, red, and gray tie he wore to work, with the half-hearted obligation of a cadet in a military academy.

"I'm not late, Davidson. I've been to Universal. Jack Wilson caught me in the parking lot this morning when I got in. He asked me to drive him to a meeting over the hill."

"Goddamn Wilson. This isn't a lousy chauffeur service down here. How does he expect me to get the mail out?"

"You'd better take that up with him, sir. Now, what would you like me to do today?"

"Get up to Candace Fielding's office right away. You were supposed to fill in for her secretary today. He didn't show up for work."

"Fielding, sir? Candace Fielding on the top floor?"

"That's right. Get up there right now. That goddamn phone is probably ringing off the hook by now."

"Excuse me, Mr. Davidson, why didn't you send one of the other guys up when I didn't show this morning?"

"Why do you think, smart ass? Because she asked specifically for you. You've been getting it on with her after hours?"

"No, sir."

Randy turned on his heels and shot out the door. He made it to the elevator in two seconds and pounded the "up" button. Candace Fielding was one of the top agents in the company. By reputation, she had some of the biggest stars in Hollywood on her client list and in her bedroom.

Candace Fielding hated her name shortened in any fashion. She dressed in what had become known as The Fielding Uniform. Tailored slacks, gray, tan, or black coordinated with a creme silk blouse, or camisole type silk shell on warmer days. Ten millimeter opera length pearls adorned her neck at all times. The only other jewelry she wore were extremely large three-karat diamond earring studs and a man's gold Cartier watch with a black lizard strap. The rumor was that the watch had belonged to Cary Grant. Guys in the mail room joked about whether Grant had given the watch to her, or if she'd yanked it off him.

Randy Stein entered Candace Fielding's office, which, like its occupant, was adorned in simple black and creme, tailored, contemporary-chic with a bit of art deco flair thrown in for high drama. Fielding was on the phone — actually, she was on several phones — and her radar picked Randy up right away as he entered. She'd had her eye on him since the day he started at the agency.

"Sorry," Randy said in a low voice. "I'll be right outside when you want me."

With one hand she motioned for him to halt, with the other, she ordered him to sit down. In the middle of several phone conversations, she also managed to offer Randy coffee without saying a single word.

"Good day, Mr. Stein," she almost shouted as she finished her calls and hung up the phone. "I've wanted to meet you now for some time."

"Thank you, Ms. Fielding. I've heard a lot about you, too."

"Like what?" Nothing got past Candace Fielding.

"You know, things like your powerful clients and your hard-driving deals." Randy was cautious.

"That's all," she said, placing and picking up two more calls simultaneously.

"No, that's not all," Randy replied in a low voice so he would not disturb her and so she would not hear.

Candace suddenly began raising her voice on the phone.

"Look, if you want to be a prick about it, I can be a bigger cunt. Your deal is bullshit and we both know it. Richard has total creative control in the contract or there is no contract. Call me in one hour or we pull the plug." With that, she gently hung up the receiver, like a lady, with her pinky finger raised.

Randy was looking at her in total awe. She caught his look. "So what else do you know about me?"

Randy hesitated. "I know you're a tough negotiator."

"You just said that."

"I know that you are feared and respected."

"Bullshit."

"Excuse me, why do you care what I know, or what I've heard about you?" Randy was direct.

"Because this is an interview," she replied.

"An interview. An interview for what?"

"For my new assistant."

"I thought Bruce Cameron was your assistant."

"*Was* is the operative word."

"Oh," said Randy. He cooled the bravado. The stakes were much higher. "Why me? You could have your pick of the ground floor."

"Honey, I could have my pick of any floor. Any floor of any building in Hollywood."

"Then I repeat, why me?" Randy asked.

"Because I like your looks. And," she paused, "I know your father."

"That's why you want me for an assistant?"

"If you are one tenth the businessman your father is, this will be a very interesting affiliation."

Randy thought to himself that he'd take the junior agent position any way he could get it. If his looks were getting him in the door, or his name, so be it.

CHAPTER 3

The year was 1975. Carol Burnett reigned as the Queen of the television network variety series. Another Carroll, named O'Connor, was the King of the contemporary sitcom on the same network. Both shows were made at CBS Television City, the absolute center of the broadcast universe. At least on the West Coast, and in the mind of Bill Parker, who desperately wanted to work at CBS. Growing up in Northern California, Bill lived back home in Oakland and commuted to L.A. whenever possible to find a job, and a passport to the dream.

Bill parked the dirty white '62 Rambler (borrowed from his closest college friend and roommate, Chris Reynolds), in the CBS lot. The windows didn't work, so the journey from the airport to Chris's apartment, then to the studio, had been hot and windy. Bill wiped the sweat from his collar and forehead. He ran a comb through his hair, put on his navy blue linen Ralph Lauren blazer with the expensive looking gold buttons that he had bought on sale for ninety bucks at the tony I. Magnin store in Beverly Hills. Straightening his creamy yellow silk tie, Bill walked down the covered ramp leading to the steel and glass entry hall of the CBS program department headquarters.

As he opened the heavy glass door, the cold air conditioning inside the lobby hit him in the face. The sticky, smoggy summer air that had stifled him was obliterated in the icy CBS lobby. Bill walked in, across the bare white and black veined Carrera marble floor to the guard's desk.

"Hi, my name is Bill Parker. I'm here to see Mr. Asher."

The guard looked up at Bill after scanning the security monitors. "Do you have an appointment?"

"No, sir. However, Mr. Asher knows me and he'll be familiar with my project when you call him."

"Have a seat. I'll call you," the guard smiled. He knew no appointment meant no entry.

Bill again crossed the smooth floor and sat down in one of the six large black leather and chrome Eames chairs in a corner of the lobby. An enormous black-on-white CBS "eye" logo was mounted prominently on the twenty-foot tall blank white wall to the side. Bill crossed his legs, then folded his arms across his chest, and waited.

"Excuse me, son," the guard called out.

Bill jumped up and rushed over to the front desk. "Yes, can I see him now?"

"I'm sorry, but Mr. Asher isn't in. His secretary said you'll have to call back and schedule an appointment."

"But I'm in from out of town, today. I may not be back for weeks."

"I'm really sorry, but there's nothing I can do. If you want to call before you leave, we have phones just outside."

Bill thanked him and headed back into the heat. Heading toward the Rambler, he accidentally stumbled upon the door to his dream. In typical CBS fashion, it was black and marked by a very small black and white sign stating simply "Personnel Department — Open 10-12, 2-4." It was 11:30 a.m. He went inside.

The office was plain and functional. It was the kind of office you'd find at any large corporation. A sorting out zone for administrative workers, clerks and secretaries. On one wall across from the seating area was a small glass sliding window, the sort found in a doctor's office. A tiny sign near a buzzer read "Push For Service." Bill pushed the buzzer, stood up straight, took a breath, and waited for the window to slide open. A very young Hispanic girl with thick, dark bangs practically covering her eyes, opened the window. She didn't bother to look up at Bill Parker, not that she could have seen him through her hair. She just handed him a clipboard with a CBS employment application attached.

"Fill this out completely on both sides and return it to me." She closed the glass door.

Bill sat on a sofa and began to fill in the blanks with the history of his life. Turning the paper over, the application called for honors and awards. Did CBS really care? Just in case they did, he filled in every line. He took his completed application and rang the buzzer once again. The girl with too much hair opened the glass gates to success.

"Finished?" she asked.

"All filled in," said Bill. "Can I schedule an appointment?"

"You might be in luck." The impersonal receptionist came to life. Was it Bill's disarming smile? Whatever the miracle, her attitude changed from cold to warm. An explanation wasn't important. The interview she could provide was all that mattered to Bill. "One of our employment counselors is available this morning. If he'll see you now, you won't have to come back tomorrow."

"Oh, God. Let him see me now," Bill muttered.

"Excuse me?"

Maybe she didn't have ears, either, he thought. "I just said that I hope he can see me now."

"Okay, just wait, I'll be right back," and the glass door shut once again with a jarring clank. Bill returned to his seat.

A Moment later, the glass slid open again and the receptionist called out Bill's name in a full voice. Bill got up and walked toward the window. As he reached the receptionist, she closed the glass door almost in his face, and opened the black door next to the window, ushering him inside.

"Mr. Donatello will see you, now. Follow me." She led Bill down a long hallway with offices on both sides. Each office was identical, primarily furnished with a plain black, metal desk, chrome-trimmed, with a faux wood-grained metal top. Each desk was placed visibly in the center of each office, with an industrial-looking fabric-covered swivel chair in the standard issue CBS Chinese red, positioned properly behind each desk. A matching metal credenza was placed against each back wall, and one guest chair, also in red, in front of each desk.

There were no windows. This was an inside sector on the subground floor level of CBS Television City. This was the Personnel Department, in all its power and glory.

17

The receptionist stopped abruptly, reaching John Donatello's office. Her worn sneakers squealed on the highly buffed, black linoleum floor. She peered into the office, then made her standard announcement.

"Your next appointment is here, John." She continued, now in a whisper, "Let's see how long this one takes." Then, the mysterious girl who had gone from cold to warm and back to cold again, vanished around the corner.

Bill stuck his head in the door. He saw John Donatello sitting behind his desk. He was thirty-five, very small, with short, straight, black hair and large, black eyes underlined by very pronounced dark circles under each one. As he stood up to greet his next interview, Donatello's dark eyes perked, and a grin took hold of his otherwise matter-of-fact face. Bill pulled the rest of his body around the corner of the office door.

"Hi, I'm John. Who are you?" asked Donatello with a smile.

"Bill Parker. Thanks very much for seeing me."

"That's what I'm here for, please, sit down."

Donatello gestured for Bill to sit.

"Would you like to see my resume?" offered Bill.

"Absolutely," John replied. As Bill reached into his blue leather portfolio, Donatello was looking at him, thinking that Bill was the perfect all-American boy. A virgin, unspoiled by the cynicism John Donatello felt sitting behind his desk.

Bill Parker radiated positive energy with a smile that was strong, genuine. His sandy blonde hair, long and pushed back to the side, exposed the full force of flashing green eyes. He looked up and handed Donatello his resume. "Here you go."

John took it from him and started to read aloud. "A U.S.C. graduate?"

Bill nodded.

"Honor Society. Trojan Chorale. Tennis team. Fraternity president. What are you doing now?" John looked up from the resume and stared at Bill.

"I'm living in Northern California with my parents. I've been working at odd jobs, earning enough money to job hunt down here in Los Angeles — in the industry."

Bill was hungry and it showed. It wasn't offensive because he was young, smart, and good-looking. A champion two-year-old thorough-bred racehorse at the starting gate of his first race just waiting for the gate to open.

"Let me take a look here." Donatello started thumbing through a three-ring black CBS binder filled with job information sheets. Bill thought that there must be something in that entire book he could do.

"Do you have accounting experience?"

"Yes, sir. I did the daily books in my uncle's store every summer."

Donatello paused, checked the black binder, then looked straight into Bill's eyes and said, "There's someone I think you should meet. Wait here, I'll go talk to him. His office is down the hall." He got up and walked out of the office, casting a final look at Bill as he left.

Bill sat nervously. He wasn't sure about Donatello. Was he gay? Maybe he was just a little nerd with a job that possessed the power to launch Bill's career, or kill it, at CBS.

Donnatello pranced back into his cubicle office. With a look of a cat that had just swallowed the canary, he spoke,"Mr. Grayson will see you. He's just about to go to lunch, but he said he'd wait and see you first."

"Who is he? Does he have a job opening?" asked a very anxious Bill Parker.

"Grayson is the head of Guest Relations. And, he might have an opening. Might."

Bill's adrenaline flowed. This was the closest he'd ever gotten. Now he had to close the deal. He would make the best usher CBS ever had. After all, that's where some of the biggest people in the industry had started, or so he'd been told. It was at the absolute bottom.

Donatello told Bill to follow him. They went through what seemed like a labyrinth of narrow hallways, corridors with black doors that finally led back to the main hallway of the building. "Okay, kid, wait here a minute," said Donatello as they arrived at the doorway of the "Guest Relations" department. "I'll go and see if Mr. Grayson is ready to see you." John left Bill standing in the hallway. He went inside the office door. As he entered, he left the door open and Bill could see a very pretty girl sitting at a desk right inside the office.

She was talking on the telephone, and her red, polished fingernails caught Bill's eye from across the hall. He was intrigued by what he sensed was a contradiction in her look. She was very slim with long, straight, blonde hair that fell casually over her shoulders. She wore no make-up, no jewelry, and her clothes were simply tailored and unpretentious.

The focus of Bill's attention looked like a Vassar co-ed. Very Eastern, and probably very smart. What was she doing sitting behind the receptionist's desk in the ticket office? Again Bill caught a glimpse of her red fingernails. She stroked one of them at the cuticle, still talking on the phone, going about her business, oblivious to Bill. He was fascinated by her.

Donatello came out of the closed office directly behind where the girl was sitting, and proceeded to the ticket office door. He waved at Bill to follow him. As Bill crossed the hall, his green eyes met the blue eyes of the Vassar co-ed with the Lolita nails. She hung up the phone as Bill entered the office.

Acknowledging Donatello without looking at him, her gaze was fixed on Bill. "John, do we have an appointment?" she asked.

"Jerry said he'd take a few minutes before going to lunch to meet this young man from U.S.C."

Bill held out his hand.

"Hello, I'm Jodi," she said. She shook his hand hard. Bill noticed her hand was slender and soft, and the smell of her hand lotion now belonged to him as well.

"I'm Bill Parker. It's very nice to meet you."

"John, did Jerry want you to bring Bill right in?"

"Yes, but check first. He was going to make a call before seeing him."

When Jodi stood up, Bill saw what had been hidden by the desk. Jodi was a knockout. Her white, tailored cotton shirt was neatly tucked into a pair of starched, tightly fitted, light blue Levi's. She was tall, almost five-foot-eight, and moved with the agility and grace of a woman who had probably spent her childhood riding horses at her Daddy's stables on the weekends. She went into Grayson's office and closed the door behind her.

20

Jodi soon reappeared from behind Grayson's door, and slipped back into the waiting area. Bill was standing erect, smiling broadly, and making small talk with Donatello.

"Mr. Grayson is ready to see you. Just go in."

"Thank you so much. Maybe he'll hire me and we'll get to work together," Bill offered as he prepared to enter Grayson's office.

"Maybe." Jodi smiled a polite, disconnected smile. "Good luck."

Bill entered the office and closed the door behind him. Jodi turned to Donatello. "Looks like a rich kid, the spoiled type."

"He was probably thinking the same thing about you," John replied.

"Touché," she grinned.

"This kid is different. There's something special. I can't put my finger on it," Donatello went on about Bill. "This kid has energy, ambition, and a certain look in his eye. He might make it. Grayson may hire this one."

"You're right about one thing," responded Jodi, never one to miss a chance to deliver the final jab.

"What's that?" inquired Donatello recklessly.

"You can't put your finger on it." Jodi turned on her heels and proceeded down the CBS hallway.

• • •

"May I see your resume, Mr. Parker?" asked Jerry Grayson. He was a tall man with a ruddy complexion, and neatly combed thinning brown hair. His clothes were tailored and he appeared well groomed, just shy of foppishness. His starched shirt, monogrammed at the left cuff, displayed his hidden ego.

"Yes, sir, here it is," Bill reached across the large desk to hand him the page he had carefully removed from his portfolio. "I want to work here so badly, sir, if there is anything at all........"

Grayson interrupted him, "We have very few opportunities. There has been a hiring freeze for nearly nine months, and, I have priorities in terms of hiring. I answer to many people, many important people with sons, daughters, friends, nephews, nieces, friends-of-friends, friends of their attorney's........"

Bill interrupted, continuing Grayson's line of thought, "Children of friends' attorneys and their friends, I know. But you don't want to hire any of them. Just think, once you hire one the flood gates will open. One boss will be happy, but another will be angry because you hired the other guy's best friend's son."

"Smart kid," Jerry interjected.

"So hire me, and nobody will be mad. Nobody will care. I don't know a soul," Bill paused for a moment. "I want a career in television. I've grown up with CBS, with Lucille Ball, Mary Tyler Moore."

"You grew up well. Very impressive friends."

Bill laughed. He liked Grayson's quick wit. This was the first comfortable meeting Bill Parker had experienced in months of begging for work. This sixty-year-old stranger had the ability to give Bill Parker his beginning in show business, and as Grayson fiddled with his necktie, Bill sensed that his time was running out to capture a job. Grayson had a lunch appointment, and he was getting ready to head out the door.

"You know, I saw more mail in your outer office than there is in the post office. Could you use help sorting it, answering it? I'm the fastest opener in town."

Grayson gave him a look as if to say, "Be careful what you wish for."

Bill caught the glance and continued, undaunted. "I'll go through it all in two weeks."

"Two weeks?" replied Grayson.

"One week?" Bill responded.

"No, two weeks would be just fine."

"It would?"

"Yes, it would, considering there is at least six months of back-logged mail out there."

"Six months of mail?" Bill grimaced.

"Six months, maybe eight. And each letter must first be opened, read, filed by show or ticket request and then answered with a CBS letter and possibly show tickets."

"When can I start?"

"Whoa — who said you could start?"

"A trial start, then? Two weeks, then you can decide?"

Grayson was about to say no. But he hesitated too long.

"Mr. Grayson, I won't disappoint you. I <u>will</u> finish the mail in two weeks."

Grayson still hesitated. Bill didn't know what else to say. He was out of begging and groveling schemes. The resume was nice, but just and only that, nice. Another white kid with a college degree, Sunday school honors and a rundown of useless summer jobs. How was he going to get to the top if he couldn't pass the first test? He was resolved to be tough, but smooth — that would be his style.

"Mr. Grayson, in just two minutes you'll be walking out of here, presumably to lunch. When you get back, the afternoon mail will have been delivered and you'll have six months and one day of backlogged mail staring at you. I'm here. I'm willing to work. How about it?"

"Okay. You're hired." Grayson came forth with an offer so fast it caught Bill off guard.

"What did you say?"

"I said okay, but just a trial, two weeks."

"Then what, if I may ask, sir?"

"Then we'll see."

"When do I start?"

"You said it, you're here, you're willing, and the mailman is on his way here. Roll up your sleeves, kid, and welcome to the Columbia Broadcasting System." Grayson held out his hand. Bill shook it with the energy of a volcano before eruption. "Sit at the desk in the back corner and start opening and sorting by show request. I'll give you more information when I get back."

Grayson straightened his tie once again. Then he left for lunch. Bill let out a celebratory shout. The loudest of his twenty-two year life. He'd never felt so excited about anything. Bill left Grayson's office facing his present and near future career, all in the form of letters. Thousands of letters in all sizes and colors, bundled up and waiting for him to open them. He walked back to a desk in the rear corner of the CBS ticket office. There were no windows. Just an old black metal desk with an old matching chair. The desk fit neatly into the small cubicle, with very little room to move. The walls, on both sides, were covered with floor-to-ceiling shelves, each one stacked with mail. Labeled and designated with a show name; "The Price Is Right," "The Dinah Shore Show," "The Sonny and Cher Show," the shelves were overflowing with mail for all the shows produced at CBS.

Bill sat down at his new desk. He slowly ran has hands over the top. He reached for the first bundle of mail, taking off his coat and rolling up his sleeves. The journey had officially begun, the race up the ladder, underway.

CHAPTER 4

C hris Reynolds got off the 405 Freeway at Sunset Boulevard just like the directions on the crumpled piece of paper told him to do. Chris didn't want to be late for his callback meeting with the big-time producer-director of the TV series he'd auditioned for. It was unusual that the man wanted him to come to his house rather than the studio. But, an unknown, twenty-one-year old actor without a job went where he was told to go.

Within two minutes, Chris saw the west gates of Bel Air off Sunset Boulevard. He turned left through the impressive creme-colored stucco pillars connected overhead by elegant, wrought iron, and drove up Chalon Road.

Winding through the narrow verdant canyons of Bel Air, Chris passed some of the most spectacular real estate in America, all surrounding the manicured greens of the prestigious, "Members Only" Bel Air Country Club.

Chris had never seen anything like this before. Growing up in Rockford, Illinois, in a comfortable two-story brick house on a street of two-story brick houses, Chris's dad was a salesman for Honeywell. By some standards, they led a good life, but not a very sophisticated one. Once a year Chris's mom and dad would take him and his two sisters to a lake for a week of vacation, usually camping out. Chris ate dinner in a restaurant once.

He left Rockford to come to L.A. to be an actor. Rather, to become a star. A rich and famous star. An actor could be anyone, go anywhere, live as grandly as he pleased. The public expected it. The movies promoted it. Chris bought it. He bought it all, he wanted it all. And he came to L.A. to make it happen. His exit visa was courtesy of swimming faster than anyone in Rockford, Illinois. With an athletic scholarship, he wrote his own ticket out of town, straight to U.S.C. in Los Angeles. He met Randy Stein on the U.S.C. swim team, and Bill Parker was his first roommate on campus.

As the car made its way around the curves and turns of Chalon Road, Chris almost missed his turn onto a street called Ambazac Way. It was a short cul-de-sac obscured by huge hedges. Driving very slowly down Ambazac, looking for number twenty, he gawked at the Disneyland of architecture spread out before him. A grand Monterey colonial hacienda to his right, a brick English Tudor on his left, and then, there it was, at the end of the street, number twenty.

The house looked like a great ocean liner on land. Its Art Deco corners were rounded and its roof flat and edged with ribbed stucco moldings. An oversized, black lacquer front door, with a massive brass knocker, faced the street at the end of the long concrete walk.

Chris pulled in and stopped the car in the motor court. He got out, locked the car, and walked proudly down the cement walk, and rang the bell.

The huge black door opened to reveal a diminutive Oriental boy dressed in a starched white Nehru-collared jacket and black slacks. Chris thought that the boy couldn't have been older than himself.

"Good afternoon, may I help you?"

"I'm Christopher Reynolds. I have an appointment with David Larkin."

"One minute, please." The houseboy closed the door almost completely in his face and went to verify Chris's claim about an appointment. As he waited, Chris scanned the front door and noticed a large metal panel that contained numerous buttons and lights. A tiny, red light illuminated one of the bulbs on the panel. Then, he saw two signs proclaiming the premises were protected by the Bel Air Patrol armed guards. Chris figured a rich and powerful Hollywood mogul like David Larkin needed a lot of security. Back in Rockford, the only building that had a security system was the First National bank. Since it had never gone off, nobody really knew if it worked.

"Please come in, Mr. Reynolds," the Oriental boy said politely, as he reopened the door. "Mr. Larkin will see you in ten minutes. You may wait inside, here."

The foyer was nothing less than spectacular. A polished, black and white checkered marble floor trimmed with inlaid brass, gave way to a room with at least a thirty-foot high ceiling. The ceiling was a deco mosaic of multi-colored tiles depicting a mythical theme of Neptune and the high seas, and the room's center focal point was a domed skylight from which a hotel lobby sized silver-toned metal and glass chandelier hung to about the twenty-foot height of the room.

In the middle of the foyer, two finely upholstered echru-colored silk chairs, with black and gold-braided trim were positioned off center, facing each other. Chris was instructed by the houseboy to have a seat in one of the chairs and wait in such awe-inspiring surroundings.

Curious about the acoustics of the large room, Chris sang the first line from Carole King's song, "You've Got a Friend" in a soft voice. Then the room sang it back to him. Chris sang another line from the song, this time in full voice, as the sound was filling the room. He did, in fact, have a voice. His friends always told him that he could make it as a singer. He had never tried that.

"So, you like Carole King?" a deep voice sounded out from behind him. Chris jumped up out of the chair. Expecting the Oriental houseboy, he turned to face David Larkin.

Since there was only room for one Rock Hudson on screen in Hollywood, the matinee idol-handsome David Larkin had followed his directorial talents behind the cameras. That particular skill had made the tall, dimple-chinned Larkin one of Tinseltown's richest and most in-demand talents. He made his own terms, called his own shots. David Larkin was a player.

"Excuse me, Mr. Larkin. I hope I didn't disturb you. I got a little carried away with the sound quality in your hall."

Chris was humble and polite, and his charm was disarming the guarded David Larkin. He'd seen them all come through his foyer. Every would-be actor and actress with any potential read for the great director. At fifty, along with his directorial reputation, Larkin was a starmaker.

"I fancy myself a bit of a singer. Actually, it was always a fantasy of mine," David said in a friendly fashion.

"I hope you don't think I was singing to get your attention. It just occurred to me that…."

"You got my attention and I'm at least glad that you really can sing." Larkin cut Chris off with kind words. "I wanted to be Frank Sinatra. I actually had a nightclub act when I first started out in the business," Larkin continued.

"Why did you stop?" Chris asked with genuine interest.

"Money."

"Money? I don't think I understand…"

"I wanted money. Performing was an uphill battle with no guarantee of a pay day. I was good, but a lot of guys are good. I was afraid of being poor."

"How did you become a director and producer?" Chris asked.

"A fluke," Larkin replied with even more candor.

"Hollywood's biggest director started as a fluke?" Chris thought that he really did have a chance if one of Hollywood's biggest moguls started as a fluke.

"Hollywood started as a fluke," Larkin told him. "A few guys got off the train in Los Angeles for a rest on their way from New York to Phoenix, Arizona. They didn't get back on the train, and an industry was born."

"Do you think you would have made it as a performer?"

"I'll never know," Larkin said with more reserve this time.

"Does that bother you?" Chris was getting a little too personal.

David changed the subject. "Let's go into my study. I want you to do some reading for me." David put his arm on Chris's shoulder and ushered him into the study through tall French doors.

The kid from Rockford immediately trusted Larkin. He was taken by his openness, and except for their differences in age, status, experience, lifestyle, and just about everything else, Chris felt like this guy Larkin was his new best friend in Hollywood. It didn't occur to him that the friendly exchange of human experiences between folks back in Rockford did not translate equally in this new arena. In Hollywood, common ground didn't always mean friendship for the common good.

CHAPTER 5

"I 'll get her, Abe. She'll sign. I know the TV package depends on it. Yes, Abe, $50 million back end, minimum. Right. When? Come on, twenty-four hours isn't much time. Okay, twenty-four hours." Candace Fielding hung up her line and looked at Randy Stein sitting across from her in the plush office. He was trying to blend in with the massive glass desk, sinking deeper into his chair. Disappearing among the one hundred silver-framed photos sprinkled around the grand space wasn't possible. It was no use, Candace had Randy right in his blue eyes.

"Can I help, Ms. Fielding?" he said.

"For Chrissakes, you've been working for me for over a month and you haven't done a goddamned thing to really prove yourself," she snapped back. "Of course, you can HELP."

"I thought you were pleased with my work," he replied. Randy was surprised, caught completely off guard by her remark. But he didn't retreat. "How can I prove myself, Ms. Fielding?"

"For starters, drop the phony respect. I've seen you in action. You can dish it with the best of them."

"Like with you," Randy said, looking right at her, square in the eye.

"Like with me." Candace shot back at him. She went on. "How do we get Laurie Dalton to sign with the agency in twenty-four hours?"

"We convince her this is the best place, the only place she belongs. This is the oldest, richest agency in town," Randy said proudly.

"That's not good enough. There's heavy-duty competition out there. Besides, a company name is nice, but the agent-client relationship is the only thing that matters."

"Then, pardon me, but how the hell do we form a relationship in twenty-four hours?"

"We don't, Stein. At least we don't at first. But you, you do." Candace was very coy.

"You want me to see her first?" he asked.

"For a clever guy, you're acting very thick today," Candace continued. "I've arranged through her publicist at the network, who is a very good friend of mine, to have you take Laurie Dalton to Ma Maison tonight. She's been invited to a private dinner party being given by the new owners of Trident Studios."

"A great opportunity to spend some quality time with Laurie Dalton on our first date," Randy replied sarcastically.

"Spend the time any way you please," Candace snapped back at him. "Just get her to sign with us. It could mean a promotion. An associate position for you."

"Candace, I've only been here for three months."

"Three months, three years, three minutes. Success in show business has nothing to do with how much time you invest, it has to do with how good your timing is." She paused and looked him in the eye. "And, in this case, I've arranged the proper timing so your job is to use your brain — and your dick. Have her in here late tomorrow so we can all talk. I won't expect you in the morning." Candace smiled and walked out of her office.

Randy nervously looked out the office window towards the hills of Bel Air. This wasn't the first time he'd been in a situation calling for brain-dick cooperation. God knows there had been plenty of similar situations, most of them resulting in his feeling more like the opposite, a dick brain. But it was the first time a woman had asked him to service another woman. That felt strange. This wasn't a frat brother at U.S.C. asking him to help out and take a date off his hands.

From his vantage point, Randy could see his parent's home, La Villa Serena. The massive tile roof and plaster walls of La Serena were a local landmark. Los Angelinos knew the estate and they knew its owners. Randy was proud to have grown up at the Villa, the only son of one of the richest, most powerful families in Los Angeles. Now, he was working for the top theatrical agency in the world, and training under one of its most influential partners. Yet, his salary was under $250 a week, and his boss had just asked him to screw some starlet to get her to sign a contract. Was he the prostitute or the pimp? Realizing that he was both, the fate of the rich, powerful Stein scion seemed questionable. Returning to his desk, papers got shuffled for the remainder of the day. Randy had absolutely no concentration, so Candace Fielding told him to leave early, go home and take a nap before meeting Laurie Dalton for dinner. Randy had called Laurie that afternoon from the office to introduce himself, and to plan their date. She sounded like an intelligent girl over the phone, and she made fun of the fact that her press people insisted on her having an escort, apologizing to Randy for getting stuck with the assignment.

Randy was impressed by her savvy and honesty. This was not some blonde bimbo he could bed and deliver to Candace Fielding for signing the next day. No longer concerned with the moral dilemma, he was worried more that he couldn't deliver.

CHAPTER 6

In a matter of weeks, Bill Parker had managed to sort out nearly a half-years' backlog of mail for the network. The once dusty shelves burdened with an abundance of rubber banded parcels of requests had been reduced to an organized assortment with only a one month waiting period for tickets.

Grayson was thrilled with his new hire. Parker had raised the class of the entire operation, and his gung-ho, "I'll do anything and I'll do it happily" attitude forced the rest of the troops, some of whom had been in the ticket office for years, to shape up. The fact that Bill dressed in a tie every day, making a special point to look like somebody, and not just the $85.00 a week temporary clerk that he was, made him a few enemies in the ranks.

The whole matter was exaggerated further by a ludicrous, but ultimately beneficial, side effect. Working with so much paper for weeks had worn the skin of Bill's fingers raw, and he developed a serious rash on his hands, forcing him to seek the help of a dermatologist. The doctor prescribed various lotions to restore the skin layer disintegrated by the paper handling. The medicine on Bill's hands were covered by thin white cotton surgical gloves. Back in his corner, Bill sat, whipping through the mail, typing the responses on the IBM Selectric in front of him, sealing the envelopes and sending them off in the proper piles wearing his jacket, tie, and white gloves. The gossip mill had a field day, and Bill was known all over the entire studio as the whiz-kid in the white gloves.

It had taken almost the same couple months to crack the iceberg Jodi Winkler, the beautiful receptionist in Bill's office with the showgirl fingernails. Jodi had definitely lived up to his first impression.

She was from the East, as he had surmised. A product of the Philadelphia Main Line, she was raised in private schools.

In college, Jodi had been a broadcast communications major at Brandeis University, with a minor in student activism. A borderline hippie, with one foot firmly planted at Sak's Fifth Avenue, she marched for equal rights and an end to American involvement in Vietnam by week, and went home on weekends to her family's elegantly traditional nineteenth century home in Bryn Mawr.

Jodi loved the East. For everything she adored about it, she hated the corresponding factor in L.A. Her biggest complaint centered on the absence of seasons in most of Southern California. It was always too hot for her. Instead of celebrating 80 degree weather in January, she cried over its absurdity. And the weather was only the beginning of her laundry list of likes and dislikes.

Yet, Bill was mesmerized by her attitude. She was at once so aloof and snotty, but also so bright and funny. He had never been exposed to anyone like her in the East Bay area hills of San Francisco, where nearly all of the girls he had grown up with were more or less younger versions of their white middle class homemaker moms.

On the flip side, Jodi couldn't quite figure Bill out. He was certainly as much a contradiction in his own way as she was in hers. Bill had the looks of the All-American athletic preppie, but he acted more like a top executive, possessed the ambition of ten men, and seemed to also have a worldliness far beyond his years and experience.

They didn't know each other that well, even though in the months since Bill had started, the two of them had become relatively fast friends, taking lunch together regularly, and talking whenever possible. Their fast friendship stopped at the studio. Jodi lived with a man who was one of the managers of the production department at the network. That's what had brought her out west, his career. Under these conditions, Bill had no intention of asking her out, even though they both were attracted to each other.

"Jodi, do you want to have lunch today?" Bill asked, knowing she'd say yes. Lunch had become their time together, time to plan and dream about their future in show business.

"Sure, can we go early? But, please, not the commissary, anywhere but there."

"How about Canter's Deli?"

"Is it Thursday?"

"Yes, why?"

"Because we went to Canter's last Thursday and the Thursday before that and I think the week before that, too," Jodi replied.

"Then we've created Tradition," explained Bill.

Canter's Deli was a block north of CBS on Fairfax Avenue. A strictly kosher block of fruit stands, newsstands, butchers, bakers, and Yiddish candlestick makers. The average age of the pedestrian on the sidewalk was better than seventy.

Jodi held the door at Canter's for Bill. The door led the customers past the bakery before going into the dining area. Row upon row of chocolate macaroon cookies lined up before them, perfectly placed on trays by Hilda, Goldie, Bertha and Mae. Ladies in beige cotton uniforms with white doily lace collars and nets in their hair. Day after day, year in, year out, placing the macaroons and cheese Danish in rows with the care of a nurse in an emergency room. Bill walked up to the glass counter and pressed his face against it. He felt five years old and wanted one of everything.

"I promise we'll stop here on the way out," Jodi told him. "I'll buy you one of those cinnamon things you like."

"Promise?" said Bill.

"Promise. Can we get a table now?" she asked.

"A booth in the corner," Bill asked the woman at the podium guarding the entrance to the dining room. She wasn't like the others behind the counter. No beige uniform with the doily collar, no hair net. She was the head yenta, joking with the customers, most of whom were familiar. But there was no familiarity with Bill and Jodi.

"Right this way, please," she motioned for them to follow her to the booth Bill had requested.

"I wonder if she realizes we come here for lunch every Thursday. We're regulars," Bill told Jodi in a loud whisper.

"The brisket is especially lean today, dear," were her last words as she waved them into the corner booth and shuffled back to her command post to attend to the line that had formed in her brief absence.

"Jodi, I've got a proposition," Bill said.

"What kind of proposition?" she inquired.

"Let's write a script together be partners."

"You and me?"

"I'll bet you're a decent writer and, well, what have we got to lose?"

"Have you got something in mind?"

"I do."

"Okay. When do we start - partner?"

"Right after the turkey sandwich comes, I need my sustenance to create."

CHAPTER 7

R andy woke up with a start from his nap. It was time to get ready for the big night, the night he would make his major career move, or at the very least save his job.

He purposely dressed down for the evening; gray slacks, brown blazer, plain brown slip-on loafers, and a simple shirt and tie. He changed two or three times before coming up with his ordinary outfit.

Ordinary was a tough call for the great Randy Stein. The hell with the fact that gray and brown were not really compatible. He remembered his boss's words. She's smart. She likes an edge. Don't let the pieces fit together too nicely. Don't look so perfect, he thought, and that would, in fact, be perfect. Not too cool, almost regular. He left his canyon cottage and drove to Ma Maison on Melrose Avenue in West Hollywood.

"Hello, Suzanne. You look incredible tonight."

Randy always said the same thing to the girl at the door every time he greeted her. "Is Miss Dalton here?"

"Yes, she's over there by the window with all those suits," she replied, continuing, "If you don't see her, just look around the room at any table. Everyone is looking at her, just follow the turned heads. You'll find her."

Suzanne wasn't exaggerating. Randy glanced at the room and every head was at a forty-five degree angle towards the northeast corner table. His first instinct was to trip a waiter coming at him with a tray of drinks to see if the angle would shift back in the opposite direction. It would take an earthquake to get the people to move.

The exact moment Randy saw her, Laurie Dalton was running both hands through her thick blonde head of hair. She wore it straight back, off her forehead, and it fell gracefully down her shoulders.

Laurie's skin was a golden tan and her enormous green eyes suddenly pierced him. The glaring stare of an owl in the blackest of nights. She had the very sultry habit of pursing her large pink valentine lips as she looked at someone. And, as her lips pulled together her nostrils would flare just slightly as she took in one last gasp of precious oxygen.

There was no question that Laurie was an exceptional female creature. Liz Taylor, Brigitte Bardot, Catherine Deneueve, Joan of Arc, all of these women were sitting there at the corner table in the body of Laurie Dalton surrounded by the ten bald men in navy suits. Ten men who had slashed their way through a long day of ruthless studio negotiations. Ten men who had threatened their underlings' job security, screamed at their competitors, hung up on their wives, lectured their children, forced their secretaries to retype the all-important letter for the third time. Ten men who now, after a day of making waves, found themselves smiling and chatting and being their most charming, outgoing, personable bald selves to win the attention of this one little captivating nineteen-year-old nobody from nowhere with the valentine lips, golden hair, and, multi-million dollar potential.

Randy wondered just how much Laurie sensed that she was in charge. He'd been warned that she was no-nonsense. That beneath the actress exterior was a brain and common sense. He also remembered how real she sounded on the phone. No bullshit, just real. How could this be the same person? She was so voluptuous and ditzy-looking, sitting there at her corner table. This was not the look of common sense.

Laurie wore a dress of the simple black silk cocktail variety, cut across her breasts, and hanging from the shoulders on minuscule spaghetti straps. The kind of dress designed to show off a woman's assets. Laurie had no hidden assets.

The dress enabled her to be her most animated. She threw her arms about, waving her hands flagrantly. Her wild swaying, marvelous, thick hair flung from side to side as she moved about. With each word she spoke, her pursing lips and nostrils sucked in and out with the regularity of a bellows. Everything moving up and down, side to side, a whirling dervish of sexual suggestion, a table-tied tornado.

All of sudden the brown shoes and the gray slacks made Randy self-conscious. Yes, he'd done it on purpose to simplify his image, to tone down the young hot-shot bravado. Seeing Laurie, the rules of the game had changed. Now he needed the Mr. Guy blazer and the yellow silk tie and the Gucci loafers more than ever. He needed his tools of instant inflatable self-confidence, and all he had were plain gray slacks and ordinary brown shoes.

He sucked in his chest and went for the table. As he approached, he noted that there was an empty chair, but it wasn't next to Laurie. It was directly across the table from her. Was he supposed to go and sit there, or move right in next to her? He was her date for the evening. Randy envisioned himself as the Future Hollywood Mogul, or FHM, as the boys at the agency liked the define this potential. He went for the spot right next to her.

"Excuse me, Laurie, I'm Randy Stein." He put out his hand to shake hers, side-swiping the cheek of one of the bald-headed men in navy suits. The guy's face was so low to the table. He was practically horizontal with Laurie's breasts. Obviously, he chose to be at that level, in spite of the potential hazards, including Randy Stein's outstretched palm.

Laurie didn't take Randy's hand. Instead, she reached up with both arms and clasped her hands behind his neck. Then she pulled him down to her head while simultaneously using the support of his strong back to raise herself out of the chair. They met midway, she kissed him on the left cheek.

"It's very nice to meet you. Please sit down here." Laurie turned to the man next to her that Randy had slapped, "Harry, love, would you be kind enough to scoot down so my date can sit here next to me?"

Harry was more than happy to oblige anything Laurie asked. Even if it meant losing the coveted position right next to her. He moved all right, and with him the entire right side of the table shifted over one place to make room for Randy.

"You're not what I expected," his first words came stumbling out, followed by a look of stupidity on his face, revealing the remorse over his choice of opening words.

"What does that mean?" she replied, pursing her lips and sucking in her nostrils.

"Well," he paused and looked for some way out of telling her his true feelings. Feelings about the contradiction he experienced meeting her, seeing her as a sex object and thinking that she was a whole lot more woman than he expected.

"I saw your first movie and you were exceptional." Randy bought some time to formulate his thoughts.

"That's sweet of you to say," she looked right at him as if none of the other men were at the table with them.

"You know," Laurie said, "that was a wonderful part because it was so finely written. It was a very lucky break for me. Did you know that the part was written with Jane Fonda in mind?"

"No, I had no idea," he said clumsily, like a fan from the Midwest with no knowledge of show business instead of the FHM associate agent-in-training that he was. The plain brown shoes and gray slacks were getting the best of him. Randy Stein was a fly in this spider's web. Hopelessly male and helpless, a victim like the rest of the ten suits attached to babbling bald heads, like all of the people in Ma Maison that night who had come to sup with the stars and couldn't take their eyes off one 19-year-old, nostril ventilating Laurie Dalton.

"Timing is everything in this business," she said next.

"It's crucial, but not everything," he said, looking at the guy still looking at her bosom. "Not everything. Talent is important. You can get the break, but you better deliver when you get it." Randy gave himself a mental slap across the face. He was coming out of the spell. At last he was saying smart things.

"You're correct," Laurie said. "But I'm not so conceited to think that I have a corner on the talent market. There are so many talented and gorgeous people here in L.A. I really consider myself very lucky to have played that part. If Jane Fonda had been available I'd still be a waitress from Laredo, Texas, trying to be an actress." She rested. The speech had been delivered. Taking a beat to reformulate her thoughts, the real Laurie blurted out, "For Chrissakes, I'm still a waitress from Laredo, Texas at heart. A girl doesn't change that much in nine months, not a girl with any sense of herself, at least. One movie is just one movie, after all. And it's a movie that's not playing anymore." It was the Laurie, the real Laurie, Randy had met on the telephone.

"It's a movie that made money and there is talk of a nomination. They're comparing you to Hepburn. I've heard the talk around the agency," Randy replied, using all the agent ease he could muster.

"Can I confess something to you?" she lowered her voice and whispered at him, moving her pursing lips and ventilating nostrils right up to his ear. Her hot breath flowed right in his eustachian tube and went right down to his crotch. Bypassed the brain entirely. "I've only seen one Katharine Hepburn film," she said.

"What?"

"I've only seen one Hepburn movie, 'The Philadelphia Story'," she repeated, blowing in more hot air.

Randy put his hand in his lap. One more swoosh of hot air and he would have an erection.

"I'll take you to a Hepburn movie festival," he told her. "I know a small theater on La Brea Avenue that plays the classics."

"I would love that," she said with another blast of air. That was it, Randy reached for the water on the table and gulped. The waiter passed by with caviar appetizers, and Randy motioned for a plate be put between them.

"Could I get another glass of Chardonnay?" Laurie asked.

"A J.B. with a twist over crushed ice for me," Randy added. "Have you ever had this caviar?" he continued.

"It's so good," she told him, "I've already had one serving, and I'd better stop. You go on, enjoy it. The capers really make it special. Make sure you eat lots of them." At that, Laurie picked up one of the delicate little green peas and placed it in Randy's mouth.

The waiter brought the drinks, Randy gulped his shot of scotch, ordering a second before the guy could escape. Laurie had turned her attention in the opposite direction so she didn't see him down the drink. For that matter, neither did the rest of the group, nor the remainder of the restaurant. When she turned the other way, so did all the rest of them. The rush of scotch to the bloodstream did help relieve his erection.

When he felt it was safe to get up, Randy excused himself to Laurie. She waved her approval and kept talking to the man on her other side. Maybe that guy was offering to take her to a Hepburn movie festival, too. Randy started to walk toward the back, past the wall that separated the tables from the partially open kitchen, to the restroom and the phone. He wanted to call his friend, Bill Parker, and tell him about his date with Laurie Dalton at Ma Maison. It was a sort of half-time break.

Scotch made Randy's way to the phone a little more treacherous than usual. He hoped he wouldn't run into anyone he knew. For no other reason, he was wearing this goddamned gray and brown outfit.

"Randy Stein. Randy! Randy Stein! Over here, darling. Look this way." Although the call was definitely coming from a female species, the voice rang out like Rommel ordering troops across the African desert. In his Laurie Dalton haze, he thought the entire restaurant had frozen because the call to him was so pervasive. Harnessing his vivid, scotch-induced imagination, Randy managed to look around the room, spotting his caller, Kelly Kurtis. By this time, she too had gotten up from her dinner table, undoubtedly with some phony excuse, and was headed in Randy's direction.

Kelly was the personification of the time-honored Hollywood starlet. She was stupid, and every move she made was a call of the wild. "Nice day we're having," loosely translated to "Fuck me now, right here" in Kelly's language. It wasn't her fault. Nature and a repressed upbringing in Iowa were to blame. Mother Nature had given her great sexual beauty and no brain. Iowa had given her the haystack and the high school football team. She fancied herself as a "Marilyn" of the 1970's.

Kelly had plenty to peddle. She was very fond of saying, "I may be stupid, but I'm not dumb," a line stolen from a favorite fifties film. Tonight at Ma Maison was proof. Kelly was having dinner with a top Hollywood gossip columnist, riding high on the success of his recent book about the lives of the famous. He was fond of being seen with the most beautiful ladies at the best restaurants. She was playing the role perfectly.

A sudden departure from her date's table was a signal to everyone in the place that it was time to come over and chat with Mr. Gossip. Besides, it was a closer vantage point to stare at Laurie Dalton.

Neither Kelly nor Randy was missed. They could have left the restaurant, driven to the airport, flown to Palm Springs and back, returned to the table, only to receive a casual mention, "Is everything all right?"

They met in a corner reserved for the phones and the john. It was ultra chic, very European, a new trend, to have only unisex bathrooms in Hollywood restaurants. Say goodbye to "MEN" and "WOMEN". It was first come, first served.

"Kelly, I've been thinking about you lately."

"Randy, I think about you always."

"You know, we should have dinner together, just the two of us," he said.

"Not in a busy place like this."

"Better thought. Let's skip dinner. Just come on over to the house. We'll have a few drinks. Talk."

"When?" she asked with one thing on her mind.

"Soon. How about… tomorrow night?" Randy replied.

"How about now?"

"Now?"

"Yes. Now. Can you think of a better time?"

"And where do you propose we go? We both are here with other people."

"Right here."

"Right where?" Randy asked.

With that, Kelly led Randy into the one bathroom and locked the door behind them. The advantage to the shared facility was having the lock on the door. Only one customer at a time. In this case, two. And, to accommodate the women and California state law, a small couch conveniently filled one corner of the lavatory. With the click of the locking door, Randy slowly pressed his body up against Kelly, moving her gently, firmly up against the wall. His hands moved up and down the sides of her back and thighs, massaging, gripping, stroking. Lowering his head to hers, he traced the outline of her mouth with his tongue, wetting his own lips and placing them on her for what was the longest French kiss.

She could feel his hard penis moving against her. It had taken no time to become erect, having just deflated only moments before at Laurie's table. Kelly moved her body in such a way that it applied pressure to his cock. Legs together, legs apart, she pleased him. Randy's hands moved to the shoulder straps of her one-piece white cotton summer dress. It fell off her shoulders like a leaf in the wind, falling at her ankles. All she wore were cotton panties. Her breasts were more beautiful than Randy had remembered. Firm, slightly upturned, and all his. He held them like the Emmy awards he hoped to someday fondle.

Randy began to kiss her breasts. His tongue circled the nipples. As his mouth moved around each hard point, Kelly bit Randy's ear and moaned slightly, a quiet, long moan. More of an extended awe.

Tearing at his brown jacket, pulling it off his shoulders and getting it twisted and turned inside out, Kelly had her partner in what became a straightjacket. Randy was sucking her harder and faster, his own excitement growing as he realized his sport coat was cutting off the circulation in his arms, which had become entangled behind his back. It broke the passion of the moment as he left Kelly's breasts long enough to pull himself free from the coat. Quickly, he pulled down the gray pants and she ripped off his shirt and tie.

Two almost naked people together in the bathroom at Ma Maison. Randy's mind wandered. What if the mirror was two-way? Good show in the kitchen. Nobody would get any service. All the waiters and the kitchen help would be lined up at the two-way, cheering.

Randy picked Kelly up and moved the two of them over to the small couch. He tore her panties off. His cock was so hard, he felt like it would break in two. It was sticking out of the top of his briefs, and Kelly went for it. She kissed him, sucked him, licked him. His pants came off fast, too. But by this time, there were people outside the bathroom, knocking at the door.

"What's going on? Anyone in there? Hurry up."

Randy did just that. He entered Kelly so hard and fast she almost screamed. It was a scream of shock. Penetration always surprised her.

At least, she let her partner think so. It was such a turn on. Suddenly, Randy's voyeuristic fantasies vanished as the knocking on the door became louder and more threatening.

The climax was disappointing. He came. They parted. Two people separated and dressed faster than at any other time in the history of modern human sex.

"We ought to be put in Ripley's." Kelly was less than complimentary.

"Yeah, a real world record."

"Don't forget your tie. It's over there."

"Thanks."

Thanks were the last words spoken. No "you were great". No "see you around". Nothing. Just thanks. Randy opened the door, and the two of them flew out amidst the knowing stares of the crowd desperately waiting to use the facilities.

Kelly didn't kiss Randy goodbye. She simply went back to her gossip columnist date, still surrounded by the adoring crowds. Just as her departure rallied them to the table, her return signaled their departure. She sat down. Mr. Gossip toasted her. Randy saw them out of the corner of his eye as he passed back through the place to his table. He thought she was very good, that Kelly. She was right. "She did look stupid, but she wasn't dumb."

Randy wondered if he would have to do some explaining. He soon realized that twenty minutes in a place like this was nothing. He knew that Hollywood never wore a watch, unless time was also money. Were it not for the sun casting a different light than the moon time all would blur together in the glamour village.

"Where have you been, Randy?" were the first words Laurie spoke upon his return. He had done his inconspicuous best to slither back into the chair beside her without attention. In fact, because Laurie was still facing the opposite direction, he was sure he hadn't been missed.

"I missed you," she continued, turning back to face him.

"You did?" he countered. "I was only gone a few minutes."

Laurie came closer, snuggling up to him and once again whispering in his ear. "You were gone for half an hour." With her words, she gave him another dose of powerful hot-sex-breath in the ear.

"Oh, shit," he muttered.

"What?"

The hot breath was doing it to him again. He'd just had all he could handle ten minutes before in the bathroom, and now he was getting aroused again.

"Please," he said, "try not to whisper in my ear."

"I'm sorry, does it irritate you?"

"No," he replied, then came very close to Laurie and whispered back in her ear, "It turns me on."

"I never heard that complaint before," Laurie was laughing. Then she reached over, once again putting her arms around his neck and pulling him towards her. Whispering in his ear with the breathiest tone she had, "Then let's go for a ride to the beach. I'm bored with this dinner. I've done my duty as centerpiece for the studio."

Laurie bolted up from her chair. She still had one hand on the nape of Randy's neck. Playing with his hair and shoving her finger down his starched white collar she said her farewells to her boys in navy blue. Randy got Laurie's signal to rise in the form of a good tug at the back of his hair. He rose so quickly from his chair that it flew over backwards to the floor. "Good-bye, Harry. Good meeting you," he said to the guy next to him, as he bent down to pick up the chair. Harry had managed to sit up straight at last as Laurie was getting up to leave.

At once, as if a cue had been given by some mysterious offstage direction, all of the studio guys stood, respectfully bidding adieu to Miss Dalton. She obligingly circled the table taking each of their hands, kissing them cheek-to-cheek, Hollywood air kiss style, and telling each of them how wonderful they were.

Randy was again spellbound by her power. She was so incredibly masterful. They all ate it up. Ten sharks, each and every one a killer, hanging on every morsel of her presence. Randy followed her around the table. He feebly shook hands with the guys after she did. He nodded. They nodded. They were jealous as hell that he was the guy taking her home. Randy knew it, but he played it cool. Low key, his gray slacks and brown shoes at work. The guy who moments before had humped Kelly Kurtis in the john and was now taking Laurie Dalton, actress extraordinaire, hot-sex-breath-turn-on, for a ride to the beach. He really couldn't believe that life could be so rewarding. But then again, he'd been blessed at birth and these were just some of the little perks of a charmed life.

CHAPTER 8

"Hey listen, why don't you come along?" Chris Reynolds wanted the security of roommate Bill Parker's company.

"No way. I don't know this guy. He didn't invite me."

"It's just a party at some rich lady's place up in Trousdale. They said to bring some friends."

Bill could see Chris in the mirror from where he sat at the makeshift desk, in the one room apartment they shared. Desk was a generous way to describe the hollow core door positioned atop a couple of piles of cement blocks the two of them had pulled out of the dirt in the empty lot next door.

Chris was pulling on his pants, tight white Levi's. He brushed his long blonde hair, pulled a red La Coste shirt over his head. He brushed his hair again. He undid his pants and pulled them down to tuck in the shirt, pulling them back up and refastening the Levi's button fly. He brushed his teeth last.

Chris came out of the tiny bathroom into the quarters the two of them had shared for the past several months, since Bill had returned to L.A. and started his job at CBS.

The apartment was south of downtown, ten blocks north of the U.S.C. campus on a numbered street off Figueroa Boulevard. The building was early 20th Century Spanish stucco. Four floors, ten single apartments to a floor, divided by a long, narrow hall illuminated by an equidistant row of a half dozen exposed 60 watt bulbs.

"The trouble with you is that you don't know how to live," Chris told Bill.

"I don't know how to live, a guy who gets dressed backwards telling me I don't know how to live?"

"Damn right. What do you mean, gets dressed backwards?" Chris was confused as Bill changed the subject.

"It makes no difference. Put your pants on anyway you like."

"I do."

"I know."

"So what of it?"

"So nothing."

"So come with me to this party, you dumb fuck."

"I said I don't care to go. I'm not looking for the great Hollywood lay."

"You could use it."

"Yeah, I could use it, you're right, but I'm still not going."

"Give me one solid excuse."

"I don't have an excuse. I don't need an excuse. I'm just not interested."

Chris crossed the room to Bill sitting at the desk. He bent down over him, and put an arm around his shoulder. "Would you go as a friend if I told you I was feeling creepy about going alone?"

"Why didn't you say so in the first place?"

"Because I didn't."

"Moral support is all you're looking for?"

"I don't know the ropes. And I sure as hell don't know the people. I'd probably trip and fall in the front entry of this rich lady's house in Ferndale."

"Not Ferndale, Trousdale," laughed Bill, correcting his buddy.

"See, I don't even know how to say it."

"Okay, I'll go."

"You won't be sorry." Chris continued, "No, really, you won't. You'll like David Larkin. Besides, it will be good for you to meet him. Who knows, it may even help your career as a writer someday."

"I'll be sorry," Bill muttered.

"Who knows, you may even get laid."

Bill gave Chris a "that'll be the day" look and got up from the desk, went to his corner of the apartment and pulled together some clothes to wear.

"How come you're dressed in jeans and a casual shirt for some big Beverly Hills party?" Bill asked.

"Larkin told me it was going to be very casual, out by the pool or something."

"So, it's okay if I look the same. I don't need a tie or anything, right?"

"You'd wear a tie to the beach."

Bill dressed quickly. He wore a blue La Coste shirt, white pleated cotton pants, cuffed at the bottom, and slip-on navy blue tasseled loafers, no socks. He tossed a navy cotton tennis sweater, with red and white striped trim, over his shoulders and tied the arms across his chest in a knot. A million dollar look, and living in a four floor tenement.

"You know, Bill, you shouldn't make fun of meeting David Larkin tonight. He's first rate, and big-time Hollywood. Right now he's got a new TV series coming on the air and he's going to be writing and directing a movie for Dustin Hoffman."

"I'm sure he'll want to sign me as the producer, and you as Dustin Hoffman's co-star." said Bill cynically.

"I'll stop pushing," said Chris. "Just go as my moral support. You can just sit there and look at the view. I'll work the party."

• • •

Will Rogers Beach lay just ahead as Randy and Laurie made the final turn on Sunset Boulevard, passing the Moroccan-looking property of the Self-Realization Fellowship. The water of the Pacific was absolutely still. It joined the cloudless sky at the horizon and was distinguishable only by the spray of white stars and planets dotting the heavens and reflecting their majesty below on the seas.

The only sounds of the night were the purr of the Porsche engine, and the music of Sweet Baby James on the 8-track tape player.

Laurie put her head back on the contoured leather headrest and watched the movement of a plane in the sky as the music of James Taylor surrounded her in the compartment of the vehicle. Randy drove on, secure and steady, certain that he had said the right things, and was doing the right thing.

"Look, there it is," he said as Will Rogers Beach came into view.

"God, it's gorgeous." She continued, "I love the ocean, do you?"

"I was practically raised at the beach. It's like home."

"Really, how lucky for you. Was this a second home for your family, or did you actually grow up on the beach?"

"It was a beach house for us. I grew up in Bel Air."

"Then you really were a lucky kid, the best of Los Angeles, and during the best of times."

"You're right about that. I remember L.A. before freeways. The only way to the beach was Sunset or Wilshire and the only way to the Valley was over Sepulveda, a winding two-lane stretch through the Bel Air hills."

"Were your parents in show business, Randy?"

"My father."

"What did he do?"

"He bought and sold, and bought again."

"Excuse me?"

"My father is Benton Stein."

"Benton Stein, the studio mogul?"

"He's been called that and a few other things."

"Then you grew up in that big mansion on the hill that you can see from all over L.A."

"That's me, just a simple country boy. Does everyone in L.A. know Benton Stein's house?"

"Come on, don't be naive. It's been in just about every form of printed media. I've even seen reporters on the TV news live from the gates."

"I am proud to be his son, don't get me wrong, let's get that straight up front, okay?"

"You sound defensive."

"Gun-shy, that's all."

"It's okay, you don't have to prove anything, you're not on trial here. I'm just curious. Besides, you've lived with this your whole life. I'm not the first woman ever to have asked you where you're from, who you are, as you drove her to the beach on a romantic date."

"This is romantic, isn't it?"

"The conversation or the setting?"

They both laughed at Laurie's remark.

"Can I confess something?" he said.

"If you need to, nobody's stopping you."

"What do you think of my gray slacks and brown sport coat?"

"They're okay, nothing great. Why?"

"Do you like the tie?"

"Not really. Why?"

"I wore plain clothes because I was told you didn't like fancy guys."

"Are you?"

"A fancy guy?" he asked.

"Yes, are you a fancy guy wearing plain clothes?" Laurie laughed.

"I'm the son of the fanciest guy in Bel Air, and yes, I take after my dad."

"So, what's the big confession, that you didn't wear your fancy clothes to impress me, or rather to deceive me into thinking that you were regular?"

"Basically, that's it."

"Are you regular, under the fancy clothes, that is?"

"No."

"Good. You're honest."

"Not always."

"Double good, you're probably a very hot agent."

"One day. For now, I'm an associate agent-in-training to Candace Fielding."

"So, we've established three things here. One, you're a fancy dude in plain clothes. Two, you're a rich kid with Daddy Warbucks for a father. Three, you're selectively honest. Was that as a person or as an agent?" she asked.

"Agents are people, too." He regretted the idiocy of his statement. They looked at each other, and Laurie fell into wild hysterics.

"It wasn't that funny. Okay. Okay. It was dumb, okay. You can stop the laughing. 'Agents are people, too.' What a great slogan. William Morris should put it on a bumper sticker. Of course, no one would dare put it on their car for fear of a major rear-ender."

Laurie continued to laugh uncontrollably.

"Look, I just wanted you to know a little something about me, that's all. I thought you'd get a kick out of the fact that I was told to dress down for the evening."

Laurie composed herself and turned toward him in the car as he drove north on the winding Pacific Coast Highway. "Unless you're into paisley ascots, silk jacquard smoking jackets tied at the waist, I happen to like a guy who dresses to kill."

"You mean I can take off this goddamned brown jacket and this ugly tie?"

"Throw them out of the car if you like."

Randy managed to slither out of the jacket in difficult circumstances for a second time that evening. He ripped off his tie and continued navigating at the same time. "Hold the wheel for a second, Laurie, will you?" She reached over with her left hand and grabbed the leather covered wheel. Randy pulled the jacket around his back and tossed it and the tie overboard into the wind. "Free," he said, "free."

"Pretty expensive freedom if you ask me," she said.

"Worth it."

"You know, clothes aren't the man. A guy that's really fancy could feel fancy in a brown jacket."

"Now you tell me. Is it too late to go back for it?"

"So where are you taking me, anyway?"

Randy was relieved that she'd changed the subject. Enough was enough about clothes. He was almost sorry he'd gone for the honesty, Laurie probably would never have given his jacket a second glance.

• • •

"Are you sure we're supposed to come here and meet Larkin?" Bill questioned Chris.

"He said to be at his house by 10:00," Chris replied.

"It's almost 10:00 on the nose. Whoever heard of going to a party at 10:00 p.m.?"

"It's Hollywood, man, not Northern California or Illinois."

"I'll wait, you go to the door."

"It'll look strange if you wait. Park the car over there and we'll both go."

Bill pulled the car in the driveway and parked it over to the far side against a stately row of tall Italian cypress trees.

They walked to the front door.

"This is a beautiful house. I'll give you that," Bill told Chris as he rang the bell.

"I told you that you wouldn't be sorry. It's worth the price of admission just seeing this place."

The Oriental houseman came to the door.

"Gentlemen, may I help you?" He obviously wasn't expecting them, and he didn't recognize Chris from the Fuller Brushman.

"I'm Chris Reynolds. Mr. Larkin's expecting us."

"One moment, please," and the door closed in their faces.

"Are you sure about this?" Bill asked again.

"Will you relax?" Chris was very confident.

"I want an Oriental houseman when I make it."

"What?"

"Pretty classy, this David Larkin, even if I do feel like an idiot standing here waiting to be taken to a party by a man I've never met, to the house of a woman I've never met at 10:00 p.m. in the middle of the week. Don't these people have to work in the morning?"

The door opened, this time it was David Larkin.

"Glad you made it, Chris."

"Thanks for inviting us."

"Us," David Larkin's response indicated his surprise at seeing "us".

"This is my roommate, Bill Parker. He works at CBS."

David Larkin made no acknowledgement and turned, going into the house. With his back to them, he asked Bill and Chris to follow him to his car. Bill gave Chris a horrified I-told-you-so look, and the two of them sheepishly followed Larkin into the house.

Shadows danced off every corner of the massive Regency-Deco mansion. There was hardly a light on throughout the place as they followed Larkin through doors, down hallways, and out to the garage.

In the garage, a mansion in its own right, were four cars, a silver Rolls Royce, a Mercedes convertible, a Ford wagon, and a navy blue Cadillac Fleetwood Limousine. The Oriental houseman became a hyphenate employee and was now houseman-chauffeur, complete with a visored cap. He held the rear door of the limousine open for David Larkin and his guests.

Larkin got in the car first and took the left corner of the rear backseat. He immediately picked up a phone. Chris got in next and sat across from Larkin in the jump seat. Bill followed and sat next to Larkin, nervously staring at Chris.

"Mr. Lee, start the motor, I need to make a call," Larkin instructed his servant. Mr. Lee scampered around the car, hit the garage door opener, jumped in the car and turned over the motor. Larkin dialed. "Mr. Lee, we're going to Sally's on Carla Ridge."

"Yes, sir. Right away, sir."

"Stop by Mr. Mark's house first on the way. I'm calling now to tell him to be ready."

"Yes, sir. Mr. Mark first."

Mr. Lee backed the limo out of Larkin's garage, down the driveway and out onto Ambazac Way. Larkin was on the phone as Lee hit Sunset Boulevard heading towards Beverly Hills.

"Mark, we're on Sunset, we'll be there in ten minutes. How did it go today at the studio?"

There was a pause. Chris and Bill hung on David's every word trying nonchalantly to look out the limo's windows at the passing estates on Sunset Boulevard.

"The producer liked the performance. How do you know? Did he tell you? Not exactly. Not exactly yes or no? Look, just keep your nose clean, show up on time, know your lines backwards and forwards. We'll talk more in the car. See you in eight minutes."

He hung up and dialed another number. The buzzing and clicking of the mobile phone was inordinately impressive. Bill thought that having a car phone was possibly even better than an Oriental houseman.

His eyes were transfixed on Larkin. An hour before he'd been at his own present residence on the fourth floor of a ramshackle building downtown, and now he was riding in a limousine with a famous Hollywood mogul driven by a houseman equipped with a phone. Los Angeles was indeed a Lotus land of dreams and opportunity. Bill was now indeed glad he hadn't fought Chris to the point of not coming along.

• • •

"So where are we going?" Laurie asked Randy again.

"I told you I had a beach house. That's our destination."

"Is it far?"

"We're about ten minutes away."

"Is it incredible?"

"Compared to San Simeon, no."

"It's incredible. Is it on the sand?"

"Yes."

"Can we go for a walk along the water, then dig a hole in the sand on the beach and sit there for an hour looking at the stars?"

"How about a glass of champagne and we'll sit in the hot tub looking at the stars?"

"Why do men always want to get a woman in the hot tub? Never mind, don't answer."

"We can do whatever you'd like," he replied.

"Can we stay all night?" she asked to his surprise.

"I've never had a woman ask that on the first date. I'm usually trying to figure that one out?"

"I didn't say we can sleep together. I said, can we stay there all night, listening to the waves crash and watching the sky."

"We can. I said we can do whatever you'd like."

"Then that's it. We'll go for a walk along the water, then dig a hole, get in and watch the stars. Then we'll have a glass of champagne. Then let's get in the hot tub and soak. Then when we're totally relaxed, we'll fall asleep listening to the waves."

"So you do like the hot tub idea."

"Divine."

Randy turned off the Pacific Coast Highway and drove up to the guard shack entrance of the Malibu Colony. The gate was nothing more than a simple wooden shed, big enough to house a couple of guards controlling a wooden arm stretched across the narrow road that was not strong enough to stop a kid on a fast bike.

"This is it?" Laurie asked.

"This is the gate to the Colony," Randy responded.

"This."

"Yes, this."

"This is the famous Malibu Colony?"

"I told you it wasn't San Simeon."

"Good evening, Mr. Stein." The guard spoke as he came out of the shed with a flashlight aimed at the car and driver.

"Good evening to you, Sam. How ya feelin' tonight?"

"Mighty good, sir. Mighty good," and he raised the wooden arm over the drive allowing Randy to pass. The entrance was a simple, black-topped, two-lane road divided by shrubs. At the end of the entrance drive was the famed Colony. A strip of real estate so precious only a select few could get in, and even fewer could afford to stay. The houses were very ordinary by any standard. Simple beach cottages with wooden clapboard siding, casement windows, and inexpensive asphalt tile shingles on the roofs.

"This isn't the French Riviera. Are you sure this is the Colony, the only Colony? Maybe this is the junior Colony?" Laurie was doing her best spoiled actress voice as she mocked the Colony on her first impression.

"You'll like the beach," was Randy's only comeback.

"I'd have liked the beach twenty miles back, too."

"This is it."

Randy hit the button on a gray and silver remote control box in his car's console and a garage door opened in front of them. He pulled into the tandem four-car garage. There was one other car parked back in the corner. Some kind of antique.

"What is that wonderful old thing?" Laurie asked.

"It's a '49 Packard, used to belong to my granddad. Mom wouldn't sell it when he died, so it sits here. I don't think it's been driven in years."

"Will it start?"

"Your guess is as good as mine."

"Let's go for a ride."

"We just did that. I thought we were going for a walk now."

"That was before I saw this car. I love old cars."

"How about later? I'll try to start it. Come on, let's go inside, I'll show you around."

Randy took Laurie's hand, then ushered her into the courtyard separating the garage from the house. A charming brick path led them to the front door. The garden was filled with bushel-sized pink and white geraniums. White lattice crisscrossed around an old barn red front door, with yellow climbing roses weaving in and out of the textured wood cutouts of the lattice. Next to the door, a giant tarnished brass cow bell was mounted on a post, and a long strand of thick braided rope hung from its innards, beckoning its use. Laurie couldn't resist; she rang the old thing with great gusto.

"Shush. You'll wake up Filipa and Jorge," Randy said as he put both his hands over the bell to deaden the ringing sound.

"It's not even ten o'clock, and who's Filipa and what's his name?"

"They live here and take care of the place. Their apartment is right up there."

Randy pointed to a wooden staircase that led up to another old red door surrounded by more lattice and more climbing yellow roses above the garage. There was no light visible in the apartment.

"Sorry. I didn't know," said Laurie. She continued, "Anyone else here I need to know about?"

"No, that's it. Other than that, the place is all ours."

"What about Filipa and ??"

"They won't bother us. I come here all the time late at night. They go to bed at 9:00."

"Do you come here alone?"

"What do you think?" Randy was proud of his direct response.

Laurie winked at him and opened the door, entering the prettiest house she had ever seen that wasn't simply a picture in a magazine.

"This isn't at all what I expected," she told Randy. "It's so romantic, cozy and homey."

The beach house was Randy's mother's escape valve from the pressure of being Mrs. Benton Stein. This was the place where she could be Jenny Hartman, the elegantly unpretentious L.A. native, waspy Westlake girl who preferred potting geraniums on her brick patio, to attending high-powered lunches and dinners at the Club. The beach house was the only true reflection of her total person.

Like the old Packard in the garage, Jennifer Hartman had inherited the house from her parents. They'd built it on the beach before World War II when "The Colony" was nothing but another strip of sand north of Los Angeles.

Inside the house, Mrs. Stein had created the warmth of a country English hideaway suitable for the pages of "House and Garden." English and French furniture, including Bombay chests of walnut and armoires of magnificent country proportions complemented over-stuffed goose down-filled upholstered furniture covered in floral prints of daffodil yellow and Wedgwood blue. Prints of English rose florals mixed with patterns of bows and more bows and baskets of flowers tied in bows. Gleaming silver and crystal picture frames adorned tabletop after tabletop filled with family history and nostalgia.

"I don't ever want to leave," Laurie said as she toured Jennifer Stein's sanctuary by the sea. "It's so special here. No wonder you love this place so much."

"If you want to know what my mother's like, just look around here. Every inch of this beach house is her."

"I'd like your mother."

"I think you would."

"How about your father, would I like him?"

"I think you would. And I think he would like you."

"Really, why's that?"

"You're like him, in a way...."

"What?"

"You have great power with people. I saw it tonight at Ma Maison. He has that power, too."

Randy once again instantly regretted his honesty. What had come over him around this girl? First he confessed his motive for dressing down, now he was telling her about his observation of her manipulative abilities.

"This is the real me, Randy. I've always been the ringleader, ever since I was a kid in grade school."

"Most actresses I've known are just the opposite. Timid, shy, insecure."

"I've got my insecurities, the rock cracks, trust me, it does."

"Why did you want to move out here to Hollywood?"

"Because I was star struck as a kid. Because I hated my life in Texas, more or less. Because every girl in Loredo dreams about getting out, moving to Hollywood, getting discovered and living like Cinderella, only most of them, the ones that try, end up as hookers, not as Cinderella."

"It was different for you?"

"I told you back at Ma Maison that I believed in luck, and I do. It's not just talent that brings success, at least not in this business. Maybe I'll change my mind at 30 or 40, but for now I'm lucky that I'm not the hooker instead of The Cinderella."

"My father would like you."

"Good, I'd like to meet him someday."

"You will. Even if it's not through me."

"What's that supposed to mean?"

"It only means that you're going places in this business, and most people on the 'A' train eventually cross tracks with Benton Stein. How about that walk on the beach now?"

. . .

Mr. Lee pulled David Larkin's limo up to the curb at the corner of Reeves Drive and Charleville in the low rent apartment district just south of Wilshire Boulevard in Beverly Hills. The streets in this neighborhood were lined with two-story, eight unit apartment buildings. The rents were low, the trees manicured and the location was ideal. The perfect place to live for a struggling actor or writer. All this and a Beverly Hills address to enhance the image.

Mark Harlander's apartment and his lifestyle fit this formula. Mr. Lee got out of the car and went into Harlander's building to get him.

"Mark is a client and a friend," David Larkin told Bill and Chris. "I saw him in a play at the Pasadena Playhouse last year and offered to help him build his career."

"You just do this for nothing?" Chris blurted out.

After a momentary silence, David responded, "We have a management contract that provides me with a standard percentage of his gross, when his gross is worth taking a standard percentage from."

"Do you manage many actors, Mr. Larkin?" Bill asked.

"I'm rather unique in that regard. I build talent for my picture stable."

The click of the car door handle meant that Mr. Lee was back with Mark Harlander. The rear door opened and in stepped a Greek god-like blonde from Central Casting. Men don't really look this good in person, Bill thought, only in clothes catalogues, movie posters, or as mannequins in storefront windows.

"Good to see you, guy," David said. Lee closed the door, and went around to the driver's compartment. "You're looking great as usual," David continued. Mark nodded his approval and looked at Bill and Chris, wondering who the extras were tonight. Larkin introduced his passengers. "Chris Reynolds and Bill... I'm sorry, what was your last name again?"

"Parker."

"How's it goin'?" Mark replied.

"Chris read for me. I'm thinking of auditioning him for a small part," David said to everyone's amazement, especially Chris's.

Larkin, now sitting next to Mark Harlander in the back seat of his limo, started talking to him about work, excluding the guys as if they were invisible. There was now an impenetrable shield between the jump seats and Larkin. Chris and Bill spent the remainder of the ride to the party alternately taking in the Disneyland-like tour of Beverly Hills real estate on the outside, and the Hollywood tour de force taking place beyond the invisible barrier in front of them, on the inside. Bill was sure this was all a materialized dream, a verse and chapter from Nathaniel West's Day of the Locust come to life.

Beneath the skepticism, beyond his cynicism, he loved every Hollywood beat of it. This was a real slice of the tinsel pie and he was a part of it. It was, in fact, what he'd always wanted, to be part of the inner circle, the powerbrokers, the movers. And at this moment, he was just a jump seat away, regrettably on the wrong side of the invisible barrier, but just a jump seat away.

• • •

"Oh my God, it's 7:30 in the morning." Laurie let out a quiet scream, as she stumbled out of bed and around the master bedroom of Jennifer Stein's Malibu Colony beach house. "Where are my shoes?" she mumbled, searching in vain for any kind of article of clothing resembling that which she believed she wore the evening before. In her futile hunt for her clothing, she found herself in front of a mirror-fronted, French Louis style carved armoire. She slapped her face and pulled her thick and tangled hair back, wrapping it all in a severe bun. Half dressed in her slip, crawling on the floor, she managed to spot the little black cocktail dress under a pastel-colored mohair bed throw that was now on the carpet.

"Wake up, Randy," she tried to be gentle and sweet as she rocked him, with both of her hands on his shoulders. Randy had fallen asleep backwards and face down on the bed. His head was practically over the bottom edge and his legs were spread-eagle, one on a pillow at the top, the other hanging over the side. He was in his white cotton boxers, his gray slacks thrown over a chair by the bed.

"Randy, please wake up. I'm due at the studio and I'm going to be very late." Laurie shook him again gently, this time making her plea right in his ear.

Randy pulled his head up, turned to the side and looked at Laurie. In his half-conscious state, he thought that she was even more beautiful in the morning. He rubbed his eyes with his free hand. The other hand was still asleep under his stomach.

"What did you say?" he said looking right at her, nose-to-nose, on the end of the bed.

"I need to get to the studio, we have to get up. By the way," she looked back over and whispered in his ear, "Good morning, you look very cute in your boxers."

The hot-sex-breath-in-the-ear Laurie brought the otherwise zonked out Randy to life. He put his one good arm around Laurie and drew her next to him.

"I like your hair pulled back like that," he said.

Then, looking into her eyes, pressed his legs against hers, and kissed her.

"That's the way I like to start off the morning," she said softly.

"Did we make love last night?" he asked.

"You don't know?" she responded coyly.

"I don't think we did. I think we fell asleep talking on the bed. Can you believe it? We fell asleep."

"We did fall asleep, but don't worry, your male ego is salvageable. You did try more than once."

"You stopped me, I remember now."

"Well, you're a fast operator. Besides, we made a deal, remember?"

Randy looked at her, then smiled, "Yes, I remember. You told me that you would put a gardenia on my pillow when you were ready to make love to me, and that if I was willing to wait for the gardenia I wouldn't be sorry. Now, did I really go for that line, or were we both just too tired anyway?" Randy smiled at her again, pulled her close and kissed her a second time.

"You went for it, and you'll have to abide by it," Laurie said. "For now, you've got to put on your old gray no, let me rephrase that, your wrinkled and rumpled old gray slacks and take me to the studio before I get fired off the TV show, before there's no work to represent me for."

"I do want to represent you," he said.

"I know."

"Do I need to wait for a gardenia on my desk to know your answer on that?"

"Not a bad idea, I'll give it some thought."

Randy got up off the bed by crawling onto the floor over the back end and doing a somersault into the corner where his clothes were thrown over a chair. He stood up and got dressed as quickly as possible, while Laurie ran into the bathroom to wash her face.

• • •

Mr. Lee navigated David Larkin's navy blue Cadillac Fleetwood limousine into the executive lot of the studio. Larkin was half asleep in the backseat with the New York Times, Daily Variety, and the Hollywood Reporter in his lap. The tires of the car tapped a concrete parking bumper jolting Larkin awake. Mr. Lee shut off the ignition and came around to open Larkin's door. Larkin stepped out of the car, forgetting the papers in his lap, and they fell to the ground, the wind blowing them in all directions as he stood up outside the limo.

Lee scurried to catch everything, putting the papers neatly back in the car. He handed David his black leather case with its long, thick, shoulder strap-like harness. The weight of his scripts and papers, personal effects, appointment book, phonebook, the phonebook alone rivaled the size of a yellow pages in any number of modern cities, required an extra heavy-duty strap so that he could carry it all.

For a while Larkin had a runner, the Hollywood euphemism for an entry level job generally given to a kid right out of U.S.C. Film School with a masters in cinema-television, following him around toting the bag. It became too pretentious, even for David Larkin. So, he lightened the load, divided the bag into baguettes, three of them to be exact, and took what he needed, when he needed it, to the various meetings, rehearsals, shooting schedules that filled his day.

With baguette number one in tow, Larkin headed from the limo to the executive suite. John Moran would be waiting there for him.

Larkin knew how much Moran hated these 8:30 a.m. meetings. It meant he had to be in the office ahead of everyone else. Yet, at 8:30, Larkin would have John Moran's complete attention for at least an hour, since Larkin had to start his shooting schedule by 9:30 and Moran couldn't sit still and concentrate on one thing for more than an hour anyway. At least there would be no phone interruptions, no secretaries barging in with emergencies.

Larkin got off the elevator and walked into Moran's third floor office. There he was, just like he always was, behind the great partners' desk, left over courtesy of the David O. Selznick days at the studio.

"Good morning, John," Larkin spoke first, as he entered. Actually, he wasn't feeling all that good himself. Sally's soirée in Trousdale had been an evening to forget. Too much wine mixed hazardously with a fondness for white powder provoked the worst in the sophisticated set. By 2 a.m., Mark Harlander was being pulled out the door by a security man attempting to keep Harlander's fists off Chris Reynold's face. Larkin could not recall how Mr. Lee got him back home. Despite the consequences of the previous evening, like the magnificent Hollywood edifice he was in, Larkin looked terrific.

"How the hell are you, you, you no good bastard calling me in for another 8:30 meeting." Moran barked at Larkin, but it was routine, and more important, it was friendly fire. David always knew when it wasn't. He could smell trouble.

"I feel terrific, John. I have never had so much energy. I think it's this new exercise regiment I've been on." Larkin lied to John Moran. He felt like crap, tired, rundown, his head ached from too much Crystal Champagne, and he knew he had a very long day ahead of him. But Larkin followed the credo taught to him by a man he considered something of a mentor early in his career. That mentor had a secret code, known only to his closest, and few comrades "in the business." The code was, if you felt a little lousy, say you're fine. If you felt more than a little lousy, say you're doing great. And, if you're feeling like pure shit, say your life was absolutely terrific, that you were on top of the world, never better.

David Larkin practiced his old mentor's philosophy like religion. He was feeling absolutely superb - like shit.

"I've been looking at the dailies and I've got some suggestions, David," Moran was starting with suggestions, a very thinly disguised term for orders from on high.

"Really, what sort?" Larkin responded.

"I've got to tell you that I'm more than pleased. In fact, I'm convinced the show is on the proper course," Moran said, setting the tone to buffer the criticism to come.

"Good, then we agree."

"We always agree, David, most of the time."

"Then what suggestions do you have?"

"You want it straight out or sugar-coated?"

"Let me have it. What is it? What change? What re-write? What re-shoot?" Larkin sat down in one of the pair of oversized Sheridon style armchairs opposite Moran's desk. "Go on, lay it on me. Go on," he repeated.

"The Dalton girl is fucking brilliant and too hot just too hot on screen."

"That's bad?" Larkin was off his guard now.

"That's bad when she's the co-star. Peter Barker looks like a male Bette Davis in a bad TV remake of 'Sunset Boulevard' next to Laurie Dalton. For Chrissakes, the chemistry is awful. She's the star, he's the tag-a-long and it's the Peter Barker Show."

"You're exaggerating," Larkin offered.

"I don't know what to suggest. Not yet, anyway. But we've got to fix this and fix it fast. The network will shit when they see this."

"It's only the first week of production, John. Don't you think we might be jumping to conclusions here a bit too quickly?"

"No. I'm sure of it."

"You're sure of it? Or they're sure of it?"

"We're sure of it, if it makes you happy, goddamn it!"

"Well, that's nice, but I'm the creator of the series and I'm not sure of anything like that, not in the first week. So give it a rest, Moran."

"You're too close to Barker and the show."

"You're damn right I'm too close. Barker is my star. I've made him. I've taught him and managed him for years, through bit parts, failed pilots, and one five year hit before this. I know the man, I know what he's got and I know this is the right vehicle for him, for you, for the network."

"And for you, David."

"Yes, for me, mostly for me. It's my show. I created it, and Barker is my boy. I created him, too."

"But it's my studio, and it's their network, and it's Proctor and Gamble and Ford and God knows what other dollars that will either finance this failure or this hit. What do you want it to be, David?"

"Come on, Moran, this is ludicrous. I simply won't agree, not now, not yet."

"Then promise me two things?"

"What?"

"Think about it. Think about it hard and watch the chemistry."

"What else?"

"Think about how to make Dalton the focal star, not Barker. Then we'll have the hit. Let's talk next week. Same time, 8:30 okay with you, David?"

"If it's okay with you, John. I'll be here."

Larkin got up and left the office with his bag in tow, which suddenly became a huge burden, and he wished for a moment that he'd kept the goddamned pretentious little runner.

A million negative thoughts hit Larkin's brain. This was no longer the show business David Larkin had flourished in for over twenty years. It was a business of constant compromise without clear and distinct leadership.

Everybody had their hands in every project. The creator of a show had the least to say, while the studio that financed the actual production tap-danced with the network that, in turn, was buying the production and putting the show on the air.

Along the way, power broker agents and their greedy clients clawed for an increasingly disproportionate slice of the pie as inexperienced actors were given directorial assignments to sweeten their deals and writers were elevated to producership in order to get them to sign on and beat the competition. Larkin felt like he was witnessing the final days of Rome. It was dog-eat-dog, only in the chaparral-covered hills of Los Angeles it was more aptly coyote-eat-coyote. They were feasting, but would there by anything left of Hollywood when they were finished? David wondered, and kept on walking towards the set.

CHAPTER 9

Randy made a quick shower-shave-change stop at his place up on Hutton Drive before making his appearance at the Candace Fielding suite in the Morris building on El Camino. He was right on time as he walked through her double door entry at 10:00 a.m., looking very dapper in a navy blue Calvin Klein double-breasted suit that sported simple, very faint, wide pinstripes. His shirt was heavily starched Egyptian cotton, and he wore a vibrant red silk tie, in a perfect Windsor knot, to complete the picture.

Still wet from his fast shower, Randy's rich wavy black hair was combed straight back off his forehead, and it looked as if he'd styled it that way to compliment his formidable suit. Candace was at her desk, on the phone as expected, when he entered.

"Is there a contract in your pocket, or are you just happy to see me?" she said to Randy flippantly, mimicking Mae West, looking up from her phone call cupping the receiver as she spoke.

"I'm always happy to see you, Candace," he responded.

"Then prove it," she hung up the phone, got up and went over to him. Randy was standing still beside his desk holding his briefcase.

"What happened last night with Dalton?" Candace was tough.

"I met her at Ma Maison. She was there with all the studio guys. We had a good time, we left, drove to the beach, went for a walk, fell asleep, and I took her to work this morning."

"You spent the night with her?"

"Yes."

"Good."

"I'm planning on picking her up tonight after she finishes shooting."

"Did you talk business?"

"Some."

"How much some?"

"I laid the groundwork."

"Did you lay her?"

"I laid the groundwork," he repeated.

"Don't be a smart ass with me, Stein. I want that girl in my stable, do you read me?"

"Candace, I will do my best to sign her."

"No, if you don't sign her, your best won't be good enough and you can climb the corporate ladder somewhere else."

"I feel that I have a shot with her. She's very smart, not just another dumb blonde that got lucky." Candace cut him off, "What are you yapping about, Stein?"

"I'm saying that she's not a simple, slam-dunk sign. She's smart."

"You said that," she interrupted again.

"And she's talented, too. She's particular, she's analytical… and she's careful," he finished.

"Brother, she's everything but a fucking boy scout, and my client." Candace started to walk back to her desk and spoke with her back to Randy, "All I know is that she is a hot property in a hot new TV series with offers galore for film and TV and she's unrepresented. It's fucking unheard of, just a lawyer to do her deals, no agency. Did you hear me, no agency." Candace reached her desk and sat at the throne. "Every two-bit pitcher in town is trying to land her and you just may have the inside track, so don't blow it. Do you hear? Don't blow it."

Candace picked up the phone and dialed. Before Randy could sit at his desk, she was at it again with someone else. Candace simply never ever let up when it came to business.

• • •

A rush of silence fell over the two hundred people on Soundstage 21 at the MGM lot, as David Larkin entered through the thirty-foot tall studio doors. The stage was at maximum capacity for a 9:00 a.m. weekday morning. Scenic artists were spray-painting variegated shades of green paint on the needles of dead pine trees in the front of the main house on the set, a six-columned antebellum colonial. This was the home of the new Larkin TV serial, "The Reilly's of San Marino".

The artists sprayed and the carpenters nailed, the hairdressers fluffed and puffed and the gaffers played with the lights. The best boy served coffee and rolls, always croissants, never doughnuts. Larkin hated doughnuts on the set, in the form of food or people. Actors were milling around rehearsing lines and checking costumes and make-up. But it all stopped as the almighty David Larkin set foot on Stage 21.

Larkin was respected by the cast and the crew largely for his talent and reputation, but also because he worked as hard and as long as any man or woman on the show. He was often the first one there and the last to leave. He expected everyone to be as dedicated. Not surprisingly, few lived up to his demands, his expectations. Actually, nobody did.

He considered himself the best, and the only real King of the Mountain at the present time in celluloid history. There was one quality in others that he supremely admired. To the point of personal adoration, he worshipped those with acting talent. Especially those he found, developed, and managed. The rewards were immense. Not just in dollars, which were extraordinary for the standards of the seventies, but in vicarious excitement. There was a certain thrill for David Larkin to be in the presence of Barbra or Sammy, Frank or Lucy. He was their junior, but their peer. It was equality in a true show business sense, a trade off. He worshipped them, they were in awe of him.

"Mr. Larkin, you're wanted in your office, sir," a skinny boy with a ginger-color complexion, who looked like he was barely fifteen and just off some corner of the male prostitute zone on Santa Monica Boulevard, ran over to Larkin with the message.

"Thank you, Danny," said the almighty David Larkin. He quickly made his way to the back of the stage where his office was located. Larkin's office was very plain, ordinary studio issue. It was quite a large contrast to the man who lived in a deco regency mansion in Bel Air and rode in a limo. He wanted it plain, no attachments or fuss. A large old desk, two wooden chairs, a bookshelf filled with scripts, an ugly green couch, two IBM Selectric typewriters and a phone. That was the almighty David Larkin's office environment at MGM.

"D.L., here are the latest script revisions." Marie, his secretary, handed him the pages as he passed by. Her phones were ringing off the hook. Marie kept track of four lines for David. In her late forties, she had worked for Larkin for almost thirty years, her entire adult life.

In the early days she'd had a huge crush on her boss. After all, he was, in so many ways, Mr. Wonderful. Talented, handsome, rich and famous, Larkin was Clark Gable to Marie. The crush faded as the scripts and letters mounted and although somewhere around year ten in David Larkin's employ she finally came to terms with the reality of her life, and the impossibility of any relationship with David other than what existed to date,Marie still adored her boss. After all, he was now her entire life. She had no family, no social life to speak of, no hobbies, no tennis or golf. Even though Marie O'Neil was still an attractive, slender brunette, she chose to devote her life to David Larkin. They were meant for each another, sort of.

"Marie, would you see if Miss Dalton is available to come to my office?" David called out through the open door separating their spaces.

"Right away, D.L." She loved to call him by his initials. It was such a fine tradition that went along with the best of the past Right away, "C.B." In a minute, "J.B." Okay, "D.W." Larkin liked it. D.L. was just fine with him.

• • •

By mid-day lunch break, the tension was omnipresent on Stage 21. Cut, cut, cut. Take 56, 57, 58, 59. Cut. Take a 5. Cut. Take another 5, Take 60, Take 61. The cast and crew knew that the morning had been a disaster. Larkin had shot and re-shot, but he had nothing acceptable in the can. The second assistant director called lunch with not a second to spare. David Larkin had become the "almighty volcano," about to erupt, and his lava would leave no one unburned.

"D.L., D.L.." Marie was chasing Larkin across the floor of the stage "D.L., please stop, I need to speak to you."

"Just follow me, Marie, I know you're there," he shouted, never turning around, stopping, or even slowing down to acknowledge her.

"Okay, Boss, I'm ten paces behind you with the news that Moran is waiting for you in your office," she said just loud enough for him and no one else to hear. It was sort of a whisper-shout. She'd mastered the technique over the years. Larkin stopped cold, and turned around.

"Thank you, Marie, join me in the executive dining room for lunch?" Before she could answer, he took her by the arm and turned her around. The almighty and Marie marched through the barn doors and out onto the studio lot.

The walk to the dining room was brisk. David had on his dark glasses and marched at the pace of a Nazi S.S. storm trooper to avoid being stopped by anyone. Marie kept up. They walked in the glass doors of the dining room and Tony, the maitre'd, bowed, greeted them and took them immediately to Larkin's regular booth in the back.

Larkin's corner booth was prime viewing territory. It was definitely the "A" table. He had a perfect vantage point of everyone in the room, and also could see anyone coming over to him with plenty of notice. There was a phone at this table. He often picked it up, pretending to make a call, if someone he didn't want to see was coming his way. The perfect deflector that phone. It worked every time.

"Marie, I've got a problem."

"I know, David."

"I really thought he'd come around."

"He can't do it."

"I coached him, I sent him to Nina Foch, she worked with him for a month."

"She told you he was wrong for the part, David."

"Yes, I know but he has the look, the draw. Women loved him in 'The Divorce Chronicles'."

"That was such a bad movie, D.L."

"Seventy-five million at the box office isn't bad."

"I didn't say unsuccessful, I said bad."

"The role of Joe Reilly should be a snap for Barker, what the hell's wrong?"

"He's dumb. How's that for starters?" Marie didn't hold back. Three decades on a job had some advantages. "Dalton is superb. She's your show."

"I know, but with Barker at her side, we're all going to be laughed off the fall schedule." Larkin knew Moran was right. He hated that Moran was right.

"David, do you want the phone?" Marie handed it to him before he could answer her. She saw Moran coming.

"Larkin," he said in a voice loud enough to silence the restaurant. "We need to talk."

David handed the phone back to Marie. It was too late for decoys. Moran sat down in the booth next to Marie, who didn't move, leaving him very little room. "That's it, David, we need to get rid of him."

"What's it? And who's him?" Larkin replied very coolly.

"You know damn well what's it," Moran snapped back. He was sweating from his near run over to the dining room from Larkin's office. He grabbed a napkin off the table and patted his forehead and neck, quickly unbuttoning his collar and loosening his suffocating tie.

"Another hot one today," Larkin said coolly.

"It's even hotter on the set. David, I know how badly the morning went. We need to do something about it. Surely you agree?" Moran was making an attempt at reason.

"Surely I agree about what? You're being very vague. And, how do you know what kind of morning I had on the set? Were you there?" Larkin was not so cool now.

"My production executive was there. He is always there, as you are fully aware. Now let's stop the bullshit and face reality. Who the fuck are you protecting anyhow?"

"I am not going to listen to the frantic demands of an executive who is basing his anxiety on the reports of a 23-year-old Princeton graduate in a Brooks Brothers suit with an MBA so new that the ink isn't dry on the parchment." David stood up. With perfect poise and total composure he folded his napkin, put his hand out to Marie, gesturing for her to get up. "We'll have lunch in my office. I can't eat here today."

Moran was angry, but he bit his lip and glared at Larkin and Marie as they began to walk out.

"John, if you'll have your secretary call Marie, we'll set up a meeting to discuss matters at a later date in private," David said. And then, he and Marie walked across the room as all eyes were glued to them in the total silence of the normally bustling dining room.

The four telephone lines were all ringing when David and Marie walked back in the door to the office off stage 21. "Don't answer any of them," Larkin declared.

"As you wish," she took a deep breath and went on, "at least they are all ringing in harmony."

He laughed anxiously. She gave him one of those, "Now what are we going to do," looks.

"Marie, if you can get a free line, call the William Morris Agency and get me that new young agent I said I liked. What was his name again?"

"Sholtz, D.L. Michael Sholtz."

"Right, call Sholtz for me. I need to speak to him right away."

"Yes, sir."

"And then, as soon as we've talked to Mr. Sholtz I need Sol Larson at CBS."

"Okay. First Shotlz, then Larson, anything else?"

"Yes, then get me Howard Hillman at Paramount."

"Sholtz, then Larson, then Hillman."

"Listen, if you can't get an open line, just pick up one of the ringing phones, hang it up, and dial fast."

"Yes, sir." Marie saluted. She loved the action, the drama. Word of the Moran-Larkin lunchroom scene had spread all over the lot, all over town, in minutes. Everyone was calling to verify the gossip. David knew he had to work fast to win the game.

"D.L., I've got Mr. Sholtz from the agency on line 2," Marie called into Larkin's office. He picked up the phone.

"Michael, I've got to move quickly and I need your help. Peter Barker is screwing up 'The Reilly's' and he's got to go, but nobody else needs to know this. I want to protect Peter and the Studio, and most of all, my show. How are your tap-dancing shoes? Word is leaking as we speak."

"Barker's contract is airtight, David. I ought to know, I helped negotiate it. How can I get him out at this point without causing a furor?"

"Isn't there an out for a movie deal?"

"There is, on seasonal hiatus, with studio and network approval."

"That won't work."

"Give me half an hour. I'll come up with something. I need to go upstairs and talk to Lou. I'll get right back, I promise, just keep the lid on it. We'll get out of this."

Larkin hung up the phone and told Marie to get Larson.

"Sol on line one, D.L."

"Sol, we've got to re-write the storyline of 'The Reilly's'. Barker is a disaster, he'll never sustain the series. Our only hope is to use him as a season opener, a hook to get the audience. Then write him out of the show, after we establish new characters and a new storyline."

David knew he could do it and he also knew his longtime associate Sol Larson, head of network programming, would back him up.

"David, this is a tricky one. The affiliates all expect Barker as the star. The network has promoted the hell out of him as the cornerstone of the show."

"We'll build a new cornerstone," Larkin replied.

"Barker is no good for this show, and we're in trouble. He's got to be released, carefully."

"What have you got in mind?"

"I want to restructure the show working Laurie Dalton as the lead. She'll play the female dynamo who controls the Reilly empire created by her late father, Joe Reilly, killed in a tragic accident. She'll do this with the help of her older brother. We'll add a new character, let's call him Eric. He was a runaway, she'll bring him back and together these two kids will conquer the world."

"Sounds interesting," Larson said. "But will it work?"

"Dalton is superb. I'll find the right boy for the brother part. Somebody unknown, with great sex appeal for the young audience. The spin on this program will be youth all the way. Uninhibited youth with power, money, looks, glamour, and a big future to enjoy it all. It's pure fantasy."

Larkin was excited with his plan and Larson went along.

"It's out there, David. It's wild, I think it may work. Get back to me with your final scenario. I'll back you, here, at the network. It won't be easy, but I'll sell it."

Larson hung up, and Larkin called for Marie to make his third call to Howard Hillman at Paramount. Hillman was an independent movie producer on the Paramount lot, making yet another of his trademark blockbuster action-adventure flicks. He'd also known Larkin for thirty years. They remained close, although competitive, as they worked in the same arena as producer-directors. In Hollywood, there was no room for two tigers in the same cage.

"Howard, it's David."

"How's it going?"

"I need a favor, Howard."

"So it's not going well?"

"It's going well enough, but not perfect. I need to dump Barker he's not right."

"Barker's out?"

"I know it's nuts, but what else is new? He's just not right."

"So what can I do?" Howard questioned.

"Give him a part in your new movie."

"We're just about done casting, David."

"But it's not done, Howard. Just about, isn't the same as signed."

"Oh, come on, you know what you're asking. You know how complicated and difficult it is to change at the last minute?"

"I know, but I also know it's done every day in this town."

"So why should I do this?"

"Because, Barker is hot property. You've used him in your last two films. You want another 'Divorce Chronicles' don't you?"

"This is a different vehicle," Hillman replied.

"Then write him a major cameo. Promote him for box office."

"You still haven't said why I should do this?"

"You want me to say it, Howard? You know why you should do this? Do I have to say it out loud on the phone. Give me a goddamned break." Larkin was angry, on the verge of yelling into the receiver.

"It's fucking blackmail. That's all it is. Call it anything else, a favor, a consideration, but it's still plain fucking blackmail." There was silence and then Hillman spoke again, "This is it. I'll do it for you, but this is it. No more. Do you read me? I want the other business forgotten and <u>never</u>, I mean <u>never</u> mentioned or hinted at again, as if it never happened." Hillman was screaming.

"David, what is it you have on Hillman?" Marie asked as she entered his section of their offices. She'd heard Larkin's side of the call, and guessed the rest.

"He used my beach house off and on last year for an affair." David was matter-of-fact and began looking through a pile of scripts on his desk.

"That's the big secret? The whole town is having affairs, why is his so secret?"

"Now you're asking too many questions, let's get back to the Barker situation. Is he back from lunch? Can you find out and get him to come in here?"

"Yes, D.L., right away." Marie left the office as David kept searching through his papers, looking for something he couldn't find.

• • •

"Los Angeles is a marvelous place to make a fortune and a terrible place to make a living." Benton Stein's words of counsel to his son Randy were often draped in poetic language but the message, nevertheless, was clear.

"There is no middle class, no in-between, no comfortable zone," he continued. "Either you're a player or you're not in the game. And if you're a player, then you better have the killer instinct, and you better play to win. Winning counts, son. In business the bottom line matters, and it's just as true in show business as it is in a cotton mill."

"Dad, where do you draw the line? Let's say you were an agent's assistant at a big agency and your boss put your future on the line, demanding you do anything you had to do, including sex, drugs, and lies to sign a new client the agency wanted."

"Do you want a career with the agency?" Benton asked.

"Yes, very much," Randy said.

"Do you think the new client is worth this effort?"

"Yes, she's worth it."

"The client is a young actress, perhaps?"

"Yes."

"Fuck her, tell her she's the next Marilyn Monroe, and sign her ass to a contract."

Randy looked at Benton and took a gulp of his white wine. The Polo Lounge at the Beverly Hills Hotel was filled to capacity for a 5:30, mid-week afternoon. The bar normally didn't get busy until around 7:00 in the evening with the after work meeting crowd and the pre-dinner drink tourists, hoping to get a look at the stars meeting their agents for a little tête-à-tête.

The deep forest green, velvet room with its starched pale pink linens and twinkling candlelight was still Benton Stein's favorite watering hole. He'd been a regular for more than three decades and he knew them all. Angelo always put him in the front room and always at the first table against the wall. He always sipped his JB Mist slowly at that table, advising C.E.O.s, candidates for national office, as well as his son, in the ways of the world. He also met his women there.

The Polo Lounge was so suited to Hollywood. It wouldn't be the same in any other city. A mix of entertainment business lore, movie stars, rich people, classy-looking people, and regular Midwestern-looking people mixed with hookers and hustlers and traveling salesmen in shiny suits with ring around the collar.

Laurie Dalton came through the door of the Polo Lounge at about 6:45, about three drinks after Randy first sat down with his father.

"Dad, there she is, at the front."

"There who is? You didn't say anyone was coming here."

"It's Laurie Dalton, the actress I was telling you about."

"I'm surprised that you didn't mention you'd invited her to join us."

"I want your opinion, honest opinion of her after you meet her, deal?"

"Deal. If she's half as gorgeous up close as she is from fifty feet away, my opinion is already set."

• • •

"David, I'm sorry, but the writing on the show is terrible. I need a new writer. I can't say the lines. I can't even remember the lines they're so bad. I'm sorry, I'm really sorry. Tomorrow I'll do better, but you've got to get me a new writer, someone who can write for me, David."

Peter Barker, nearly fifty-nine and still pretending to be a thirty-five year-old stud bachelor, faced the career crisis of his lifetime. On film, he still had that magic charisma. In person, Barker looked used, tired and scared like a cat in a corner. Too many years of living on the Hollywood rollercoaster. Barker was sweating and his eyes twitched violently, as he confessed to his producer and begged for forgiveness. It was late, the set was dark, and everyone had long since gone home.

"Peter, you're missing the point."

"I don't get it," the sweating, twitching, actor feebly replied.

"You're a big star, Peter, not some two-bit actor who can't remember a line."

"What are you saying, David?"

"It's not working, Peter. You're wrong for this part, for this show."

"I can play this part. This is a piece of cake. I told you, it's the writing, not me." He was getting more nervous and his voice was shaking. David could see he was almost in tears.

"We talked at lunch, didn't we?"

"Yes."

"Was the afternoon better?"

"Worse."

"Did I make you more nervous?"

"It just got worse."

"I know. And I believe it won't get better, because the whole thing is wrong."

"What do you want me to do, quit?"

"I'm thinking..." David replied.

"You know, it's not me, D.L. I think it's that Dalton chick. She's trouble, that one. The upstage queen she is. She steps on every one of my lines, she makes me look stupid, throws off my timing. If you just got rid of her, and get me a new writer, David, it would all work out. I know it would."

"You're right. The chemistry between you and Laurie is way off."

"Then you'll think about it, re-casting her, giving me another chance."

"I already have thought about it. Peter, that's not the way the deck is going to be played."

Peter started sobbing. The echo of his angst encircled the room, bouncing off the four barren walls magnified three-fold in the solemn empty space. He cupped his hands over his eyes, putting his elbows to his knees. Peter Barker, film legend, reduced to tears over the role of Joe Reilly on a TV series. The Oscar he'd won five years earlier for his leading role in "The Sinner" all but forgotten, just a foggy memory. He was only as good as his latest role. It was the actor's curse. Now, in this moment of weakness, the past, his glorious past, was worthless to him.

David was amazed by Barker's reaction. To him it was the Achilles heel of the insecure performer. And, it was in nearly all of them, great and small alike. He also knew that nothing short of giving in completely to Peter, which was out of the question, would console him. So, David gave Peter a hug, put his arm around his shoulder, and the two almighty titans of tinsel walked out of the barren office into the vast silhouette of night at the studio. They headed across the lot for the parking structure, where their cars and drivers would be dutifully waiting.

CHAPTER 10

T he studio provided Peter Barker with a chauffeur and limousine. Jimmy, the driver, had only known Peter for a few weeks, picking him up daily since the start of rehearsals for the series.

"Shall I take you home, Mr. Barker?" Jimmy asked, as he got into his driver's seat. The glass partition separating them was open. There was silence. "Excuse me, sir, Mr. Barker, shall I take you home, sir?" Jimmy asked again.

"Yes, okay, fine," Peter answered abruptly in a staccato voice. He reached over and closed the partition with a bang. He'd never closed the translucent border between them before. Jimmy figured Barker had a rough day on the set, so he'd leave him alone, and get him home quickly.

• • •

Pulling the slate gray stretch Lincoln Town Car Custom Limousine out of the MGM gate into the Washington Boulevard traffic, Jimmy headed north, zigzagging throughout the time-worn business district of downtown Culver City. He turned right on Venice Boulevard, then a quick left onto Robertson, the gateway to Beverly Hills.

Jimmy was now on a steady course, when Peter yanked open the glass partition.

"Jimmy, stop the car. Stop here pull over."

"Here, sir?"

"Just stop the goddamn car now."

Jimmy pulled the stretch over to the right side of Robertson and stopped at a red curb in front of Sid's Liquors. Heavy burglar bars covered the large plate glass windows of Sid's. A yellow and red neon sign flashed over the open door, leading to a brightly lit den of discount liquor.

"Wait here. I'll be right back," Peter said, as he threw open the rear door and got out of the limo on the sidewalk.

"Tell me what you want. I'll get it for you," Jimmy shouted back, but Peter was already out of the car.

He was buying booze. Bourbon to be exact. Three fifths of Jack Daniels to go, and fast. The black man behind the counter threw the liquor into a brown bag, Peter threw two twenty-dollar Bills on the counter and took off without waiting for nearly nineteen dollars in change. He jumped back into the limo and told Jimmy to drive.

Peter was drinking the Jack Daniels straight out of the bottle the second he got back in the car. He didn't bother to use the cut crystal glasses provided in the plush vehicle. For that matter, if he had looked, he would have discovered that the limo bar already had a bottle of Jack Daniels. It didn't matter, he was in his own world and wanted nothing the studio provided.

By the time Jimmy the driver crossed Olympic Boulevard entering Beverly Hills, Peter was starting his second fifth of Jack Daniels.

"Turn left, Billy, turn here, do you hear me, Billy?" Peter's directions were slurred and he couldn't remember his driver's name. It didn't matter, "Billy" would do.

"Bill, hey, Bill, turn. Do you read me, man, I want to make a fast stop before we go home, okay, so turn, okay?"

"Where to sir?" Jimmy responded.

"Chasen's, Billy. Take me to Chasen's."

"Yes, sir. Right away."

The classic white brick facade and green awnings of Chasen's Restaurant hadn't changed in years. It was the most venerable of the old Hollywood establishments. Inside, Gregor stood guard at the main dining room entrance just as he'd done for the past umpteen years. Beyond him, the polished, old world knotty pine paneled walls, lined with red leather booths, catered to kings and queens, movie stars, presidents, and the Forbes 400.

Peter stumbled out of the back of the car, tripping over the valet and nearly landing on his face. The red coated doorman caught him.

The next few paces into the foyer of Chasen's were no easier. He smashed the door into the back of the coat check girl in the lobby. Excusing himself from that disaster, he backed into a woman waiting for her husband, stepping on her arch with all his weight sending her screaming in pain to the floor. He tried to help her up, and even though she recognized him as him, Peter Barker, the pain had the best of her and she wanted no help from her assailant, even if it was an accidental assault by a major movie star.

Peter cowered away from the scene of the ruckus he'd created. The woman's husband, the coat check girl and the valet were now all at the fallen lady's side. Peter went to Gregor and asked to sit at the bar in the back. Gregor reluctantly agreed and escorted him to the large curving wooden bar at the rear of the establishment. The bar was packed with good-looking businessmen types in expensive-looking English tailored suits. The women with them were blonde and buxom and sat legs crossed on the red leather stools.

Peter spotted his pal, Bill Holden, nursing a drink with a lady friend.

"Bill how's it going guy?" he said.

"Not too bad. Haven't seen you in a while, where have you been holed up?"

"Working on a new TV series." Peter could hardly get the words out.

"Have you met my friend, Cynthia Carter," Holden introduced the buxom blonde sitting next to him. She was overwhelmed to be sandwiched between two idols.

"Oh my God," she squealed, "Bill Holden and Peter Barker talking to me." She held out her hand presumably for Barker to kiss. He ignored her, ignored her hand, and kept talking to Holden.

"To tell you the truth, I got fired tonight." Barker was practically shouting.

"Hey, Pete, cool down. You don't need to tell the entire restaurant. Sshhhh." Holden got off his stool, put his arm around Pete and sat him down on the stool next to Cynthia.

"I don't care if the whole FUCKING CITY HEARS ME." Peter yelled, pounding on the counter, sending Cynthia's wine flying.

She jumped back to avoid getting soaked and crashed into Holden. Now he was holding her steady along with Peter. The rest of the bar was watching them while Gregor was on a direct course across the dining room to the problem zone.

"Mr. Holden, Mr. Barker, is anything wrong?" Gregor asked in the typical hushed tones of a well trained maitre'd.

"No, nothing's wrong," Barker shouted back at him. The bar and the dining room grew silent. It was that instantaneous kind of silence, like taking the needle off a record mid-track.

"Mr. Barker, I must ask you to keep your voice down. You are a valued patron, but please, please, you are disturbing our other guests." Gregor was gentle but firm.

"It's okay, Gregor. I'll take care of him," Bill Holden said.

"Mr. Holden, sir, if you need my assistance…" Gregor walked away as things seemed to return to normal. The needle was back on the record, the silence replaced by multiple conversations and the clatter of service dishes and flaming sauce pans.

"What happened at the studio, man?" Holden asked.

"They fired me the star of the series before it even got going. They fired me because they told me I was wrong for the role." Peter was regaining some of his composure sitting reasonably erect at the bar.

"Sounds odd. Is that it? Just hello, you're fired," Holden pressed for the truth.

"That's all. They decided I was a giant mistake. I asked for a new writer, I asked for a new leading lady, but nothing granted, just vamoose." Peter was starting to cry again. His emotions had gone from anger to tears in seconds. Cynthia had never seen a major movie star cry off screen.

"Hey, hey, come on, let me buy you a drink, then you'll join Cynthia and me for a little dinner. Big fucking deal, it's a lousy TV series. You're a goddamned movie star, man. Forget it, it's nothing." Holden waved at Bud, the bartender, to get a drink for his friend. As Bud crossed over to him behind the enormous bar, Peter saw John Moran sitting at the very far end of the restaurant in a corner booth. He was with two other men and they were all huddled in conversation.

"No thanks, Bud, I'm feeling fine, thanks," Peter said to the bartender. Then he got up and excused himself.

A waiter was busy tossing Caesar salad at a cart in front of John Moran's booth. He added the oil and vinegar and tossed in some anchovies as Peter walked by. Moran spotted Barker. The pair had an uncomfortable moment of eye contact. But Moran looked away, feigning not to see him and kept on talking business with his dinner companions. Peter picked up the large wooden salad bowl off the waiters' cart and before the poor server knew his Caesar was missing, Peter dumped it all on top of John Moran's head. The raw egg and Parmesan cheese sat in a lump centered on Moran's bald spot, while the rest of the dressing ran down his face behind his ears and onto his dark blue suit.

"Recognize me now, Mr. Moran?" Peter said looking at him, right in the eye. At least in one eye, his other one was forced closed by the onslaught of falling Caesar dressing. "You remember me Peter Barker. I was the star of 'The Reilly's of San Marino' until you and Larkin had me fired today, fired without discussion, fired without trying to correct the problems, just fired like some two-bit day player."

The needle was off the record once again. This time it had been removed with a jolting scratch. People were frozen in their tracks. Bill Holden was the exception as he made his way across the room to help his friend. He grabbed Peter from behind and pulled him away from Moran's table. Peter struggled, but Holden had a firm grip on him.

"Let the fuck go of me," Peter protested.

"It's for your own good, pal. Just come with me," Holden replied.

Moran was wiping off his head and face with the multitude of napkins that an army of servants had rushed to his table. He stood up and faced Peter as Holden was still dragging him away.

"You're the problem. The entire problem," Moran spoke loudly and slowly at Peter. "And the problem has now been eradicated."

Peter broke away from Holden at Moran's final insult and lunged at Moran with a powerful hook under his chin. Moran flew back into the booth knocking over the waiter's cart, landing across the center of the table. The food, the drink, the silver took off in all directions, hitting Moran's dinner partners with Chasen's shrapnel. Inasmuch as they were trapped in the semi-circular red leather booth, pinned to their seats, they simply watched as Peter served Moran to them on a silver platter.

Holden again grabbed Peter, this time pushing him through the restaurant. Gregor had already summoned Jimmy and the car. He was waiting, the motor running.

Bill Holden put his longtime friend Peter Barker in the limousine and Jimmy drove off.

• • •

The limousine reeked of bourbon by the time Jimmy arrived at the Sierra Towers on Doheny Road. Peter Barker lived in the Penthouse, some twenty-six stories in the sky, in one of the posh condominium towers man had managed to create on earth. Barker's residence in the sky was as close as man could get to heaven without dying. The residents had views that spanned the entire L.A. basin from downtown to Catalina Island and beyond. Peter Barker's view was the best the building offered, as was his condominium, which spanned over five thousand feet of space on two floors with terraces that wrapped around the rooms on all sides.

Peter had lived at The Sierra for a few years since his last divorce had cost him the home he'd built on nearby Foothill Road in Beverly Hills. The big Mediterranean house on Foothill was now occupied by Karen, his third wife of two years, and her current 26-year-old boyfriend, a surfer called J.J.

Karen Barker had left Peter for the other man that she had been seeing for over a year. It was rumored that the mystery man was a Hollywood big shot who was married. Supposedly he was going to divorce his wife for Karen. Karen and Peter split when Peter found out, but Mr. Big Shot never left his wife, dumping Karen instead. Within three months, Karen and her share of Peter's divorce settlement were living in Peter's house with a surf stud body builder fourteen years her junior. Despite the circumstances, Peter still thought that Karen was the best of his three wives.

Barker had no children. No close living family to speak of, either. He was a 59-year-old superstar with a reasonably fat bank account, living alone in a luxury penthouse. He said that's the way he wanted it. He would never marry again, not after Karen.

The concierge at The Sierra Towers, a tall handsome black man called Mr. Simpson, assisted Barker on the elevator ride up. He made sure he was inside his home before descending the twenty-six floors to his post in the massive marble foyer of the lobby. Once in the apartment, Barker stumbled around in the darkness, but managed to make his way up the floating curved staircase in his very own massive marble foyer in the sky. A light burned in the master bedroom at the top of the stairs. The double doors to the bedroom suite were cracked open, and the light drew him in the proper direction. He pushed the doors open wide and found his masseur, Don Robertson, in the room by the massage table which was already draped in pristine white cotton sheets.

Don was sitting on the floor in a yoga position reading a paperback. Don Robertson, the masseur, was also Don Robertson the personal trainer to the stars, along with Don Robertson the "would-be" actor. But perhaps most important, and most deadly, was Don Robertson, the cocaine supplier.

Robertson was all of these things to Peter Barker. Sometimes, all of these things at once. "Ten more sit-ups, then a good rubdown. How about an extra ounce of coke this week, I've got a deal, oh, and here is my new 8 x 10 'glossy'. What do you think?"

"Mr. Barker, you look like you need a massage tonight," he said as Peter flopped on his bed.

"Yes, that sounds…like… a plan," Peter barely got the words out.

Robertson came over to him and sat him up on the bed.

"First, you need a shower to sober you up, my friend." Robertson picked Barker up and flung him over his massive shoulder.

"I feel like a bag of potatoes up here," Peter said.

"We'll get you fixed up in no time," Robertson carried him into the bathroom. It was a white marble mausoleum of a bathroom fitted with gold-plated faucets. The shower was big enough for six people, with showerheads in all directions. A floor-to-ceiling clear plate glass enclosure surrounded it. Robertson put Barker down, leaning him against the sink, and opened the shower door, turning on three of the heads. Massive water gushed forth, lowering the water table of the Hoover Dam.

Robertson stripped Barker naked, his clothes left in a heaped pile on the floor. Peter was in very good shape. His six-foot frame still had the proportions of a thirty-year-old, not an ounce of excess fat on his movie star body. His arms, shoulders and chest were developed by Robertson's thrice weekly visits, toned without being body-builder muscled. The legs and butt were trim and solid. His body hair was predominantly blonde with only a small amount of gray chest hair to reveal his age.

Robertson picked up the naked movie idol and started to put him in the shower. There was no way Peter was going to stand up on his own. So he put him down on the floor, stripped off his own clothes and took him in the shower.

The cold water brought Barker back to life, at least enough to realize that he was naked in the shower with Robertson. He regained enough self control to stand upright without Robertson's support, and the two of them finished the shower quickly and without conversation.

Peter was about to open up to Robertson, tell him his story of woe, but decided instead to keep his mouth shut. How odd it was, he thought, that he could control himself with the masseur, but not with the studio boss. He laid his bare body face down on the massage table in the middle of the bedroom, where it remained on a permanent basis, and Don Robertson, also naked, and still wet from the shower, went to work on him. Robertson had the reputation for being the best rubdown in town, and he'd earned the rap. His hands were "magic." That's what everybody said. Barker thought so. Robertson worked every muscle and joint in Barker's body. He squeezed the poisonous liquor right out of his pores.

"You really should cool it with the booze it'll kill you," Don said, finishing the massage and heading for the bathroom to get dressed.

Peter was thinking that a cocaine offering was just around the corner. Robertson had a way of making the white powder sound like medicine.

"You need anything?" Robertson asked from the bathroom. There it was, thought Barker.

"No. No thanks, I don't need anything," he replied.

Robertson came out of Barker's bathroom dressed and ready to go to his next appointment with his next star client. Peter had already left the bedroom and was out on the terrace. Los Angeles was spread out before him. The crisscrossing grid of twinkling lights below pulsated for miles in all directions.

Peter stood naked at the ledge breathing in the air and watching the planes in the sky get in line for their approach to LAX in the distance.

Robertson came up behind him and grabbed his shoulders. "I've got some great stuff tonight. The best I've had in months. I'd hate to see you miss out," he said.

"No, I think I'll pass. Another time, okay?" Barker tried to release himself from Robertson's strong grip.

Robertson held on tight. "I'm going to do you a big favor," he said. "I'm going to let you have a sample." He took a scoop of cocaine out of the vial in his pocket, and shoved it up Barker's nose with the aid of a small "coc" spoon. Holding his head back with his hand so that none of the precious powder would be wasted, Barker inhaled and reeled.

"How about that?" Robertson asked. "Pretty incredible stuff, right?" he continued.

Barker said nothing. He was flying like the planes on approach, in line for landing, too.

"I'll leave your regular order on your bed table in that silver box on my way out and charge your exercise account," Don said as he let Peter go, and went back inside the condo. He dropped the pouch of powder by the bed, as promised, made a notation of the sale in his book, and left.

Peter was still naked and began reeling from the effects of the cocaine and alcohol. Somehow he had climbed up on the three-foot-wide cement ledge and was standing with his arms outstretched, legs apart, as if he was trying to reach the planes overhead. Higher and higher he stretched upwards, almost catching one. Another leap, his fingers spread wide, his palms open, his head thrown back, his eyes on the stars… his feet… off the ledge.

Peter Barker fell twenty-six stories to his death. His nude, perfectly shaped, fifty-nine-year-old body crushed on the pavement below in front of the lobby of the Sierra Towers.

At the moment Barker's body hit the pavement, David Larkin entered the dark penthouse on the 26th floor. The door was open.

CHAPTER 11

P eter Barker's death twenty-six floors below created a three-ring circus. He nearly landed on a schnauzer named Titan, belonging to Mrs. Rolfson, a lady who lived in the building. Actually, Barker missed both Titan and Mrs. Rolfson by mere inches. Her screams echoed off the massive south facade of the Sierra Towers bouncing back and forth between the complex and the City National Bank Office Building across the street. Mr. Simpson, the doorman, was the first to arrive on the scene, racing from his desk in the lobby. Moments later, half of the residents of the Sierra Towers flooded the street to see what was happening. Motorists on Doheny Road came to a screeching halt, backing up traffic for several miles to the east, down the Sunset Strip.

• • •

Police were arriving in droves. The entire area was being cordoned off with yellow plastic disaster ribbon while officers were trying to disperse the crowd and get the traffic moving.

Upstairs in the penthouse, David Larkin was unaware of the events below. He had come in through the rear door and darted into the elevator unnoticed, to avoid dealing with the bureaucracy of signing in and being announced. The sounds of the sirens were ignored by David, after all, he heard them all the time. The condo was dark, just as it had been earlier when Barker himself had arrived home. David called out for the star. There was, of course, no answer. He, too, was drawn to the light escaping from the cracked door upstairs. Climbing the curving stairway of the two-story condominium, David continued to call out for Peter.

Larkin stepped carefully and quietly as he approached the master bedroom door. Peering through, he saw that no one was in the bed, so he entered.

"Peter, are you in here?" he called out again. "Peter, it's me, David. I want to talk to you," he said.

Larkin had come over to explain. David wanted to tell Peter that the studio wasn't giving him any room. He would tell him of his deal at Paramount to get Peter right into a movie. He would also tell him that Moran had just called him, from Chasen's, with the news of their eventful meeting.

David Larkin had come to make peace. Mostly for his own good. He had plenty riding on this new series. But also, peace for Barker and Moran. Hollywood was too small a town. He'd seen these sort of rifts grow into major decade-long feuds poisoning all the players, including himself, just by association. He wanted to avoid this, at all costs.

"Peter, are you in the bathroom?" he called out, approaching the door.

Still no answer. He passed by the bed table and saw the pouch of cocaine in its familiar plastic baggie wrapping, sitting in an open silver box on the bedside table. David recognized the goods, delivered by Don Robertson. While Larkin was not an abuser of drugs or alcohol, in fact not an abuser of anything except himself and those people close to him from time to time, he did indulge himself with stimulants when he wanted to. He also was known for sharing them generously with those who played games with the almighty.

There was no question, this had been a killer day, for all of them. David reached for Peter Barker's cocaine and took a portion. Inhaling it quickly, he clumsily dropped the monogrammed silver box, spilling half of its powdered contents onto the floor. David got down on his hands and knees and picked up as much as he could. The rest he dusted away in all directions slapping the carpet with furious energy.

Having wasted the better portion of the cache, he stuck the little box in his pocket with the intention of replacing its contents in full for Peter with some of his own. David would send Mr. Lee right back to the condo with a refilled package.

Feeling the high from the powder, David made his way back down the curving stairs, out the foyer and into the waiting elevator. Once again, his timing was nothing less than theatrical. Moments after he got in one elevator and descended, the other opened and troops of police burst onto the twenty-sixth floor to begin their investigation.

He arrived in the lobby of the Sierra, discovering all the commotion. There was the old lady in the corner sobbing uncontrollably, Simpson holding her with one arm and fanning her with a magazine using the other. Her dog yipped as it pulled and tugged on a makeshift leash made from a section of curtain rope that Simpson was also managing to hold onto. Police were everywhere. Residents were standing around in a fog talking in hushed tones. Poor old woman, David thought. Her husband must have died tonight.

He walked quickly out of the lobby feeling a bit paranoid, carting a half empty container of coke in his pocket, while L.A.'s finest in blue surrounded him. Nevertheless, he made it outside and found the rest of the circus. The hook and ladders were there, along with the coroner's vans. People were walking in all directions, just milling around. Mr. Lee came from out of nowhere and tapped his boss on the shoulder.

"This way, Mr. Larkin. I parked around the corner."

"What happened, Lee?"

"I don't know, sir. I move the car to the side to get out of commotion, since you told me you be a while. All of sudden I hear a woman screaming, then police and fire trucks and lots of people. By the time I came around, there were <u>so</u> many people, I couldn't see. But I think somebody get killed. I saw a bag get put into the police truck that look like a body."

"Can you get us out of here?" David asked.

"Yes, sir, there's back driveway. No problem."

CHAPTER 12

"Why is it always so goddamned hot at funerals?" David Larkin wiped the sweat off his forehead with his black silk hankie. He was dressed totally in black. Were it not for his long hair and oversized Italian dark glasses people might have mistaken him for the priest.

"Because it's L.A. You want a cold funeral, die in Maine," John Moran replied.

"The studio could have provided a tent. Look at all those wilting starlets. How will the shots look in the papers?" The whole scene was getting on his nerves, and it showed.

"The man is dead, will you show some respect?" Moran demanded.

"Oh, look at you, Mr. Holier Than Thou. You're goddamned thrilled about it." David was really dripping now. The noonday sun was fierce. There must have been nearly a thousand people, all decked out in their best Hollywood black, melting in the high eighty-degree heat out on Forest Lawn's back forty.

"What's eating you, Larkin? Fate has taken care of our dirty business more perfectly than we could have ever concocted. The publicity will send the first episodes of 'The Reilly's' right into the Top 10. You'll kill him off in the series, rewrite the plot line, and bingo, you stay in the Top 10 for seven years. I'll retire on it," said Moran.

"Good. Then you'll be out of my hair."

"I'll haunt you in retirement, David. You can count on it."

Directly across the burial site, David watched his star, Laurie Dalton.

"Is that Benton Stein over there?" Moran asked.

"You can bet your stock options on it," D.L. answered. "And he's sitting with my star."

"Our star," said Moran. "I didn't know they were acquainted," he added.

"Terrific. My new star is a close friend of the studio's controlling stock holder. Perfect." David gave up using the handkerchief to wipe the sweat. It was ringing wet. He threw it on the ground in a wad. A sixty-dollar square of hand-finished Chinese silk tossed like a piece of used Kleenex.

"Don't get excited. The broad on the other side is his wife. Maybe they just sat next to each other by accident."

It wasn't the funeral, or the heat, or Laurie Dalton sitting next to Benton Stein that was eating David Larkin. He was completely undone, spooked by coming to terms with the notion that Peter had jumped or was pushed, perhaps only seconds before he'd arrived at his penthouse that night a week ago.

David envisioned Peter leaping when he first entered the place calling out his name, "Peter, are you home? Are you here? Peter, Peter." In matter of fact, Larkin was traumatized by the fact that Barker's deathly act had come too close to touching his precious little life. He didn't lament over his own culpability possibly attributing to Peter's actions.

Neither did John Moran. They didn't discuss their feelings of regret. That didn't come up. In truth, neither one felt the tiniest twinge of remorse. They weren't responsible for anyone but themselves. They're own asses were well covered at all times, the hell with the next guy. That's just the way it was.

"I read today that the police are investigating. They think it may have been a murder," Laurie told Benton Stein.

"I heard that yesterday," he replied.

"Who would want to kill Peter?" she asked.

"I don't know," he said. "But if it was murder, whoever did it sure went to a lot of trouble to make it look like a suicide."

"Dad, if it was a murder, how did the killer get Barker to strip off all his clothes?" Randy asked. He was sitting on the other side of Laurie.

"Maybe he was already naked," he said.

"A jealous lover?" Laurie questioned.

"Perhaps. Evidence will tell when they reveal the autopsy results."

"They must know. The man's being buried," Randy added.

"They know. They're just not saying yet. I think something's brewing. The so-called accident is about to be exposed," Laurie jumped in with her two cents.

"We'll see," Benton said. "We'll see."

Jennifer Hartman was silent throughout the exchange of death views going on next to her. Her stoic respect was punctuated by silent tears running down the sides of her cheeks. She didn't try to hide them, to wipe them discreetly away. They fell gracefully to the earth where her long time friend, Peter Barker, was being laid to rest in front of her.

Jennifer tried to focus on the good times. The early romance, the career, the thirty years of friendship. They had remained close. She'd consoled him through three divorces and hundreds of romances. He'd been her shoulder to cry on over the escapades of her husband, Benton. Jennifer had no other confidantes. Certainly not the ladies at lunch. Her only true friend was now being covered with dirt and roses. With him went her deepest feelings, desires, and dreams.

"I hope they hang whoever was responsible for this," were her only words spoken, as the priest finished his blessing and the mourners began to parade past the open grave tossing in their final floral tributes.

The press was roped off behind another piece of the yellow "DO NOT CROSS" disaster tape. But, they were roped off conveniently enough to get plenty of pictures of the celebrity crowd. The cameras clicked wildly as Laurie Dalton walked by. Flanked by Benton Stein, the press was ecstatic. The paparazzi would make big bucks with these shots, selling them to news services and papers and magazines worldwide.

David Larkin and John Moran were behind them, their faces in the background of all the shots.

• • •

CBS Television City buzzed in high gear. Chairman William S. Paley and his New York entourage of society and business comrades were in town for meetings. Bill Parker loved the excitement. Paley was something of a hero to him. He hoped to get a good look.

The factory acted like dad and mom were coming over to the kids' house for Thanksgiving. The facility was immaculate, fresh flowers were everywhere, on every available glass-topped table surface. The trees in the parking lot were pruned beyond the perfection of Mother Nature, and the football field-sized green lawn in front of the executive office building was greener than the money the complex generated. All the employees had been warned of the chief's visit. They'd been asked to dress up for the occasion. Most complied willingly, happily. Bill always dressed. Each day was a potential opportunity to meet someone, to advance the career. Unlike the rest of the multitude, he would be in a tie when the opportunity came, not in a tank top.

Bill asked his boss Jerry Grayson if they'd see Paley. "Does he make rounds, an inspection?" Bill questioned.

Grayson laughed, "I've never seen him and I've worked here for almost fifteen years."

"How could that be?" Bill continued.

"I figure he doesn't need tickets, and his relatives don't need jobs down here amongst the privates." Jerry was warm, but caustic.

"You're kidding me, you've really never seen the man?" Bill persisted.

"To tell you the truth, he arrives here in a limo which drives him right up to the front. He gets out, goes in the executive entrance, up the elevator to the third floor and into Asher's office. They meet, he leaves the same way he came, the limo goes back to the Beverly Hills Hotel, or wherever he might be staying." Grayson said matter-of-factly.

"So what's all the fanfare around the plant? There are secretaries actually wearing carnation corsages," Bill told him.

"Tradition, my young friend. And who knows, one day The Chief might take 'the tour'. We're all waiting." Grayson smiled. "Get back to work. The 'Price is Right' mail is building up back there."

Bill went back to his desk. He was sitting and unbundling the mail when Grayson reappeared.

"Is he here?" Bill asked.

"No. No. He's not here," Jerry replied. "But I think I've got news that might be better."

"Okay. I like the sound of that. What is it?" Bill asked.

"You're wanted upstairs," Grayson told him. "You're wanted in Asher's office, top floor."

"Excuse me?"

"That's right. You heard me. Asher's office. Get going."

"But why? Do you know why? What's up?"

"I believe you're going to be offered a promotion, a job that will make heads spin down here in the catacombs," Jerry Grayson told him with great pride. "Now, get going, and let me know everything that they say, OKAY?"

Security was much tighter than usual due to Paley's impending arrival. Guards checked Bill for his CBS photo badge I.D. at every corner as he made his way to the executive suites. Friendly ground awaited him at the main reception desk in the person of Curly, a handsome black woman he'd talked to the last time he'd been upstairs.

As she was visiting with Bill, the elevator door opened and out stepped CBS Chairman and founder, William S. Paley. With him, two very distinguished men, a magnificent woman, and two security guards. Curly jumped up from her desk at near military attention. Bill stepped back, out of the way, and the platoon of generals passed by.

"Good morning," Mr. Paley said to both Curly and Bill.

"Good morning, sir," she replied. Bill nodded his head and repeated the same words. They went through the massive double black doors and vanished into the executive chambers.

"My God," Bill said. "That was really him."

"Yes, and the Mrs., too. It's been a long time since she's come here with him," Curly said.

"That was his wife?" Bill said. "I not only saw him but his wife, too? Grayson's worked here for almost fifteen years and he's never seen Paley. I've been here for less than four months and I'm saying good morning to him, and to his wife and friends." Bill was nearly in a trance.

"It's all timing, Mr. Parker," Curly told him.

• • •

Chris Reynolds walked into David Larkin's office near Stage 21 at MGM. It was not what he expected. It was an army barracks.

"Hello. Is this Mr. Larkin's office?" he asked.

"Yes. Can I help you?" Marie replied.

"I'm Chris Reynolds. I was asked to come in for a meeting."

"Oh, yes, I called you. I'm Marie O'Neil, Mr. Larkin's aide-de-camp. Mr. Larkin gave me your number and asked me to interview you for a job," she continued.

"Really," said Chris. "That would be terrific. I'm a good actor, and I'll do anything for a break, any part at all."

"That's good, because this part is off camera," Marie smiled.

"I don't understand," he replied with a deflated look on his face.

"We are in need of a guy-Friday around here," Marie said directly.

"A guy-what?"

"Friday. Guy-Friday."

"I don't know what that is." The deflated look had shifted to embarrassment.

"A general assistant, an office boy, a runner of errands. Like a gal-Friday, only we want a guy-Friday," she explained looking directly at him.

"So it's not a part on the show. It's a job on the show, sort of."

"Right. We'll pay you $150.00 per week, plus car expenses gas and mileage. The regular hours will be 10:00 to 7:00, but you can count on some late nights. There is no overtime, and it's expected that you do what it takes."

"No overtime," he repeated.

"None," she said from experience.

"But it's a foot in the door, isn't it?" he asked.

"A lot of young men would think so," she told him.

"When would I start?" he asked.

"Now," she said.

"Right now, today, like in after we finish the interview now?"

"Now," she repeated.

"Okay, then, yes, I'll take it, and I'll start now. What do you want me to do?" he said.

"Well, start by organizing all the scripts in D.L.'s office. He likes them in alphabetical and chronological order. Author and date of submission."

Chris went to work in Larkin's office sorting out the scripts. He had come to the studio only moments before expecting to read for a part, perhaps even get a small part on "The Reilly's of San Marino." Instead, he was now David Larkin's new office boy, guy-Friday.

Even though this was a bit of a detour from the dream, Chris was excited to be working for Larkin. He would hang around the set and eventually it would happen — he'd get to audition for a part. He would turn the job into what he really wanted. It was just a matter of time.

• • •

"Randy, I'll do it," Laurie blurted out after fifteen minutes of silence in the car during the ride from Forest Lawn back to the studio.

"Where's the gardenia? I don't see any gardenias?"

"Not that," she laughed.

"Damn. I thought I was going to get lucky on the 405 Freeway," he said, joyfully suspecting the truth of what she was going to do.

"I'll sign," she told him straight away.

"You will. That's great. That's phenomenal." He leaned over and kissed her at 75 m.p.h. "Now we can really make plans. I'll do great things for your career," he added. "You'll get everything you always dreamed of - the right parts, the right deals to develop your own properties, produce and star in your own packages. And you'll get paid top dollar, the highest standard in the business." Randy was jubilant.

"And then I'll run for President," she added.

"Huh?"

"Oh, I'm just kidding. You're getting so carried away and all." She put her hand on his knee.

"Well, this is big news. I hoped you'd come around." He put his free hand on top of hers and drove on.

"I'm excited about it, too," she told him, adding, "I think we'll make a good team."

"We'll be the A-team. We'll take Hollywood by storm."

"Can you do it in six months?" she asked.

"What? Six months. What does that mean, six months? Are you planning on going back to Laredo?" he joked nervously.

"No, although I'm overdue for a visit home."

"I've always wanted to see Laredo," Randy responded tongue-in-cheek. "But what does the six months thing mean? I don't get it." He was still worried.

"It means I'll only sign with you if you'll give me six month options, for the first two years. After that, I'll sign a long-term contract." She was very direct and business-like. One minute she was a 19-year-old girl from Laredo, the next, she was a Hollywood negotiator. Randy was impressed by the challenge, but didn't like the terms.

"The agency never signs a six month deal," he protested.

"They'll make an exception," she told him.

"They don't make exceptions," he told her.

"Then The Artists Agency will make an exception, or ICM, or I'll just continue to be a free agent with a high-powered, big bucks lawyer."

"Did he tell you to demand a six month option?" he questioned.

"Yes. He did."

"Typical lawyer bullshit. He knows it's never done. He's just throwing his weight around to impress you. It's not done and he knows it and it's foul play to lead you on, to make you think that you are special that you can change the system."

"I am special. I can change the system. And there are no rules in Hollywood. No rules that aren't broken, that is."

"I suppose he told you that, too. Don't you get it? Laurie, you're too smart not to see through this. He's setting you up. He can't lose. If you can't get one of the big three agencies to buckle under, he says 'tough shit' to all of them and continues to hold your career tight in his hands. But that's not good enough for you. He may be a powerful lawyer, but he's just another schlockmeister dealmaker. What about your career? Can he guide you? Can he put you in the right films with the right studios and get you the roles that will make you into the actress and the star you want to be? I don't think so." Randy was at his best.

"And you can? Why do you think you can? You're only twenty-two years old and you're barely starting out yourself. What makes you so special?" She was cruelly direct.

"I have it in my blood. I've grown up in the business. I know how it works and I've seen the best and worst all my life. I have a clear vision for myself and for you, too, and I'm young enough and bold enough to take the risks and make it all happen — for both of us," he finished his plea.

"I must be crazy, but I believe you. I hardly know you, but I believe you," she said.

"I think I can get them to do a one year option at first," he added.

"Okay, one year. It's a deal," she said.

Randy turned into the MGM lot and pulled up to the guard with his new client.

• • •

"Marie, Marie, are you here?" Larkin screamed out for his assistant. He'd lost the best part of the day at Peter's funeral.

"Yes, D.L., I'm here," she yelled back as she came towards him from his office, leaving Chris to sort out the scripts.

"Any calls?" he asked.

"Plenty. Jim Stinson at The Hollywood Reporter, Art Bondemeir from The L.A. Times, Harold Hulch from The New York Times, Bill Jones from The National Enquirer, and a Sergeant Arnold from the L.A.P.D." She finished reading off the pink message pad, then handed the little slips with the phone numbers to David.

"Did this Sergeant Arnold say what he wanted?"

"Only that he needed to speak with you as soon as possible. He left two numbers to call him back. Shall I call for you?" she asked.

"In a minute. Let me get my thoughts together first, and get organized. We've got a cast and crew meeting on the set in a half hour with Moran. Who's that in my office?" David asked, seeing Chris on the floor from the back.

"That's the young man you asked me to call and hire as your new assistant, Chris Reynolds," she told him.

"Right. How's he doing?" he asked.

"Fine. He's only been here a short while, but he seems eager to please. He's sorting out your scripts now."

"Good. That's good." D.L. walked into his office and shut the door. Chris turned, saw him, and jumped to his feet.

"Mr. Larkin, good to see you again," Chris said as he rose.

"Don't get up, Chris," David was his charming best.

"Thanks for this job. It's a great opportunity to work for you."

"Glad you feel that way. I think we'll get along very well."

Chris wanted to ask him about the possibility of reading for him again, but decided not to bring it up at this moment. Instead he would be the hard working, loyal aid and impress the boss.

"I hope I'm doing these scripts right for you, Mr. Larkin," he asked. David was sitting next to him at his desk going through some notes.

"Did Marie tell you how to do them?"

"Yes, she helped me get started, too."

"Then, I'm sure you'll get it right. Oh, and from now on, you may call me David. Drop the Mr., okay?" He looked down at Chris on the floor.

"Thank you…David. That's super." Chris was beaming. The big mogul wanted him to call him by his first name. Things were looking up for him in Hollywood.

"Marie, will you try that police detective now,"

David gave his instructions to his secretary via the intercom. He looked down at Chris, still sorting out the roomful of colored papers bound with two-and-a-half-cent gleaming brass brads, called scripts. David envied his youth, his clean slate. "Chris, there's one thing we need to get straight between us right now," Larkin said. "Anything and everything that you hear me say, or see me do, in this room, in the car, or anywhere we are together, is just between us. If you ever repeat anything you hear, you're gone. Fired. Finished. You understand?" David looked right at his young charge.

"Yes, sir, I mean, David, you've got my word. I'm not a talker anyway."

David stared at him for a long moment, then Marie's buzz broke their union. David picked up the phone. "Yes, he's on, okay." He turned once again to Chris. "Starting now, Chris," he said. Chris nodded, David picked up the line and the flashing light stopped signaling. "Hello, Sergeant Arnold? Yes, I'm David Larkin. Yes, that's correct. Yes. Okay, when would be convenient? Later today? Okay, how about six o'clock in my office. Yes, on the MGM lot, Stage 21. Okay, see you then." David hung up the phone and called for Marie. She came running.

"Yes, D.L., what is it?" she asked.

"Leave a gate pass for this Sergeant Arnold. Although he probably can get in without one. He's coming to see me at 6:00 tonight."

"What for, D.L.?" She looked concerned.

"The Peter Barker case," he answered.

"I didn't know it was one, a case, that is."

"It is now. They're investigating his death."

"You mean it wasn't suicide?"

"No, I mean they're investigating, that's all, nothing to get overly alarmed about. Standard procedure, especially when someone famous dies under these circumstances." David went on, "Are the actors back yet from the funeral? I want to have a meeting with the cast in here before the studio meeting on the set later. Can you check for me, Marie?" He smiled at her, and she melted. Of course she'd check for him. She'd do anything for him, even after thirty years. Even without a romance, Marie still loved her boss.

"Chris, put all the scripts over in one corner of the office. I want them out of sight when the cast comes in here."

Chris moved the scripts at once. He, too, loved being in the company of the boss. This was the real business.

• • •

Curly looked at Bill, who had been sitting, waiting for his interview for over an hour.

"This is it, the beginning for you. Go in there and impress the hell out of Mr. Asher. Go get him." She gave him a pat on the behind as he passed her desk heading for the big black doors behind them. He was surprised by her familiarity and went through the black doors with a big smile on his face.

Bill walked down the long aisle of secretaries fronting executive offices on both the right and left sides. At the end of the hall there was another reception area, another set of double black doors. This was the inner sanctum-sanctorum of the CBS Television network. The buck stopped here. Asher held program court daily behind that set of double black doors. Producers, writers, actors, agents, executives, they all came here to pay homage, to sell their wares. Few walked away with anything. But for those who did, potential immortality and certain fortune was in their back pocket.

What did Asher want with him? Bill Parker wondered. His usual confidence eroded by the overwhelming power and glory of his surroundings.

The secretary at the reception desk at the far end greeted him, and asked him to sit down. Asher would be with him momentarily.

Out of the large glass corner window beside him Bill looked down at the big green lawn in front of CBS. The gardeners were watering. Bill saw Mr. Paley's limo pull up in the front drive. With the timing and precision of The Secret Service, the chief and his entourage exited the main lobby, boarded the VIP shuttle, and drove away. Bill blinked. Was it all real or simply a mogul mirage? How did he get downstairs? Paley had been in Asher's office and Bill thought that the only way out was the way in.

"Mr. Asher will see you now, Mr. Parker," the tall thin lady behind the desk summoned him. He went inside.

"Hello, Bill. Please come in." Harry Asher offered him a seat in what Bill felt was the Oval Office of Television. The room was actually square, perfectly square. And large, nearly forty-by-forty feet with full floor to ceiling windows on two sides meeting at the corner. The other two walls were solid. An oblong oval table of white veined marble with black metal pedestal bases on either end, surrounded by CBS red leather upholstered chairs, was positioned in one section of the room. In another corner, a living room area with two matching black leather sofas, was an enormous square glass coffee table with handsome art books and crystal objects adorning its top. Another section housed a second large table. Presumably Asher's work space. This one made of highly polished mahogany and brass. Behind it, a large gray and black, fabric-covered chair. A fine English mahogany secretary was against the back wall bookended by drawings of the stars. The secretary was a

FAME FARM

beautiful old antique, in stark contrast to the contemporary state of the rest of the suite. In still another corner, a full bar service and behind it, a door, flush with the wall. Bill wondered where the panel door led to an escape tunnel? Realizing that Paley must have left the building through some back hallway, Asher's door now held magical intrigue.

A bit of the magic vanished when an older gentleman, replete in black trousers and a white starched Nehru jacket, came through the door with lunch for Mr. Asher, and asked Bill if he would like anything to eat or drink. Bill was dumbfounded. Did he dare accept the offer? Was it polite to pass? Asher made the decision for him.

"Bring the young man a plate, will you, Stauffer? What do you drink, Parker?" Asher asked.

"Iced tea, or water if you don't have any iced tea," he answered.

"I'll have an iced tea as well, Stauffer," Asher told the man who promptly left.

"You're probably wondering why I asked you to come up here today?" Asher said. The dapper, top reigning network boss stood only five-five, six inches. He was bald, with deeply recessed gray eyes shrouded by over-sized black-rimmed glasses. Impeccably tailored, a dark lavender Gucci tie, embroidered with small silver interconnecting "G"'s complimented the starkness of his deep gray suit. Asher had been born and raised in Brooklyn, but he spoke with the refinement of an English gentleman. "The human resources folks have had an eye on you since you began working here."

Stauffer came back through the vanishing panel door with more lunch and iced tea. He set the food down in front of Bill on the marble table where they were conferencing.

"Thank you," Bill said. Stauffer left again quietly.

"Anyway, we have a program here at the network to develop our talent from within. We like to take young people we believe have ability and test them. If they succeed, they move up the CBS ranks. I am in need of a personal assistant, not a secretary now, but an aide, and the human resources office thought I should meet with you and some others, too, I might add." Asher took a mouthful of the cobb salad Stauffer had prepared for lunch.

If Bill had taken a portion of the salad, he would have choked on Asher's words. Fortunately, he was too in awe of his surroundings, his good fortune, to eat. He pushed the salad around the plate to avoid insulting his host. Asher ate heartily and kept talking.

"What are your goals, my friend?" he questioned Bill.

"I would like to write and produce," he answered, instantly realizing that the network would be looking to groom executive material, not writers and producers. He covered his error as best as possible under the circumstances. "But first, I'd like to learn about production and programming. I am, or at least I believe I am, a creative person. Writing is something that comes naturally to me. And I enjoy it and I've got a lot of ideas." Asher seemed interested, so Bill kept talking. "But I don't know how the system works. I've tried to sell some of my ideas and my scripts without success. My contacts are very limited, and I would greatly benefit from any network experience, any at all. And, it would be an honor, and if I may say so, like being struck by lightning, to get the opportunity to work for you." Bill was out of breath. Asher looked at him as he finished the cobb salad in front of him.

"Salad not to your liking, young man?" Asher asked.

"No, no, no, it's very good." Bill took several large bites as fast as he could shove it in. "It's very good. May I have some more?" He couldn't believe he'd just asked for more. Where did the words come from? The door slid open and Stauffer appeared.

"More salad for my guest, please?"

"For you, sir, anything else?"

"No, I'm fine, Stauffer. Thanks."

He picked up Bill's plate, left and returned seconds later with an over-flowing plate of salad.

"That's very generous," Bill said, wondering how he was going to eat it all. Actually, it was lucky, he thought. The huge salad bought him extra time with Asher, extra time to impress him any way he could find. Bill Parker wanted to hold onto the lightning that had just struck him. He couldn't let go. He couldn't let someone else have this opportunity. He knew enough to know that lightning never struck twice in the same place.

CHAPTER 13

"I want you all to take these new scripts home, study them, know your new lines and be ready to go by 8:00 a.m. in the morning." D.L. spoke with the authority of the great white father, instructing his slaves on the set. "We've lost too much time already, with all due respect to our late star and friend, Peter Barker, the show must go on. It's going to be a new show, with a new thrust and energy. There will be many changes over the next few weeks, and months. I expect all of you to roll with the changes. There will be no excuse for backstabbing and politics during this time. I won't have it. Do you all hear me loud and clear?"

The crowd of some seventy people, including cast and crew right down to the valet parking man, rumbled. David took the grunts and sighs as an affirmative signal, a "yes" to his challenge of total loyalty.

He went on, "Also, I won't tolerate chronic complaining, bitching and moaning over schedules, casting or anything, including the flavor of the morning pastry." He changed his tone from the stern white father to his benevolent great communicator voice and said, "And now, ladies and gentlemen, I'd like to introduce the new star of 'The Reilly's of San Marino.'" The crowd was silent. "A star who will be so important by virtue of the success created by and from this new role, this new series, that all of America and half of the rest of the world reached by American television programming will watch this individual's every move. Ladies and gentlemen, a star whose face will be on every magazine cover worldwide ... Miss Laurie Dalton!"

Laurie was horrified. Like the rest of the seventy people sitting on every corner and stool and tabletop of the "Reilly's" set listening to the boss, she expected Charleton Heston or maybe John Forsythe to be coming out after that introduction. Each and every one expected a new leading man to fill Barker's formidable shoes.

She froze for a moment. What was he talking about? One hundred forty eyes pierced her flesh. Some were red hot hostile over the news. Others just green and cold with envy. Most were as shocked as she was. Not because she wasn't a star on her own, or because she couldn't rise to the occasion. But she was a baby star, a one-hit-movie baby star with so little experience.

She got up off the floor where she sat cross-legged, surrounded by her fellow cast members. With the grace and confidence of the star she was introduced as, Laurie Dalton walked the few steps to David Larkin with regal agility. She was able to command the room with the single act of her walk. She knew it. Why not here, she thought? Why not here, where it really mattered, now, when it mattered more than ever before?

"David, I'm not deserving of your very, very important introduction." Laurie was genuinely humble. "I guess I should say something profound, but I am not prepared. All I can say to everyone is that I will do my best, as an actress, to play this part. If it is now the leading part in our series, I will play it to the best of my ability. I'll promise you all this, I'll keep us all working for a whole bunch of years. I won't be the only one getting rich around here. I promise you that."

Someone in the shadows yelled out "Right on, girl!"

The cast began to get up and move toward Laurie and David, surrounding them. It was as if she'd just won an election and the campaign workers were closing in with congratulations. Laurie knew there would still be resistance, envy. It wouldn't vanish with a speech, or even the promise of money. She was going to rise to the occasion, professionally, and be the leading lady that would carry the series, no matter what envy or no envy.

"Good God," she said to David as the throngs came closer, "things do happen fast in show business."

David looked at her, eyeball to eyeball, "Hold on for dear life, the rocket is about to lift off."

• • •

It had been a lost day at the agency. For that matter, most of Hollywood had virtually shut down for Peter Barker's funeral. No big deals made on this day. A tribute to the death of a star.

Candace Fielding was in a foul mood. She hated funerals even more than she appeared to hate everyday life. She had eaten her two secretaries alive before going to Forest Lawn and she'd managed to fire one of her junior agents after getting back from the burial site.

Randy Stein knew that the particular guy fired wished it had been Candace's funeral instead of Barker's. She was beyond horrible, but he couldn't hold in his big news much longer. The perfect moment just wasn't availing itself. As he began to tell her, Candace cut him off.

"Did you see that little queer power monger, Michael Stoltz? He was actually crying, crying big, watery tears. Did you see it? I'm talking to you, Stein!" she blasted him at his desk.

"Yes, Candace, I did see him crying," he answered dutifully. He dared to challenge her tirade with the addition of a "So?"

"So, you say 'so'?" She walked over to Randy and sat on the edge of his small desk, knocking off a stack of scripts and other papers. She didn't attempt to bend over and pick them up. "So, what a FUCKING HYPOCRITE!" she screamed.

"He represented the man." Randy was cool.

"He used the man. He was about to agree to letting the studio dump him, cut him loose from his contract, a contract that he made for him only a month ago."

"So?" Randy dared to challenge her with another "so?"

"Is that all you can say so? So, hot-shot, why am I so riled over all this?" she asked him.

"Because Peter Barker was your client for more than ten years before he switched to Michael," Randy said.

"Michael was my associate agent. He had your job. He stole Barker from me, and three other clients, went to the big boys and demanded his own desk, no more associateship."

"Maybe he was ready to move on."

"He was ready to move on with my clients," she snapped.

"They wouldn't have left you unless they wanted to make the change." Randy was very sure of himself, which of course only he understood.

"It's the business. Steal or be stolen from, but no one ever stole from me before or since Stoltz. No one." She looked at Randy, then slid off his desk, stepped over the pile of papers she knocked to the floor and paced the office. "I would never have done that to Barker. I would never sell out my clients to a studio, a network, to a whim, for a better deal, for a bigger client. Never. I may be the biggest bitch in Hollywood, but I'm not a two-timing bitch. And he had the nerve to cry, to ball at the man's funeral."

"I see your point, Candace. I didn't have all the facts," Randy said. "Candace," Randy was demonstrative as he approached, taking her by the arm and turning her around to face him.

"Yes," she said, glaring at his hand on her arm.

"My timing is bad, in fact, it's terrible. But, my news is good. Laurie Dalton will sign with the agency."

"That's excellent news, Randy." Her mood was much lighter at once. "We'll serve her interests well."

"I will serve her interests, Candace. I want her to be my client, not our client." He was very direct.

She was flabbergasted. "You're damn right, your timing sucks," she spit the words at him. "You're my associate not a full agent. You've got fucking nerve, especially after what I just told you."

"I've given the matter a lot of thought, Candace. I realize that I'm young and inexperienced."

"You said it, kid. You said it." She crossed her arms and paraded the office.

"And I also know that you gave me a break bringing me upstairs to work with you." His efforts to appease her were rapidly failing.

"You're damn right about that, too. You thanked me all right. Wow, what a thanks!" She continued to pace wildly.

"But, this opportunity is mine. I can't turn it over to you like a good private serving his general. Besides, she wants to work with me, not you. She doesn't know you," he added.

"She wants to turn her career over to a twenty-two-year-old nobody without experience?" Candace stopped short, "You fucked her good, Stein. Congratulations. You fucked her good, and screwed me at the same time."

Randy wanted to tell her that she was wrong. But somehow, saying the right thing while he was doing the wrong thing made matters worse. Instead he compounded the fracture by telling her that he was only following her orders "fuck her and sign her" she'd told him.

"So, see, now you've got me saying so, so, so." She was still spitting the words. Her demeanor was rattlesnake-like, coiled and ready to strike. "So, you think you'll get your own commission from this one, do you? Full agent status in less than a handful of months. You've got to be the fastest rising stud punk agent in the whole goddamned stud farm stable. From the mailroom to the top floor without wasting any time in between to learn a goddamned anything."

Her anger was at its apex now. Candace unfolded her tense, crossed arms and went back to Randy at his desk. She pounded her fist to add a bit of drama to her last words to him. "Pack up your goddamned briefcase, and get the hell out of here now! They'll find you a new desk somewhere in the joint. I don't want to look at your face for one more minute." With her final slam, she caught her long, opera length pearls between fist and tabletop. The force of the blow ripped the pearls apart, sending the delicate, round beads flying in all directions, bullets from a ten millimeter machine gun.

"Fucking nightmare!" she howled. "What else can go wrong today?"

Randy put on his coat, picked up the briefcase and walked out of the room. He wasn't entirely sure where to go, who to see with his news and with his demands for his own agency responsibilities. Randy walked down the empty top floor hall of the agency. Most of the secretaries had gone, doors were closed left and right. He went to the end of the hall to find Lou Jacobs, the chief. He would still be there. He never left, not since his latest divorce anyway. It was safer at work.

Randy could hear noise coming from Lou's office as he approached. The door was closed and his usual cadre of assistants and secretaries had left early with the rest of the pack. Barker's death was like a national holiday. Only thing missing was the barbecue and the bunting.

As he got closer, the voices got angrier. He hesitated, and listened.

"You'll give me exactly who I want for the series, do you understand?"

"The network wants to develop an unknown, have an open casting call, maybe do a promotional national search for the right actor."

"I don't give a FUCK what they want. This is my most important package and I came to you to be sure that it lasts in the first place. Apply some pressure, trade off, scratch their back on some other deal, but don't let me down on this one."

Randy couldn't make out who was in the office with Lou Jacobs. He knew the voice, but couldn't finger it.

"We need a young star for the role of 'Eric' — a little name value, goddamn it. We need to put some heat back in the series." The other guy was practically screaming. "Laurie Dalton is your star, John."

Laurie Dalton... John... Randy realized they were talking about Laurie and her show. John, who was John? Moran! Lou was yelling at John Moran about Laurie's show. Providence, pure and simple. Randy knocked.

"Who is it?" Lou snapped.

Randy opened the door and went in.

"Randy Stein, sir. Sorry to interrupt."

"Then why are you?" Jacobs came back at him.

"Because I overheard the last piece of your conversation, as I stood outside, trying to decide whether or not to interrupt, and I decided to come in because I believe your conversation concerns me." Randy was bold.

Lou, nonplussed, "What are you talking about, Mr. Stein?" he asked.

"Laurie Dalton, sir. I heard you mention her name. She's my new client."

Moran went through the roof at this new bit of information. "She's your client. Oh, that's perfect. Just perfect. With all the goddamned superstar agents in this company this is who she picks - a punk kid. Do I know you?" he ripped into Randy.

"You will, Mr. Moran." His response was piercing. Lou Jacobs, slightly out of character, but nevertheless in his shrewd and savvy way, went over to young Randy and put an arm around his shoulder.

"Randy is my hottest new agent, John. You better get to know him. He now handles one of your most important stars." Lou smiled. It was the smile of a predator bringing food back to its young after a successful hunt. His teeth sparkled.

"We feel, that is, Lou and I and the network, that Laurie is the star of 'The Reilly's'. We don't want the package to get complicated by the addition of some hot young actor who will come on board demanding a huge salary, a share in the backend profits, thinking his ass is saving ours," offered the new super agent Randy Stein.

"That's right," Lou added. "Go on, Mr. Stein." He looked at Randy, who got the message to continue as if it had all been prearranged, prediscussed, agreed upon in some fictitious meeting in the limousine or the lunchroom.

"You are overruled, Mr. Moran. The star, her agent, the packaging agency and the network want an unknown. I suggest we start thinking together on this same plan to insure we get the right person in the part. If we do this properly we'll have the hit series we all believe we can have."

Randy looked at Lou again. Now his eyes and his teeth sparkled. Providence had indeed been fulfilled. The entire scenario was genius. It was a pure example of timing and opportunity colliding with the force of dynamite. Not only did Randy get his full agent status without begging or cajoling or threatening, he became a full-blown hero in the eyes of the big boss. All this in the course of ten minutes. What if he'd gone home, or to the men's room? He thought the hand of God was on him. Moran left Lou Jacob's office saying he would take the matter under advisement and get back to them later. Lou shook hands with his new twenty-year-old star agent and offered to buy him a drink.

• • •

"Jodi, do you think I have any chance of getting the job with Asher?" Bill wanted that opportunity more than he'd ever wanted anything in his entire life. He felt so close to Jodi as they sat together on the sofa in the small Hollywood Hills apartment that she shared with her boyfriend. Grayson had closed the ticket office early, like the rest of Hollywood at half mast for Barker. Bill and Jodi went back to her apartment in West Hollywood to work on their script, <u>The Divine LaVine</u>, a comedy they had co-created. Bill nearly always felt uncomfortable working there. After all, she was engaged, and her fiancé lived with her. But he was never there. Jodi explained that he traveled a lot for CBS. He was a staff production executive and was working on a bowling tournament in Seattle.

"You said the meeting went well. You put your best out there on the table, right?" she responded.

"But how do I know that my best is good enough?"

"You don't. You can't. And none of us ever will know unless we become king or pope or something."

"I wish I knew my competition."

"Grayson told me who one of them is, do you want to know?"

"Are you kidding? How come you didn't tell me?" He begged for any tidbits of information to ease his agony.

"Jim Stanton, in the scheduling office," Jodi replied.

"Stanton, no way, he wouldn't hire him, he's such a dummy."

"That's what we think, but somebody likes him. He got the meeting, he's being considered." Bill got up from the sofa, picked up the phone sitting on a rickety side table, and started to dial.

"Who are you calling?" Jodi asked.

"Randy Stein, my old buddy from U.S.C. The one I told you about that works at William Morris."

The main switchboard receptionist at William Morris answered. She told Bill that nobody was answering Mr. Stein's line. Bill left a message. He hung up, and began to dial again.

"Now who are you calling?" Jodi asked impatiently. She wanted to get off the job conversation and back to work on their script. It was getting good and she was on a writing roll that she didn't want to fade.

"I'm trying Randy at home," Bill said. Sensing her frustration, "We'll get back to work in a second, okay?" The phone rang and rang. No answer. Bill hung up. "He may be able to get a good word about me to Asher. His dad is Benton Stein. He practically owns the town, probably knows Asher well. For all I know he may owe him a big favor," Bill said.

"Will you come back to earth?" she pleaded. "Do you really think, if he did owe him a favor, or even if he just knew him, that Benton Stein would make a special effort to help you?"

"You're right, Jodi. God, I'm lucky to have you as a friend," he said continuing, "but it wouldn't hurt to mention it, right?"

"So go ahead and mention it, but don't count on it. Your best bet is to work through your channels at the studio. Grayson really thinks the world of you, you know, you dumb ass. He can help you more than you think," she told him.

"How's that?"

"He may be the lowly head of Guest Relations, but he's well-respected all over the plant, including the top floor. If he's rooting for you, you've got a chance."

"Really."

"Yes, really. Now, there's nothing more you can do, so relax. Let's get back to writing, here. We're on to something. Who knows, maybe we'll get lucky and sell a script before you become president of the network." They both laughed.

"Want some coffee?" she asked him.

"No thanks, but I'll take a coke if you've got one. Actually, any kind of soda," he replied.

"Okay, I think I do," she said, going through the cafe-style louver doors. "How about 7-up?" she called back to him.

"Fine," he said. She came back out with the drinks and sat next to Bill on the couch. Their script was laid out in front of both of them all over the small, wooden coffee table. Papers were also on the floor, on the back of the couch, everywhere.

"I think Barry LeVine needs a love interest," Bill said.

"I thought we agreed that the character was stronger if he always wanted the girl, but never got her. You know, constant crushes. Infatuations but no sex."

"He's too flat, one-dimensional. He needs a woman," Bill went on.

Jodi stopped, looked right at him and said, "So do you."

"Let's not get personal here," Bill replied immediately. "Besides, how do you know I don't have one, or maybe several," he said.

"Who's kidding who? Your social life is nonexistent." She went on, "You are a great guy. Look at all you've got going for yourself, looks, brains, ambition. How come you don't have a girl?"

"The only girl I've been interested in lately isn't interested in me. She's with someone else," he told her. "But you know what? I think it's time to throw caution to the wind, let my feelings out and face whatever the consequences are," he continued.

"Good. That's always the best way to be, true to yourself. It will always work out for the best. Look, even if she rejects you, you will have been honest and you'll know that you weren't missing out because you were afraid." Jodi went on talking. Bill was looking at her, barely listening, comprehending nothing. The secret love for Jodi that he'd held inside was tearing him apart. As she advised him of how to handle his mystery love, the only thought he had was of how incredible it would be to have his arms around her, his lips on her lips.

"It's the same with the Asher job," Jodi continued. "Put it out there, and do your best, then it's out of your hands. Let the chips fall and all that b.s., but it's true you know, it's really true."

Bill was ready to explode. She didn't get it at all. How could she be so blind, this smart, sensitive girl he idolized. Maybe she would reject him. Maybe she would throw him out, end their friendship? Was it worth the risk? What if he couldn't see her again, have lunch with her, plan and dream and scheme about a future with her? He would miss all that too much. Maybe he should leave it alone, wait for another time, and another place.

There would be no other time, no other place. Bill put his arms around her and kissed her. He was strong and held her very tight, pulling her up to him. At first, she struggled somewhat to regain her freedom, to break away and think about what was happening. But his lips held her as tightly as his arms held her body, and she soon gave in willingly to his desire.

Bill kissed Jodi for what seemed like an eternity and a millisecond at once. They were both blissfully confused by the encounter. But, it was right, and they both knew it. He gently, and softly, touched the back of her neck, beneath her long, silky flowing blonde hair. His nails stroked her skin and he moved his hands up the back of her long slim neck further into her hair, as he kissed her more passionately.

Jodi's tongue teased him. She went deeper inside him, bathing his entire mouth. His tongue, united with hers, his thoughts, at last in unison with hers. It was so perfect. The risk had been worth it. The fear unwarranted. The waiting unnecessary. Bill had wanted Jodi from the moment he saw her that first day at CBS. Now, so many months later, she was in his arms.

They fell back on the sofa — Bill kissing Jodi slowly, moving from her mouth to her cheek and then to her ear. She shivered as he licked her ear. He moved his lips down the side of her neck, and under her blouse. Caressing her, pushing her breasts gently and tightly together with his arms, he firmly and lovingly kissed her, lower and lower until his head was between her full bosom. Feeling her nipples hard beneath the blouse, he moved his hands to them and stroked them slowly back and forth, then around in circles. His mouth and tongue replaced his hand movement as he pulled her blouse carefully apart exposing her beautiful body for the first time. His mind raced. Was this really happening to him? It was so wonderful, too good to be true.

Jodi reached around Bill and pulled his shirt off his shoulder, responding in kind to his actions. It was all too incredible. They wanted to be undressed with one another. To feel the softness, and the hardness of flesh and body, heart and soul. They groped a bit, and then the groping turned to exploration of one another. Sensually, and gently, they took time to smell and taste the pleasure of each new discovery as they revealed their bodies to the other.

Jodi was very thin, almost frail for her size. Bill was surprised at how fragile she was naked. She was so formidable fully dressed.

Without the tight designer jeans, and fancy shoes, and expensive tops, she was very vulnerable and more beautiful than ever. More astonishing, her defenses were tossed aside, the snobby aloof, Eastern co-ed became a tender, sweet, loving creature of nature. She gave of herself fully and completely. Behind the initial shock of Bill's actions, both of them found love. It was all there, the love, hidden under layers of complicated human barriers established by the two of them to protect themselves from the most important experience of their lives.

Bill was very strong, very masculine. Jodi was as surprised at his manliness as Bill was taken by her vulnerability. She had thought of him as cool and distant, consumed by career drive. To her, he had been handsome, but not very sexy. Now he was the ultimate. The perfect man for her. She loved his broad shoulders and tight stomach. His long muscular legs wrapped around her, holding her in to him, shielding her from everything the entire world.

She spread her legs apart and raised her knees. Bill pushed himself up off of her, his biceps flexing and glistening fromsweet-smelling sweat.

Jodi saw his cock. It was exquisite. Perfectly straight, and round, full of manly power. Bill entered her with great care.

She was very moist, and very ready for him to penetrate, to reach inside her body all the way in, until his cock was inside her so far that it touched her heart. He slid in, slowly, very slowly, all the way, and she wrapped her lifted legs around him tying him to her with her feet as he lowered his entire body on top of hers, until they were as one, and remained as one, in love, into the night.

CHAPTER 14

S ergeant Arnold had called to say he was going to be late, and it was nearly 9:00 p.m. Larkin waited for him, using the quiet time at the studio to work on the script, and to plan his auditions for the new character, "Eric."

Marie typed up a storm. Steam rose from the keys. Larkin had Chris taking dictated notes and running them into Marie's outer office for inclusion in the script that she was assembling. Never mind that Chris had never taken notes of any kind, much less dictation. For that matter Chris had barely been a "C" student, worse in English. But, there he was, assistant to the almighty David Larkin, taking fast notes on a new script.

"Marie? When did that police detective say he would be here?" Larkin called out to his assistant. She managed to hear and understand him without letting up on the pounding of her IBM. She had developed Larkin-radar over the many years with the boss. Chris was amazed.

"Arnold called at about six forty-five, said he was running late. I told him we were going to be working until 10:00 or so. He said he'd be here. That's all." She kept working. "Any more pages? I'm caught up," she called out. David handed Chris a pile of papers to take in to Marie.

"Is it always like this around here?" Chris asked Marie, handing her new pages.

"This is nothing, kid. It's usually much wilder." She winked at him and grabbed the pages, ordering them in her own fashion.

"This is amazing. Does anyone ever eat?" he asked.

"Hungry?" she asked.

"Well, sure, it's almost 9:00," he said, feeling guilty for mentioning it at all.

"There are some snacks in the cabinet over there. Cokes in the fridge. Help yourself."

"Thanks," Chris said sheepishly. "Could I get you something?"

"No, thanks. Too late for me," she told him, making him really feel awful about even considering food when there was work to be done.

"Excuse me, is this David Larkin's office?" The voice accompanied a big, tall man, six foot four, weighing two-hundred-fifty pounds. He wore a navy blue blazer, gray slacks, a white shirt, open, with no tie. "I'm Sergeant Hector Arnold, L.A.P.D., Homicide." He displayed his credentials to Marie. She stopped typing. At last, Chris thought, the police could make her take a break.

"Sergeant Arnold, yes, I spoke to you earlier. I'm Marie O'Neill, Mr. Larkin's associate. We've been expecting you, sir."

"Sorry I'm so late. Got tied up on another murder case downtown," he said.

"Another murder case?" she asked politely.

"Yeah, but it looks like we pretty much got that one wrapped up. I'll have more time to concentrate on this one," he told her without reserve.

"This murder case? You mean Peter Barker?" she said. "It was murder?"

"Looks that way, ma'am."

"Wait one minute. I'll tell Mr. Larkin you're here. Chris, offer the sergeant a coke or some coffee."

Marie hustled into D.L.'s office and Chris obliged the sergeant with coffee, following Marie's orders. Marie shut the door between the rooms gently as she went into David's headquarters.

"Never mind, Marie, I heard it all," David said before she could warn him.

"Good God! He was murdered. How awful!" She put a hand on David's arm. He looked down at her gesture of protection, then glanced at her.

"Marie, I'm sorry for Peter. All I know is that we've got a show to launch. Send the man in and we'll get this over with as soon as possible. Okay?" He patted her hand reassuringly. "Everything is going to be fine, really. Just send him in," he repeated.

Marie went back to the outer office. "Mr. Larkin will see you now, Sergeant Arnold." She escorted the big man into D.L.'s office, then left, closing the door once again at David's request.

"Please sit down, Sergeant," David said like a gracious Hollywood host.

"Thank you, Mr. Larkin. It's exciting to meet you. I've seen your movies and TV shows. I guess I'm a fan," Arnold said awkwardly.

"Well, I guess that's a compliment," D.L. came back, then laughed a little to break the ice. "What can I do for you, Sergeant?" he continued.

"I need to ask you a few questions about Peter Barker," he replied.

"Anything," was D.L.'s response.

"The standard first question, then. When was the last time you saw Mr. Barker alive?" Hector Arnold took out a small notebook and pen and prepared to make notes.

"It was late afternoon, the day he died, here at the studio," Larkin told him.

"About what time?"

"Oh...," D.L. paused, "Four or five o'clock, then he left the set for the day."

"Did he say where he was going?"

"No, he just left. But...," D.L. hesitated.

"But what?"

"But I know that he went to Chasen's Restaurant for a drink at the bar," David finished.

"And how do you know that?"

"Peter ran into an associate of mine, and he told me." David was very circumspect, which naturally piqued the sergeant's curiosity. It was what David wanted, although he had not planned it that way. Sort of instantaneous malevolence, a way to throw a little dirt in Moran's direction.

"Who was that?" the detective asked.

"Just a co-worker who happened to be at the restaurant at the same time. A coincidence I assure you."

"May I have the name, please?"

"John Moran, VP of Production here at the studio." D.L. gave over the name like he was offering candy on Mother's Day.

"And this Mr. Moran, he told you about seeing Peter Barker at Chasen's after you heard about his death?"

"No, not exactly." D.L. wasn't sure about this next move, should he tell him the truth or just let the facts jumble? He chose jumble to avoid implicating himself in any fashion.

"What then?" the policeman asked.

"Moran called me from Chasen's," which was true. Moran would certainly tell the detective the same thing. "He, Moran that is, had an argument with Barker in the restaurant."

"About what, do you know?"

"Barker was about to be let go from the series." David paused then said, "Moran wanted him out, off the show. They got into a row over it…" he paused again. "I heard it was some argument at Chasen's."

"Why did he, Moran, call you from the place?"

D.L. thought he was off the hook until the detective asked this question. He came back with truth disguised with jumble. "He wanted me to help him do something about Barker. Get him off his back, control him." D.L. realized he'd said it the wrong way, making himself look involved.

"How could you do that, Mr. Larkin?" he asked.

"Peter and I were friends," he said with conviction, and with relief. "We went back a long way. I gave him his first starring role in a movie years ago. He did this TV series because I asked him to do it, Sergeant Arnold. He didn't need the job."

"So what did Mr. Moran want you to do about Mr. Barker?"

"The dailies, that's the term for what's shot each day, looked bad. That is, Barker looked bad. He wasn't giving the show his all, phoning it in you might say. And he didn't click with the rest of the cast, bad chemistry. Anyway, the studio was panicked. The network was angry and pressuring Moran to do something. He was in turn pressuring me to fix the problem. That's all." D.L. finished his long explanation.

Sergeant Arnold was buried in his notes. "How were you planning to… fix the problem as you put it?"

"Well, as you can imagine, this was a very delicate issue. Peter was a good friend. He'd done me a favor in the first place doing the show, and now it wasn't working. Worse, he didn't see it. He blamed everyone else, the writer, the other actors, the network, Moran. Peter behaved like this was the end of his career."

"It was the end of his career, Mr. Larkin." The irony of the moment's revelation was haunting. David looked at the cop.

"Indeed it was, Sergeant. Very sad. Very sad ending. The wrong ending, if I may say so. He was a great man, a great star, he deserved better."

"Would you say that Mr. Barker was upset over the potential firing, depressed perhaps?"

"Oh, yes, very much so. That's why we all thought he'd jumped. Didn't he jump?"

"We're investigating the possibilities, including the one that he was pushed," the cop said directly.

"Barker was loved, Sergeant. It's hard to believe anyone, anyone at all would do such a thing."

"Well, thank you for your time, and for the information. May I call you again if I need to?" he asked politely.

"Anything. I'll help any way I can," David said, showing the detective to the door.

Marie and Chris were working on the script as David and Sergeant Arnold came out. Marie's typing and Chris's Xeroxing came to a fast halt, their eyes glued to the unlikely duo.

"It was nice meeting you, Mr. Larkin. Can I get an autograph for my wife, Dianne, before I go?"

"Certainly. Marie, do we have a picture handy?" D.L. asked.

"Here you are," she handed him an 8 x 10 black and white studio shot of David sitting in a director's chair on a set with cameras and crew all around him. It was very Hollywood. David was even touched up. His skin was perfect in the photo. Chris looked over Marie's shoulder at the shot as she handed it to D.L. for a signature. It was C.B. Demille of 1975, Chris surmised.

David signed the photo, personalized it "To Dianne," and gave it to the cop. Arnold was very grateful for the gesture, and he departed.

"What did he want?" Marie asked immediately.

"Routine," was all David Larkin said as he walked back into the office.

"We're about done with the new script, D.L.," Marie called out to her boss as if nothing, no police, no questioning had ever interrupted the "all important" Hollywood process.

"Good. Then let's get the hell out of here," he replied. "Chris, come in here, please."

"Yes, Mr. Larkin, I mean, D.L."

"I let Mr. Lee go home, would you mind driving me so I don't have to call him back to pick me up tonight?"

"Sure, that's no problem."

"I'll be ready in five minutes, okay?"

"Okay, I'll be outside waiting. I'll get my car."

• • •

The soft radio tones of the Bee Gees harmony was the perfect way to end a remarkable evening, Bill told Jodi, whispering the lyrics of the song into her ear, "If I can't have you, I don't want nobody, baby."

"Can I tell you something?" she asked quietly.

"Of course, anything."

"Are you sure? Anything?" she persisted. "I don't want to make you feel uncomfortable."

"Did I do something wrong? Did I hurt you?" he asked with a horrified look, the beauty of the moment after lovemaking all but lost with the utterance of a single word - uncomfortable. Bill thought about the fragility of his life. He was a pane of glass, one moment strong and translucent, the next, after a single blow, shattered, useless, crumbling.

For a blinking moment he almost wished he'd kept the distance between them. She was, after all, engaged to someone else. How could he do this to her, to her fiancé, to himself? He should have resisted. In one moment of weakness, by virtue of a single action, everything was changed in his life.

"I have never felt love before, true bell-ringing, foot-stomping love," Jodi said softly. "And now I know what all the fuss is about."

"Huh?" Bill was in shock. Having just prepared himself for rejection, he'd just been told he was the ultimate lover. "I... love... you... too," he managed to stutter out. "I did from the first moment I saw you behind that stupid little front desk you sit at."

"What took you so long?" Jodi asked.

"I thought my feelings were that, my feelings. Until tonight, here, I didn't believe you shared them. Part of me still thinks this is all a dream, all of it, I mean us here together in your apartment, the script we're writing, my interview with Asher, even our lousy little jobs in the ticket office at CBS. Is all of this happening to us?"

Jodi sat up, and kissed Bill on the side of his face, down his neck, and over onto his shoulder. A series of tiny, quick little bites to assure him that all of it was very real. He put his arms around her once again and pushed her back down on the sofa.

"Let's get married. Tonight, right away," he said gleefully.

"You're a nut," she said.

"No, I mean it. Let's do it. It's going to happen eventually anyway, so what's wrong with a Tuesday night in West Hollywood? Look at the bright side, there wouldn't be a need for sneaking around, the big emotional break with Greg. It would all be right there, out in the open, self-explanatory, you know, they fell in love, they married, that's all."

"You're serious." Jodi was astonished. "You mean it, don't you?"

"I sure do. I love you. And I'd do anything to move out of that apartment downtown with Chris." Jodi took a breath then whacked Bill with one of the pillows off the couch. "If we can't get married tonight then I want to finish our script, okay?" Bill said. "Let's work in the nude."

"What?"

"Sure, it'll be our trademark. When we're big time writers, the interviewers will ask how we work so well together, and we'll tell them we always write in the nude - to strip away the inhibitions."

• • •

Benton Stein's silver Lincoln Continental Mark V coupe came around the corner with a screech. The gas crisis of '73 didn't scare Stein, or Detroit for that matter. Benton loved his car. He managed to give it a relatively inconspicuous once-over glance to be sure the valet had not damaged his capitalist tool while he dined at the California Yacht Club in the Marina del Rey.

It was after 11:00 and all of the other dinner guests had left their tables at a respectable 9:00 p.m. on this Tuesday night. Benton had not even arrived by 9:00, which was not unusual at all. Business usually kept him occupied until about 8:15, and then, as he was leaving his office at MGM, he ran into an acquaintance. He invited her to dine with him, suggesting the Cal Yacht Club, where he was a member. It was private, and close to the studio, just a few miles down Washington Boulevard to the Marina.

Dinner had been a delight. The mogul and his female acquaintance sat at a window side table looking out at the full moon casting its incredible beacon down on the rippling waters of the Pacific. Dingys and yachts, side by side, filled the slips all around them. The cling and clang of the bells and ropes, block and tackle, provided a constant din of maritime "dinner music."

The Cal Yacht Club was very elegantly unpretentious. Benton kept his yacht there. It was christened "All Heart," named for his wife Jennifer Hartman. The one hundred and twenty-foot motorcraft slept twenty in ten absolutely luxurious staterooms, and its main salon could accommodate two hundred guests. The ship had been meticulously crafted in Europe, and its interiors outfitted by California's premiere designer du monde, Arthur Elrod of Palm Springs.

The red-jacketed valet handed Benton the keys to the Lincoln.

"Would you like to see my baby up close before we go?" he asked his dinner date.

"Why not?" she answered. "I'd love to see her."

"Okay, then, follow me." Benton put out his arm for his companion. She took it like a daughter being led down the aisle by her father. He tossed the keys to the Lincoln back to the valet.

"We'll be back in a few minutes, son. Just keep the car up front."

The valet smiled, knowing full well that he was stuck until Commodore Stein decided to come back for his car. Ten minutes or ten hours. He couldn't leave until Stein let him go. The kid walked back to his station and sat down on a stool in the darkness, staring at the big silver Lincoln illuminated by the glowing moonlight, alone, in front of the club. He would wait for the boss to return.

"Here she is," Benton said proudly. "She's beautiful at a distance, but up close, she's incomparable," he continued. "Come aboard?"

"Aye, aye, captain," his companion said, and he took her by the hand and led her up the steps into the yacht. Benton opened a pair of highly polished solid brass and beveled glass inlaid doors and they entered the main salon. A sculpted white wool carpet, at least four inches thick, was the initial sensation of luxury to all who entered. Enormous overstuffed settees were custom-fitted to the parlor.

"It's absolutely breathtaking," she told her host.

"Please sit down, we'll have a little after-dinner drink before we go," he said. "What would you like?"

"Nothing, really, I don't need another drink, not after all that champagne at dinner."

"Then, one more glass of champagne to toast our new friendship," he said, going behind a finely carved wooden bar and displaying a bottle of chilled Dom Perignon champagne he'd removed from a refrigerator cooler.

"How can I refuse?" she answered.

Benton popped the cork and it blew skyward hitting the ceiling square in the center.

"Bull's-eye," she said, laughing.

"I'm a pretty good shot," he replied, pouring the elixir into two long stemmed flutes. He handed one to his guest, then toasted her.

"To a very beautiful and talented young lady with a future of unlimited potential."

She took a sip. "You are a very attractive man, and very generous and I'll bet you toast all the women you bring here just like that," she told him with a knowing wink.

"What makes you think I bring other women here?" he asked, pouring more champagne.

"I would, if I were you," she said, adding, "besides, your reputation precedes you."

"Did Randy tell you that?" Benton asked.

Benton Stein's female acquaintance for the evening was Laurie Dalton.

Her nostril flared, and her hot-sex-breath, along with the voluptuous animated body, was capturing father in the same way it had seized the son. Only this time, Miss powerful, man-melting starlet had met her match. Benton Stein had hot breath, too. His was the fire breath of the dragon, and Laurie Dalton was totally at his mercy.

"Would it matter who told me about you?" Laurie answered.

"No, I suppose not," he said. "And yes, I do bring many women here."

"Has your wife ever been here?" Laurie asked.

"Once. She christened the ship. We had a party and took her out." Benton smiled a half-hearted grin.

"That's a shame. It's such a lovely boat, and so romantic."

"Yes, it is romantic and I assure you it is used happily to that end."

"Happily and frequently I imagine. Ever the same girl twice?" she said, cutting through the smoke, but not surprising Benton.

"Never," he paused. "Maybe you'll be the first, that is, the first girl to come here twice."

"Who says I want to come back?" Laurie said, keeping up with his come-on, one-to-one, eye-to-eye, fearless prey facing her predator.

"You will, I promise it," Benton said.

He moved closer to her, and carefully positioned himself to kiss her. Benton waited for her to pull back, to resist him. She didn't retreat. She looked him in the eye, daring him to kiss her. He couldn't, wouldn't wait any longer. Their lips met. It was a long, luxurious kiss, suitable to their surroundings, so deluxe and soft, and rich. Laurie was the first to break the moment, thinking it was a mistake, but liking it so much. She wanted more. These were dangerous waters, she thought. The Marina del Rey was shark-infested, and she was with one of the sharks, if not one herself.

Having tasted the flesh, there was no turning back, and a second long kiss led to a second bottle of after-dinner champagne, and then to the satin sheets of the master stateroom. Benton Stein was nearly three times Laurie Dalton's age but he made love to her like no man she'd ever known. Maybe it was his wealth and power that attracted her, or maybe it was the fact that he was married, or maybe it was the fact that his son also wanted her, or maybe she just found him irresistible. It was all of these things, Laurie thought, all of them.

Their lovemaking led to a deep sleep, induced no doubt by their mutual alcohol content and the gentle movement of the ship in the Marina waters. The light of day came all too soon, piercing the many portholes of the stateroom, filling it with laser beams of sunshine crisscrossing in all directions.

"Is there a shower on board?" Laurie asked as she kissed her mogul lover good morning.

"Through that door there, a full bath, everything you could need," he replied.

"That's handy. How many new toothbrushes do you buy a month?" she laughed at him, and kissed him again. Benton wanted her again, and they hadn't even parted.

The Lincoln was waiting for them in the same spot the valet had left it the night before. So was the valet, only he was sleeping on his stool, leaning against the wall of his little hut. The 6:00 a.m. eastern sun hadn't landed on him yet. Benton walked over and removed the keys to his car from a hook on the wall. They were the only keys.

He left a hundred dollar bill in the kid's lap, for his loyalty, then he and Laurie got in the car and drove off. The engine noise woke the kid, who jumped to attention as his one hundred dollar tip fell to the floor without his noticing.

CHAPTER 15

P eter Barker's death, the continuing police investigation, and the press following every step of it, put Laurie Dalton on the cover of virtually all of the tabloids, and three national magazines within a month.

News crews were stationed at the studio entrance daily waiting for a shot of anyone connected with the story, especially the star, Ms. Dalton. Word on the street was that an imminent announcement would soon be due from City Hall, calling the death murder.

Moran was jubilant. "The Reilly's of San Marino" ratings doubled to a near 40 share. He'd even endured two sessions with Detective Arnold, answering his questions about the dispute at Chasen's, the matter of some salad tossed over his head.

As the show went into its second month on the air, Moran was not alone in celebration. Asher at the network was offering new deals to both Moran and Larkin. The entire Friday night line-up of shows on CBS was pulled out of the basement by "The Reilly's." It meant multi-millions in profits for everyone, as long as it kept going. Moran's job was to make sure it did.

Larkin had tastefully written Peter Barker out of the show, giving him a fatal heart attack while on business in another city. The news brought Emmy-winning tears on screen to his favorite child, "Susan Reilly," played by Laurie. The next week, the ratings went up again as America tuned in to see what "Susan" would do next.

She took over. Larkin, with great skill, was building his lead into a major TV star. He liked the challenge, loved the fact that his scheme was working, and working so fast. The best part of TV, he thought, was that success came right away. Not like making a movie where it takes two years to write it, another two to sell it, package it, and then another year to make it, before one ticket is sold.

Yet, Larkin was still on thin ice. The show wasn't a solid hit. And he wasn't used to working with a solo female lead, especially a 19-year-old female star. Larkin wanted to balance the show with a male. He decided that he would discover a male hunk to play the new role of "Eric," the long-lost brother. Moran and CBS both were saying no. They wanted an established name in a lesser role. Larkin was holding open auditions in spite of the protests.

Hundreds of hopeful young men with 8 x 10 glossy photos of themselves, a resume, and no agent, stood in line at the studio gate waiting to get in, to be seen. It was the Hollywood cattle call. A chance for the masses of actors without agents to get their break. All of the represented actors would be seen by appointment, later.

The pressure of delivering a weekly hour of television was all-consuming. The entire staff worked eighty-hour weeks without blinking. Chris Reynolds hadn't even been home. Most nights he slept on a couch in the office after finishing work at 2, 3, 4 in the morning. No wonder he was on a flat weekly salary, no overtime. But thoughts of overtime had long since vanished from Chris's mind. He was fully immersed in the grind. The regular filming of the series had to continue while the auditions were held. Larkin had arranged to use an adjacent soundstage for the auditions so he could run back and forth between the filming of the show and the call.

Sergeant Arnold arrived on the set in the middle of it all. Marie saw him coming across the lot and dashed to get him in order to orchestrate his arrival on the set, giving Larkin warning.

"Sergeant Arnold," she said, a bit out of breath as she ran up to him, darting between groups of the best looking men she'd seen in one place in years, "I didn't know you were coming to see us today. Can I help you?"

"I hope I'm not disturbing anything. I've got a few more questions for Mr. Larkin, and I would also like to talk to some of the other cast and crew," he replied.

"Today!" Marie let out her horror without check. "I mean, today, of all days, it's a madhouse around here. Can you come back later or tomorrow?" she asked.

"I wish I could ma'am, but no, it'll have to be today. I'll just wait around until you folks have a break," he said.

"If you insist, Sergeant," Marie replied and started to usher him back to the studio office.

"I'll be inconspicuous, stay in the background. Haven't spent much time on a set before, it'll be interesting for me," Arnold told her cheerfully.

"We don't break for lunch for another hour, are you sure you want to hang around?" Marie repeated.

"I think it's best," was all he said.

• • •

Jodi and Bill walked down Fairfax Avenue back to CBS from their weekly lunch at Canter's at a leisurely pace. The same characters were always there, selling the fruit, squeezing the fruit. They passed a gift shop window with all the displayed merchandise covered in cobwebs. The tarnished brass menorah, the dust caked white porcelain soup tureen "on special." It had all been there, in the same spot for God knows how many years.

The two wunderkinds with so much ahead of them, so much future to celebrate, kept on their journey back to the plant. It was mere steps away, just across Beverly Boulevard through the public parking lot, past the lines of tourists waiting for tickets to all the shows Bill and Jodi spent their days sorting out, mailing out, passing out. Their work was all for these tourists, for America, Bill told Jodi as they excused themselves cutting through the bottleneck line to get in the artists' entrance, back to work.

"I hate to admit this," Bill said holding the artists' entrance door open for Jodi, "but I always feel special coming through this door. They're all out there waiting in line, and we get to come in. Is it crazy? It makes me feel privileged," Bill said.

"You feel privileged when the mail is delivered on time," Jodi remarked, as she entered the ticket office ahead of him.

Grayson was standing in the door to his inner office. He looked angry. Bill came in a moment later and saw the look on Grayson's face right away. "Is something wrong, Mr. Grayson?" Bill asked quickly, losing his happy grin.

"Come in my office," Grayson said, and showed him in, then closed the door behind them.

Bill caught one last look at Jodi before it shut. He saw the look in her eyes. She was worried.

"Sit down, Bill." He did.

"What's wrong?" Bill persisted. Grayson hesitated, making matters worse. "Did I do something?"

Grayson didn't have the heart to tell him. He hesitated further, finally speaking. "We lost. We didn't get it," he said.

"I don't understand, what did we…"

"The job, the job with Asher. He didn't hire…"

"Oh," Bill understood. His chest sunk as if he was in a plane losing altitude fast at thirty thousand feet. His heart was in his stomach. Grayson felt the same way. "We didn't get the job." It was just as important to Grayson. It was a "we lost," not you lost.

"Who got it?" Bill asked.

"A guy named Franklin, Jim Franklin. A new kid, worked as an assistant to the head of casting in New York. Princeton graduate, East Coast family, all of that."

"There's some consolation in knowing the job was filled after a global search." Bill tried to lighten the mood, even though he felt like he'd been kicked in the balls, hard. "Asher was looking in New York, too?" he asked.

"Apparently." Grayson got up and came around the desk. He put an arm on Bill's shoulder. "You've got what it takes, don't forget that. Someday you'll be the President of the network, bigger than Asher. This is only a minor setback. Seems like a lot now, but it's not."

Bill knew Grayson was a good friend. It was great to have a champion, only he wished his champion had more clout.

Jodi had been waiting nervously at her desk outside Grayson's door.

"I didn't get the job with Asher," he said quietly to her as he came out of the office. "He hired some guy from New York, a Princeton grad."

"Probably his alma mater," Jodi came back. "See, if you'd just interview with a guy from U.S.C." She tried to ease the pain, without much success.

"I'm going back to my corner and open the goddamn mail." Bill went on, "I'll be fine, just need to be alone with the mail for a few hours. Thanks for the sympathy." He walked back to his corner, put on his white gloves to protect his skin, and dove in.

• • •

There was only one bad element to Randy's new deal as a full agent at William Morris. Lou Jacobs had insisted that he remain under Candace Fielding's supervision, and that his new office was next door to hers. At least it wasn't shared space.

Randy had his own territory, his own secretary, which he'd hand-plucked from the mailroom ranks. The secretary's name was Gary Smith, and he was green as grass. Nearly the lowest guy on the mailroom totem pole, but he typed like the wind, nearly ninety words per minute. He would work as hard as Randy pushed him and, he had no connections, none.

Jennifer Stein hired her interior designer to do Randy's office as a present for his promotion. The best of the best, a class triple AAA designer with taste, talent, and a client roster that included movie stars, moguls, and maharajahs.

The designer created a mini masterpiece for young Mr. Stein. It was the talk of the agency. Army Archerd even mentioned the item in his daily column in Variety.

Jennifer meant well. So did the designer. In the end, despite its elegance, it was all just too much for a twenty-two-year-old first-time agent. Even if he was the son of Benton Stein. And even if his client was the hottest new star in the universe.

Randy was about to take off for the studio, to drop in on Laurie. His departure was delayed by the unexpected arrival of his "office benefactor" mother, Jennifer Hartman Stein. She entered her new office.

Everything about it was her style — grand, grand style. It reeked of taste and old money. Randy had grown up around it all, but it wasn't him, not yet anyway, the shoes were still a few sizes too big.

"It's so marvelous," she said. "What a splendid job. Are you happy with the office, dear?" she asked.

"It's beautiful, mom, you shouldn't have done it, though."

"Nothing is too good for my son. Besides, next year we'll be expanding into the space next door and we'll have to re-do. You'll see, just wait."

"Into Candace Fielding's office!" Randy screamed with laughter. "That'll be one hell of a day. So, mom, did you come to see the office?" he asked.

"Yes, and to invite you to a party in your honor. Your father and I want to throw you the best party Hollywood has seen this year for the best new agent in town. We'll have it at the estate, and we'll invite everyone. What do you say? How about that for a send off?" Jennifer was excited with her idea. She hadn't thrown a big party in a long time. Her son's good fortune was the best reason she could imagine. And when it came to parties, she was the queen.

Randy put his arms around his adored mother and hugged her. "You're too much, mom. Do you know that?"

"Yes, of course I know it."

"I think the party is a great idea."

"It will give us a chance, the three of us, to celebrate as a family again. I think it will be good for all of us, you know what I mean?" she said.

"Yes, mom, I agree."

"Your father is very proud of you, too, Randy. Laurie seems to be a fabulous girl. Bring her as your date, the guest of honor, next to you of course. I've set the date with the caterers for next month. The first of December, a Saturday night, we'll have a winter ball this town has never seen the likes of, in honor of you."

Randy kissed Jennifer on the cheek and they left his office together. The secretaries that lined the outer hall from one end to the other turned and watched as the golden boy and his twenty-four carat mom paraded toward the elevator.

• • •

"Mr. Larkin, as you've probably read in the papers the autopsy of Mr. Barker revealed heavy amounts of alcohol mixed with equally dangerous levels of cocaine in his bloodstream. The two together were, in fact, potentially lethal themselves, regardless of the top floor plunge." Detective Arnold looked at a harried David Larkin who was barely concentrating on the policeman's words. He had hundreds of "Erics" to sift through, and he was falling behind shooting the show. On top of everything, the script wasn't working as well as he'd hoped. The writers were frantically revising at his orders while the cast and crew were on break, and he was being interrogated by Arnold.

"Mr. Larkin, I have to ask you some personal questions," the detective pressed forward. David's attention focused momentarily.

"Yes, oh, what is it?"

"Were you aware that Mr. Barker drank excessively?"

"I knew he drank socially, but he was not a heavy drinker, certainly not an alcoholic. I knew him for many years."

"Did he take drugs?"

"Again, he may have, but never in front of me. He wasn't an addict, if that's what you're asking." Larkin lied. He had done drugs with Peter, bought and sold them with Peter. Both of them were very fond of cocaine. Both of them were supplied by Don Robertson.

"Did you know Mr. Barker was drinking or taking drugs the night of his death?"

"How could I have known that? I just told you he never did that sort of thing in front of me."

"I thought you said the two of you had been friends for years. Didn't you socialize with Mr. Barker?"

"We were friends, and we did go out. But not so much in recent years. And even if we did I didn't keep tabs on the guy's habits. It wasn't any of my business."

"Mr. Moran stated that you knew he'd been drinking that night because Moran had called you from Chasen's Restaurant and told you what had happened. Is that correct?"

"I suppose so. But, Moran called to tell me to get Barker 'off his back.' I think those were his words exactly. He told me he had been attacked by Peter in the restaurant and they had fought. He may have mentioned that Peter was drunk, but I don't recall. Besides, that wasn't the purpose of his call, to tell me Peter was drunk."

"How did you plan to follow Mr. Moran's instructions? That is, how could you keep Mr. Barker off his back?" Detective Arnold asked pointedly.

"We've been over this before, Sergeant. I tried to call Peter, to talk to him about what happened," Larkin replied. "I wanted to reason with him and also to let him know what I was doing to help him save face when he left the show."

"What do you mean, save face?" Arnold wondered.

"I had arranged for a favor, a part in a new movie at Paramount that would get him off the show without embarrassing him. Peter could say he broke the TV deal to do the movie, that it was always part of his contract, an out for a great film, his first love."

"Did you reach him on the phone, Mr. Larkin?"

"No. I never did. He never knew," David replied.

"Mr. Larkin, do you use alcohol or drugs?" David was taken aback by the directness of the detective. Again, what purpose could the truth serve in answering honestly. The lie was preferred, it was acceptable, palatable, better than the truth.

"No, I do not use them. If you are suggesting that I take either one frequently or regularly, you're off base. I'm into physical and mental health, Detective. Ask anyone who knows me. I diet, I exercise, and I don't indulge in booze or drugs." Larkin was extremely convincing.

"Thank you, Mr. Larkin, again, for your time. I need to talk to Ms. Dalton now, and then I'd like to hang around the set, pick up some information if I can from other cast and crew members. I'll try and stay clear, disappear into the sets, so to speak."

Larkin looked at the six-foot-four, two-hundred-fifty pound detective, and thought he would be invisible on the set like an elephant in a grass field. "You can do whatever you must. Please don't upset Ms. Dalton, though. We're running behind and I can't afford any more problems on the set." Arnold was generous, took his directions with good spirit and again reassured the almighty that he'd be good.

"Where can I find Laurie Dalton?" Arnold asked.

"Marie. Marie," David called out for his assistant. She wasn't there, Chris came in instead.

"Is Marie around, Chris?"

"No sir, she's grabbing lunch, can I help you?"

"Yes, show Detective Arnold to Ms. Dalton's dressing room."

"Yes, D.L. Follow me, Detective Arnold."

Chris took the big guy wearing his standard issue blue sport coat out of Larkin's office. David was glad to be rid of him. Maybe that was the last of the big investigation. He didn't kill Peter Barker, and frankly, he didn't particularly care who did, except for the fact that until the case was resolved Arnold might continue to bother him. That he didn't like.

• • •

Randy knocked loudly on Laurie's dressing room door so she could hear him above all the hammering and construction on the set outside.

"I'll be right there. Hold on," she called back. She was sitting in a chair at a makeup and hair table outfitted in her portable trailer dressing room. All of the actors, from the extras to the major stars, had trailers for dressing rooms. They rolled in the trailers for the stars, then rolled them out when they were out. Bigger star, bigger trailer. Laurie had a medium-sized tin can. But the parking space beside it was empty, so there was definitely room to expand, a very good sign.

Laurie's hair was pulled back, wet, a hair stylist was working on her. Another stylist was finishing her makeup. And a third person was giving her a pedicure. Four people jammed into a 6 x 12 tin can filled with clothes, more clothes and more clothes. Laurie asked her hairdresser to get the door for the detective she was expecting.

"Be nice, Sally. It's the police," she told the hairdresser.

"The police. Why?" Sally asked.

"That was D.L. on the phone calling to let me know a police detective is coming to talk to me about Peter. His name is Arnold, Sergeant Arnold. Will you let him in?"

Sally left her post with comb in one hand and brush in the other and went to let the detective in the already overcrowded star's dressing room.

138

"Come in, Sergeant Arnold," Sally said, actually greeting Randy Stein, whom she'd not met before. "Ms. Dalton is right here, behind all this mess. Follow me, don't trip over anything. It's an obstacle course in here."

Randy didn't know what she was talking about, deciding that not asking was surely the simpler approach. He followed Sally through the maze to Laurie's dressing table.

"Randy, it's you!" she exclaimed.

"I gather you were expecting someone else. Who's Sergeant Arnold?" he said.

"You're not Sergeant Arnold!" Sally exclaimed. "I knew you were too young and too cute to be a cop."

There was another knock at the door.

"That's the cop," Sally quickly added. "I'll get it again." And she went back through the clothes racks to the door.

"How's it going, Laurie?" Randy asked, bending down to give her a kiss on the cheek. Laurie puckered her lips and blew him a return kiss in the mirror. She was unable to move otherwise.

"The show going well?" Randy questioned her further. "Everybody treating you right?" Laurie smiled and nodded.

Her makeup lady finished applying the final touches of lip liner with the grace of Michelangelo.

"You can talk now," she said, putting the brush down. "What do you think?"

Randy loved the new look and raved about it. The three stylists concurred eagerly. Laurie looked in the mirror for a long moment at herself. Randy was behind her, therefore also fully visible in the mirror. He was smiling at her and their eyes met in the glass. The guilt was colossal, especially for a girl who always did what she wanted without guilt. Laurie never felt she owed anyone an explanation for her actions. Now she was reconsidering her modus operandi.

Over the past few weeks Laurie had been with Randy's father six times since their first casual dinner turned into an all night romp. Benton had told Randy about their chance meeting at the studio and then dinner at the yacht club, not about the affair. Randy was glad his father liked her. But neither Benton nor Laurie had said a word to a soul about the other half dozen times they had met, bedded, and parted in secrecy.

Laurie harnessed the best actress genes in her to continue smiling at Randy in the mirror. Laurie knew that Randy wanted to make love to her. The gardenia jokes persisted, and every other kind of flower was delivered in profusion to the set, to her apartment, to her dressing room. All the cards said the same thing - "I love you, Randy."

She wanted them to say "I love you, Benton" because that's what was happening to her. She was falling for a man old enough to be her grandfather. At first it was a dalliance with power, money and danger. But with each subsequent time, it was less about power, money and danger and more about desire. Laurie loved the way Benton loved her.

"Excuse me, Laurie, Detective Arnold is here to see you from the police department." Sally interrupted Laurie's eye contact with Randy in the mirror. Laurie got up and shook Arnold's hand. She had the grip of a man, which men generally loved. Arnold was surprised.

"Is there somewhere we can talk, Ms. Dalton?"

"Other than in here, Detective?"

"No, this is fine. I meant in private."

"I really don't think there is anything I could tell you that these people couldn't hear."

"Very well."

Laurie sat down and Sally went to work finishing the French braid in her hair. Randy stood guard at her side, while the makeup ladies made themselves scarce amongst the costume racks.

"When was the last time you saw Mr. Barker?" Arnold began.

"The afternoon of his death, here at the studio."

"What happened at the studio that day?"

"It was a bad day, for Peter, for all of us. Every line was a struggle, every shot was a retake three, four, five, ten times. We were getting nowhere, friction on the set was intense, even the crew was feeling it."

"What do you mean by that, Ms. Dalton?"

"Well, Sergeant, the crew, that is, the grips and prop guys that move the set and the gaffers that do the lights, they're paid by the hour to do their job regardless of whether we actors are failing or succeeding at our task. These guys do their best, and get paid, and go home.

When they start to get upset with what's happening on the set, well, then you know things aren't going well."

"In your opinion, did Mr. Barker seem upset or behave in any way unusual that you recall?"

"No, not really. He was having a hard time, but I think he felt it was our fault, not his. He seemed kind of aloof through it all."

"Were there any arguments with anyone?"

"Only one. He and D.L. — David Larkin — had some words."

"Can you tell me more?"

"D.L. wanted Peter to give a little more in his performance, stretch the character of Reilly. D.L. felt Peter wasn't playing it with depth, just phoning it in because Peter was such a big star."

"How did Peter react?"

"He told him to shove it up his, you know where, that the problem wasn't him, it was the writing and…" Laurie hesitated.

"And what?"

"And, the rest of the cast, meaning me mostly I suppose. We had no chemistry together. Just didn't spark."

Randy interrupted at this point correctly thinking Laurie was telling too much to the sergeant. It was time to get to the set and back to work.

"Thank you, Miss Dalton. You've been helpful and I hope I didn't take up too much of your time. If it's any consolation, you spark me! You are great in the show. My wife and I watch every week." Sergeant Arnold shook her hand and left the trailer, nearly taking a rack of dresses with him that caught the pleat of his sport coat from behind. The rack fell to the floor with all the wardrobe, sending Laurie's assistants scampering to pick it all up, garnering belabored and effusive apologies from Arnold as he made his way out.

"Nothing is calm and simple around here, ever," Laurie told Randy. He took her by the hand and they went to the set for the remainder of the day's filming.

CHAPTER 16

B oth the auditions for "Eric", and the filming of the "The Reilly's of San Marino," ended around 7:00 p.m.

David Larkin asked Laurie to stay and come back to the office for a few minutes. Randy was with her, having come back to the studio to pick her up, and take her to dinner.

"Here are your messages, D.L.," Marie said, handing David a stack of little pink papers two inches thick.

"Thanks. I think." David walked into his office with Laurie and Randy right behind him. Randy winked a silent hello to his old U.S.C. pal Chris Reynolds. They hadn't seen each other in some time. Chris was insulted by the quick brush-off. After all, they'd been good pals in school, which meant bonded for life. To Randy it meant nothing. He didn't have time for Chris anymore. David Larkin's office boy could do nothing for the future Hollywood mogul, Randy Stein.

"Please sit down," David said to Laurie and Randy. "Everybody come on in here, and bring the contenders," he shouted out to the staff in the outer office. They came in immediately, bringing with them the pictures of all the young men that wanted to change their name from Jim or Bob or Bill or Joe to ERIC.

"We got some good ones today. Let's see if our choices match," David said to Kim and Andy, his two casting executives. Kim was the guy and Andy the girl, only sometimes it was hard to tell even without the confusion of names. Kim and Andy were neutral. Neither outwardly masculine or feminine, they exuded no sexuality. At least not in their dress or their manner. Behind closed doors, each of them most probably preferred the mystery of the same sex. Kim handed David the "A" stack of pictures and resumes and the room became silent waiting for the almighty to go through the pile and pick his favorites.

"No, not this one, I hated him." David threw a picture across the room. Before the group had a chance to be horrified by the discard, David was raving about another picture. "He was one of my top choices. Yes, this one is a definite possibility," he said holding up the picture.

Chris saw the picture, but didn't smile. It was Mark Harlander, the Greek God guy that had gone with them to his first big "Hollywood" party. Chris was sure Mark had the part, that it would be no use to even ask David for an audition. The casting people knew that David and Mark were friends. Harlander had been making the rounds for a couple of years with Larkin pushing him. Despite the relationship, the casting duo just acted as if they'd done their job brilliantly, selecting Harlander.

"Laurie, what do you think of him?" D.L. handed her the picture.

"He's gorgeous," she replied, giving the 8 x 10 to Randy for a look.

"The ladies will go for this one," Randy added.

"Kim, arrange a screen test tomorrow for this one with Laurie." David handed him Harlander's pictures.

"And now, show me your five or six runners-up."

Kim and Andy nervously fumbled through the bios and picked out their other choices, handing them to David. He glanced at them briefly, handed them back and told his casting people to audition all of them on film. They were now excused, they'd done their job for the day.

"Maybe he'll get an even better 'Eric' tomorrow," Kim said as he and Andy left the office. The second day of auditions were primarily reserved for candidates submitted by agents. Kim and Andy had scheduled nearly one hundred appointments.

David turned to Laurie to give her a hug and express his appreciation for her support, and for her incredible talent. She was delivering in a big way, he told her. Randy was even more excited than Laurie by Larkin's praise.

"Would you care to join us for dinner?" Randy asked David, putting his arm around Laurie to define his territory in the aftermath of David's glowing tribute.

"No thank you, another time?" he replied. "I think I'll just have Chris take me home. I've got a lot of work to do."

Larkin asked Chris to get the car to drive him home as he had been doing for several weeks since he started working for David. With the arrival of Chris Reynolds, Mr. Lee, Larkin's houseman-chauffeur, had been getting a few hours off. The first time David asked Chris to drive, he went for his own broken down old white Rambler. Larkin had an amused look on his face when Chris pulled up to the office in the Rambler to get David, but he got in anyway and didn't say a word about the car all the way home to Bel Air. The next day, Marie gave Chris a set of keys to a studio car, a brand new black Lincoln Continental assigned to David for his use off the lot. On the lot, Teamsters Union personnel had total jurisdiction driving all vehicles. David didn't want teamsters driving him home, so the studio had managed to quietly arrange for the Lincoln, which nobody knew about. From that day on, Chris was the only one that had access to the car for Larkin.

"Before I forget," Randy addressed both Laurie and David. "Mom and Dad want to have a party in our honor next month, Saturday night, December first, at the house."

"Really?" Laurie was shocked, but her response managed to come out sounding pleased. This was one event where her performance would no doubt win an Emmy. Whose date would she be, father or son?

"That's very generous," David said not particularly interested. But it was good for the show.

"Great, then I'll tell them you both approve. Mom will be especially excited."

"I bet she will," Laurie said in a whisper.

"You'll finally get to meet her," Randy offered.

"I'm looking forward to it," Laurie smiled, then looked into Randy's eyes as they left the office for dinner. Randy didn't know that she'd be having dessert, with his father.

• • •

Larkin came out of the office and got into the front seat. He never treated Chris like a driver, more like a friend driving him home. Chris looked forward to this task as it was his only time to talk to David, one to one.

Some nights, the ride to Bel Air was in silence, if David wanted it that way. Other nights, David talked nonstop, and Chris felt like he was really getting to know the almighty Larkin.

The news of Mark Harlander as the number one contender for the part of "Eric" had put a damper on Chris's enthusiasm and added a new dimension to his conflict over asking David for an audition. This was the biggest crisis to date in his life, and David didn't even notice. To make matters worse, tonight was one of Larkin's talking nights. All Chris wanted to talk about was auditioning for the part of Eric, and that was the only thing they didn't talk about on the twenty minute drive from MGM to Bel Air.

On all other nights, David had simply gotten out of the car, thanked Chris and gone into his house. Tonight, on this most confusing of nights, he did the impossible, he invited Chris in for dinner. Why tonight, Chris thought, realizing that maybe this would be the perfect opportunity to bring up his desire to audition for Eric.

"Lee is making steaks tonight. We'll have a little red wine before dinner to relax. How's that sound?" David asked as they entered the foyer.

Chris hesitated, then replied nervously, "It sounds very good, thank you." He was not himself and David sensed it.

"Everything all right with you?" he asked Chris.

"Sure. Great. Couldn't be better."

They went into the study, and Mr. Lee appeared from out of nowhere, following them and asking for drink orders. David told him to get one of his best bottles of cabernet and to light the fireplace.

"Okay, let's have it. What's eating you?" It was unlike David Larkin to persistently inquire into someone else's state of mind. He was always more concerned with his own.

"I guess I'm a little tired, and also surprised to be invited for dinner," Chris said.

"An invitation to dinner at my home generally produces a smile on the face of the person invited, not a frown."

"I'm really sorry. Maybe I should go."

"Nonsense, you deserve a little R & R. After a glass or two of wine you'll feel like yourself. By the way, if I haven't told you how pleased I am with the job you're doing take this dinner invitation as a hint that I am very happy with you."

"Thank you, sir, I mean David," Chris said, beginning to feel better, but still unable to find the words to ask for the audition. David telling him what a good job he was doing made it even harder.

Mr. Lee brought in several bottles of cabernet sauvignon from the wine cellar. He handed the fruit of the vine to his boss for inspection and went over to the bar to get the obligatory silver tray, corkscrew, and glasses.

"This is a good vintage. Lee, open the Chateau Lafite first." Lee came back over and wrapped a white linen towel around the bottle. He set it down on top of the silver tray, placing the wine on an antique pedestal table beside David. With great elegance, Mr. Lee applied the corkscrew to the bottle and retired the thirty- or forty-year-old cork from it's job of keeping the red liquid gold inside the container. He handed the cork to David who pressed it to his nostrils and inhaled its rich aroma. David handed it to Chris, who first looked at it, then copied the almighty, inhaling what fragrance was left after David had sucked in all he could.

"Nice, yes?" David asked his guest.

"I suppose so, but I don't know much about wine," Chris said honestly.

"Then a special treat awaits you, and a bit of history to boot."

"History?"

"Take a look at this bottle," David said, handing the Château Lafitte to Chris, removing the linen towel.

"1941, was that a special year?" Chris asked.

"Indeed it was if you were in Paris under Nazi occupation. Most of the best wines, like this one, were confiscated by the German conquerors, sent to Berlin or just enjoyed by the top ranking German officials in charge of the occupation. This was the last year that this wine was bottled until after the war was over."

"How did you get it?" Chris was genuinely impressed by the mystery. Now, he savored every sip that he took from the heavy Baccarat wine glass.

"My father was a pilot in the air force during the war, one of the soldiers who liberated France. Apparently the wine was one of his spoils of the victory. He probably found it in some deserted villa held by the Nazis, and shipped it home to the states. A case of this remained stored in his garage for the next thirty years. I found it a year ago, after he died, cleaning out the house."

"He never drank it?"

"My inheritance," David replied, taking a drink from his glass.

Mr. Lee was busy stacking logs in the fireplace. With the turn of a small chrome key on the wall, gas jets ignited the wood. Presto, instant fall fireplace mood, Bel Air style. David poured another glass of wine for himself, and for his guest.

Fall in Los Angeles was two-faced. The November days were warm, practically balmy with temperatures ranging into the eighties. But it all changed rapidly with the setting sun. The nights were cold, forty degree cold, and the fire in David's hearth along with the vintage red wine, warmed Chris and for a fleeting moment he felt at home in his grand surroundings.

"Dinner is served," Mr. Lee announced, while quickly exiting back to his dinner command post in the formal dining room. David filled Chris's glass for a third time as they got up for dinner.

"Wait, I've got a better idea," David said. "Let's eat in here. Lee, can you bring the dinner into the study?" he called out.

"I feel a little funny drinking your inheritance, David," Chris said as he sat back down on the deep leather sofa.

"What did you say? Oh, that's right, that's what I told you." Larkin was the master story teller. He invented truth to suit the occasion. The evening wine became so much more enjoyable rescued from the stash of Nazi invaders. "Well, don't think another thing about it. We'll open another bottle and drink some more."

Mr. Lee re-entered the study bringing dinner. He laid out the food on the coffee table before the two men as if it had always been intended to be served that way: Linen placemats with sterling silver utensils, folded cloth napkins, china service, a water pitcher with crystal goblets, even a small flower arrangement of yellow and orange birds of paradise mixed with fall foliage. Everything was so deluxe in David Larkin's life. A casual dinner in the den was more elegant than Christmas dinner at the dining table had been at Chris's home back in Rockford.

"Are you enjoying the work at the studio, Chris?" David's question took him by surprise.

"I have learned so much. I appreciate the opportunity more than I can say. There is one…"

David cut him off just as he was about to find the words to talk about the audition.

"Is your steak cooked to your liking?"

"Yes, just fine thanks, anyway, I was wondering if I might ask…"

Lee came in, cutting Chris off again, to tell David that he had a phone call. David got up and left the room to take his call in privacy, telling Chris to finish his dinner and not wait for him.

Returning about fifteen minutes later, as Chris was finishing his steak and the rest of the second bottle of wine, David explained his absence. "That was John Moran at the studio calling to ask about the 'Eric' auditions."

"That's okay. I just finished the rest of your inheritance." Chris was drunk, but not sloppy. The wine had taken away all of his uptightness. "Speaking of Eric," Chris went on, "I need to talk to you about that."

"I think Mark Harlander is right for the part, don't you?" David interjected immediately. He knew what Chris wanted, giving him no satisfaction.

"You're asking me?" Chris now slurred his response a bit, "or telling me?"

"I'm asking," the almighty said in another very unusual moment of generosity as he sat down on the sofa next to Chris.

"Well then, he may be right for the part, but I believe I could play it better."

"You do, do you?"

"Yes, I do and, David, if it's not asking too much, I would like to audition. I know that's not my job and you probably want me to stay where I'm at as your assistant, but that's not what I came to Hollywood to do. As much as I appreciate the job, I came here to be an actor."

"Have you ever been with a man?" David asked.

Chris was so proud of himself for getting out his request that he missed David's response completely.

"Have I what?" he asked.

"Been with another man?" David repeated.

"I don't think I know what you mean."

"I mean have you ever had sex with a man?"

"You mean, am I gay? I'm not gay."

"No, I mean have you ever sucked cock?"

Chris was confused. "What are you asking me, David?"

"Just what I said. Would you like to know what it's like to be with another man? You've been with plenty of women, I presume. How about a new experience, one you won't forget?"

David took a small box from the antique pedestal table next to the sofa and emptied its contents onto the glass-topped cocktail table. Chris recognized cocaine, even though he'd never tried it. David carefully divided the powder into sections with a blunt-edge razor, making small, thin lines, and then, with a golden metal straw he'd removed from the box, inhaled one of the lines up his nostrils. David handed the utensil to Chris.

Tired from working six twelve hour days in a row, drunk on two bottles of questionably inherited Nazi wine, tense and nervous from the self-inflicted fear about asking David for an audition, sated from too much food, totally confused by David's blunt proposition of sex, Chris took the golden coke straw and sucked in the fine white powder like a pro, but some of it missed his nose, landing on his upper lip. Chris licked his face around the mouth, his wet tongue encircling his lips, a cat finishing a bowl of milk.

As the cocaine hit Chris's brain, David was hitting on him. He was all over him, pulling at his shirt and rubbing his leg with one hand moving it up into his crotch, goosing him firmly. Chris could feel David's hand grasping his cock, rubbing it up and down, squeezing and tickling his balls right through the cloth of his tight Levis.

Chris closed his eyes, his mind was not functioning. Should he stop David, making up some excuse that wouldn't insult him too much. Did he want David to continue? If he went along, would he get the audition, and the part? And if he cut David off, would that be the end of his audition, his job, his future?

David stroked Chris's cock until it was hard, bulging in his tight Levis. It was too late to turn back, his erection was the final invitation. David unzipped Chris's fly and let his penis soar. Chris could feel David's tongue on him and then his entire mouth stroking him up and down, faster and wetter.

Chris was leaning back on the deeply cushioned leather sofa, his head back over the top, and turned away from the action taking place below his belt. Out of the corner of his eye he caught Mr. Lee nonchalantly entering the room, and quickly turning around to leave. It really was too late to stop. Now, even the butler knew.

At that moment, Chris changed forever. He became a willing participant, no longer the innocent victim. David sucked him harder, his cock traveling deeper into the unknown territory of David's throat.

He had never had a man do this to him before. David was good at it, and Chris became more involved as David brought him closer to orgasm. His formerly limp body started to move with David's movements. Chris put his hands on David's shoulders and pressed hard as he came closer and closer to letting go. He warned David as he was about to come, but this suitor sucked him harder, rather than pulling away. Chris came full force into David's mouth as his orgasm built to a crescendo, letting out a holler along with his semen.

As the two men laid back on the leather sofa next to one another, Chris stopped trying to figure out what was happening to him. "Why" didn't matter anymore, at least not at the moment. For now, he was stripping off the rest of his clothes along with David Larkin, the almighty Producer and Star Maker, and was about to step further into the abyss of the unknown, sucking the cock of a man, a man more than twice his age who happened to hold the key to his future, not in the proverbial palm, but in the crotch. He was going for it all the way now. Damn the cost. Chris would suck David off better than Mark Harlander, better than anyone had ever sucked him before if that's what David wanted. If that's what it took, he'd do it like he'd Xeroxed and filed and drove.

The morning came quickly for the men who'd been playing around until about 3:30 a.m. They shaved together, shared coffee in David's thick terrycloth robes in the bedroom, dressed and left the house. In the black Lincoln on the way to the studio David read his papers in silence, as he always did.

Just before they entered the studio lot, he looked up at Chris, smiled at him and reminded him of what he'd told him when he hired him. Everything and anything that Chris heard, or in this case shared with David, remained just between the two of them.

Then he told Chris that he would be auditioned for the part of Eric at the end of the day. That was all, nothing more was said. Chris parked the Lincoln, and they got out and went their separate ways. David to Moran's office, Chris to Stage 21. There was no turning back for Chris Reynolds now, he was a part of Hollywood for good.

CHAPTER 17

B ill Parker smelled Fall in the October air. The scent unique to L.A. was a combination of fresh fertilizer and winter grass applied by the city's army of Hispanic gardeners to countless lawns. Bill felt like he could create a spark in the dry, sharp air with just the snap of his fingers. The tall sycamore trees that lined both sides of the street in Beverly Hills where Bill had parked his car were dropping their summer leaves. No color change, just green leaves quickly turning to crackling, dry, gray brown fossils, then vanishing as the gardeners blew them away before they could pile up, or be walked on or rolled around in.

Fall was somehow a time of new beginnings for Bill, like a new school year, a chance to rev up the engine and make things happen. He was on that very mission as he walked in the front door of the William Morris Agency.

"Good morning, may I help you?" the receptionist asked.

"I'm here to see Randy Stein," Bill said.

"Is he expecting you?"

"Yes, my name is Bill Parker."

The receptionist was an octopus, wearing the headset of a phone operator and juggling a dozen phone lines while greeting visitors.

"He'll see you now, take the elevator behind you to the top floor," she told him.

"Thanks." Bill got in the elevator with a dozen other hopefuls and went up.

The top floor of the William Morris Agency was not unlike the top floor at CBS. Impressive and austere at the same time, with a long line up of secretaries and agents' offices on both sides of a long hall, culminating in the president's suite. Bill found Randy's spot almost immediately, a few doors down from the elevator.

There was no secretary outside Randy's office, so Bill poked his head in the open door and found Randy at his desk talking on the phone. Randy waved his friend in. Entering the impressive space, Bill looked around nonchalantly, then sat down, waiting for Randy to finish his call.

By the appearance of things, Bill was sure that Randy Stein had the world by the tail. He was young, smart, good-looking, he had a great job with a fancy office and his family had wealth and power to back him up. Bill watched him on the phone. He was masterful. And he looked masterful. His suit and tie were perfect, his shirt fit like it was made for him, which it no doubt was.

"Okay, so how's it hanging, friend?" Randy asked as he hung up the phone.

"Good. Things are really good."

"Getting any action?"

"Well..." Bill paused. "I've met someone."

"So, give me all the facts, man."

"The fact is I could be in love with her but she's living with someone else."

"Does she know how you feel? You done anything with this chick?"

"Once."

"She's still with another guy?"

"At the moment."

"You always pick the complicated ones. The trouble with you, pal, is that you like trouble, you like the goddamned intrigue, the drama." Randy finished his speech and Bill changed the subject.

"I need your help, Randy."

"Name it."

"I've been writing, or I should say we've been writing, and we work well together. We've done an original sitcom pilot that's salable, I think. The truth is, I don't know how to sell."

"You brought it with you?" Randy questioned.

"Yes." Bill took a copy of "The Divine LaVine" and handed it to Randy, who threw it up in the air and caught the script in the palms of his hands like pizza dough.

"Feels good, right weight. And the color choice is good for the cover. Yellow is bright, optimistic. I like the title, 'The Divine LaVine', kind of comical, fantasy oriented. But maybe, maybe too Jewish with the LaVine. You know, the networks don't go for Jewish stuff too often. It scares them. And you know what the biggest unwritten rule is?"

"No, I don't," Bill responded.

"No shows about show business. All the network guys think they're the kiss of death. They hear a pitch about a comedy that centers around a show business theme and the executives run for the hills."

"That's nuts. What about 'I Love Lucy' or 'The Mary Tyler Moore Show'? They're all about people in show business, and they're the best sitcoms on TV."

"I know, I know, it's true, what can I tell you? So this 'Divine LaVine', what's it about?"

"A Jew...in show business," Bill said stone-faced. They both shared a moment of silence then broke into uncontrollable laughter.

"I'll read it anyway," Randy said, "and if it's good I'll help you get some meetings to pitch the concept. It's the least I can do for my old friend."

"That would be super. I can't ask for more."

"Yes, you could. You could ask that it sells."

"Even better." Bill hesitated, continuing, "How can I get you to be my agent?"

"That's not as easy. I'd like to just say let's go, but William Morris doesn't just sign anybody because they're a friend. You haven't got any juice yet."

"Juice?" Bill questioned the term.

"Credits, references, sales, you don't have a track record, no momentum. I couldn't convince my superiors that you'd be a profitable client, not yet, that is. I'll help you unofficially. We'll see what we can do. In the meantime, if you're gonna be partners with the girl, writing partners, that is, you need to write a couple of original scripts for existing shows. Maybe I can sell you and your girl as a writing team to an existing show if the producers like your work."

"Do you know of any shows where that would be possible?"

Randy thought for a minute, posturing for Bill's sake. "There's a new show, 'The Reilly's of San Marino', a David Larkin Production. There could be some staff turn-over soon."

"I know David Larkin," Bill told Randy.

"You do?" Randy was surprised.

"Chris Reynolds works for Larkin as a runner. I went to a party with Larkin that Chris invited me to."

"That's right. I saw Chris at the studio. I forgot he was your roommate. That's perfect, you already have a connection, just get me some of your material and I'll submit it."

"You're a real friend. I mean it, thank you very much, this could be the step that opens the big door for me. I've watched 'The Reilly's'... I think I could, or we could, write an episode. Should we try?"

"Sure, why not, go for it. Like I said, when you're ready, I'll submit the script, unofficially, not as William Morris property, but as a favor, sort of under the table."

"When it sells, we'll sign a deal, okay?" Bill replied.

"Yes, we'll work together," Randy said. They shook hands and Bill got up to leave. "Wait," Randy called out as Bill left his office. Bill turned back at once. "My parents are having a party in a few weeks at the old homestead, a celebration for the holidays, and for my new position here at WMA, how about coming and bringing your new lady?"

"That's one party I would never miss. When is it?" Bill replied.

"Saturday night, December first, seven o'clock. Do you remember the house?" Randy knew he did, but he asked anyway.

"We'll be there, and thanks again. Maybe we'll have the sample script ready for you by then, I'll make it a goal."

"Good idea," Randy said as Bill finally left. "Make it a goal."

• • •

It had been the most difficult day of Chris Reynolds' life. Just looking at himself in the men's room mirror made him sick to his stomach. The previous night he'd traded his body for an acting audition. It was a trade that had also included his rather fragile soul and all of his ego.

Feelings of guilt and confusion consumed him, and the day passed painfully slow. There weren't enough chores, enough things to keep him spinning like a whirling top so he wouldn't have ten seconds to sit, to think, to be with himself.

His co-workers noticed that something was wrong. All day long they'd asked him if he felt all right. Was he sick? Did he have the flu? Did he want to go home? His responses were lame. Chris was in a walking trance.

David was the same old David. It was business as usual, with one exception. Chris was on the list for a casting meeting and on-camera audition.

By almost five o'clock in the afteroon, the casting team, Kim and Andy, had seen over one hundred potential "Eric's" sent in by the biggest and best agents in town. Mark Harlander, Larkin's front runner who had come the previous day on the open audition, was back for an on-camera reading at the end of the call. After he was finished, it would be Chris's turn.

Word spread all day long that Chris Reynolds was getting an audition. This information helped to explain his near hypnotic state to most of the concerned co-workers who'd been asking him if he wanted to go home. The best part about the news was that the entire group was for him. He'd made it known to everyone that acting was his dream, and the dreamer was about to have his day.

Nervously, Chris watched from behind one of the sets as Mark Harlander finished his second audition. Mark was good. He had the look, the attitude, and he also had David Larkin's vote. At least he had it yesterday. Chris had literally given everything he had to change that vote, but Mark probably had been on Larkin's couch as well.

Now, it was Chris's moment of truth. Could he live up to his own expectations and give the best performance of his life in the next five minutes, or was everything he'd ever wanted for the past twenty years about to evaporate right in front of him? The assistant director called out his name over the studio public address system.

"Chris Reynolds, Chris Reynolds, report center stage for your audition."

The message was repeated again as Chris stood in momentary suspension behind the set searching for his motivation and the energy to face up to the dream. It was so easy to be brave in a dream. On the third call from the assistant director, Chris could stall no longer. He emerged from hiding and walked to a center stage table to meet with the casting people that he already knew quite well.

"I'm happy David gave you this opportunity," were the first words out of Andy's mouth. Kim followed with similar support, although less effusively given. Still, in his trance, Chris believed they were sincere.

Yes, they liked Chris, and maybe they were even happy for him, although it was unlikely. Not for one second did they believe he could be good enough for the role. They wanted Mark Harlander. He'd paid his dues. They'd known him from countless auditions around town and many bit part castings. He played the game right and it was his turn. David Larkin had already picked him. Auditioning Chris was just another kiss-off Hollywood favor. They played along.

Chris was handed the "sides," those precious excerpts of the script for his audition.

"I don't need this," he said handing them back. "I know the dialogue, all of it, both parts, like I know The Pledge of Allegiance."

The casting people laughed — a little.

"Sally, are you ready to audition Chris?" The assistant director called for the actress, who was Laurie Dalton's stand-in and who was being paid an additional fee to audition with all of the men.

"I'm here," she called out and walked over to Chris.

"Okay, then places please and get ready," the assistant director requested.

"Wait. Stop. Hold the phone," a female voice called out from the darkness across the set. "I'm coming, just wait one second."

Laurie Dalton emerged from the shadows and to everyone's surprise asked Sally if she would mind if she did this one audition.

"You would do that for me, Laurie?" Chris said, nearly in tears from the emotional tidal wave in his brain.

Laurie whispered, "I think it's the least I can do for someone like you. Besides, if we click, they'll all see it, right here and now, and maybe you'll have a chance. I don't like Mark, anyway, he gives me the creeps."

"Are we ready?" the assistant director shouted.

"Yes," both Laurie and Chris called back.

"Places. Lights. Cameras. In 5,4,3,2, ACTION."

Show business magic took over the sound stage as Chris and Laurie recited the familiar dialogue. The room crackled with their energy. From the first line delivered the chemistry was devastating. This would be an audition that used to make history. A new star was born. A new team created before the very eyes of cast, crew, executives alike.

The casting people were talking at a feverish pace behind their table, as the entire stage broke into thunderous applause for Chris as the pair finished the scene. As the assistant director called, "Cut and print," Chris approached the casting table and shook hands, and thanked them for their support. He was told he'd hear soon about the outcome. Leaving the sound stage with his arm around Laurie Dalton, Chris no longer felt the guilt, the confusion created by his motives and actions the night before. On the way out they both saw Mark Harlander come out of the men's dressing room. Nobody said a word.

"Watch out for that one," Laurie broke the silence when Mark was out of earshot. "He's trouble," she added.

"Did I really do well?" Chris begged for an additional boosting.

"No," Laurie paused. "You were a star."

• • •

Jodi had heard plenty about Bill's apartment, "Casa de no Dinero," but seeing was definitely believing. The traffic leading downtown from CBS had been very heavy. Stop and go, jolt, wait and stop again. It had worn both Jodi and Bill out.

Jodi looked around at the neighborhood as Bill parked his car in the rear dirt lot. She was amazed that people lived with so little. Her new lover was one of those people, and she was going home with him.

Jodi had no place else to go. No place that she wanted to go, that is, other than home with Bill. She'd told Greg that it was over between them. The bomb was dropped during lunch at the CBS Commissary, not over the free weekend as planned. It was a terrible mistake, bad timing of the worst kind, but Jodi couldn't lie to him any longer.

The scene that followed rivaled anything being shot down the hall on the CBS soap opera, "The Young and the Restless."

Before storming out of the commissary, Greg told Jodi to clear out of his apartment. She'd left work early to get her clothes, which were now filling the trunk and backseat of Bill's car. All of her worldly possessions were parked in a car on a dirt lot behind a tenement in the Mexican ghetto of Los Angeles.

In spite of everything, Jodi walked in the back door of "The Casa" happier than she had ever been before. Bill kissed his lover, picking her up in his arms and carrying her across the threshold. The pressure of their combined weight made the floor boards creak so loudly that Bill put Jodi down and they ran together hand-in-hand, laughing, up the narrow stairs towards Bill and Chris's room.

Bill unlocked the door, all three locks, and opened it for Jodi. They entered and stared at each other. Home was crowded with two people standing in the middle of it. Jodi looked at the single bed in one corner of the room and the bed roll on the floor in the other. The yellowed and torn window shade flapped in the breeze from the open casement window that had no screen. She looked above her at the bare light bulb in the ceiling socket and noted the large stain resembling a sketch of the outline of The Great Lakes to the left of the light.

Jodi's new home was everything Bill had told her it was. She was wishing that he'd been exaggerating the facts, but no such luck.

"Where do I sleep?" she asked.

"Would you like the Blue Room or the Windsor Suite?"

"I'd like the mattress instead of the bed roll on the floor."

"Good, that's the Windsor Suite, my room, we'll share."

"And will we be alone in our suite, or can we expect visitors?"

"We do have a permanent guest, you know. He is usually in the Blue Room, over there. However, he hasn't been in lately. Frankly, I don't know if he'll be back tonight."

"Will there be a crowd, should he return?"

"If it is, we'll both leave. But Chris is the greatest. You'll love him, but not too much, he's very handsome, the movie star type."

By 8:30 that evening they were hungry. Bill ran down to the corner store and bought a few items promising to concoct a romantic dinner. Jodi organized the Windsor Suite, folding what she could of her clothes and stacking them in the corner next to Bill's. Love made spoiled girls from Philadelphia do the damndest things. If her mother could only see her now.

Returning from Morrie's 32nd Street Market with a can of tuna, a head of lettuce, a tomato, a loaf of half-price day old French bread, a bottle of cheap French white wine and one votive candle, Bill set about to prepare his evening feast.

Clearing his desk, made of the old door, and turning it into a dining room table, Bill made a tuna salad, sliced the bread, poured the wine and lit the single candle. Dinner was served.

"I've never had French wine in a dixie cup," Jodi said, holding up the paper cup to make a toast. "Here's to us. Two broke lovers against the world."

"To us, to the future, to the dream," Bill replied.

They drank from their dixie cups and ate off the two plastic plates Bill had saved for this special occasion.

"Is your movie star good-looking friend ever coming home?" Jodi asked.

"He works on 'The Reilly's of San Marino' and sometimes he's there half the night. I'm sure he'll turn up eventually."

"That's the show with Laurie Dalton and all the Peter Barker controversy."

"That's the one, and get this, we're going to write a sample script for that show, can we do it?" Bill asked her like a pep squad leader.

"Of course we can. I've watched it, have you?"

"Every week since it debuted in September. I like the show. It's an old-fashioned nighttime soap opera. We could dish some dirt, write some intrigue."

"It won't be 'The Divine LaVine'," Jodi kidded him.

"No. We're switching gears from comedy to drama," he said.

"Just like that?"

"Just like that."

"How come? We haven't even pitched our comedy yet."

"My agent friend, Randy Stein, told me today we might have a shot as junior writers on this show if we write a good sample script.

He's got connections there, and so do I, sort of. After all, Chris works for the producer."

"Chris may never come home again."

"The Blue Room will always be his," Bill joked, continuing, "Let's start writing it tonight, after dinner, how about it?"

"Isn't the show on the air tonight at 9:00?"

"You're right. We'll watch it first, then write, we'll be inspired," Bill said.

"It's five of nine now," Laurie looked at her watch. "Where's the TV?"

"It's hidden under a towel in the bathroom, in case we get robbed they might not find it. I'll go get it and plug it in."

"Bill," Jodi called out to him as he went into the bathroom to get the portable TV, "do you think we could move soon?"

"As soon as we sell a script. We'll move the next day, I promise."

"Then let's start writing now, before we watch the show. There isn't a moment to waste."

CHAPTER 18

The 11:00 p.m. TV newscast was broadcasting its opening headlines when Jodi began shaking Bill to wake him up. He had fallen asleep next to her on the single bed they had been sharing for the past ten days. Jodi was between Bill and the wall, and the force of her sudden push to awaken him practically threw Bill off the edge of the bed onto the floor.

"What's the matter?"

"Someone is trying to get in. Listen. There's a noise at the door," Jodi said in a nervous whisper. Bill sat up in the bed next to her and they both saw the tarnished brass doorknob turn. The door swung open.

"Chris, is that you?" Bill recognized the intruder to be his long lost roommate.

"Yes, it's me. Who did you think it would be?"

"Jodi thought someone was breaking in."

"Jodi?"

Jodi, who had been nude, dashed into the bathroom upon the opening of the door, and now came out with a towel wrapped around her.

"Hi. I'm Jodi Winkler and I've heard a lot of good things about you." She held out one hand to shake his, holding on to her towel with the other hand behind her back.

"Where have you been for the past week? I know this place is ever so humble, but it's home, man, it's home," Bill kidded his long lost best friend.

"It's been a zoo at work. I've been staying over instead of coming here. Just easier, that's all," he replied.

"Not even a phone call?"

"Who are you, my mother?"

"Okay, okay, I'll let up. I just wanted to know that you were still alive, give you about six-hundred messages from every female in town looking for you, and introduce you to our new third roommate, Jodi — is it okay with you?" Bill said.

"Of course it's okay. It'll be fun to have a woman's touch around here." Chris didn't look at either of them as he spoke, walking over to his bedroll. Then he laid down, fully dressed, falling asleep in seconds.

"He must be really beat," Jodi said to Bill quietly, not wanting to wake Chris up.

"Let's go to sleep, too. We'll all talk again in the morning."

Nobody slept well at "Casa de no Dinero" that night. Chris punctuated the silence with a succession of screams in his disturbed sleep. A startled Jodi and Bill jumped up on four separate occasions. Morning came as a blessing.

Jodi was up first and into the bathroom for a shower to help revive her so she could attempt to face the day. They all felt like they had hangovers without the benefit of alcohol. Chris was semi-conscious on the bedroll, sprawled out half onto the floor.

Bill was last to rise. He could barely open his eyes as he turned and sat on the edge of the single bed looking over at Chris, who was somewhat awake but absolutely still. Chris glanced at his friend sitting on the bed with his eyes shut, his hair standing straight on end as if he'd stuck a finger in an electric socket. Bill pulled the blanket off the bed and covered himself over the shoulders to fend off the morning chill.

Through his morning squint, Bill looked back at his friend across the room. The running water from Jodi's shower was so loud Bill thought the pipes were about to burst in the wall next to his bed. He practically had to shout at Chris to be heard over the plumbing.

"Good morning, have you been up long?"

Chris was slow to answer. "About an hour."

"Are you okay?" Bill was beginning to function as a human being, his eyes were at least opening.

Chris didn't answer at all. Bill got up off the bed and crossed the room, sitting on the floor next to him. Bill was still wrapped in the old, faded brown blanket.

"Look, I'm your friend. If something's wrong, maybe I can help. Are things bad at work?" he questioned Chris.

Chris looked at Bill again, staring, not saying a word. His expression was painful, as if he were about to cry.

"Chris, what's wrong?" Bill pleaded.

"I've been living with someone for the past week and a half, that's why I haven't come home."

"That's got you so upset?" Bill interrupted.

"I don't know who I am anymore."

"She must be a real dozy." Bill said smiling. "Come on, you can't be that far gone over some girl in a week."

Chris looked at Bill and almost froze, unable to speak the truth. But, finally he knew it was time to tell someone and he knew that Bill could be trusted. He told him that he'd been living with David Larkin, sharing his bed for most of the past ten days. He told Bill how it had all begun, about the audition for "Eric." He said he didn't understand it, but he'd done it, so he must have wanted things to turn out this way.

Bill had always been Mr. Cool and Sensible, but this news rendered him speechless. He had no words of comfort or advice. He just sat and listened as his best friend, his roommate, the guy he'd always been a little jealous of because of his meltdown effect on most women, told him about his gay relationship with his boss, one of the most powerful men in Hollywood.

"Did you do this just to get the part?" Bill finally spoke.

"At first, that's what I told myself. But after a week, can I lie to myself? Besides, I don't know if I got the part. The jury is still out."

"Why did you come home last night?"

"I needed a time-out, that's all. David didn't want me to leave. But, on top of what I just told you, I've been working sixteen-hour days and doing coke to keep me going. My head feels like it's going to explode."

"Oh, my God," was all Bill could say. He stared at his friend, completely overwhelmed by the situation.

"I'm going back," Chris said. "You and Jodi can stay here in the apartment, until I figure out just who and what I am." Chris got up off the floor and took off his clothes, dropping them in a pile on the floor. He went over to his suitcase-dresser to find some clean gear and began dressing.

"I guess I won't be getting a shower," Chris said, cracking his first smile at Bill as he dressed. The plumbing was still moaning loudly from Jodi's use of the bathroom.

"You know women and bathrooms," was the only dumb thing Bill could say.

His relationship with Chris was changed forever. Modesty had never been a concern for either of them before, especially living in their ten-by-twelve environment. Bill watched as Chris turned away from him while slipping on his clean underwear.

After Chris finished dressing, he grabbed the jacket that had been used as his blanket during the night and started to leave. Opening the front door, the flow of water stopped abruptly as Jodi finished her shower, and the noise of the pipes was silenced.

"I don't know how you're going to leave all this luxury behind." Bill said to his friend standing in the door.

"I may need to come back," Chris answered.

"Hell, why not? It's your apartment, you sonofabitch." Bill got up off the floor and went over to Chris. "You call me, do you hear? You call me anytime you need to talk."

Chris put his arms around Bill, hugged him tight and left, waving good-bye to his friend as he walked down the long hallway to the stairs. Bill watched him, wrapped in the brown blanket in the doorway.

"What are you doing? Where's Chris?" Jodi said as she came out of the bathroom wrapped in a towel. "Boy, is it cold in here this morning!" She ran over to Bill and slipped next to him under the blanket. He wrapped it around the two of them, then he kissed her in the open doorway. A bunch of Latino kids came out of the apartment directly across the hall and began laughing at the sight of the two lovers under their blanket, bare feet exposed. Just another typical morning in the ghetto.

• • •

Chris arrived at the studio early. It was only about 8:30 on this particular Friday morning. He expected to be alone until at least 9:00, when Marie generally arrived. He needed some time to get his act together before the rest of Larkin's staff converged for another non-stop day in the business of creating fantasy. Chris realized that he wasn't going to get a head start today, hearing the keys of the IBM clanking away as he neared the door to the office.

Marie was hard at work and to his surprise, David was also there in his office. The door was open, and he saw John Moran and the back of another man he couldn't make out. He recognized the voice of a third, it was Randy Stein, but he couldn't see him. The door shut abruptly just as he caught David's glance. Marie looked up at him offering a cup of coffee.

"Big pow wow in the chief's office?" Chris asked.

"You can say that again. The head of network programming, agents, and all the rest of the moguls here for a breakfast meeting." Marie responded.

"Trouble?" Chris pressed for more details.

"Oh, there's always trouble. The ratings have slipped a bit in the last week, so the panic is growing that we better fix the writing problem and cast 'Eric' and do this and do that and change this and get rid of that. You haven't been around long enough to know how it goes. I've seen it so many times I can predict the exact sequence of events. When a new show has problems, the first wave of blame goes to the writers. If they don't fix it, they're fired."

"What if the writing wasn't the problem in the first place?" Chris interrupted.

"Since when did reality get in the way?" she responded. "The next wave of blame goes to the director, then it's the cast, then it's the producer, unless he's also the creator and the owner of the show. You can't blame an owner!"

"What about interference from the network or the studio? What about just getting rid of a bad plan or idea and going with the instinct or flow of the original concept?" Chris was making sense, but Marie quickly put him in his place.

"Boy, have you got a lot to learn," she said. "The networks and the studios do whatever they want. It's their money, so it's their show. They don't care about instinct or concept, they look at research and demographics and placement."

"So what's gonna happen?"

"Like I said, I think heads will role on the writing staff first, then 'Eric' will be cast."

"Do you think I still have a chance?" he asked. She didn't answer right away, but did break from the typewriter to look at him.

"I hope you do, but I don't know. On the one hand, anything is possible. But so many forces are at work here. What's important is that you did very well in the audition. You proved yourself that day. You demonstrated that you have the talent and validated all your claims around here about wanting to be an actor. I believe that someday you'll get a shot but I don't know if it'll be here and now, as Eric." Marie looked at Chris for a second and went back to work.

"But I deserve it. I did the best, everyone said so, doesn't that count?"

She stopped typing again and answered simply, "No. It doesn't."

• • •

"Where are you going?" Jodi caught Bill as he was running out of the ticket office putting on his Polo blazer.

"Another interview," he called back.

"With Asher? I thought the job was filled?" she called out.

"No, no. This is with Copley in the Production Department. I'll fill you in later, I'm late." Bill ran down the hall towards the elevator. His Bass Weejuns were marking the highly buffed linoleum floor leaving a trail of black lines from the ticket office to the elevator door.

The interview was for a production control supervisor post, a job Bill had never heard of and knew absolutely nothing about. It didn't matter. It was a step up. Grayson told him it was a springboard job to much bigger and better positions in the network hierarchy.

It was nearly noon when Bill returned to the ticket office. Jodi was anxious to hear all about the interview over lunch.

"Oh, by the way, before we go, you got a call from Chris. Here's a number at the studio where he said you can reach him. He said it was important." Jodi handed Bill the slip of pink message paper with the phone number. He took it and went back to call his friend in the relative privacy of his corner. Bill dialed the number. The phone rang and rang, and rang some more. At last, a gruff voice answered, "Stage 21."

"Is Chris Reynolds there?"

"Just a minute." The phone dropped. No "hold" button. Bill envisioned the receiver just hanging there in some big studio barn. He could hear the echo of many voices in the background.

"Hello."

"Chris, is that you? It's Bill. Are you okay?"

"Yeah, sure. Listen, I've got some news for you. Most of the writing staff over here on 'The Reilly's' was just fired. If you've got some sample scripts I'd get them over here as soon as possible."

"That is news. Randy Stein offered to help me do the same thing last week."

"That's fine, too, but if you get some material over here I'll see if I can get David to look at it directly."

"What a favor. I don't deserve it, but I'll take it," Bill replied. "Are you coming to the apartment tonight?"

"No, why?"

"Jodi and I could finish our 'Reilly's' script tonight if we work all night on it. You could take it in the morning."

"I won't be there tonight. It's better anyway if you two need to work. Call me here tomorrow on your lunch break or after work and let me know how it's going with the script."

"That's really great, Chris. Thanks a million. Are you sure you're okay? What about the part? Did you hear?"

"No, I didn't hear. And yes, I'm okay." Chris hung up.

Bill went to Jodi, who was tapping her nails on her desk waiting for him. "What took you so long back there?" she asked.

"I've got big news. Let's go." Bill dragged her out of the office, on to the streets of Dream Town.

CHAPTER 19

It was the Wednesday before Thanksgiving and workers were stringing Christmas decorations up and down Wilshire Boulevard. The tall palm trees lining the main drag of Beverly Hills were being wrapped in strands of tiny white lights, becoming enormous tropical candy canes. Snowflakes of Styrofoam floated overhead on wires strung between traffic lights and street signs. Jodi hated them. They were so obnoxious. Giant Styrofoam snowflakes in 80 degree, dry winter. Her lips were chapped from the heat and her hands were beginning to chafe like Bill's. Soon, she envisioned, she'd be wearing the white gloves, too. An epidemic.

Driving into CBS together that morning, Jodi and Bill talked about the Thanksgiving break. They needed the time off. It would be a chance to get away from the CBS shuffle, clear the head. Bill wanted to use the time on the "Reilly's" script with Jodi. The work had to be the best possible.

While the days off ahead were welcomed, the prospect of Thanksgiving dinner at the "Casa de No Dinero" was bleak. Philadelphia was out of the question for Jodi this year, and Bill didn't want to spend the holiday with his family in Oakland.

There would be so many questions about Jodi, and the ultimate problem of deciding where she would sleep. So, he made alternate plans.

Breaking the piggybank and mortgaging the upper limits of his VISA, Bill reserved a room for two nights at the Hotel Bel Air. On Thanksgiving Day, he would take Jodi for a drive up Stone Canyon, destination the pale pink Hotel Bel Air. They would check in, and spend Thanksgiving in their room with the shutters closed, the fireplace constantly smoking, room service, The New York Times, their script, and the bed. Hopefully they would do everything in the bed.

Bill figured that there would be no need for clothes of any kind. The luxurious crested terrycloth robes that the hotel provided for its guests would be their only garments. That is, if either one of them ever emerged from under the sheets. Since somebody would have to open the door for room service, the robes would get some use. Turning into the CBS parking lot, Bill's surprise Thanksgiving plans were placed on hold.

All of this bliss would start tomorrow.

• • •

The assistant director yelled "CUT" "PRINT" "WRAP" and filming on the set of "The Reilly's" stopped for the day. Thanksgiving recess began early for the troops. D.L. came down on the set to let everyone know that they could have the rest of the day off, thanking them for their continuing contribution to the success of the show. Then he asked for a hand of applause for their star, Laurie Dalton. Last, he told the cast and crew that the writing staff had been let go, which everyone already knew. Hearing it directly from the boss made it somehow okay. Soon, there would be a new group of scribes, their predecessors nothing more than a memory.

"What are you doing for Thanksgiving?" D.L. asked Laurie as the troops began to disperse in all directions.

"A friend has invited me to Palm Springs for the weekend. I've never been."

"That's perfect. I'll be there as well. Would you care to be my guest for dinner?"

"Can I call you with an answer? I don't know what our plans are yet."

D.L. handed Laurie a card with his Palm Springs number on it and told her to call him any time reaffirming his open invitation to her and her friend.

"Do we have new writers yet?" she inquired.

"Working on it. They'll be in place over the next couple of weeks, before the Christmas hiatus."

"I know about 'Eric'," she said.

"Randy Stein told you, did he?"

"Yes."

"Brian Jamison is the right choice. He's perfect for you," D.L. said to Laurie.

Larkin spent the previous day negotiating with the studio, the network, the casting crew, and what seemed like every other soul in Hollywood who had two-cents worth of opinion concerning the role of "Eric." The final draw ended up casting a young actor named Brian Jamison. Mark Harlander lost out because David Larkin liked him too much, and Chris Reynolds lost out because everyone else knew too little about him. So, in Solomonesque fashion, the guy in the middle became a choice of compromise, the lesser evil of powerful opposition forces. Out of nowhere, a new star was born.

"Has anyone told Chris?" Laurie asked somewhat anxiously.

"No. I'll tell him myself," D.L. responded with sharp confidence.

• • •

Bill could hardly wait to get Jodi in the car and drive her to his Thanksgiving present in Bel Air. Despite her persistent inquiries that were beginning to sound like protests, Bill refused to give in. Heading west on the Santa Monica freeway, leaving downtown and their ghetto apartment in the rear view mirror, nirvana was less than a fifteen minute drive away.

"You never told me how the second interview went with Jay Copley." Jodi held back from asking Bill about his big opportunity for nearly twenty-four hours. The fact that he hadn't volunteered any information was not a good sign.

Bill's mind was on "The Reilly's" script, and his first response to her probe was nothing more than "huh?"

"Have you forgotten so soon?" she said sharply. "Jay Copley, the job promotion to the production department twelve-hundred dollars a month, a raise of about five that's five times your present salary."

"It went fine. I think he likes me," Bill said casually as if he didn't care, which he didn't.

"You think he likes you. That's all?"

"Yeah, that's all, so what?"

"Don't you want the job?" Jodi was perplexed.

Bill was still thinking about changes he wanted to make in their script.

Turning on Stone Canyon, he felt like he was now a million miles out of L.A. The Canyon was his favorite street in the city, an amazing contradiction. Right in the middle of one of the biggest cities in the world, Stone Canyon was more like a country lane in an Elizabethan fairy tale. Towering Sycamore trees arched the canyon road on both sides forming a tunnel of branches. The crisp blue sky peeked through at unpredictable intervals sending crossing vectors of light down, resembling spotlights on a stage. A perfect metaphor of nature for a would-be Hollywood wunderkind.

About half way up the canyon lane sat the Hotel Bel Air with its pale pink stucco walls and old world Mediterranean towers gracefully set back from the road by a running brook, replete with white swans, and awning-covered bridges. The musty smell of the damp fall sycamore leaves blended with the scent of burning oak creeping from the chimneys of the many cottages on the hotel grounds.

"This is a wonderful idea. Breakfast at the Bel Air on Thanksgiving!" Jodi looked around with obvious pleasure. The surroundings had a similar, albeit western version, feel to her parents' neighborhood on Philadelphia's Main Line.

"Who said anything about breakfast?" Bill gave the car to the green-jacketed valet.

"We came all this way and we can't even have breakfast?"

"I guess we can get something... after we check in." Bill came up behind her and put his arms around her waist, leaning his chin on her shoulder.

"Check in? Did you say what I think you said?"

"You got it right. We're checking in and having the best Thanksgiving, ever." Bill kissed her on the cheek as the swans looked up at them.

"Let's go!" Jodi replied excitedly. "What are we waiting for?" Bill took her hand and they crossed the bridge leading to the front door of the happiness hotel.

• • •

Just two hours to the east of Los Angeles and the Hotel Bel Air, the setting on Thanksgiving Day was quite different. The town, Palm Springs, the temperature approaching a warm seventy-eight-degrees by late morning.

The desert sun was so bright that David Larkin and Chris Reynolds wore dark glasses sitting on the flagstone terrace of Larkin's adobe hacienda. They drank orange juice freshly squeezed from the morning harvest, picked by Blanca the housekeeper, off one of the more than fifty citrus trees surrounding the swimming pool. Chris had never been to such a glorious place. On his first morning in the California desert he was almost glad the events in his life had taken him on such a remarkable journey.

Up at sunrise, Chris explored the grounds of D.L.'s estate. His first discovery was tantamount to Columbus landing in the New World. Arriving in Palm Springs in the dark of night Chris didn't realize that he was surrounded by mountains rivaling the Alps. Opening the French doors of his room he stepped outside facing the western slopes of Mount San Jacinto, rising thousands of feet to a rocky snow-capped summit. It was breathtaking.

A manicured green lawn stretched out before him. At its edge, a movie star fantasy swimming pool that was at least fifty feet long. Twenty chaise lounges lined either side of the pool with bright yellow terrycloth-covered cushions ready to greet sun-worshipping guests. Date-bearing palm trees with trunks of elephant skin, lined the property enclosed by an eight-foot-high, white stucco wall. Grapefruit, lemon, orange, and tangerine trees blossomed forth a bounty of perfect fruit. Everywhere hibiscus flowers bloomed. Chris had found the Garden of Eden. If only the folks back in Rockford, Illinois could have seen him now.

On his morning hike around the grounds he found his boss, his lover, jogging the perimeter of the property. Chris joined him for the final thirty laps as Larkin finished his two mile morning run.

After the exercise, they landed on the flagstone patio by the dining room where Blanca served them juice and toast. D.L. had hardly spoken a word since the day before. He didn't ask Chris to spend the night with him, and now they sat in silence drinking orange juice and staring at the jagged peaks of Mount San Jacinto through dark glasses. Chris excused himself, and jogged back around the house to the French doors leading to his room.

He went over to his duffle bag and started throwing out its contents. Tossing his clothes and personal effects around the room, he madly searched, finally locating what he sought at the bottom of the bag. Pulling out a small package of cocaine that he'd bought from Dan Robertson the last time Robertson had been at D.L.'s house for a workout, Chris emptied the contents onto the small, glass-topped desk in his room. With the skill of an expert user, he divided the coke and inhaled two lines. At once his insecurity over D.L.'s silent treatment faded. He felt better, and ran back outside to return to the splendid sensation of desert life that was so new to him, as the pungent smell of the nearby cacti, mingled with the taste and smell of cocaine, filled up his nostrils and took control of his brain.

• • •

About two miles to the south, in a large, contemporary home on the ninth fairway of the posh Canyon Country Club, D.L.'s star, Laurie Dalton, lay in bed with Benton Stein. Benton slowly separated his lips from Laurie's, and hopped out of bed, quickly moving across the three-inch thick white, wool carpeting to the bathroom. He shut the door.

Laurie called out for him to return without success. She then picked up the phone and called David Larkin. The phone rang several times before Blanca answered in broken English.

"Is Mr. Larkin there?"

"Si. Yes, un momento. One minute please."

"Hello," D.L. said as he came on the line.

"D.L., it's Laurie. Is your Thanksgiving invitation still good?"

"I'm delighted you called. Of course it's still good. We'd love to have you." D.L. was truly pleased. He liked the thought of having his star at his table. The bonus would be meeting her date. "The two of you come to my house at 5:30 for cocktails. Dinner will be at 7:00. Where are you staying?"

"I'm at a house in the canyon," she replied.

"Let me give you directions, then." D.L. rattled off the street by street roadmap to his estate.

"It will just be me, D.L. My date has been unexpectedly called back to L.A." Laurie emphasized the "unexpectedly." She was clearly displeased.

"His loss, my gain." D.L. now knew why his star was joining him for Thanksgiving. It didn't matter.

Benton came out of the bathroom dressed and ready to go. Laurie was hanging up the phone and he wanted to know who she was calling.

"Your wife," she answered coyly.

"Very funny." Benton sat down on the bed next to her.

"I just made a dinner date since you've chosen to desert me in the desert. 'Deserted in the Desert', my next movie, a real tear jerker." Laurie was sarcastic.

"Look, it's Thanksgiving. How can I not go home to my wife?" Benton became the cheating husband instead of the passionate lover in Laurie's eyes.

"So go on. Who's stopping you?" she told him.

"I thought I made it clear to you that I would have to leave you for one lousy turkey dinner. I'll be back by midnight tonight and we'll have the rest of the weekend together."

"I said split. I've made other plans. I'll be just fine. Go home to your family. Feed the facade, it's hungry. It's holiday season. Live the lie, go." Laurie retreated to the corner of the bed as Benton moved closer to kiss her and hold her, to tell her it was all okay. She pulled away from him as he came within inches of her face. He took her head in his hands and pressed his lips to hers. They kissed passionately and Laurie gave in to his touch.

"I'll be back by midnight. Will you be here?" Benton asked as he got up off the bed. Laurie paused a moment, looking at her lover. He was damn good-looking for a man old enough to be her grandfather.

"I'm having Thanksgiving with David Larkin. I'll be back here by ten, waiting." Laurie brought the sheet down, exposing one of her breasts. She smiled at Benton. He dove on top of her. As fast as he had showered and dressed to leave for Los Angeles, he was now stripping off his clothes to make love, one last time for the road.

• • •

Bill set to work on "The Reilly's" script immediately after check-in at the hotel. The plot wasn't strong enough and he wanted to add some intrigue. He told Jodi that he might throw out the subplot entirely and work on a new one. She was too tired and too happy to be in a comfortable bed to get involved.

By midday, Jodi finally pulled herself out of the peach-colored cotton sheets. She managed to make it all the way to the peach-colored bubble bath in the peach marble bathroom. Jodi hadn't had a bath of any kind or color since moving into the ghetto, leaving her bathtub and boyfriend behind in West Hollywood. A shower that was very often cold in a bathroom that was even colder was all Bill could give her.

Bill had left Jodi in bed, searching for a place to write on the grounds of the hotel. After nearly six hours, which had passed with the snap of a finger, Bill realized that he'd better go back to the room and spend a little quality time with the woman in his life.

Jodi reclined in the warmth of the bath, reflecting on her feelings about Bill. She admired his drive, the obsession with succeeding in the business, but it had begun to chip away at their relationship. Jodi wondered if Bill loved her because they were partners in his dream. After all, it was his dream. She often felt shut out, a vehicle to success instead of an integral part of his life. She believed in him, and she also believed that she loved him, yet it was Thanksgiving Day and he had left her in bed alone to work. That was the truth she didn't like facing. Work was his true love.

"I'm in the bath," Jodi called out when she heard Bill enter the room. He walked into the peach spa and found her resting in the tub, her head against a pillow built into the fixture.

"Not bad," he said.

"Want to join me? There's room."

"Best offer I've had today, but no, I can't."

"Sure you can. Just do it."

"I've got to keep working. The whole script is upside down at the moment. I've torn it apart."

"So why did you come back in here?" Jodi looked at the marble tiled walls of the spa tub instead of Bill.

"I wanted to see you and tell you how excited I am about this script. What I've done is going to make it work. We could get jobs from this."

"We could. I've hardly done a thing on it. Who's we?" she protested.

"Come on. You're part of the team. I'm not counting words here, Jodi."

"Yeah. Well, I am. And I'm not much of a team member. If you sell this, it's your success, not mine." Jodi slipped down, completely underwater, the thick bubbles covering her head as she disappeared beneath the surface. Bill left the bathroom and went back to the corner of the lobby he'd set up as his writing spot.

• • •

By early afternoon the sun had reached a very warm, sultry 84 degrees in Palm Springs. David Larkin had invited about a dozen local friends over for an afternoon by his tiled pool. What a sight. The gay marines had landed in Speedos.

His dozen guests were from all walks of gay life — militant to closeted, macho to mainstream. But, they all had something in common: youth and muscles. It wasn't long before the effects of overflowing frozen margaritas released all inhibitions and the muscle men exposed their ultimate muscle. Speedos littered the lawn.

Chris was new to all this. He'd never been to a totally gay party. What was he supposed to talk about? Was he supposed to make friends, or make a date? His only refuge was the remainder of the coke he'd tucked away in his room. An additional dose of white powder helped him to see clearly that he was the focal point of the event. They were all looking at him, analyzing him, staring at his formidable body. The stares became more pronounced when he too dropped his pants in favor of sun tanning the entire body. When in Rome...

Chris had it all over the rest. His face, more handsome, his body in better shape, even his dick was bigger than all of theirs. Most importantly, he belonged to the almighty host. Chris finally came to terms with his position and his power at that moment in time. He didn't need to talk to anyone about anything. He just held court, like the prince that he was for a few fleeting hours one lost afternoon in Palm Springs.

Laurie Dalton arrived at Hacienda Azul Agua, that's what David Larkin had named his Palm Springs pad, just as the last marine was saying goodbye. Blanca had switched gears from poolside nachos and frozen cocktails to a formidable traditional Thanksgiving dinner with a south-of-the-border accent. She was serving in the main dining room. Chris greeted Laurie at the door, explaining that David was taking a short nap and would be up and about soon.

"What are you doing here?" Laurie questioned Chris.

"Sounds like you're not happy to see me," he teased, still flying high on coke and tequila.

"Are you kidding? I'm thrilled to see you. What a relief, a mirage in the desert, that's what you are!" She hugged and kissed him hello. "What the hell are you doing here? Did your job expand?" she asked.

"Sort of. Let's talk before D.L. gets up. It's beautiful outside." Chris motioned for Laurie to follow him to the patio.

"Can I tell you something confidential?" Chris looked Laurie in the eye. She could see he was high.

"My ears are open, and my mind. My mouth is closed," she replied.

"I've been with David for the last few weeks."

Laurie looked at Chris, not getting his revelation. She never considered the possibility that he was gay. Chris was so manly. She found him very sexy, even fantasizing about making love to him in her studio trailer.

"I've been sleeping with Larkin."

"You mean he's fucking you," Laurie said.

"Maybe at first. But I'm not innocent. Not anymore."

"Forgive me if I'm shocked." She went on," I thought you were making it with every girl on the set."

"I've had my share," Chris told her. "I don't really know what's going on in my life right now. I'm on a ride and I can't get off. Don't know if I want to get off."

FAME FARM

"Sounds like you're pretty mixed up," Laurie said sharply. Almost immediately it occurred to her that Chris might be sleeping with the almighty in order to get the part of "Eric." "If it's 'Eric' you're after, this may be the wrong way to get him," she told Chris in a very serious tone.

"God, I wish I'd known that a month ago. I thought it would make the difference."

"What do you think now?"

"Hell if I know." Chris broke the somber mood and laughed. "What the fuck matters anyhow?" He asked Laurie if she wanted a drink, then went into the house to get her a glass of white wine.

The sun slid gently down behind Mount San Jacinto and the sky gradually turned black as it disappeared, filling with millions of pulsating stars. Blanca came outside and lit an array of candles on the patio.

Chris returned and handed the glass of wine to Laurie. He had one for himself as well. "You're sleeping with D.L., too?" he asked.

"Ha, ha, ha," she said. "But there is something I'll share with you."

Chris took another big gulp of wine, finishing his glass. "Hold the secret, I'll be right back with the bottle." He ran off into the house.

Laurie was feeling guilty knowing that Brian Jamison had the part of "Eric." She was going to ask Chris if D.L. had talked to him about the part when he got back with the wine. Instead, she ended up telling him about her affair with Benton Stein. The gossip exchange ended when David Larkin came out of the house to join them on the patio.

• • •

Thanksgiving dinner was uneventful all around the southland. In Bel Air, at La Villa Serena, the Stein family ate gourmet turkey and smiled at each other. Servants cleared the silver trays of sumptuous, but hardly touched food. They kissed each other good night and Randy and Benton left, going their separate ways in search of a Thanksgiving fuck. Jennifer Hartman Stein closed the front door on her men. She cried out loud as they drove out of the motor court. This was her first Thanksgiving without her very best friend, Peter Barker.

Nearby on Stone Canyon, at the Hotel Bel Air, Jodi stared at Bill as he raced through turkey dinner in the hotel dining room. All around them, beautiful, wealthy families with their designer children in matching velvet holiday outfits, shared Thanksgiving. Bill and Jodi shared a table, but that was all. Bill was a million miles away thinking about the script, the career move, the dream.

Small talk was the name of the game at David Larkin's Thanksgiving dinner table in Palm Springs. He'd invited four couples to his table. Blanca served smoked turkey stuffed with chili and jalapeños, and the cabernet flowed.

Chris was generally quiet through most of dinner. The coke and tequila had worn off and the wine was putting him to sleep. Besides, he was no longer the prince holding court that he'd been that afternoon by the pool. The king, the almighty D.L. was at the head of his table, and Laurie Dalton was unquestionably the queen of the night. No one even cared who Chris was or even wondered why he was there.

Long after the Larkin's friends were gone, and hours after Laurie had returned to Benton's bed in his desert house on the golf course, D.L. decided it was time to talk to Chris. D.L. asked him to join him on the terrace. Chris brought the remainder of a bottle of Cabernet with him, and found David bent over, lighting an outdoor fireplace with the turn of a gas jet and the flick of a match.

D.L. sat down in a deeply cushioned chair by the fire and invited Chris to take the one beside him. Chris sat and filled each of their glasses with the final red drops of the evening's consumption.

"I toast you, young Chris Reynolds. A remarkable man, my friend," D.L. said loudly, looking directly at Chris. He drank from his glass as Chris watched him carefully, finally believing the toast, and following suit with a large swig of his own wine. David put down his glass and removed a small vile of cocaine from his pants pocket, then offered some to his friend.

"You're not getting the part of 'Eric'," D.L. suddenly said to Chris directly.

Chris was caught totally off guard. "Excuse me?"

"I said, you didn't get the part," David repeated. His tone was gentle, especially for David Larkin.

"What do you mean, I didn't get the part, I was the best one for the part, I saw…"

David cut him off. "You were good. Maybe you were even the best, I'll offer that. But you weren't the first choice of all the powers that be. We went with a known quantity, Brian Jamison."

"I could act circles around him. Just give me the chance. You're the producer, the boss, you can tell them to trust me. Tell them that I can do it." Chris was upset. It was a devastating blow. He'd given everything for the part, literally everything, including his soul.

David wasn't surprised at his reaction. Even though Chris was so macho, as an actor he had yet had to deal with rejection. This would be only one failure in a long line to come before the big break. D.L. had hoped that Chris had understood the rules of the game better. He looked at his young friend bent over in anguish, watching him regain his composure in spite of the wine and the coke and the rejection.

Chris slowly pulled himself together and sat back up in his chair. He looked across the fire at David. "Did you fight for me?" he asked.

David said nothing, looking back at Chris with equal intensity. After a minute of silence, he spoke. "Yes. I fought for you," he lied. The truth would have served nobody.

Chris rose from his chair and walked over to David. He looked at him, deeply hurt, then passed by, walking around the outer perimeter of the property to go to his room. He spent the remainder of the Thanksgiving weekend there in seclusion.

CHAPTER 20

The Monday after Thanksgiving was a real nightmare for the police department. The drunk tanks were overflowing with a full populace of now sober humanity, while the pale green halls of the jailhouse bulged with pinstriped barristers clutching the greenbacks necessary for their clients' bail.

Today, Sergeant Hector Arnold had been summoned downtown to the central jail to interrogate someone the cops had picked up over the weekend in what had been labeled by the press as the third largest coke bust in the city.

A detective on the drug case had called Arnold at six-thirty that morning with some important information he'd gotten on a homicide from one of the suspected dealers. The information pertained to the Peter Barker case.

Entering interrogation room B-7, Arnold found several civilian-suited detectives questioning a muscular and tanned blonde man in his thirties wearing a city-issued orange-colored body suit that was far too small for this man's developed physique. The prisoner was constantly pulling at the neck, in order to breathe, then yanking at the sleeves to permit circulation in his arms. Just as Arnold approached him at the table, the man raised both his arms and removed the top portion of the bodysuit-turned-straightjacket, by pulling the garment off his back with a loud grunt. He then tied the arms of the suit around his waist, fashioning a makeshift belt to keep the pants from falling to the floor.

"I'm Sergeant Hector Arnold." The detective put out his hand to shake the hand of the suspect. He responded. His grip was rather limp and fishy, not the handshake of a strongman, to Arnold's surprise.

Arnold knew who the guy was. He didn't need an introduction. Don Robertson had been on his investigation list from day one of the

Barker affair. In fact, Arnold had planned to interview Robertson during the coming week, anyway. This big guy with the small fish handshake wasn't the murderer. That's what Arnold thought. Robertson had signed in and out of the Sierra Towers with witnesses to verify his coming and going. But maybe he knew the killer, or saw the killer.

"My name is Robertson," the man said rather meekly.

"Do you realize the seriousness of the charges against you, Mr. Robertson?" Arnold dove in.

"Yes sir, I do."

"And that's why you've decided to cooperate with us, tell us all you know?"

"Yes, sir. This other guy said I could make a deal."

"Do you have an attorney, Mr. Robertson?"

"No sir, I don't."

"I see." Arnold paused and looked over at his fellow detectives. "Then the city will appoint a public defender on your behalf. Your rights have been explained to you, Mr. Robertson?"

"Yes sir. I'm willing to talk if it'll help me. I don't want to go to jail. I can't go to jail." Robertson broke down. The big muscle man was sobbing. Arnold knew at once that Robertson would tell him anything and everything.

"You're an actor I'm told, Mr. Robertson," Arnold continued his investigation.

"Yes, sir."

"And you also train people, that is, you're an exercise coach?"

"Yes."

"Who are your clients, Mr. Robertson?"

"Mostly Hollywood big-shots, sir, actors, and producers and directors, the whole town really. I'm the best trainer in Hollywood." Robertson smiled a bit and sat up.

"Did you train Peter Barker, Mr. Robertson?"

"Yes, I did."

"When was the last time you saw him?" Robertson hesitated, then looked around the room at his formidable captors.

"The night he died, sir. I was with him in the apartment that night. I can't believe that he's dead. He had so much to live for, sir."

"What time did you leave the apartment?"

"I don't recall exactly. Around nine, I think."

"And Barker was still alive when you left?"

"Oh, yes, sir. He was alive."

"Did you work out with Mr. Barker that night?"

"No sir. He was too tired. He just wanted a massage."

"Did you give him one?"

"Yes, sir."

"Did he say anything that you can recall?"

"No, nothing. He was very quiet, not a word."

"Mr. Robertson, did you sell drugs to Mr. Barker?" Robertson was silent, Arnold repeated his question. "Did you sell drugs to Mr. Barker - coke, marijuana, pills?" Robertson was still silent. "Mr. Robertson, do you wish to cooperate with us or not? I ask you again, did you sell drugs of any kind to Mr. Barker?"

Robertson broke down again, sobbing hysterically. "Yes, yes, I sold him drugs!" he shouted between sobs. "I've sold them all drugs! Why do you think I'm the biggest trainer in Hollywood? Do you think it's because of my acting? It's because I supply them all, all the bastards that never gave me a goddamn break in their goddamn business. That's all I ever wanted… to have a chance… to be an actor. I didn't want this. Look at me…" Robertson held his head in his hands. "Barker had been buying coke from me for two or three years. His ex-wife got him hooked on the stuff. She loved it and got him into it before they split. I used to train both of them together, and leave my little packets for them after each session. I still train her and her new boyfriend. He sucks the stuff up his nose, too. She buys for both of them with Barker's money."

Arnold interrupted Robertson's confession.

"Did you give Barker coke the night he died?"

"I left him his usual order, wrapped in a package and put in his silver box on the night table by the bed." He didn't bother to tell the police that he'd shoved coke up Barker's nostrils because he didn't want to lose a sale.

"You mean after you finished the massage, you packed up, putting a delivery of coke for Barker on his table, then you left?"

"That's what I said."

"Barker didn't have any of it while you were there?"

"No, sir. He was already flying high when I got there. God knows how much he'd already had. I gave him the massage, left the coke on the table and went to my next appointment."

"Did anyone see you leave?"

"Sure, I talked to some old lady in the lobby on my way out. I think she lives there. I've seen her before. She could verify my story."

The detective made a note to find the little old lady at The Sierra.

"Who was your next appointment?"

"A producer named Larkin. David Larkin."

Arnold turned away from Robertson and glanced at the detective who had called him at six-thirty that morning. It was a look of "Thanks, you can call me at any hour." Arnold continued his questioning. "What time was your appointment with Mr. Larkin?"

"About 9:30. He was the last one of the night. He was always late. He never got home early."

"And did you work out Mr. Larkin or just give him a massage, then leave him a little packet?" Arnold's sarcasm went right over Robertson's head.

"Oh, no sir, I did nothing with Mr. Larkin. He wasn't home. Nobody was there. So I just went home myself."

"Larkin wasn't home when you got to his house? Are you sure?"

"Oh yes, sir. I'm sure. I rang several times. I waited for almost half an hour. Then I left figuring he was late at the studio. He missed appointments now and then when he got tied up. But he always paid me anyway."

"Did David Larkin buy drugs from you, Mr. Robertson?"

Don Robertson was silent once again. But this time there were no tears. "Yes, sir. He is a good customer. I've been training... and dealing to Mr. Larkin for about five years. You got my book, or somebody has it. It's all in there." One of the detectives handed a little black book to Arnold. "That's it. That's my book. It's all in there. Now can we make a deal? I'll do anything you ask, just don't send me back to jail. You've got the book."

• • •

After spending a couple of days and nights in the pampered luxury of the Hotel Bel Air, it was nearly impossible to go back to 23rd and Figueroa, especially for Jodi. Bill had enjoyed the break and the beauty of the Bel Air, but the return was less traumatic for him. He had blinders on, and the task at hand was "The Reilly's" script and getting it to Randy Stein. He was not tuned-in to Jodi's rapidly declining morale. She was withdrawing from him, but Bill couldn't feel the change. He thought they were still on the same train.

It wasn't just the reality shock of returning to 23rd Place that complicated their relationship. Chris Reynolds had come home that Sunday night. There they were, the three of them, living in one room.

Jodi wrapped herself in the sleeping bag, practically pulling it over her head, and cocooned in the corner of the apartment for the night, clinging to the one mattress and the wall. She was embarrassed, ashamed and confused. The situation wasn't romantic any longer. She wanted out.

Bill and Chris were up all night. Bill sat and worked at the door-turned-into-desk-top, with the light of one small censor lamp glaring onto the paper of the manuscript. Chris didn't want to sleep, so he sat up with Bill and kept him company. Chris offered insight into the direction of the show and the tone of the characters, especially Laurie and the new older brother, "Eric." Bill quickly wrote "Eric" into his scenario, going back into the script and tearing it apart to fit in the new character. This would surely impress Larkin, for no other writer would know about "Eric," Bill thought.

The two of them were close that night, like the best friends they had once been in college. It was the therapy Chris needed to go back to work, to face Larkin and himself. Bill finished the script, putting the final typed papers together at 7:00 a.m. in the morning.

He had done his best to be as quiet as possible typing all night. But the drone of the clanking typewriter keys - click-click-click-click - in the small room, tortured Jodi. The sleeping bag had muffled some of the noise, but she awoke with a headache from the all night barrage of the clanging metal. Without so much as an acknowledgement of morning, Jodi got up and went into the bathroom, closing the door behind her with a bang.

"Let me take the script to work, I'll give it to Larkin. You don't need Randy Stein to help you," Chris told Bill as they dressed. "Let me take a copy in to David. We can stop at the Xerox place around the corner before we leave for work and copy the script."

Bill was happy at his friend's generous offer. "I'd be honored if you tried to help me by turning this in to Larkin, but, I'm still going to give a copy to Randy and go through the channels. Is that alright with you, buddy?" Chris nodded his approval as they dressed for work.

• • •

Chris arrived at Stage 21 by 9:00 that Monday morning after Thanksgiving.

Marie was at her post, as usual. The phone rang, the Xerox gurgled and spit out pages, and Larkin could be heard barking out orders in his adjacent office. It was business as usual. Everyone was back to work to do another episode of "The Reilly's of San Marino."

The events of the weekend were history. Was Larkin remorseful over denying Chris the part? No. Was the crew worrying about the staff of former writers now out of work? No. This was show business. It moved on, it flowed.

Larkin bolted out of his office and saw Chris. He shouted for him to follow him to the stage at once.

"How about dinner tonight?" D.L. said when Chris had caught up with him.

"That would be interesting," Chris replied, realizing that he was carting around Bill's sample script. The sweat of his hands were leaving an indelible smudge across the cover page. "D.L., can I ask a favor?"

"You can ask… you can always ask," D.L. answered briskly.

"Would you read a script my friend Bill Parker has written for the show?"

"Bill Parker, I know that name, don't I?"

"You met him a couple of months ago. We all went to that party with you."

"Oh, yes. The kid that was so self-confident — aloof". D.L. had never called anyone aloof or self-assured. He was the only one who held that label. Chris didn't know how to read his response, but he persisted as he'd promised his friend.

"I think you'll be impressed with the writing, D.L. He's a talented guy. Will you read it?"

Larkin put out his hand as if to say "Okay, I owe you one, I'll do it. I don't want to, but I'll do it."

Chris handed him the manuscript. "I think you've just found a new head writer."

• • •

"I got it! I really got it!" Bill yelled his words of jubilation to Jodi as he entered his now former place of employment, the ticket office. "I've typed my last envelope, sorted my last pile of mail. I'm free, I'm rich - three hundred a week rich. We're moving just as soon as I get my first paycheck. Do you hear, we're moving out of 23rd Place! How about Beverly Hills? Are we ready for Beverly Hills?"

Bill grabbed Jodi by the shoulders and picked her up from her chair. He swung her around like a tetherball on a rope, kissing her and kissing her again as her body twirled around him. She nearly clobbered Mr. Grayson as he came out of his office to join in the celebration.

"That's exceptionally good news, Bill." Grayson patted his protégé on the back. "When do you start?"

"I'm not exactly sure. Copley told me it might not be for a few weeks, possibly even after the first of the year. What a Christmas present." Bill put Jodi down before she turned green from being spun around the room.

She embraced him, saying how proud she was of him.

Bill was so elated with the news of a promotion that he couldn't hear the pain between the lines of Jodi's words of congratulations. She felt more shut out than ever.

Grayson proudly trooped his boy wonder around to show him off to the rest of the flock. It was his way of letting them all know that hard work and a smart attitude paid off.

In a matter of moments the mood became New Year's Eve, a month early. Grayson popped a bottle of champagne that he kept on hand in a small bar refrigerator in the corner of his office. The promotion was a wonderful excuse to quit work early and rally round the boss and his protégé. Jodi sat at her desk through it all.

CHAPTER 21

Rain was coming down in sheets. It hadn't stopped all week. What was supposed to be a tropical storm blowing over from down Mexico way had landed on top of Los Angeles. The fury of the torrential downpour was unseasonable, and unexpected. Storm drains couldn't handle the water, streets flooded, trees uprooted, and the auto repair shops were having a land office Christmas business with smash-ups on every other block, every other minute.

Jodi begged Bill to drive slower. Waves of water hit the sides of the Mustang with the force of ocean currents slapping the shore.

"This isn't a surfboard, Bill. Be careful. Watch out for that car over there," she moaned.

"I grew up with rain like this every winter. It never stopped, and it's nothing new to me. Relax. We'll be at the party in a couple of minutes." Bill had no fear of the rain. He was anxious to get to Randy's house for the big affair. Rather, he was anxious to meet with Larkin to find out if he'd read his script.

Three or four unreturned phone calls to Randy that week did not dampen Bill's spirits. Randy must have been busy at work, Bill thought, or busy with the party preparations, or maybe he just didn't get the messages. In any event, the mystery would be resolved tonight. They would all be there, Randy, of course, and Larkin and Chris and most of Hollywood. A little rain wasn't going to get in Bill's way.

The downpour wasn't getting in Jennifer Stein's way either. Lots of money sometimes had a way of conquering nature. Mount Rushmore, The Panama Canal, The Aswan Dam, and now the waterproof tent erected over an acre of lawn behind La Villa Serena. All symbols of man's conquests on earth.

Jennifer Stein was expecting nearly a thousand people to honor Randy, and a little storm out of Mexico was no match for Hurricane Jennifer when she was putting on a "do."

Bill and Jodi drove into the driveway after being cleared by a guard with a list and heavy rain gear at the gates. A line-up of Mercedes and Cadillacs and Rolls Royces filled the road up to the house.

"It's a wonder they let us in, driving a Mustang," Bill said.

"We stand out in the crowd," Jodi replied. "I'm just glad we're here and dry," she added.

"Have you ever seen anything like this before in your entire life?" Bill asked her.

"I've seen traffic jams before," she answered sarcastically.

The line-up of cars started to move up the driveway. Bill was gazing out his side window taking in the sights, and didn't notice that the cars in front of him had finally moved forward, which caused the cars behind him to start blasting their horns. He quickly pressed on the gas pedal and flooded the already soggy engine of his Mustang. The car spit and shook and stopped with a jolt. He tried in vain to turn the engine, but it just didn't want to go.

Jodi looked at him. "I told you we stood out in the crowd," she said.

Bill hit the steering wheel with both fists, which, of course, accidentally slammed down on the horn. The sound of the horn from Bill's tantrum reached four valets dressed as nutcracker soldiers, who had run down from the entrance galleria to assist moving the stalled car. One of them opened Bill's door without warning and he nearly fell out of the car.

"Having trouble, sir?" the valet asked.

"It won't start," Jodi offered.

"Men, take a corner," the lead valet shouted, and with the precision of a military corps the four valets pushed the Mustang up the drive to the front porte cochere.

At the front entrance, a second troop of nutcracker-clad valets rushed the vehicle to assist Bill and Jodi out of the car and into the event of the year. They walked in, and the men walked their car away and out of sight. Bill wondered if they'd push him all the way home later.

The twenty-foot ceiling of the porte corchere was draped in twinkle lights hung to resemble icicles in a cave. Velvet carpet the color of emerald green flowed from the valets into the mansion, while half of the Los Angeles Philharmonic Orchestra lined the velvet path, donning black tie, playing Mozart for the glitterati.

The centerpieces were the talk of the evening. A tier of three grand scale glass bowls in decreasing size rose from the tables. In the bottom bowl were hundreds of clear and silver glass marbles. The magic was all in the center bowl, as dozens of tiny silver-colored fish swam in clear waters, mesmerizing each table. The top bowl of glass held a display of white orchids and lilies that emptied the floral coffers of nearly every designer in Los Angeles. At each place setting a gift box wrapped in silver foil paper and tied with an enormous white bow featuring a porcelain white dove in its center, awaited the lucky guest. The gift in each box was a large silver bowl in the Revere style that had been monogrammed with Benton Stein's international corporate logo, then personally engraved to each and every attendee. "Presented to Mr. and Mrs. John Desmond Maatta, Christmas, 1975."

Champagne flowed as dozens of waiters in white tie passed the finest hors d'oeuvres Milton Williams, Jennifer Steins' chief of staff, could create. An assemblage of one hundred employees toiled in an auxiliary tent behind the big top preparing the food using portable stoves, barbecues, and ovens brought in for the night. The entire production was of military proportions, and it came off without a hitch.

Bill and Jodi made their way down the green velvet path towards the reception line. Jodi was impressed, although quick to point out the excess of it all. Rich folks back on The Main Line would be appalled by such flash. Bill was completely awed by the splendor. He'd never seen such glamour. This was the Hollywood fantasy he'd only imagined existed. Only now it was reality.

As they reached their host and hostess, who were attired in regal splendor, Bill introduced himself to Mr. and Mrs. Stein and presented

Jodi. Randy reminded his parents that he and Bill were friends from U.S.C., and that they had all met before.

Jennifer remembered, Benton pretended, and gave Bill an insincere "Good to have you here again, young man," welcome. Jodi was introduced to Randy by Bill. Their eyes met like lightning bolts of sexual desire. That kind of instant, unmistakable animal attraction that makes people go to bed without asking for a name. It lasted for an orgasmic moment before the butler in red broke the bond announcing, "Mr. William Parker and Miss Jodi Winkler," to the crowd. There was no silent gasp as they walked down the flower-laidened entrance.

Not far behind Bill and Jodi, a young woman arrived who did produce a moment of silence when the butler introduced her. It was the lady of honor, Laurie Dalton. The studio had provided her with a limousine and she'd asked her friend Chris Reynolds to escort her for the evening. Randy had wanted her to attend the affair as his date, but Benton had advised him to host the affair unattached.

Jennifer Stein was extremely warm and gracious to Laurie upon her arrival. Benton feigned a detached, yet warm hospitality to the second guest of honor for the evening's festivities, trying to hold back his immediate desire to take her in his arms. Laurie looked so stunning, so radiantly beautiful and sexy.

Laurie maintained her poise in spite of a similar reaction to seeing Benton looking very distinguished and handsome in his black tuxedo. Benton's eyes pierced Laurie's well-guarded shield of composure, and for a moment she almost gave herself away. She regrouped quickly, however, and introduced Chris Reynolds to the elder Stein's.

Randy reinforced her introduction with the message that Chris was another friend from U.S.C. Chris proudly shook Benton's hand, did the same with Jennifer, and took Laurie by the arm, escorting her into the affair to the wild applause of the guests under the big top. Les Brown played the theme music from "The Reilly's of San Marino," and the most beautiful male and female flesh and blood on earth took a bow for the adoring mass of who's who. Benton didn't take his eyes off them. Who was this handsome young man on her arm? Had his advice to Randy been a mistake?

Then, the almighty David Larkin arrived. His date was a tall raven-haired young woman with deep dark eyes, white skin and Chanel red lips. Her gown was a sheath of limp black velvet fastened on her model figure at one shoulder with an elegant art deco period onyx and diamond brooch set in platinum. She said nothing. Only a small smile taking the form of an upturn of either side of her mouth gave any indication of her mood. D.L. introduced her to his hosts as Monique Du Barry, and the butler in red announced their very elegant entry into the tent.

Laurie was now dancing with Chris. He held her close as Laurie rested her head on his manly shoulder. They turned back and forth and all the way around to the Big Band's rendition of "As Time Goes By."

Far from the dance floor, Bill and Jodi were seated at a table at the rear perimeter of the tent. Their silver bowl had not been personally engraved like the majority of other guests, but their champagne was just as fine and they were there with the powerful and the famous.

Bill put his arm around Jodi's waist, leaning over to her. "Can you believe this?" he asked. The dream was all so real. Farah Fawcett and Ryan O'Neal chatted with Ali McGraw and Bob Evans directly in front of them. Super agent Swifty Lazar walked by with his wife, Mary, on his arm.

Looking across the tent, Bill spotted David Larkin sitting alone at his table up near the dance floor, in the "A" section. Excusing himself, he left Jodi to sit alone in the back as he crossed the bustling party tent towards Larkin.

"Excuse me, sir, I'm Bill Parker," he said, putting out his hand to shake with the producer. Larkin turned towards him, but didn't offer a hand in return. Bill tried not to look too silly while reeling in his outstretched arm as he continued. "My agent, Randy Stein, sent you a script that I'd written for your show. I understand you're looking for new writers?" Bill was his direct, all-American boy, confident self.

Larkin loved to taunt the really straight ones.

"Who did you say you were?" he asked, knowing Bill immediately and remembering him as Chris's friend that went with him to the party in Trousdale.

"Bill Parker, sir. I work at CBS. We went out one night a few months ago with my friend Chris Reynolds, he works for you…"

"Oh yes, that's right. I thought you looked familiar," D.L. told him. He went on. "Did you say Randy is your agent? That he gave me a script of yours?"

"That's right. He would have sent it to you about a week ago," Bill replied.

"I can't recall Randy giving me a script by you. He's given me several dozen scripts in the past week or two, from all the agency clients, but I'm certain yours wasn't among them. You see, as a writer, I make it a point never to forget another writer." D.L. looked at Bill, waiting for the straight kid with the ambition of a bulldozer to regroup and hit him again.

Bill was momentarily nonplussed. He hesitated, speechless, about to retreat and go back to his table. "Sorry to have…" Bill began to make his exit, Larkin interrupted him.

"Randy didn't give me your script, Mr. Parker, but Chris Reynolds did. Last Monday, in fact. I have not read it yet, but if Chris tells me once more how good it is, or how talented you are, I may be forced to read it… out of self defense." D.L. glared at Bill.

"Oh, sir, I would appreciate it. I'm sorry if Chris has pushed too hard. He's a good friend and…" Bill was regrouping and getting the old pitch back in high gear, when Larkin cut him off again.

"I will read it, Mr. Parker, and you will hear from my people one way or the other."

"Thank you, sir. I hope you like the work."

Bill offered to shake hands again. D.L. turned back around. This time it wasn't a snub, he simply didn't see the offer of Bill's hand. Bill turned away and shuffled back to the table with his news, dodging between and around some of the most glamorous and famous people "the dream" had ever envisioned. Given the excitement created by Larkin's promise to read his work, he saw nobody. Bill was in his own world, his dream, and he was all that much closer to turning it into reality.

When he finally worked his way back to the table, Jodi was nowhere to be found. Bill looked around the massive tent but didn't see her. First he sat down, but after about ten minutes alone he felt conspicuous and decided to mingle around, cruise the tent. Maybe he would find Chris, tell him how grateful he was for his support, and meet Laurie Dalton on top of it.

It wasn't hard to find Chris that night, since he was Laurie's date, and they had barely stopped dancing for a second since they had arrived. Laurie loved to dance and Chris loved being her partner. She could see Benton Stein watching them out of the corner of her eye. His stare nearly melted her. Instead of watching her lover, Laurie concentrated on dancing, on Chris, on being the center of attention.

The strength of Chris's entire body enveloped the feminine star. His massive shoulders pressed up against her, and her entire body fit in the hollow of his chest. They danced on as Benton was coming toward them.

"Thank God, the music is coming to an end," Laurie thought to herself. Chris released her from his grasp. She stepped back and smiled at him. He took her hand and then walked down to their table. Waiters at attention filled their glasses instantly. Chris raised his glass and toasted his evening's partner.

"To the most beautiful girl in the world and to the best female friend a guy in Hollywood could ever ask for!" Glasses clicked, and Benton Stein stepped up to the table.

"Good evening, Miss Dalton," he said.

"And good evening to you, sir," she replied.

"Who is your young companion here?" Benton went right to the heart of the matter.

"Why, you know Chris Reynolds. He's a college friend of Randy's and we work together on the show," Laurie teased Benton with her coy and taunting tone. She didn't really mean to do it, but the situation demanded it. She could feel his jealousy and she didn't like it.

"Ms. Dalton, would you join me for a few minutes. I would like you to meet some of my guests."

"Now, Mr. Stein?" she continued to taunt him.

"Yes, I think now would be a superb time," he answered.

"Well, then, now it will be," she said, getting up, excusing herself and telling Chris she'd be back, "just as soon as the big boss is through with me."

Bill saw Laurie leave Chris's table with Benton Stein, so the timing was good to make his way over to see his friend. The crowd in the tent had grown to proportions prohibiting much movement. It was a hazardous maneuver, dodging an assortment of ladies in sequined gowns guzzling champagne and talking with their outstretched arms all at once. Groups of huddling moguls in black tux puffed on foot long cigars. Despite all the obstacles, Bill made it over to Chris intact.

"Chris, what a great party, huh?" Bill said, surprising his buddy from behind.

"Bill, good to see you, man. Yeah, this is some party all right."

"Not a bad date you've got," Bill told Chris as he pulled up Laurie's vacant chair to sit down.

"She's a wonderful girl, Bill. If I wasn't so fucked up, I could be in love with her."

"Oh, come on, you're not so bad," Bill tried to lighten the mood sensing Chris was disturbed.

"Really man, I'm in trouble. Who the hell am I anymore? What am I doing?"

"All I know is that you're the best friend I've got," Bill said. Chris was surprised by Bill's unsolicited pat on the back. "Larkin just told me that you gave him my script."

"So? I told you I was going to do it," Chris answered.

"Yeah. But he also told me that Randy has never given him my script. So, I'm humble. If it weren't for your help I'd be nowhere." Bill asked the waiter for a glass of champagne from the silver tray he was carrying. Bill held his glass up to drink with his friend. "To the best friend I've got," Bill said. They drank.

Laurie followed Benton through the crowd. He tried to be as inconspicuous as possible, which of course wasn't possible at all. Eventually they made their way into the house, cutting between the barriers of poinsettia trees and into the private sanctuary of the Villa. Benton took Laurie by the hand down a series of halls and through a door into a small room at the end of the house.

"Where are we?" Laurie asked.

"In the maid's quarters," Benton told her.

"Why are we in the maid's quarters?"

"Perhaps you'd prefer the master bedroom?" he said.

"Actually, I would," Laurie replied. Benton took her in his arms and kissed her as passionately as he had ever kissed anyone in his life. He could not remember ever feeling jealous of his mistress.

"Where's the maid?" Laurie asked jokingly as their passion took a momentary breather.

"She's working. There are about a thousand people out there, remember?" Benton was sarcastic. He wanted to stop talking and start making love. Reaching for Laurie's breasts, she stopped him.

"Oh, no you don't."

"Why not?"

"If you want to make love to me, it will be in the master bedroom of this house or not at all," she said.

"That's impossible," Benton told her.

"Then it's impossible," Laurie said.

"What if Jennifer came in?" Benton pleaded with her. He wanted her more than ever before.

"You said it yourself. There are about a thousand people out there at her party. Why would she leave the affair to go up to her bedroom? Besides, you told me that you have adjoining master suites — his and hers. Why couldn't we go to yours? Would she, or anyone for that matter, have reason to enter your suite?"

Benton took her by the hand and they began a journey back through the halls, up the massive stairs to the second floor to Benton's bedroom. He had never taken another woman to his own bed. This was going to be special.

The room was more like a hotel club suite than the bedroom of a house. An entrance foyer beyond the door gave way to a large room that was elegantly and masculinely paneled in a dark cherry wood. A fireplace centered a major wall, flanked by floor-to-ceiling bookshelves overflowing with everything from best-sellers to classics. The furniture was sparse and simple. An extra large king-size bed on a raised platform was against the opposite wall. The headboard was a thick soft beige-colored Italian leather. Night tables on either side were covered with phone lines, remote controls for the TV, the stereo, every possible electronic apparatus available to man in 1975. Benton even had a machine to play tapes of TV shows and movies. It was a huge ugly thing to have in a bedroom, but very convenient for the ultimate mogul. In front of a large bay window on the far wall of the room, two very contemporary Italian leather chaise lounges flanked either side of an antique sofa upholstered in a green and red tapestry fabric. A dozen current magazines were neatly arranged next to a vase of fresh flowers on the coffee table. To the side of the seating arrangement were a pair of large, closed double doors. The doors led into Jennifer's suite. They were locked.

As Benton went back to lock the front door to his bedroom, Laurie stripped off her clothes and sat down on the bed, legs crossed, wearing only her high-heeled black pumps.

"Well, isn't this nice," Benton said as he came back around the corner, looking at Laurie's beautifully nude body. He went into the top drawer of his bed table and removed a beautiful black box.

"Here, this will go nicely with your…shoes," he said, dropping the black velvet box in Laurie's velvet lap. "You better put them on, you'll catch cold," Benton teased her.

Laurie opened the box and found a magnificent strand of large white pearls clasped together with a diamond. She picked up the necklace and fondled it, rubbing the pearls gently, back and forth in her hands. She looked at Benton. He smiled.

"Go on, put it on. I told you that you were going to catch cold dressed like that. They'll warm you up," he said, moving closer to her.

Laurie put the strand of pearls around her neck and Benton assisted, fastening the diamond clasp. As the platinum latch clicked closed, Benton gently pushed Laurie back onto his bed with the weight of his body. He began to lick her behind the ear, slowing coming around her neck, up onto her face. Their lips met, and they kissed long and hard, holding one another, embracing as lovers.

Benton put his arms behind and underneath his tender, soft Lady Godiva, enveloping her naked flesh with his tuxedo-clad body.

The silk of his jacket lapel rubbed her flesh so sensuously, hardening the nipples of her breasts.

Laurie tried to undress her lover, but the studs of Benton's formal shirt were difficult to remove. She pulled and pulled at one until finally he came to her aid, ripping the shirt open with both hands. She stroked his masculine hairy gray chest, her hands moving up onto his strong shoulders. Using her delicate fingernails she tickled him, then firmly dug into the flesh of his neck and upper back. The turn-on was potent and powerful. Laurie could feel Benton's hard penis trapped inside his suspendered tuxedo trousers. She reached down and found his fly, unzipping him, freeing him. He entered her instantly. She was moist, and very ready for him.

Their lovemaking was immediately the best they'd ever shared. Benton could feel Laurie's response. She loved him inside her and he knew it. Every move was one move. Their pleasure was symmetrical, equal, constant. Benton moved deeper and deeper inside her. She held him close, and wanted more. He gave her what she wanted.

Randy's sudden and unexpected entrance was an unwelcome end to their lovemaking. The passion vanished instantly with his uninvited arrival. The heir apparent bolted through the double doors leading from his mother's suite with the innocence of an eight-year-old kid. The last thing he expected was to find his father making love to his client, a girl he wanted desperately to make love to himself. It was a completely dreadful moment of compromise and revelation - for all of them.

Benton moved off Laurie, horrified to see his only son standing there, over them, staring. Laurie pulled the cover of the bed over her. It was an instant reflex of self protection. Unfortunately, Benton didn't have the same reflex. His fat, hard cock stuck out of his pants like the smoking gun it was.

Randy didn't say a word. He just looked at them for what seemed like six hours but was actually less than thirty seconds. Finally he turned and left his father's room through the same doors he had entered, his mother's. Benton followed him, finally putting his privates back inside the tux.

What had begun as their most passionate lovemaking had ended as their most disastrous. Without satisfaction, and with deep regret, Laurie was on her back, alone in Benton's bed, staring at the moldings of his formidable ceiling. At first she was as stone; frozen and rigid. But soon, the facade cracked, and she cried. The tears ran down the sides of her face dropping onto the silk coverlet of Benton's bed. It took more strength than she'd ever mustered to pick herself up off that bed to get dressed, to return to the party, to pretend that the worst had not just happened.

Benton had lost Randy, chasing his son through a half dozen upstairs chambers. Giving up, he ducked into one of his guest bathrooms to put himself back together. He'd never been in this particular bathroom in all the years he'd lived in the house. How odd it was to be a stranger in one of his own bathrooms, to be fixing his tuxedo studs in such unfamiliar territory.

Rejoining the party, and finding her abandoned date Chris Reynolds, Laurie was never questioned about her absence. Chris had used his free time to duck into another one of Benton Stein's bathrooms and to take more of the cocaine he'd brought with him from David Larkin's supply at home.

Benton appeared only moments later. He deliberately passed by Laurie, giving her a smile of reassurance. It was such a small insignificant gesture, but it won her over completely. She felt so much better.

Bill Parker had been nervously pacing the lavish party, looking for his date for over half an hour. Jodi had not come back to their table and nobody had seen her. For that matter, nobody even knew who she was.

Bill finally realized that things had not been exactly perfect between them over the past weeks. They had not made love since their weekend at the Hotel Bel Air, and even that had seemed forced to him, but he hadn't dwelled on it, assuming it would all pass with a little good fortune.

Convinced that his good fortune was around the corner, Bill had become more obsessed with his work, leaving Jodi further outside. Even though he knew she was unhappy about it, he didn't believe it was serious. He loved her and she loved him, and her mood would pass.

Jodi's disappearance at the party changed his simplistic viewpoint. Bill feared that she had left him, and had gone home, unable to stand the pressure of his maneuvering for recognition. This was the first time his shell of ambition allowed emotion. He didn't like the feeling. There was no room for vulnerability in "the dream." What if he lost his edge? Would his love for her be enough to make him happy in life? For Bill Parker, at twenty-two years of age, love of career and love of woman could not be combined into a whole package that translated into love of life. He wasn't capable of a balanced scale. They were totally separate parts of him, and they didn't mix.

His frustration over losing Jodi at the party grew proportionately with the shots of scotch he was consuming to try to maintain his cool. The "cool" was turning to anger, as he went from inside the tent to inside the house to the front entrance drive and back again, looking for her. How could she have just left? The rain was still coming down in torrents. She couldn't have simply walked away, and the car was still with the valets. Bill had checked twice. He returned to the tent, found another scotch, and went back to his friend Chris Reynolds' table. Bill sat down and watched as Chris and Laurie continued to dance in each other's arms, waiting for some sign of Jodi.

The sign came. A piercing scream cut across the tent obliterating the music of the thirty-piece orchestra, and the chatter of one thousand people came to a halt. At the front entrance to the tent, where everyone had been announced by the butler in red, a young woman fell to one knee sobbing hysterically. Her dress was torn and her hair tangled and pulled to one side of her head. Guards, waiters, rushed to her. Two large men in tuxedos picked her up and walked her into the house. Bill stood up to see what was wrong. The girl that the men were whisking away was Jodi. He ran through the mumbling crowd to her, as the orchestra played on to revive the party.

Forcing his way into the house, parting a platoon of burly men in tuxedo guard uniforms, Bill demanded to see Jodi. They finally let him pass thinking he could help to calm the screaming woman and explain what had happened. He found her curled up in a ball in the corner of a downstairs library. Nothing more than a giant human wad of discarded, crumpled paper, crying and shaking, her arms covering her head, and her face buried in her lap. Bill went over to Jodi and knelt down on the floor next to her. He put his arms around her to calm her, but she shook him off violently and screamed at him to leave her alone.

"Can't you tell me what's wrong?" Bill pleaded. She cried harder, louder, then began pounding on him with her fists, using every last ounce of strength in her body, finally collapsing into her corner, exhausted.

"Jodi, did someone hurt you?" Bill asked. "Did I do this to you?" he asked compassionately, thinking that he'd hurt her so badly that she'd gotten drunk, perhaps fallen, injuring herself. She was silent.

"Please, Jodi, let me help you. I love you, Jodi. I love you."

She began to sob again. Her entire body convulsed with each outburst of emotion. Bill reached for her yet again, this time able to hold on, embracing her. He put his head firmly on her shoulder, pressing hard against Jodi and against the wall. The security of his unrelenting hold on her, enabled her to find the words to speak to him.

"I'm so sorry. I'm so sorry...," her first words were barely audible.

"Sorry? About what?" Bill asked, still holding onto her, his head against hers.

"I didn't want this to happen. I was hurting, losing you, confused. I didn't think I loved you anymore and didn't know where to turn."

"Jodi, it's okay, I'm here. No matter what, it's okay."

"No, it's not okay. It'll never work. Never."

"Jodi, please try to calm down. Nothing is that terrible. I'll try to change, Jodi. Really, I'll try to, I promise."

"He raped me," she screamed out.

Bill released his hold on Jodi and sat back, horrified by her words. He grabbed her hands in his and clutched them firmly, looking into her eyes for an answer, any kind of an answer.

There was no answer, only sadness. The deepest, darkest sadness Bill had ever seen. He felt even more helpless, adrift between his two worlds that had both crashed, slamming into one another on this night at the most spectacular event the dream had ever materialized.

"Who raped you, Jodi? Who did this to you?" Bill began to cry as he begged for information.

"Randy did it," she finally told him, repeating," It was Randy."

Bill jumped to his feet, a madman looking for revenge. Jodi grabbed his sleeve as tightly as she could to keep him from leaving her, from running after Randy.

"It's my fault," she told him. "We met in the hallway and I was attracted to him. We talked for a moment, then he kissed me. I let him kiss me. He kissed me again and moved me up against the wall, kissing me harder. I liked it, I gave in to him. The next thing I knew we were in some room and he was pulling at my clothes. I tried to stop him, I really tried, but he wouldn't stop. He just kept coming at me, forcing me to make love to him. I started to scream and he gagged me with his coat, I thought I was going to choke to death. He ripped my dress up my body and then…" Jodi started to sob, unable to finish her story. Finding the resolve to continue, to tell what had happened, she went on, "He jammed his penis in me as hard as he could. He wanted to hurt me. The bastard didn't even take off his goddamned pants. All I can remember seeing was this goddamned bastard standing there afterwards… standing there over me as I cowered on the floor… standing there in his tuxedo with his penis hanging out of his fly. He looked so goddamned smug and satisfied with himself, calling me a bitch, a whore, and a tease, and every goddamned other name he could think of… blaming me for his actions, for his failure to act like a man instead of an animal."

Bill was unable to speak. He stared at her.

"I want to leave now," Jodi said.

"I'll call an ambulance for you, and get the police to arrest the bastard," Bill told her.

"No. Just get me out of here in your car. I don't want an ambulance, or the police."

Bill picked Jodi up in his arms, and carried her out of the Villa into the rain. They were surrounded by the team of tuxedoed guards, preventing any incident to spoil the party of the year. A valet had Bill's car waiting, to his amazement. They got in and drove back down the magical drive full of twinkling white lights.

CHAPTER 22

Jodi didn't go out of the apartment on 23rd Place for nearly two weeks. She wouldn't leave to see a doctor, so Bill arranged for her Beverly Hills gynecologist to pay a visit to the ghetto. Physically, Jodi was okay. That was all that could be said about her.

Bill lied to Mr. Grayson at the network, telling him that Jodi wanted to take all the accumulated vacation time she had coming to her. She wanted the cover. Bill wanted to blow the roof off Villa Serena, to get his good friend Randy Stein, Mr. Macho-one-track-sex-mind. All their years of good old boy get-any-lately? Talk had culminated in the rape of his girlfriend. His only real girlfriend.

Bill finally backed off when he saw that his indignation was making matters worse. Right or wrong, it had happened. For Jodi, the road to recovery was not paved with police reports and legal depositions. Bill was supportive, but more confused and more depressed than ever over their relationship. He loved Jodi but she was slipping away from him and he felt helpless to do anything.

On Monday, one week before Christmas, Jodi packed her Louis Vitton college graduation gift luggage and left. Bill was hard at work, keeping up the image and pounding out the CBS mail, anxiously waiting for his promotion to Jay Copley's department. Jodi got in a yellow cab that took her down ten long miles of Century Boulevard to the Los Angeles International Airport, and a non-stop TWA flight back to Philadelphia.

She left a note for Bill on his door-top desk.

• • •

Bill raced up the four flights of stairs to his apartment, calling out for Jodi as he neared the door. She didn't open it as he expected, so he fumbled around in his pockets to find the keys.

Unlocking the series of deadbolts, he gained entry and found darkness. She wasn't there. Bill hoped that Jodi had gone to meet a friend for dinner. She needed to start to come out of her shell. Then he saw the note on the desk.

"Dear Bill — God, I hate letters. Especially ones that say good-bye. But right now, or maybe always, I'm too much of a coward to face the truth in person. Without your love and support I don't think I would have survived the past couple of weeks. I will never be able to thank you enough for that.

I also hope you know that I do love you. But right now that love must be wrong, because it won't keep us together. I want to go home. I need to be with my family, sleep in my bed, forget what has happened to me.

Someday I will see your name on the screen in big letters. I'll probably read about you in the papers and tell my kids that we were once very close. They'll ask what you were really like, what Hollywood was like, and I'll tell them the truth. I'll tell them that it was all such a fabulous dream. I'll tell them how handsome and smart you were, and how we had such big plans together. Most important, I'll tell them that you were a good friend, and that I will always love you. Jodi"

Reading her letter slowly in the dimly lit room, a cold chill ran through his body. The tension was far greater than any anxiety he could ever remember feeling in his life. A tear ran down his cheek, and he quickly wiped it away with his free hand.

Holding back, reining in his emotions, Bill sat down on Chris's bedroll by the open window and looked out at the Mexican kids playing soccer in the dark empty lot behind the building.

• • •

The remainder of the week was murder. Had it not been for the daily revelry of the Christmas Holidays, a lunch with Grayson and two or three office parties in the network building, Bill would have gone mad. He called Jodi everyday, leaving messages, but she never called him back.

Bill also waited for Copley's call. Copley was supposed to let him know his official start date, but there was no communication. On Wednesday, Bill decided to call him. He left word. Now it was Friday, and Copley still had not called him back.

By midday everyone was packing up and leaving for the Christmas Holiday. By three p.m., the giant communications factory was a deserted hub. With no intention of leaving before the end of the day, Bill finished his stack of mail, alone. There was still hope that Copley would call, so Bill waited. At five o'clock, with still no word from Copley, he decided to initiate another call. If nothing else, he could wish Copley a Merry Christmas, tell him to have a great holiday and they'd talk next week. Copley picked up his own phone.

"Hello, it's Bill Parker, Mr. Copley."

"Parker, yes…" Copley coughed loudly into the receiver.

"Mr. Copley, I hadn't heard from you all week, so I thought I'd call to check the status of my start date on the new job, and also to wish you Merry Christmas."

"Well," Copley cleared his throat, "I'm afraid there's some bad news."

Bill knew instantly that somehow he'd lost the job. His heart sank into his stomach.

"What happened?" he asked.

"I'm embarrassed to tell you that Paretti, my boss, has hired someone else for your job, without telling any of us. We went about the interview process, selected you, and then found out that he wanted someone else. I had a meeting with him on Monday, it was my last ditch effort to convince him you were the man for the job. But, there was no chance. I just found out about it today."

"Jesus Christ," Bill said in disbelief.

"I'm sorry, too. Maybe next time. Try to have a good Christmas anyway."

CHAPTER 23

"Chris, where the hell are you?" Larkin called out for him in full voice. It was barely eight-thirty in the morning the day after Christmas and they were back at the studio preparing for a week of hell. The rest of Hollywood was skiing in Aspen and swimming in the bay of Banderas, Acapulco. But Larkin had a show to get back on its feet. By the first of the year he would have a completely new writing staff and he would be ready for production on the second half of the first season. These all-important shows would make or break the series.

"I'm Xeroxing, I'll be there in a second," Chris called back to D.L.

"Screw the Xeroxing. Get in here now!" D.L. summoned him.

"Okay. Here I am," Chris said, entering the almighty's office.

"This is the best script I've read in a year," D.L. proclaimed.

"That's nice, boss. Can I go back and finish my work now before you let me have it for not getting you your pages?" Chris knew when he could take a few liberties and talk back to D.L. This was one such time.

"You don't understand, Chris. With writing like this, our show could be on the air ten seasons." D.L. was foaming at the mouth.

"Okay. So hire the writer," Chris told him.

"I plan to," D.L. replied.

"Good. Can I go?" Chris asked.

"Not until I thank you."

"Thank me? For what, putting up with you?" Chris was really taking liberties. At least they both laughed at his remark.

"Thank you for this incredible script," D.L. said.

Chris went over to D.L. at his desk to look at the script. He didn't know what he was talking about until he saw the cover page, written by Bill Parker and Jodi Winkler.

"I told you he was a good writer," Chris said.

"These two are great writers, Chris. Who's this Jodi Winkler?"

"That's his girlfriend and partner."

"I should have read this six weeks ago, goddamn it!" D.L. barked. Chris had an I-told-you-so expression on his face. They laughed again. "The important thing is to get the two of them working here tomorrow. How can we get them?" D.L. asked Chris.

"Shouldn't be too hard. They live in my apartment."

"Well, call. Right now."

Chris picked up the phone and dialed. The phone rang about six times while D.L. impatiently paced the office. Bill finally picked up. His voice was muffled.

"Bill, is that you?" Chris asked.

"Yeah. But you got me out of the shower. I'm dripping on the floor, what is it?"

D.L. was motioning to Chris to give him the phone. Chris handed it over mid-sentence.

"Bill, this is David Larkin. I just read your script and I'd like you and your partner Jodi Winkler to come in and see me this morning."

There was silence.

"Hello? Are you there?" D.L. repeated.

"Yes, sir. I'm here. What time do you want me to come?" Bill said. He was shivering, standing wet and naked in the unheated apartment, a steady stream of cold air from the broken window blowing across his backside.

"I want you both in my office at the studio by ten this morning,"

Bill hesitated again. He didn't know how to tell Larkin that Jodi wouldn't be there. "Okay, sir. Ten o'clock."

• • •

The studio lot was Disneyland, Fairyland, Outer Space, all rolled into one spectacular magical experience. For someone who had dreamed of show business, this was nirvana. Bill's excitement pulsated with the blood in his veins.

Reaching the Larkin bungalow, Bill entered ready to face his future. His vision of show business glory vanished as he looked around the dismal office. CBS-TV City was so electric. There was a sense of purpose everywhere in the factory. Here, on the inside of a powerful movie studio, Bill felt like the cobwebs were overtaking the humans. Layers of dirty beige paint obliterated the architectural moldings of the thirties vintage bungalow. The walls were cracked, the wood floor barren and unpolished. Bill had just left the identical surroundings on 23rd Place.

The outer office was empty. Larkin had given Marie the week off for her annual pilgrimage home to visit relatives in the Midwest. Hearing Chris talking through a door, Bill entered after knocking once, not waiting for any response. He found Chris, and he also found David Larkin.

"Sit down, Bill." Larkin was effusively generous.

"Where's your partner?" he asked.

"She's not coming, Mr. Larkin," Bill answered directly. Chris gave Bill a surprised look.

"What do you mean, Bill? I need you both here to discuss your script," Larkin said, a little less generosity in his tone.

"Mr. Larkin, we are no longer partners," Bill told him. Larkin looked dismayed. "If you can only use us as a team, then I'm afraid I've wasted your time. But I want you to know that I am a strong writer on my own, and I'd like you to consider me alone for a job." Bill wanted to tell Larkin that he'd written the entire script on his own, but he didn't.

Larkin was thumbing through his script like it was a deck of cards. Bill waited for the deal. Chris spoke first.

"Look, David. I told you Bill was a good writer. Ten minutes ago you were patting me on the back and now you're doubting your own conclusions. Give him a shot, for chrissakes. He'll deliver, you'll see. I know that he will."

"You sound like his fucking agent," D.L. told Chris.

"Better," Chris replied, "I believe in him with no strings attached, no ten percent riding on this recommendation," he said.

"Okay," Larkin finally said after thumbing the script so violently that he broke the spine of the brads binding it together. "Okay. I'll bring you on board for thirty days. Deliver quality like this piece or perish. Got it, Mr. Parker?"

Larkin had run the gamut from generous host to killer boss. "Who do I make your deal with Mr. Parker?" D.L. asked.

"I'm sorry, sir?" Bill was confused.

"Your agent, Mr. Parker? Do you have one, other than Mr. Reynolds here?" D.L. was sarcastic, but he did smile.

"Randy Stein, Mr. Larkin," Bill spit out without thinking. "Wait a minute, Mr. Stein and I are no longer associated..." Bill said nervously.

"Well, that makes two divorces for you, Mr. Parker. No partner, no agent. Sounds like you'll fit right in, here in Hollywood." D.L. continued to smile at the two of them.

"How's that, Mr. Larkin?" Bill asked honestly.

"In love today, not speaking tomorrow. That's how this whole town, this whole business works. Everything changes constantly." The almighty imparted his wisdom on his followers, and started to walk out of the office. "I'll pay you Writer's Guild scale for a month, and then we'll see. In the meantime, get yourself an agent or a lawyer or a new partner or something. You are a member of the Writer's Guild, aren't you, Mr. Parker?" D.L. asked.

Bill nodded an affirmative yes, and looked at Chris as D.L. walked out of the office. "How do I join the Writer's Guild?"

• • •

The writers' bungalow was small. Actually, it was about the same size as Larkin's bungalow down the street, but Larkin's place was divided into two offices and this was divided into eight. Nobody else had been hired yet, not even a new secretary. Bill had his pick of the eight tiny rooms with bricked-in windows. He took door number one and settled in. He was excited and anxious to get on with his work, further bolstered with confidence through the encouragement given to him from Grayson earlier that morning when Bill had called to give him the news, and to resign his post at the ticket office.

Chris gave Bill an insider's tour of the studio lot showing him the vital things — the closest men's room, the closest parking lot, the fastest route to the commissary, a secret way in and out of the lot without being seen. Then, they went to the stage where "The Reilly's" was filmed, and to the executive building where Moran's top floor office overlooked the entire studio and west to the Pacific Ocean. By noon-time, a studio teamster driver came by Bill's new office with a typewriter and some other supplies that Chris had ordered the instant that Bill was hired by D.L. The driver found Bill sitting there, in his new office, looking at the brick window. Chris had gone back to D.L. to resume his own duties.

Bill took the machine gratefully and organized his desk. It was time to begin, but begin what? He had no instruction. As if by mental telepathy, a studio messenger entered the bungalow with a manila folder and handed it to Bill, leaving before Bill could even say hello, how are you, who are you?

Inside the packet were his orders. Pages of notes on new show direction, character breakdowns and motivations, and a show-by-show outline from Larkin for the next three episodes. A small post-it type note was attached to the first of the outlines. It read, "Get busy, Mr. Parker. Here are your guidelines. Follow them for structure and plot, but overwhelm me with your creative license otherwise. First draft due on shows one and two by Friday, close of business."

It was already nearly half-past noon on Monday. Bill took off his jacket and tie and papered the IBM. Smoke was rising from the keys within minutes. He would deliver first drafts of all three scripts to Larkin by Friday, and they would be the best first drafts ever submitted to the Almighty. The bleak surroundings, even the brick windows all but disappeared as Bill escaped into his writing, consumed by his deadline, his energy, and the dream.

• • •

Pressure was mounting at City Hall to wrap up the Peter Barker case. Detective Arnold was feeling the heat from his superiors to make an arrest. It wasn't that the public was clamoring for some sort of justice. Barker's death was old news, forgotten. But the system demanded a resolution to a case one of its payrolled detectives had spent months investigating. Arnold was told in no uncertain terms to put on some heat and wrap it up. But Arnold had no prime suspect, just a pack of Hollywood heavyweights, and every one of them was covering something up. To him it was a question of weeding out the biggest liar with the clearest motive and finding the evidence to corroborate his charges. With the chief demanding some action, Arnold decided to make a deal with a felon, already in custody, to help himself. The scales of justice would tip a little for a trade off. Arnold was simply trading away a conviction on one small crime for a possible conviction on a greater one. It all made such convenient good sense.

Don Robertson had been rotting in the downtown jail for weeks, stuck in limbo, lacking parole and unable to make a move. His court-appointed attorney, a tall, thin, balding, nervous woman in her late thirties, met Detective Arnold at the jail house to finalize the arrangements.

The deal was that Robertson would go to work for Detective Arnold, back in business as a work-out trainer and drug dealer to the stars. The only difference would be the wire in his jock strap. In exchange for his services, the felony cocaine pushing charges would be reduced to possession, and a recommendation from the police to the court for leniency.

A signature here, a signature there, and iron doors started swinging open. Don Robertson was free, as long as he behaved. He traded in the standard issue orange uniform for his personal clothes and walked out the door with Detective Arnold and the twitching-balding lady public defender. Freedom came at a big price, but it was worth it. Robertson's pretty-boy blonde face and steroid built body had made him a prime target in the society of men behind bars. He hadn't slept in weeks.

They walked over to the administration building at Parker Center Police Headquarters, then into a private room outfitted with only a table and chairs. Arnold told Robertson to sit down and listen. The Lady defender paced the room relentlessly.

"You'll check in with me three times a day — seven a.m., three p.m., ten p.m. Here's my card and the number you'll call to get me." Robertson took the card, nodding in agreement. "We'll place a small article in the paper about your release, say something about mistaken identity or something, to let your Hollywood folks know you're out.

In a day or two, you start calling your clients to tell them the heat is off and you're back in business. Set a new schedule and let me know all of it. You got that?" Arnold asked firmly.

"Yes, sir. I do," Robertson replied.

"As soon as you get a new schedule you go to work, only you wear this wire. We'll have to figure out some way to put it in your goddamned crotch if you don't wear a shirt to exercise," Arnold said.

"How about my gym bag, sir? We can just put it in there. I always have it with me," Robertson offered sheepishly. He was tired of men touching his crotch. First the guys in jail, now the police attaching microphones.

"We'll see. Whatever works," Arnold thought, continuing, "You'll have an undercover team following you in a van everywhere. They'll record what you pick up. You got that?" Robertson nodded again. "And if you get yourself in trouble, we'll be there, right there to back you up," he added.

The public defender came over from her place to concur on that piece of information. After all, her client's rights had to be covered. That was the law in these situations.

"What about the stuff?" Robertson asked. "The stuff. The junk?" he asked again.

"We'll provide you with the bait. Your undercover associate will supply you, and collect the money, too. You'll give him all the money you collect. Got that?" Arnold put his finger into Robertson's shoulder blade and pushed.

"How will I live if I give you all the money?"

"You'll live, besides, you can keep the money you make as a workout instructor. That is what you do, isn't it Mr. Robertson?" Robertson said nothing. "We'll get started by week's end. Your first assignment is to get re-acquainted with Karen Barker and her boyfriend. Work on that. And don't forget, your first check-in call to me is coming up — three p.m. today."

Arnold walked out of the interrogation room leaving the lady attorney to dot the "i"s and cross the "t"s. The heat was now back on again. Robertson would be Detective Arnold's ticket to wrapping up the Barker case.

CHAPTER 24

Without packing, Bill moved out of 23rd Place. During the first week of his new job as a writer on "The Reilly's of San Marino," Bill hadn't left the studio lot. It was hard enough to deliver one decent script outline in a week, but three was Herculean. There was no time to go home.

Chris gave Bill a key to one of the actor's trailers, which he used to sleep for a few hours and shower in the mornings. He looked like he'd lost ten pounds in a week, scavenging bits of food in the office, or a fast hot dog from the truck that came around to feed the working crews on the lot. Gone was the rehearsed and polished image of success, the starched shirt, the suit and tie. Bill was holed up in his bunker, and the only thing that mattered was that he delivered great work. For the first time in his life he even let his beard grow.

After weeks of unsuccessful attempts, Bill finally connected with Jodi on the phone. He told her about the job and about how Larkin had wanted both of them. But there was no sound of remorse in her voice. She didn't want it.

Jodi was genuinely thrilled for Bill, reassuring him that his talent would open many doors as soon as it was recognized. She also told him that she was feeling much better, and that she had started going to a therapist for counseling. The therapist had helped her realize that her life in Hollywood was a phase that was over, and more importantly, that it wasn't a career in show business that had attracted her west, but her boyfriend, whom she'd left for another boyfriend — Bill. And now that was over, too. The therapist attributed Randy's attack to the permissive society in Hollywood and, in particular, to a very spoiled, maladjusted young man in need of help. Bill said he thought it sounded like the therapist wasn't too fond of men in general, or Hollywood. In the end, Jodi told Bill to deliver a killer script and to get out of 23rd Place with his first paycheck. Then she said good-bye, and asked him not to call her again.

• • •

At the end of the week, Bill entered D.L.'s bungalow with the results of his sleepless first week as a Hollywood writer. It was very quiet in the office. Chris wasn't working at his desk or standing over the Xerox machine as usual. Bill could hear D.L. in his office, so at least he knew that the boss was there to receive his work. He knocked on the partially open door and waited for word to enter.

D.L. waved him in the office and continued his phone conversation. Whoever was on the other end, or whatever they said, put Larkin in a finer mood than Bill had ever witnessed. Incredible luck, super timing, Bill thought, handing his scripts over to Larkin like a mother giving over her baby to adopting parents. Bill actually tugged on the paper as Larkin grasped hold.

"It's a little long for two episodes, Parker," Larkin said immediately.

"That's because I did three, sir," Bill told D.L. proudly.

"Three? But I only gave you outlines for two, how could you have done a third?"

"I expanded the plot based on the directions you clearly laid out for the first two. If you don't like it, nothing lost, but hopefully you will like it. I think it's the direction you want the show to go."

"I'll be the judge," D.L. said. "But I appreciate the initiative no matter what, okay?"

"Okay." Bill was glad he'd done the extra work, even if Larkin tossed it just to make the point that he was boss. The effort had shown the king workaholic that he had a prince standing in line for the throne. If Bill could make Larkin his ally and mentor rather than foe, he'd have it made.

"I'll read them over the weekend. You'll have my comments Monday morning. By the way, if I don't like what I read, there will be no Tuesday morning here for you. If I do, you'll join the rest of the new staff starting next week, at least you'll join them for the remainder of your month try-out until I make a final decision." Larkin was packing up his case to leave. He seemed to be in a rush.

"Have you seen Chris? I've got to get going early tonight." Larkin asked Bill to look for him. Chris was coming in the door as Bill was on his way to find him. The two of them went back into Larkin's office.

"I'm here, boss," Chris said. "How come we're out of here so early tonight?"

"I've got a workout and massage at 7:30 tonight with Robertson." D.L. smiled at Chris.

"I thought he was in jail?" Chris said.

"Was, my boy, is the operative word. Let's go."

Larkin and Chris left the bungalow huddled in secret conversation. Bill watched them walk across the dark lot towards the parking structure. He felt sorry for Chris, somehow, wondering what the night had in store for him and his own new boss, David Larkin.

• • •

Don Robertson had been unable to reach Karen Barker to set up his first appointment for Detective Arnold. She and her surfer boyfriend had apparently gone out of town. Arnold told him to call "whoever the hell" he wanted, but to get going, or he'd end up back in jail "faster than he could set up his goddamned massage table."

David Larkin had always been one of Robertson's very best customers, so he called him right away. Unable to find a replacement source of cocaine with product as good as Robertson provided, D.L. was anxious to have Robertson come around.

By the time Chris drove in the driveway of Larkin's Ambazac Way mansion, the familiar black Chevy Camaro belonging to Don Robertson was parked in its old spot, out of the way, on the side against the hedges. D.L. hit the button that operated the electronic garage door, and the massive aluminum sheath began rolling up into the eaves, permitting Chris to pull the studio Lincoln into its berth.

D.L. got out of the car without saying a word and did double-time into the house.

Parked up the street, in a dark panel truck, Detective Arnold and his staff of electronic surveillance operators hoped David Larkin would be glad to see Robertson. Glad enough to impart some piece of information that might give Arnold his case.

He had been told, in no uncertain terms, that his undercover plans were not simply to produce a giant Hollywood drug bust among the big shots. The chief didn't want Arnold hauling in the stars, producers, and studio moguls on cocaine charges without a murder one charge to go along with it.

Arnold had prepped Robertson unmercifully off and on all week. His direction was to turn any conversation back to Peter Barker.

As Arnold was checking his equipment in the van, adjusting the frequency, the voice levels, double-checking the tape recorder and the back up recorder, he heard Larkin enter the room over the hidden microphone on Robertson. The massage table was already set up in Larkin's exercise room upstairs.

The customary hellos were even more friendlier. Larkin actually hugged Robertson as he expressed relief over his release from jail. The pressure of his body against Robertson sent a jarring blast of static through Robertson's jock strap microphone. The crew in Arnold's van let out a "Jesus Christ!" in unison. The volume was turned down a notch on the speakers.

Robertson asked Larkin to change into his gym shorts while he set up the weights for their exercise regimen. Chris came in the gym as Larkin was going into the bathroom to change. Robertson asked him to join as well. Before Robertson's arrest, Larkin had started exercising with Chris. It made him feel younger keeping up with his virile twenty-two-year-old lover.

Chris expressed his own welcome at Robertson's return, sans the hug. Detective Arnold's crew was happy about that.

And then Chris went for the bulls-eye, asking Robertson about his cocaine supply.

Robertson was standoffish at first. The kid wasn't his client. Was he supposed to tell him that he was back in business, and that his gym bag was loaded with the finest Central American powder he'd ever had? Robertson decided to go for it, and since Detective Arnold's orders were practically tattooed across his chest, he used the kid's question about the coke to steer the conversation right to Peter Barker.

"Man, since my bust, right after Peter Barker's murder, my sources have dried up," Robertson told Chris.

"You were there with Barker the night he died, weren't you?" Chris was a willing candidate right off the top. There was silence in the police van.

"Yeah, I left just before he was killed, but I don't know what happened. Didn't see anyone."

"The paper said Barker had coke in him." Chris was nearly hitting a homer for the boys in blue up the street.

"So?"

"So. Was it yours?"

"Yeah, it was mine, but so what?"

"Maybe he was so high that he fell off his terrace. Maybe nobody else was there at all. Maybe it was your fault for selling him the coke." Chris was judge and jury. It unnerved Robertson. Detective Arnold's chief deputy gave him a look, but Arnold had already digested that idea months before. He didn't think it was that simple. Somebody else was there, he firmly believed, and that somebody killed Barker.

His best hunch told him it was the ex-wife, or more likely her boyfriend. If only he and his officers were parked in Beverly Hills tonight listening to their private confessions to Robertson, the case would be closed.

"Look kid," Robertson said to Chris in a stern tone, attempting to shift the responsibility off himself. "Don't go getting holier-than-thou with me. Mr. Larkin was pretty generous with you with his white powder. I didn't hear you ever saying, no thanks."

"What's that got to do with Peter Barker's death?" Chris slapped back at him.

Larkin walked back in the exercise room to find his young lover arguing with his coke dealer. "What's wrong in here?" he said. "I thought this was going to be a happy reunion — for all of us."

"Why don't you find yourself a stud with less of a mouth?" Robertson sarcastically asked D.L.

"We're getting a little personal here, aren't we Don?" Larkin responded.

"This little bastard just accused me of killing Peter Barker." Robertson was nervous, he paced the room and looked away from Larkin and Chris.

"What are you talking about?" Larkin asked.

Before Robertson could answer, Chris shouted at David.

"You were there, David, didn't you see this asshole selling Peter more coke than he could handle?"

Detective Arnold and his men nearly wet their pants. The information surprised them so much the van nearly vibrated from their combined excitement.

"This guy's a real jerk, David. I think the cops made a big mistake letting him out of the slammer. Count me out of the exercise." Chris left the room with the slam of the bedroom door behind him.

"You could have any dude in town, David. Why that jerk?" Robertson asked him as he counted his sit-ups, holding his ankles down on the mat.

"A little jealous of his youth, Don? We're not twenty-two anymore, eh?"

"No, I just think he's bad news. The moody type. Short fuse, too. Hey, what did he mean, you were there?" Robertson asked. Detective Arnold checked to make sure his machines were recording.

"There, where?" Larkin had already forgotten Chris's comment out of context.

"There, with Barker, the night he died. I was there, I didn't see you. When were you there?"

Larkin didn't answer him right away. Instead, he turned over and started doing push ups without letting Robertson conduct the exercise. Robertson asked him again when he was there. Larkin stopped abruptly and turned back over.

"Look, are we here to exercise or talk? If you're that interested, I was there after you left, but Barker wasn't there, okay?"

"Well, how do you know?" Robertson dug deeper.

"Because he wasn't there, that's all."

"How do you know you were there after me?"

"Because I saw your usual coke delivery on the nightstand and the whole goddamned place smelled like you, Aramis and massage oil is a pretty distinctive scent."

"Oh."

Arnold took off his headset and asked his deputy if they'd found a coke stash in the search of Barker's apartment for evidence. The deputy shook his head, "No," but reminded him that there were traces of the drug found in the rug by the bed. So where was Robertson's delivery to Barker?

"Look Don, first you upset Chris, and now you've got me out of the mood here. I think we better call it quits for tonight." Larkin got up off the exercise mat and admired himself in the full-length wall of mirror.

"I've got some real choice stuff here, David. You do still want that, don't you?" Again Robertson was sarcastic.

"Okay. I'll take some. Just leave it in the usual place on your way out." Larkin paused and turned to Robertson who was already folding up his table to leave.

"You know, Don, jail doesn't agree with you. You're not the same guy. Try to relax and unwind a little before you come back here next week. You got that, friend?" Larkin looked right at him, then he left the room to go and find Chris.

Mr. Lee was downstairs crossing the foyer to bring some refrigerated mineral water up to "the almighty" when "the almighty" appeared.

"Lee, have you seen Chris?"

"He went out the front a few minutes ago. I think he go for walk."

"Thanks." Larkin went out the massive front doors leaving Lee standing in the hall holding the tray and water. Moments later, Robertson came down the stairs and walked right by him as well. He didn't even say good-bye, just slammed the doors on his way out. The giant chandelier shook, the giant windows shook, and Lee shook, standing there with his glass of water. Robertson got in the Camaro and reached down into his crotch to pull off his wired third ball. The microphone was small and fuzzy and the wire was taped to his inner thigh and then ran around back to a very small battery/transmitter hidden in his waistband. He screamed a "fuck" or two as the tape pulled his pubic hairs out of the tender flesh. Then he held the tiny instrument up to his mouth and spoke into it in a heightened pitch.

"How's that for undercover work?" He went on. "Pretty damn good, huh? There's your suspect. Now, am I off the hook?"

CHAPTER 25

M onday at the studio was absolutely wild. The whole town had come back to life. The holidays were over and it was wheel and deal as usual. On the set of "The Reilly's," the writers' bungalow, formerly deserted, was now bulging at the seams. Six new writers, and a head writer, Gary Burger, instantly brought Larkin's writing staff back to eight, including Bill.

They were earning different weekly increments in the thousands. Starting with two grand a week for the lowest member, Bill Parker, and finishing with Gary Burger, as head writer, pulling in better than ten big ones each and every week. At forty-one, he'd worked on enough network shows to fill a single-spaced two-page resume. Divorced, balding, and angry that he wasn't David Larkin, Burger came on to the lot ready to kick butt. He had a great deal to prove.

Laurie Dalton looked incredibly beautiful her first day back at work. Everyone fawned over her. Laurie's presence shot life into the arm of the show, and the energy level was high all over the set, whenever she appeared.

There was no question in Bill Parker's mind that Laurie Dalton was the show. Without her it was just another dramatic serial. Fortunately, he'd thrust the focus of his scripts in Laurie's direction.

All the writers were joking and posturing and checking each other out in the bungalow. It was a chicken coupe in pursuit of a pecking order. First came the battery of questions about credits. "What have you done lately?" Then, a "Who do you know?" Next, "Where did you go to school?" "Have you ever written a feature film?" "Who's your agent?" "Do you play racquetball?" "What color BMW do you drive?"

It was a first day of school at High School Writers Hell, and Bill hated the pretense of it all, immediately withdrawing. Most of the writers knew each other from past shows, or at least knew each other's reputation. Bill was a stranger, and strangers in Hollywood were suspect.

By the end of the first day, the "suspect" status had its advantages. For one thing, he had a clean slate, no preconceived notions of his ability or his personality. He could see that he would be able to orchestrate his own image, and he was going to be very careful about the process. Second, he had no baggage, owed no favors, except to Chris. His allegiance was to Larkin for the opportunity and to himself to build a strong base for career development.

While the rest of the guys spent the remainder of the afternoon bonding in the bungalow, shooting rubber ball baskets into a makeshift hoop taped to a wall, Bill decided to make himself scarce. He'd already had what he felt was a run-in with Burger. The guy had given him the third degree about who he was and why he was there a week before anyone else. Bill had tried to be vague without sounding aloof, but he'd failed, and Burger was suspicious of him and his connection to Larkin.

Escaping Burger, Bill found that life on the set was far more interesting in the company of Laurie Dalton. He hung out in her trailer with Chris. Laurie talked about the incredible time she had in Hawaii over the holidays with Benton. He had flown to Laredo, where she had been visiting her family, and picked her up in his private jet. When he got back to L.A., he surprised her with his plan to take her to the islands for a few days.

The afternoon passed quickly, and the hide-out in Laurie's trailer came to an end for Bill. The creative "nerd herd" huddled around Marie starting at about 5:45 in anticipation of the 6:00 p.m. writer's meeting.

When D.L. opened his door, the procession flowed in. Bill managed to be last and took a spot standing in a corner of Larkin's office, leaning up against the wall. He was blocked by a couple of the other guys, one sitting on the arm of the sofa in front of him, and another taking a chair that cut him off completely from the waist down. Burger was sitting in another chair adjacent to D.L.'s desk. The major at the general's side, ready to implement his orders.

D.L. began to speak and the chatter went immediately silent. Burger was the first to tell everyone to keep it down, even though they already had. D.L. gave him an odd look. Bill realized at that moment that he had a real jerk for a head writer, but none of the rest of the writers seemed annoyed by Burger.

"First, welcome to 'The Reilly's of San Marino'," Larkin began. "You were all selected and hired because of your talent. We have an opportunity here to create a lasting television series and I expect you'll all contribute your utmost effort to that end. As far as the law and order goes around here, I am your dictator, king, president, and occasional despot. What I say goes at all times. Mr. Burger is your direct link to my leadership. As your head writer, he will make assignments based on my direction, and his estimation of your individual strengths. All of you will report to him."

Bill had a sick feeling as D.L.'s words sunk in. A week in show business as a writer and the proverbial writing was on the wall. Burger didn't like Bill, didn't trust him, and he knew it.

"You're probably all wondering what we're going to do for a shooting script next week since the cameras are set to roll on Monday?"

D.L. broke away from his speech and called out for Chris, who entered the room with a stack of freshly mimeographed scripts. The material was so freshly copied that the delicious smell of fresh ink permeated the room.

Chris passed out the scripts on orders from D.L. The first one went to Gary Burger, and the last copy to Bill back in his corner of the office. Bill took it with great trepidation. What had happened to his work? Larkin had never said a word. Perhaps his fear of Burger was moot, his days numbered as the Hollywood writer.

Then he looked down at the cover page. It was his script. There was his name. "Written by Bill Parker." He looked again to make sure it was real. He ran his fingers across the page to feel the print as if it was in Braille. Then Bill put the script up to his face and sucked it in, all of it, breathing in the ether-like smell of the wet ink on the paper. It was intoxicating. The other writers were reading through the pages, skipping around to get a feel for the work and for the show they were all hired to write. The script was a first example of what they now had to follow. Burger was the only one looking at Bill, who caught his glance, but looked down to avoid recognition.

"Staff, this is our first script," D.L. continued. "It is an outstanding screenplay, making the absolute most of the storyline and giving our actors, particularly our female star Ms. Dalton, and her new co-star brother, tremendous opportunity to act. The dialogue is crisp and fast-paced - just the way I like it. This is an excellent example of what I want from all of you each and every week."

Bill was still inhaling the ether. He was practically drunk listening to D.L.'s praises. The whole thing was too good to be true. Was he really talking about his script? Chris had left the room and returned with a box load of material, setting it down on the coffee table.

"What Chris has just brought us will be your bible for the next thirteen weeks. These pages are my notes and outlines for each of the next dozen shows. We will, of course, revise as we go, but in general, this is our course. Mr. Burger will make his assignments from this bible. Please make a permanent note that we'll have a writers' meeting every Wednesday at 3 p.m., here in my office. By the way, there is some good news. I am currently three weeks ahead on scripts, so there is some luxury of time to really dig in and do great work. Gentlemen, that will be all. Gary, do you want to take over from here?"

D.L. turned the meeting over to Burger, who did exactly what Bill, even in his ink-induced high, expected: he repeated everything that Larkin had already said. Bill was thinking that this redundant procedure was absurd, but again, none of the other writers seemed to blink at the obvious absurdity. Maybe this was just standard operating procedure in Hollywood. After all, Bill thought, what did he know about how things went?

CHAPTER 26

Detective Arnold had been using Don Robertson undercover, all over town, non-stop. Robertson's legs were raw from pulling off the adhesive tape holding the recording apparatus in his shorts. He'd also been dealing more coke in a month than he normally sold in three. The supply, courtesy of the authorities, was an amazing inducement to his clients to spill forth information useful to Arnold.

The most important fact picked up came from none other than one of his prime suspects. Karen Barker told Robertson about an affair she had with someone her former husband knew and trusted. She never gave the name, although Robertson did his sly best to pull it out of her. This was not new information to Arnold, he'd heard it before. Howard Hillman at Paramount had alluded to it without saying it, and so had Karen on their last meeting, but now it was substantiated again by the source to a third party.

The real break came in Karen's further revelation of the affair's locale. She told Robertson that she missed the sunset cocktails at the Malibu Sea Lion Bar. A moonlight walk down the beach to her lover's beach house followed, where they'd spend the night making love with the bedroom windows open to the pounding surf.

La Costa Beach was just north of The Sea Lion Restaurant and Bar. It was second only to "The Colony" as a Hollywood playground on the sand. Movie stars and moguls crowded the tiny strip of white sandy beach, their simple beach houses next to one another on fifty-foot-wide lots right off the Pacific Coast Highway.

Checking the La Costa Beach real estate tax logs downtown at the county recorders office turned up one owner's name. A name that definitely captured Detective Arnold's attention - David Larkin. Now he had three pieces of evidence and all of it connected to Larkin.

First, there was the drug issue. Larkin had categorically denied using cocaine, and was in fact a major customer of Robertson's. Second, Larkin had been to see Peter Barker at his home sometime the night he died, a fact he'd also denied in questioning that had been revealed by the admission of Chris Reynolds on tape through Robertson's first undercover assignment at the Larkin house. And third, Karen Barker had been having an affair with someone at what was potentially Larkin's house in Malibu. Perhaps her lover was Larkin? He was the only suspect with a house in the area. But he was gay? Or maybe bisexual? Was that what ended his affair with Karen Barker? Did Peter Barker find out, confronting Larkin? Or did Barker's rage over being fired by his ex-wife's lover provoke a fight between the men, ultimately sending Peter Barker over the ledge to his death?

Arnold was making progress. If he could prove that Larkin was in Barker's apartment by finding some kind of physical evidence, he'd have enough to bring to the D.A. to instigate charges. Arnold filed papers, requesting a search warrant be issued for Larkin's beach house and his main residence in Bel Air.

• • •

Gary Burger made the ego-driven error of writing the fourth week's script himself, cutting out not only Bill, who was the rising star, but also the input of six other highly paid staff writers.

Making matters worse, Burger gave the script to Larkin only three days before shooting was due to begin. His supreme self-confidence overshadowed any sense of caution or self-preservation that might have compelled him to turn the work in with at least a week's notice, permitting revisions. Larkin was furious.

Not only did he find the script "pedestrian," but the audacity of turning in anything at the eleventh hour was inexcusable. Larkin's screaming could be heard all over the lot. Glass windows nearly shattered from the pitch. Secretaries were running for higher ground. He summoned Burger to his office and verbally stripped him of his manhood, his creative ability, and his rank on the staff. Finally, he was instructed to have Bill Parker re-write the script on a twenty-four hour turnaround and was told that the results would weigh heavily on the value of his contractual renewal.

For the previous several weeks, Gary Burger had demeaned, isolated, and abused Bill in an attempt to have him fired or force his resignation. He'd tried to use his considerable authority and connections to rally his staff against Bill. What he had succeeded in doing was sending all the writers into their own foxholes, scrambling for their own self-preservation, and ultimately destroying any unity or camaraderie that might have existed.

Bill had taken the abuse for three weeks, unloading his anxiety and frustration only to Chris. His best friend had in turn let Larkin know what was going on in the privacy of their bed. Burger's mediocre script was a marvelous theatrical moment for the almighty manipulator Larkin to turn the tables.

Gary Burger left Larkin's office with his tail between his legs. The first thing he did was call Randy Stein, who was his agent, to solicit support. Stein didn't take the call, fearing the worst. If Burger was out and Bill was in, he needed to get busy mending fences.

The second thing Burger did was to go to Bill and apologize. He confessed that he was scared to death because he was on a four-week trial and he couldn't afford to lose the job. He even pretended that he liked Bill, that they could be friends.

Bill was dumbstruck. He'd never seen such an instantaneous transformation of character. It was no surprise when Burger's apology was followed by the request for a twenty-four hour turnaround rewrite. Bill accepted the challenge, and asked his head writer to leave so he could get to work.

The all night session produced what Bill thought was his very best work to date. Despite the unbearable pressure of time, he'd found dialogue and plot twists only a 3:00 a.m. daze could have concocted. But it all worked, or so he hoped. Chris had come in early, by 6:00 a.m., to help Bill finish the manuscript and prepare the mimeo machine so that Larkin would have the completed work no later than 9:00 a.m.

By eleven, Larkin had barely found enough uninterrupted time to read the entire script. Across the lot, John Moran had read his copy.

And across town, the program executives at CBS had also read their early morning messenger-delivered copies. The jury was unanimous. The writing was brilliant. Phone lines were buzzing. Larkin was a hero. Parker was a star. Everyone was counting their future profits. Bill went home to 23rd Place to get some sleep. Burger was given a reprieve, and with it came the hope that his all-important contract would be picked up after all.

• • •

Randy had not spoken to his father since he'd found him with Laurie at the Christmas party. In turn, Benton had not made any attempt to discuss his affair, preferring to keep the whole thing his own business as much as possible. He figured his son would get over the shock.

He didn't get over it. The shock turned to anger, then to rage. Randy wanted Laurie to be *his* lover. His father had every other woman in town. Not only had Randy avoided his father, but he'd also stayed away from Laurie. His daily calls to her had become weekly calls. He'd stopped asking about the smell of gardenias altogether.

Avoiding both his star client and his powerful father couldn't go on forever, consequently Randy accepted Benton's offer to meet for dinner at the Polo Lounge. They had a great deal at stake.

The initial reunion was chilling, especially from Randy's point of view. The two of them sat in the familiar green velvet booth and glared at each other. The waiter brought a second round of drinks without asking. Benton broke the formidable ice.

"Okay, you hate your old man, so what do you want me to do?"

"You're a fucking bastard, do you know that?" Randy's venom was lethal, even though he spoke in hushed tones to keep their strife private.

"I love her," Benton told his son, calmly and easily.

"You love her. That's a joke. You love them all. What about mom, do you love her, too?"

"Yes, I love her, too, but not like I love Laurie. I need to be with Laurie. In fact, I am seriously thinking of asking for a divorce from your mother. Laurie is not a passing fancy to me, son."

"Oh, that's great. And what about me? Does it matter to you that she's my client? Do you care that maybe I had a thing for her as well?"

"I'm sorry, son. I didn't do this to hurt you. Laurie has been even more concerned about your feelings than I have."

Randy was feeling mean. "What's next, dad? Does she love you, or are you just the big fat wallet meal ticket for the bimbo starlet?"

"Is that all you think of your client? I thought you knew Laurie better. She doesn't need me for my money. This girl has power of her own, and she knows that her future is in her own hands, her own control."

"Come on, she's good, but she's not that good. This little piece of work has sure got you fooled. And there's no fool like an old one."

Despite his father's attempt at a reconciliation, Randy was too spoiled and too stubborn to face the reality. Restraining an emotional urge to hit his father, Randy quickly slipped out of the booth and quickly left the Polo Lounge. He couldn't talk to his father any more, couldn't look at him. The anger and hurt feelings had overcome him. In times of great distress, Randy had run to his dad to fix life — Dad was not the cause and not the solution. All he could think of was the need to get out of the room, to get in his car and drive, letting the cold February night air slap his face in order to get some grip on his sanity and some idea of what to do next.

• • •

The demands of Larkin's Hollywood world kept Chris working at the studio late. He had so much paper to collate and distribute that he told D.L. not to wait dinner for him, or for that matter to even expect him home at all. If the work kept him there past midnight, it was easier to catch some sleep in one of the trailers. Chris kept extra clothes in the office for such occasions. They had become more and more frequent.

On this evening, however, with Marie's help, all the script and schedule work was done by just past ten, so Chris decided to go home after all. In the driveway of Larkin's Bel Air residence by 10:30, Chris saw that the house was dark, but there was a car in the driveway he didn't recognize. It was nothing particularly unusual, just an old VW bug.

Inside, it was dark and quiet. Most of the lights were out, no laughing voices or clinking wine glasses. Lee was in his quarters, probably asleep with the TV on. Chris heard the theme music from "MANNIX" playing as he passed by his room coming in the back way through the kitchen.

Chris presumed that David was in his room, probably reading scripts. Hearing nothing as he passed by Larkin's door off the upstairs corridor, Chris did notice that there was a dim light emanating from beneath the door, so he quietly entered.

Larkin was in bed, but he wasn't reading. He jumped up as Chris appeared, and so did his companion for the evening, Mark Harlander. Not a word was spoken by either of them. No explanation, no attempt to conceal their activity, no embarrassment on the part of Larkin or Harlander. In fact, Harlander smiled. It was some sort of sick victory for him. He'd won after all. Not with the part of "Eric," but with the part he really wanted all along.

It was no big deal for Larkin. Harlander meant nothing, just another good-looking guy trading favors in Hollywood. There would be no lovers' quarrel. Chris, in haste, left the room, closing the door behind him. Larkin and Harlander didn't lose a beat. The interruption had only heightened the excitement of their relations.

Walking down the long upstairs corridor to his room at the opposite end of the hall, Chris could only think about doing exactly what he had become hooked on doing over the past nine months whenever the going got too rough for him. Robertson's renewed visits to Larkin had re-opened a free pipeline to the very best white powder available. Inhaling enormous doses of the substance, Chris buried his confusion deeper and deeper until he could no longer feel any pain.

In the months that he'd lived with David Larkin, the young man from the Midwest had slowly come to terms with his homosexuality. He was still unsure of his feelings and unable to openly admit his lifestyle, but he was beginning to accept the truth about himself.

Unfortunately, Chris had no capacity to understand, or accept the truth about David Larkin and his lifestyle of self-gratification. The producer was not in love with him. There was no deep friendship or lasting commitment on Larkin's part. Everything potentially good about the entire situation was all made up in Chris's mind.

While he had been somewhat promiscuous in his high school and college years, he never worried about long-term relationships, monogamous affairs, or feelings, the least important part of the equation, except for the feeling of pleasure.

Yet now, his entire life had turned in the other direction. Something he'd buried deep in his psyche had surfaced, and with it the expectation of feelings. He rejected promiscuity, and was stung by Larkin's affair with Harlander. The cocaine became a pain killer, at least for the moment. Chris needed the pain killer now more than ever before.

CHAPTER 27

By midnight Chris was so stoned on cocaine that his body shook uncontrollably. Literally bouncing off the walls of his quarters, his body dripping with sweat from the manic activity, he bolted from the room and ran towards Larkin's main staircase. Missing the first step, he tumbled down the curricular structure, nearly smashing his head directly on the marble floor below.

The thud of his body on the steps failed to attract anyone's attention. Chris pulled himself up off the floor, miraculously unscathed from the fall, and darted outside.

The street was totally deserted. A pitch black night surrounded him as he made his way up Ambazac Way and down onto Sunset Boulevard, a street that was busy twenty-four hours a day. Traffic sped past him as Sunset curved and snaked through Bel Air heading west towards Brentwood and the Pacific Ocean. There were no sidewalks, just steep embankments and the walls of million-dollar estates. Walking sober was treacherous along this stretch of dream town. High as a kite, walking down Sunset was Russian roulette.

The brisk night air was cold and he hadn't bothered to take a jacket. He stood shivering on Sunset jumping in fear with the onslaught of headlights chasing him. The steady stream of speeding luxury vehicles whizzed past blowing dust, dirt, and exhaust in his face. He put out his thumb to hitch a ride aimed west, toward the beach.

It seemed to Chris that at least a million cars passed him without stopping. He just kept walking with his arm extended and thumb out. At first he walked backwards, facing the oncoming traffic. With no success, Chris gave up on that approach and simply turned around keeping his thumb extended as he walked on. Another million cars passed him by.

All he could think of was making it to the ocean. At lands end, he could free himself of this horrible nightmare. The sea would cleanse his soul, make everything better. Just getting there was the mission… and how he completed it, on foot or by car, in half an hour or half the week, mattered not.

About an hour down Sunset, through Brentwood and into the Pacific Palisades, the road narrowed and climbed steeply up into the Santa Monica Mountains past Will Rogers Park. It was nearly 1:00 a.m., the temperature had dropped into the high forties, and the cars kept coming. Chris still had his thumb out. He decided to stand still and face the traffic for a few minutes and rest.

Suddenly, a small sports car pulled over. Its headlights blinded Chris. He squinted to see if someone had really stopped, or if it was a guy with a flat tire, or just a mirage.

"Chris, is that you?" a voice called out. "Hey, Chris, what the hell are you doing here?"

Chris still couldn't see the voice, only the bright glaring lights of the little car beaming down upon him. Searchlights in a prison camp from some distant tower. He walked closer, moving toward the lights, and the voice.

"Chris, hurry up, get in," the voice said. It was coming from above the car, on top of the lights. Chris was sure the cocaine was playing tricks on him. Maybe the voice wasn't calling him at all, maybe there was no voice.

"Hey man, get in. What the fuck are you doing out here in the middle of the fucking night?"

"Who is it?" Chris asked, squinting to see the voice.

"Well, who do you think it is, pal it's fucking Randy Stein, that's who's saving your hitchhiking ass at 1:30 in the morning!"

Chris got in the car. Randy hit the accelerator and swerved back onto Sunset, his wheels leaving a cloud of spurning dust behind him.

"Thanks Randy… for picking me up," Chris said.

"I thought it was you. Where are you going?"

"To the beach."

"Any particular beach?"

"The first one I can find."

"Isn't it a little late for a swim?"

"I just want to be at the ocean."

"Can I ask why?" Randy was sarcastic.

"I need to think, that's all."

"Hard to think at Larkin's house in Bel Air?" Randy knew that Chris was high, so he jabbed him even harder with his remarks. Randy's lack of inhibition also came from the consumption of far too much beer. The car reeked of alcohol.

Chris looked down at his feet, which had been butting up against something on the floor. Eight or ten empty beer bottles sloshed back and forth from under the seat of Randy's passenger compartment with every swerve of the Sunset travel.

"You're drunk," he said.

"And you're Jesus Christ," Randy answered.

Randy stepped on the gas as hard as he could, pushing his foot to the floor. The car became a projectile missile, no longer a passenger vehicle but a sortie flying a mission.

"I'll get you to the beach," Randy said. "We both can think there," he added. "I need to think, too. I've got a lot to think about, too," he said repeating himself.

"Watch out," Chris screamed as Randy drifted into the oncoming lane of traffic, right in front of a Buick station wagon. He managed to pull back just in time, but the guy in the wagon went off the curb trying to avoid him and took out a couple of mailboxes before coming to a stop. Chris looked behind them but could only see the small, glaring, red taillights of the wagon and clouds of dust. Randy said nothing, he just kept going, his foot to the floor.

Fortunately, at 1:30 in the morning, mothers with strollers aren't crossing the quaint downtown village shopping streets of the Pacific Palisades. If so, Randy would have murdered them all. He ignored all of the stoplights, racing through the reds without even flinching. The cops were apparently asleep, too.

"Relax, man, I've traveled this stretch a million times," Randy said to an increasingly uncomfortable Chris, "I know every inch of it. We'll be at the beach in two minutes." He reached down between his legs and found another bottle of beer. He handed it to Chris, then reached down again searching for more. When he couldn't feel the next bottle with his one free hand he looked down under the seat, completely ignoring the road.

"Watch OUT!" Chris screamed. This time the car was headed directly at a city work crew fixing something beneath the street. Flashing cones warned of the impending obstacles. The familiar yellow city truck was parked center, mid-Sunset, and sawhorses with black and white painted stripes surrounded the vehicle as well as the open manhole in the street.

"Watch out, goddamn it!" Chris yelled again. "What are you looking for under the seat?" he screamed.

Randy calmly raised his body revealing the treasure he'd located. Another bottle of beer.

"One for each of us," he said. Then he pulled the car to the left just in time to avoid catastrophe with the City of Los Angeles.

Randy told him to look for the bottle opener. It had fallen off the console and was probably somewhere on the floor beneath him. Chris managed to obey the order out of self-preservation. He just wanted Randy to drive. He'd do all the looking.

Finding the bottle opener just where he'd been told to look, Chris sat up and offered to open Randy's bottle. He handed it over directly. Then he opened his own, and took a giant gulp.

At last, they reached the final few miles of Sunset, past the Pacific Palisades High School and Temescal Canyon, when behind them, from seemingly out of nowhere, red, flashing lights of the police were on their tail. Apparently, not all of the cops were asleep at 1:30 a.m. Chris saw the police first out of the corner of his eye, and alerted Randy to stop while he began throwing the empty beer bottles out of the open Porsche helter skelter, as fast as he could.

The flying glass projectiles were bombs released from the careening sortie. They hit the dark pavement, exploding, sending their sparkling fragments out in multi-directions, causing the police to dodge the destruction coming at them. Randy pressed on faster, rather than listening to Chris's demands to pull over.

Within two minutes time they had two more vehicles with flashing red lights in pursuit. They were no match for Randy and his German getaway machine. A few old Ford Galaxies with red lights couldn't get him.

He deliberately swerved his car into the eastbound lane of Sunset. Even though it was the middle of the night, there was still some traffic in both directions. Eastbound cars were forced to run off the road or into the westbound lanes. Randy pulled the car in and out of the oncoming vehicles like an expert race driver despite his drunken condition. Chris managed to rid the car of all the evidence of beer. Not that it was going to matter at this point, with the armada of the LAPD chasing them.

Chris could see the Pacific Ocean beyond the final cliffs of Sunset Boulevard. Adrenalin raced through his body along with the cocaine, the beer, and the effects of the very cold night air against his T-shirt-clad chest. Randy seemed so much in control. He was the master who would prevail. Above the law, he would elude the little pests trying to curtail his fun.

They were so close to the beach, Chris could really smell the pungent sea air. The light of the moon illuminated the rippling tides below them and the glass-like Pacific spread out in all directions. Solace was around the corner, down the hill. Randy was actually going to escape the police. Nobody really ever got away like this. Chris was amazed. The police sirens were dimmer, the red lights smaller in the distance, as the Porsche hit the home stretch.

Randy floored the car again as he came around the final curve at the top of Sunset before descending the hill to the ocean. The car jumped like a horse kicked in its sides, and took off into the eastbound lane to avoid flipping from the excessive speed on the turn. Coming up the hill going no more than fifteen or twenty miles an hour was a big old U-haul truck. Both Randy and Chris saw it instantaneously. There were three passengers in the van sitting close, side-by-side. The six whites of their collective eyes were illuminated by the searchlights of Randy's speeding car hitting them directly across the face.

Chris reached over, reacting to the doom in front of them, and grabbed the wheel of the car. His athletic left arm locked on the wheel as he turned it with all his strength to the left, sending the car off the road in order to avoid a head on with the U-haul.

"Hit the brakes," Chris screamed at Randy who was still flooring the gas pedal. "Hit the brakes!"

It was too late for brakes. The sortie flew over the side of the Sunset-Palisades cliffs at one-hundred-twenty miles per hour. Hitting the jagged rocks of the five hundred foot drop to the ocean below, the car burst apart in flames before landing in the dirt beside the Pacific Coast Highway at the bottom.

At the top of the hill the three police cars arrived to find the people from the U-haul looking down over the cliff at the flaming wreck.

"It wasn't our fault. We didn't do it. It wasn't our fault," the men from the old truck kept repeating and repeating in shock.

One of the cops radioed for help and the three swirling red light-crowned black-and-whites multiplied into twenty. The fire department, a half-dozen ambulances, and two high-beamed helicopters overhead arrived on site as well.

They found the lifeless broken body of Chris Reynolds on top of the rocks, midway down the cliff. He had been thrown from the car, onto the jagged, sharp, rocks. Chris faced the Pacific, his eyes wide open and his hands still clutching tight to the bottle of beer.

Randy had been consumed by the flames of the wreckage. His unrecognizable body still smelled of alcohol as officers were finally able to remove the remains from the vehicle after the fire was extinguished. They stood back in horror, the stench of alcohol mixing with the smell of burning fuel, metal and human flesh. One policeman said it was the worst crash he'd ever witnessed.

"Poor bastards… poor drunken bastards."

The 4:00 a.m. call from the police to The Villa Serena with news of Randy's death was a bullet through Jennifer Hartman Stein's heart. Benton Stein had not come home that night after his argument with Randy at the Polo Lounge. He was, instead, in Laurie Dalton's arms, as Jennifer took the news alone. It was one time in her independent, stoic existence that being alone was unacceptable. She fell apart. Her sobbing echoed throughout the giant mansion as a platoon of loyal household servants rallied around her.

Bill was the first to hear the news about Chris. A student library card from U.S.C. found in Chris's wallet had the 23rd Place address on it. The police cross-checked the address with the phone company to come up with a number, and called.

Half asleep in dreamland, enjoying his newfound success and recovering from the previous all night work session, Bill was at first incoherent with the news. All he could say was "What! Who's this? What?" as the officer tried to explain the situation.

The horrible reality finally sunk in, and Bill began screaming out his emotions. He pounded on the walls of the tiny apartment that belonged to his dead best friend, and kicked in the door with his bare feet. Neighbors, awakened by his cries and his pounding, rushed sleepy-eyed, scantily covered to see what had happened in their normally quiet hovel. They found Bill weeping, sitting on the edge of his mattress, and they came to his side to comfort him, in Spanish.

Nobody called David Larkin. He spent the rest of the night with Mark Harlander, unaware of what he would find the next morning as he turned on the TV news in his dressing room prior to leaving for work at the studio.

CHAPTER 28

The papers and the TV journalists called the accident a "drunken midnight joy ride" that claimed the lives of two young friends, recent U.S.C. grads. One, the son of prominent LA industrialist/movie mogul Benton Stein and the other a boy from Illinois. All the press went to Benton Stein, not Randy or Chris. It wasn't that Randy Stein had died, it was that Benton Stein's son had died... along with a friend. Chris Reynold's name was only mentioned sporadically.

There were front page pictures of Benton and Jennifer, TV news crews stalked the gates of The Villa and transmitted the video image of the mansion across TV screens throughout the day.

Benton wanted the entire incident buried along with his son. The publicity in one day was killing Jennifer and hurting his own fragile public image. The boy was dead. The evidence was reckless drunken driving. That was it. He never bothered to explore the whys, or talk about their confrontation over Laurie Dalton in the Polo Lounge earlier that night. These facts would go to the grave with Randy Stein.

Everyone wanted to know how Randy and Chris ended up together. The L.A. Times reported that Chris worked late at the studio, leaving after ten, quoting a statement from co-worker "Marjorie Neal," Marie's name, spelled wrong. The woman told the press that there had been no drinking, and that Chris was in a very good mood. So what happened between 10:30 and 1:30?

The mood at the studio was, in a word, bizarre. Laurie was crying in her trailer and wouldn't talk to anyone. Larkin had shut his door and ordered Marie to keep away all strangers. Bill was no stranger, so he did get in to see him.

D.L. sat behind his desk working on scripts, totally immersed in his show. His outward appearance showed no sign of grief or strain.

"What happened, David?" Bill asked.

"I don't know. I only know what the press is reporting."

"Did you see Chris last night? Did he come home to your house?"

"I saw him for a second. Then he left and went out again. I spent a quiet evening at home. I was in bed by ten."

"Was he mad or upset, did he act strange at all?"

"I'm telling you, he didn't say anything."

"So that's it end of chapter good-bye Chris. He was my best friend he was your goddamned lover! Show some goddamned feeling, goddamn you! He wasn't some stranger that went over a cliff. Don't you care at all? Doesn't anyone mean anything to you?" Bill was relentless. Despite Larkin's repeated pleas for him to control himself, Bill pressed on, looking for some remorse, some bit of feeling in Larkin. "It's not business as usual around here, David! Hiding behind your TV show will not make the memory of Chris go away. Do you think you're going to shoot anything decent today when your star is locked in her dressing room sobbing uncontrollably?" Bill couldn't crack D.L. He remained stoically calm in the face of the truth.

"I'm very sorry about Chris." D.L. said, finally addressing Bill's cry for response. "But there's nothing I can say or do to bring him back. I don't know what happened, and I have no idea why he was with Randy Stein. I do know we have work to do here, and we're going to do it. We are fighting for survival here, Mr. Parker. Next week when the ratings come in, the nation is not going to excuse us for a bad show because our runner was killed in a drunken auto accident."

Bill lost all composure at Larkin's cold assessment.

He slammed his fist down on Larkin's desk and screamed at him, "Chris was not...our runner... He was your lover your lover, goddamn you and he was my best friend." He left Larkin's office in disgust and slammed the door behind him.

• • •

February in LA was not generally so cold. By mid-morning, mist still hung low to the ground creating a "fog in the moors" kind of image amidst the alleyways of the old studio lot. Through the haze, sets were being rolled in and out of the old cavernous soundstages. Wardrobe racks filled with all variety of costumes rolled by, as Bill made his way back to the writers' bungalow.

He passed by Laurie's trailer and decided to knock. To his surprise, Benton Stein opened the door. Bill didn't know what to say. He just stood there facing Stein, whose face was as red as a tomato, swollen and puffy, his eyes bloodshot.

"I'm sorry, Mr. Stein." Bill's first words were brief. Benton Stein nodded his head. Laurie was somewhere in the back of the tin can crying.

"Are you here to see Miss Dalton, young man?" Benton didn't remember Bill, and assumed he was some kid working on the lot just doing his job.

"What happened, sir?" Bill said, taking Benton by surprise. "Do you know how this happened?"

"Excuse me?" was Stein's only response. This stranger had no business questioning him about the events of his son's death. "I have to be going now," he said matter-of-factly. Benton Stein stepped out of the trailer and down the two metal steps onto the studio pavement, leaving Bill with his questions unanswered as he walked off around the corner and vanished.

"Laurie, it's Bill, are you back here?" Bill could hear her weeping and wanted to warn her that he was there. Passing through the crowded trailer he found the star sitting at her makeup table, just as she did every morning before shooting began. The table was a mess, she was a mess. Makeup was spilled everywhere, and what little she had managed to apply to her face was running down in streaks carried by her waves of tears.

Laurie was totally inconsolable. Bill did not know that the young star had not only lost her good friend Chris, her agent Randy, but also her lover, Benton Stein.

Benton had come to the trailer to say goodbye, to tell her that he could never see her again. There was no explanation, and the more she protested the less he would say. Finally, he told her that he loved her, but he would never leave Jennifer, especially now, and that it was best to part friends.

Bill let Laurie know that he was there for her, but he couldn't find any additional words to comfort her. He left Laurie to cry by herself in her trailer and went back to his bungalow.

Back at the writers' quarters it was a different story. The guys didn't really know Chris, or Randy for that matter, so it was "too bad" and on with the business of the show.

Gary Burger was due in Larkin's office for an eleven a.m. script overhaul meeting. Bill walked in amidst the final throes of preparation for the conference with Larkin.

"Where the hell have you been?" Burger demanded, as Bill entered the small reception area of the writers' quarters. Thirty-six hours earlier he had been kissing Bill's ass, begging forgiveness, telling him that they could be friends.

Bill had stayed at the bungalow all night to rework Burger's script, save his job, and this cocky attitude was his reward. Burger knew that Bill's best friend had died only hours ago. He also knew that Chris had been Bill's connection to Larkin.

Bill looked at Burger and seethed with hatred for this low, insecure, and two-faced man. Burger could surely feel Bill's animosity. He was nervous about his meeting with Larkin, so he pressed Bill for an answer concerning his whereabouts.

"You got my script yesterday before I went home to sleep. I've done my share...so get off my fucking back," Bill replied.

"Don't talk to me like that, you little piss-ant nothing," Burger said.

"What did you call me?"

"You heard it. Who do you think you are? You've got no credentials what do you know about writing for television?"

Bill stepped back, paused, then returned the fire. "Apparently I know enough. My scripts are in production yours are in the wastepaper basket."

As Bill turned away, Burger reached out and grabbed him by the back of his shirt and yanked Bill back towards him. The force of the jerk ripped his shirt and spun Bill around. Coming around he leveled a right hook into Burger's jaw, which sent him flying back against the wall of the bungalow. The entire building shook from the hit.

The ensuing fight brought the rest of the writers scrambling out of their corners to watch. No one tried to break it up. They just watched with eyes popping and mouths open, catching flies. This sort of thing only happened in the scripts they wrote not in real life.

The excitement was over after Bill delivered a knee to Burger's groin, followed by a powerful elbow to his gut, sending Burger to the floor holding his balls and moaning.

Finally, picking himself up, Burger glared at Bill, then headed for Larkin's office for their meeting out of breath and out of sorts. Piles of script pages were in his hands and despite his bruised ego and sore balls he was prepared to save his job. This was, after all, week four, and his option was due for renewal.

Larkin flagged him in and shut the door. "Parker's rewrite was damn good. Do you agree?" Larkin asked.

"Yes. It was good, D.L. Did you make any further revisions?"

"I did did you?"

"As a matter of fact, I did. The fourth act break was still weak I wrote in an argument between Laurie and 'Eric'." Burger fumbled through his massive pile of papers finally locating what he was after, giving the scene to Larkin.

D.L. took the pages and read them in front of Burger who sat in anxious silence. D.L. finished, then looked up at the ten-thousand-dollar-a-week head writer. "You think this improves the fourth act?" he asked matter-of-factly, seeming to solicit an affirmative response from Burger.

"Yes, D.L. I think it makes it better."

"When did you do this? This morning?"

"Yes, D.L. This morning."

"I see." Larkin buzzed Marie on the intercom. "Bring me those pages from the staff, will you?"

Marie soon entered with a stack of papers matching Burger's load. D.L. thumbed through and pulled out two pages that matched the ones Burger had given him with the rewrite of act four.

"Funny," D.L. said, "I have the same pages here in my pile, only Ken Lindt's name is on the top right corner of each page. He's that young writer we hired off that ABC soap, isn't he?"

Burger just stared at D.L. Where did he get all of the writer's pages? How did he know who was doing what?

"You see, Mr. Burger, I have a long standing policy of having my associate Marie collect copies of all my writers' work each and every day from the writers' secretary. I review all of it, even the work they feel is sub-standard. I knew that Mr. Lindt had written that new ending for act four, and you're quite right, it is good a definite improvement. Oh, and one other thing…you're fired."

Burger left the room destroyed. The man limped off the lot and drove away, never bothering to go back to the writers' bungalow. Marie made sure his office was neatly packed and shipped out by the studio teamsters.

Ultimately, Larkin postponed filming for half the day in response to the death of Randy and Chris. He'd use the time to fine-tune Bill's script revisions and allow all the production service technicians to gear up for the new show. The morning off had, in fact, served Larkin well. The entire crew went to lunch at noon, and by one they were ready to roll.

Bill walked into Studio 21 at about 1:30. He'd been jogging the studio perimeter for two hours thinking and trying to release some of his pain. Expecting to find a still empty soundstage, he barged right in the door, slamming it accidentally behind him. Bill ignored the red light outside the studio which was flashing, warning everyone that work was in progress. He figured the light was left on by mistake. But, D.L. was back to work.

The director called "cut" as the slamming door ruined the scene in progress. Bill was more surprised by his actions than anyone. He apologized to the cast and crew and slithered to the back of the stage, out of the way, and the director regrouped his actors for the next take.

As he crossed to the rear, Bill caught Laurie's eye. There she was, the sobbing, inconsolable girl he'd seen only hours before in her trailer covered in running makeup. Laurie now looked absolutely beautiful. Not only was she gorgeous, she was in total control of the set, and specifically, the particular scene. The director was ready, and the cameras rolled. Bill leaned up against the back wall in the dark, folded his arms across his chest and watched an incredible performance of his very own work. He didn't hear anyone coming up next to him, but when the scene finished, the lights came on revealing David Larkin leaning up against the wall beside him.

"Pretty good, don't you think?" D.L. said to Bill.

Following a moment of uncomfortable silence, Bill agreed. It was better than pretty good. It was remarkable.

"Burger is no longer with us," D.L. told Bill, catching him totally by surprise.

"What?"

"His option was not picked up... yours is... do you have an agent yet, Mr. Parker?"

CHAPTER 29

etective Arnold could hear the commotion coming down the hall. He had created the avalanche himself by sending his men out on a round-up, bringing in some of his favorite suspects. Just an attempt to flush out a killer... or maybe two. Three separate squad cars had been dispatched to bring in Karen Barker and her boyfriend, J.J., Howard Hillman and Mr. Lee, David Larkin's butler. They were timed to arrive back at the station fifteen minutes apart so none of the people would see the others. At the same time, three investigative teams were dispatched with search warrants in hand to raid both the beach house and the Bel Air residence of David Larkin, along with the Beverly Hills mansion belonging to Karen Barker. Arnold was tired of "pussy-footing" around with the Hollywood folks.

"Get your arm off of me," Karen Barker protested loud enough for the entire station to hear her. "Police brutality, that's what it is. I'm calling my lawyer," she yelled at the top of her lungs. The former wife of the deceased movie star, Peter Barker, looked frail. Thin, haggard, her blonde hair hanging straight down over her bony shoulders, Karen Barker bore little resemblance to the former model and beauty queen she had been in her prior life.

Arnold's detectives entered, escorting Barker and her boyfriend, J.J., a stereotypical muscle-bound southern California surfer. Barker immediately lunged at Arnold, who was safely planted behind his massive left-over World War II, federal government-issue desk.

"What's the big idea dragging us downtown?"

"We've cooperated with you all along," added her muscular boyfriend wearing his trademark tank top.

"I want to call my lawyer. I'm not saying one word until he's present." Karen looked like a mad dog on a short, tangled leash.

Her blonde hair was swinging over her face in all directions, while her lips curled and her eyes popped with each expletive. Arnold tried to calm her down.

"Mrs. Barker, this is standard procedure. Nothing to be alarmed about. We needed to ask you downtown to ask some additional questions that could only be completed here. You may call your lawyer right now if you like use my phone." Arnold handed Karen Barker his black phone. It was an old-fashioned multi-line model, and a row of discolored plastic buttons on the bottom were all flashing in succession.

"There's no free line," she said.

"Just push one down and dial as soon as it frees up," Arnold instructed her.

"This is insane, absolutely outrageous," she mumbled as she caught a free line. In a rush to push down on the plastic button, Karen broke the nail her index finger and the expletives began to fly once again.

Arnold finally told her to "cool it" and make her call, then left her with his investigators and went to another office where still another team of his men were waiting with Mr. Lee.

Lee looked nervous and guilty, like he had committed a crime himself. He was a small man to begin with, but sitting hunched over in a folding chair in the large empty interrogation room, he became a tiny creature, drawing inward, like a snail retreating into its shell. When Detective Arnold walked in the room, Lee sat up, somewhat raising his head slowly as he stared at the John Wayne-sized Hispanic inspector. The look of Arnold sent Lee sliding back down, further into the small chair.

Arnold put out a hand to greet Lee, introducing himself and explaining that he had a few questions pertaining to the death of Mr. Peter Barker. Lee was visibly surprised, assuming that all of this had something to do with Chris Reynolds. Lee had liked Chris, and his death saddened him.

"Did you say Mr. Barker?" Lee asked Sergeant Arnold.

"That's right, Peter Barker, the movie star. He worked for your boss Mr. Larkin, didn't he?" Arnold questioned him directly, over-annunciating each of his words, presuming Mr. Lee didn't understand English clearly because of his thick Chinese accent.

"I don't know if he work for Mr. Larkin. I think so, but I don't know, can't say for sure. Sorry," Lee replied.

"Mr. Barker was a friend of your boss, Mr. Larkin, for many years," Arnold said, again very slowly and deliberately, hoping to get a response.

"I don't know, I only work for Mr. Larkin for a few years, couldn't say how long he knows Mr. Barker."

"But he did know him?" Arnold rephrased his question.

"Yes. He come to house before."

"Mr. Lee, what are your duties for Mr. Larkin?" Arnold asked.

"I am major domo for Mr. Larkin. I do all things for him."

"Such as could you give us a list, please? Do you always drive him?" Arnold asked.

"No. Sometimes he drive himself and sometimes Mr. Chris would drive him." Lee began to break with the mention of Chris's name. Arnold didn't understand.

"Mr. Chris? Who's Mr. Chris?" Arnold asked.

"He Mr. Larkin's friend who died last night in terrible car crash off Sunset," Lee told him. Arnold looked over at his other men. One of them handed him a newspaper. The story about Chris and Randy was front page. Arnold took the paper and read it, then set it aside. Lee waited.

"Now Mr. Lee, I want you to think back many months to when Mr. Barker was alive. Did you ever drive Mr. Larkin to Mr. Barker's condominium at The Sierra Towers?"

Lee hesitated, then answered fully and simply. "Many times, we go there."

"Do you remember when Mr. Barker died?" Larkin asked.

Lee hesitated again, then answered simply, "Yes."

"Did you drive Mr. Larkin over to see Mr. Barker on that night, the night Mr. Barker died?" Arnold moved right up to Mr. Lee in the small chair. He used his physical dominance to intimidate Mr. Lee.

Again, a long hesitation from Lee, then a simple answer, "Yes."

Arnold was flabbergasted. In his wildest dreams he didn't expect this from Lee. Arnold figured he would to answer with an, "I don't remember," a lie, or a simple no. The truth had been so far from the reality of this case from the start.

"What time did you drive Mr. Larkin over to Mr. Barker's building? Can you recall?" Cracking the truth had been so simple, a floodgate of questions from Arnold flowed forth.

By the end of the questioning Mr. Lee had said enough for Detective Arnold to have cause to arrest David Larkin. The limo out the back way, a nervous, silent David Larkin in the back seat coming out of The Sierra Towers just after Barker's plunge… this was finally real evidence for Detective Hector Arnold. He left Lee in the interrogation room and moved on.

Howard Hillman was just as unhappy about being a guest of the police department as Karen Barker. Arnold's two men had literally taken him off the studio lot. Their departure was witnessed by countless people, and the news was now fueling a relentless and starving rumor mill that Hillman feared he would never be quite able to turn around no matter what. The producer had called his attorney from the studio office the moment the detectives arrived to "bring him downtown" for further questioning. The lawyer was now present with him in the police headquarters.

"Hello, Mr. Hillman," Arnold spoke in a friendly fashion as he entered the room. "I'm sorry to have to bring you here like this, but there are some further matters that need resolving."

"I'm David Wooten, Mr. Hillman's counsel and voice," the lawyer said to Arnold in a less cordial tone.

"Nice to meet you, sir. Shall we proceed?" Arnold asked.

"It's your sideshow, Detective Arnold. What was so vital that my client had to come downtown? Couldn't this have been resolved in his office, or at my office by appointment?"

Arnold's response was a cool "No."

Wooten turned to Hillman with a look of "We'll see" on his Ivy League, waspy, horn-rimmed face. The detectives shut off the lights in the room and illuminated a large panel on the wall that turned out to be a one-way glass looking into the next room. He then hit a switch that allowed the conversation from that room to be heard through a large speaker overhead.

Hillman at once recognized Karen Barker and J.J. as they continued talking with two police investigators. She was still spitting mad, complaining about the inconvenience and embarrassment of being hauled downtown. Between her bitter complaints, Karen Barker continued to plead total ignorance about her ex-husband's death. There was nothing that she could tell the police, she just had nothing to do with it. Her boyfriend was quick to agree. Hillman watched in silence.

Perhaps Arnold had given some sort of signal, or maybe it was just perfect timing, but one of the investigators began a new line of questioning that sparked everyone's interest.

"Mrs. Barker, we have information that indicates you may have had a relationship with one of your ex-husband's good friends."

The complaining stopped. Karen Barker said nothing.

"Is it true that prior to your ex-husband's death you were meeting a man secretly in Malibu?"

Karen still said nothing. Arnold looked over at Hillman in the dark. The sweat on his forehead glistened. Karen finally spoke.

"So what?" she said defiantly.

"Mrs. Barker, we have sources that confirm you were seeing someone at a certain Malibu beach house on a weekly basis for over a year."

Karen became more defensive.

As the investigator pressed, she increasingly refused to cooperate. The sweat was pouring off Howard Hillman as he watched the entire charade through the one-way glass. His attorney told him to sit down and relax, no doubt trying to figure out some excuse to give Arnold concerning his client's guilty behavior. Then the detectives in the other room with Karen Barker broke her resolve.

"How long were you seeing David Larkin at his beach house?"

"What?" Karen Barker screamed. "Seeing David Larkin at his beach house? That's what your sources told you? You've got some pretty incredible sources, stupid sources, but incredible," she snapped.

"Were you or were you not seeing your former husband's good friend and producer at his beach house in Malibu?" The detectives demanded a straight answer. Karen stalled, then answered confidently, "Yes, you goddamned fools. Yes, David's beach house became my love nest. What does this have to do with Peter's death anyway? The affair was over months and months before he died. Even if he had known, what would it have mattered? I had a new love, anyway." Karen looked over to see if she still had the new surfer love. He was there, ever the obedient dog.

"I thought Larkin was gay." The puppy dog spoke in hushed tones. The detectives didn't respond; they looked right in the one-way glass as if to somehow get a clue of direction that might come from Arnold on the other side. Nothing happened. Karen looked at all of them and smiled. She winked at her boyfriend.

"That'll be all for the moment, Mrs. Barker. Please relax for a few minutes until Detective Arnold returns." The investigators left the room.

Arnold turned the lights back on in his room, and faced Hillman and his attorney. "Are you warm, Mr. Hillman?" he asked the sweating producer.

"I'm just getting over a cold. My body is out of whack. Can you get me some water?" Hillman responded in his newly composed, secure manner. Wooten was off the hook. His client had been provided with a convoluted visa, all courtesy of the outcome of twisted police questioning.

"Mr. Hillman, you indicated to me in our last meeting that Karen Barker might have been having an affair with one of her husband's friends, but you didn't elaborate. Do you wish to now confirm Mrs. Barker's own admission of her relationship with David Larkin?"

Hillman was astounded. Karen had never said that she was having an affair with David, only that she was having an affair at his beach house. Was he the only one listening carefully? Hillman didn't know what to say. If he told the truth, implicating himself as the lover she had been meeting at Larkin's house, he would jeopardize his own marriage, his career, and possibly his freedom. Karen Barker had kept her promise under impossible circumstances not to reveal their affair, an affair that had been over for more than a year. More importantly, Hillman's dalliance with Karen had been the only deviance in a twenty-eight year marriage.

"Look," Hillman began to speak. Wooten stopped him, telling Arnold that he had nothing to say. Hillman spoke again anyway.

"He's right. I don't have anything to say. Karen Barker's private life is none of my business. I told you that before, and that's all I can say now."

"Did David Larkin ever discuss with you the fact that he and Mrs. Barker were having an affair?" repeated Detective Arnold relentlessly.

"No. Never. He never did that." Hillman was very secure with that answer. It would have passed any lie detector test in the nation.

"Do you have knowledge of Mr. Larkin's sexual preference, Mr. Hillman?"

"What?" he replied indignantly.

"Does Mr. Larkin like women… or men… or both?"

"You'll have to ask him yourself, Detective," Hillman said. "Now, if you don't have further questions that I can answer, I need to get back to the studio."

"May we go now?" Wooten asked.

"Yes, you may go. Thanks for your time, Mr. Hillman, and good luck with your new movie."

Detective Arnold was pathetically, but slyly patronizing to the exiting mogul. Hillman made no comment.

• • •

As David Larkin masterfully orchestrated his actors on "The Reilly's of San Marino" set, the police systematically tore apart both his residences with the authority of a court-ordered search warrant. Uniformed officers pulled apart every drawer, searching the most remote corners of his ordered and elegant existence. Years of painstaking care protecting the perfection of his amassed material wealth, undone in a matter of hours. The fingerprint marks of a dozen official hands smudged the silk wall coverings of his Bel Air estate, and heavy soled rubber, official-issue shoes, blackened and scuffed the polished blonde herringbone wood floors of his beach getaway.

On orders from the officer in charge, the crews were as careful as bulls in a pen could be. The worst part was pulling apart the closets. Thousand-dollar silk suits strewn across furniture. Shoes, dozens of pairs of fine English boots and Italian loafers turned upside down and inside out in the pursuit of evidence.

By late afternoon the exhaustive searching had turned up nothing more than some pornographic men's magazines. The crews were instructed to start putting everything back in order, as best they could. It was like telling a troop of conquering World War II GI's to re-hang the Rothschild collection in a war torn chateau. One of the policemen actually placed one of Larkin's Salvador Dali lithographs back on the wall, upside down, without noticing. Another one of the rookie members of the team called out from a downstairs coat closet in the Bel Air search.

"Hey, sergeant, I think I've found something," he said. The officer came running.

"What is it?"

"Look at this." The rookie revealed a small silver box with the initials P.B. engraved on its hinged lid. Inside the box, a plastic baggie with the remains of a white powdered substance that looked, smelled, and tasted like cocaine. The officer examined the find carefully.

"Where did you get this?" he asked.

"Here, in the pocket of this leather jacket, sir." The rookie pointed to a jacket hanging in the closet.

The sergeant put the silver box in the evidence bag and instructed the young officer to take the jacket as well to be examined by the lab.

• • •

Larkin called "cut" on the final scene of filming for the day, joining his weekly staff director on Stage 21 to provide "leadership" and "moral support" in time of crisis. Laurie Dalton had indeed risen to the occasion. Her performance was better than ever. It amazed Bill how an actress could override a crushing reality to give such a performance. It was indeed part of the skill. Laurie used the deaths of Randy and Chris, and the breakup with Benton to act the hell out of her script. Perhaps later, after the final scene, she would fall apart again, drink herself into oblivion, or, take an entire bottle of sleeping pills. But when the cameras rolled she was one-hundred-percent there, in front of them.

The same was true for Larkin, behind the cameras. He was the almighty producer. Against all odds he'd pulled together a distraught, emotional crew and cast, and pulled out of them an excellent days' work, in half a day. For the first time, Bill was actually feeling guilty about mourning his friend, not writing anything all day. Everyone else had performed but him. What was his excuse, what were his feelings?

Larkin asked Bill to meet with him in his office before leaving the studio. When Bill got there around 5:30, he found John Moran also waiting to see him.

"You've done a rather remarkable job here in just five weeks," Moran told Bill. "The scripts I've seen are the best I've read around this place in some time. We, that is myself and the rest of the production heads here at the studio, want you to know that we appreciate your work and we'd like to offer you a long-term deal to make you a permanent member of the studio family." Moran sounded like the President conferring a Congressional Medal of Honor.

Bill's head swam. "I'm flattered," he said to Moran. "I'd like to continue writing for this show," he added.

"There will be much more for you, Parker. We'd like to talk to you about writing a film script for us in May when 'The Reilly's' goes on hiatus." Moran looked at Bill, who was caught completely off-guard by the adulation.

"A film script?" Bill repeated.

"That's right," Moran said. "I understand Mr. Burger is leaving us today. David has agreed not to replace him with another head writer, for the time being. We've got our eyes on you. Keep up this performance for the rest of this season and the job might be yours next year, not to mention an Emmy nomination, maybe even the actual award."

"An Emmy," Bill was shocked. They were talking Emmys and he'd only been a writer for five weeks. He wasn't even officially on staff, he didn't have an agent and he'd never joined the Writer's Guild, although he'd lied and told them he was a member, intending to join with his first paycheck and a writing credit or two.

"Your confidence in me is very flattering," he told Moran and Larkin, even though he felt their timing was lousy. His success was a bittersweet victory. Bill couldn't stop thinking about Chris, and finally after John Moran left and Bill was alone with D.L. he tried again to talk about Chris with the boss.

"David, don't get me wrong. I couldn't be more grateful for your support. Writing for you is exactly what I wanted to do. I consider myself very lucky,"

"But," Larkin added, anticipating the "but" to follow.

"But don't you care about what happened to Chris? How can you act like everything is fine? I'm really having trouble with the 'business must go on' approach. I need to know where you stand and why you don't show any emotion over his death."

David Larkin walked around his office before answering. "You're not going to like my response, Bill, but I'm going to give it to you anyway. What I'm about to say is between us. I want you to know my personal view because I believe you have great talent and I want to develop a long standing working relationship with you. But I also caution you that I'm not talking to you as a close friend, or as a confidante, I am neither one to you."

"Okay, I understand," Bill replied. Larkin turned and faced him.

"I am sad over his death, but I'm not broken up. We were not that close. I used him a little, I admit it. He used me, and he didn't get what he wanted. Chris was in a hurry to please, in a hurry to make it as an actor, in a hurry to score, in a hurry to live, and to ultimately die. He wasn't prepared for the uphill struggle. He didn't really know himself, his strengths and weaknesses. Mostly, he hadn't a clue about life in the Hollywood fast lane, but he certainly liked the perks. I don't know what Chris expected from me, a career, a home, a loyal friendship, a committed relationship. Maybe he wanted all of this. But I certainly wasn't prepared to give him any of it. Not all at once, anyway. If I'm to blame for what happened in any way it's only that I indulged him too much, that I made the good life too accessible, that I didn't stop him from overdoing the coke. But I wasn't his father, and

I wasn't even his best friend. You were. Whatever our relationship was, it was short, and sweet. Life goes on. This business certainly goes on, never stopping, never letting up for one second. I, for one, never intend to allow it to get the better of me. I plan to stay on top, to fight to stay on top. There's always somebody waiting to take it all away from those on top. Maybe it's you, Bill Parker. Maybe you are the one waiting to dethrone the almighty David Larkin. Should I be wary of you? Are you planning my demise, and your rise to glory, as we sit and speak of Chris's death?"

Bill was horrified listening to Larkin. He didn't know what to say, which was fine because Larkin didn't want him to speak, anyway.

Larkin continued, "So let this be a warning to you, Bill Parker. I'm admitting you to the club of those that count in Hollywood. But the membership comes with a steep price. I will always watch my back that you are not there to stab it, and I will continue to support you and elevate your career as long as you deliver for me. So then, you see, that the business is not just the mythical "who you know gets you ahead," it's really the "how good you are" that ultimately counts. And if you want to be a member of the Club, you better be damn good and play by the rules. My rules. Do you read me, Mr. Parker?"

Bill looked at Larkin. His harsh words of reality destroyed all the fantasy of the dream. It was not supposed to be like this. Bill felt like he was making a pact with the devil. His talent and hard work had tipped the scales in his direction. But now, facing a giant leap in success, the dream was more elusive than ever before, further away, harder to grasp, impossible to believe. Worse, the dream was suddenly tainted, dirty.

"Here, take these story outlines for the next month of shows. I want your written comments by close of business tomorrow. We'll start working on the next few scripts together, okay?" Larkin handed the pages to Bill.

Taking them, Bill shook D.L.'s hand without responding.

"And by the way, I offered to hold an open house at my home following Randy's funeral at Benton Stein's request. The service is scheduled for Saturday morning at Forest Lawn in Glendale. I think you should attend."

Bill didn't answer. He left Larkin's office with the script outlines in hand and went back to his bungalow to work, to release his anger and guilt, and to refocus the dream.

CHAPTER 30

The remainder of the week was an emotional roller coaster ride that wouldn't stop. David Larkin had gone in to a fit of rage upon discovering that the police had turned both his homes inside-out searching for evidence linking him to the Peter Barker death. The controlling almighty producer became ultra-controlling, totally circumspect, and distant. He retreated into a protective shell patrolled by the best lawyers money could buy. Larkin was outraged that the police had invaded his privacy with such recklessness. He'd cooperated with the police, or so he thought. Besides, he didn't kill Barker. He knew that. But now he was obviously a prime suspect in what the police were calling a murder. The revelation of Mr. Lee's testimony downtown, and the rumor about a recovery of secretive, incriminating evidence from the search put Larkin's attorneys on full alert. On their advice, Larkin assumed a low profile and took cover.

Filming on "The Reilly's" was slow, but not disastrous without D.L. calling every shot behind the studio director. Everybody did their jobs and completed the work within a reasonable schedule, but it seemed mechanical without Larkin's omnipresence.

Laurie Dalton was especially flat. The great young star needed the prodding of Larkin in order to shine during her week of crisis. Now he was concentrating on his own problems and she had to fend for herself. Adrift in a sea of rewrites without David Larkin there constantly inducing her best instincts, making her give her very best performances, all Laurie could think about was Benton Stein.

The deflated energy of the star transmitted to everyone. News released by the coroner regarding Randy and Chris didn't help. The alcohol and cocaine levels found were of lethal proportions in the bodies of both victims. Naturally, the local and national media used the information to their exploitive best. Ironically, Larkin's retreat further created even greater opportunity for Bill. John Moran summoned him to the executive suite daily to go over story outlines, script development, and weekly casting layouts. By default Bill had been elevated to the rank of writer-producer without even a negotiation. A more experienced writer would have put on the brakes and called in the agents for a fast and healthy renegotiation of salary and title. But the new kid with the big dream accepted the challenge without demand and was more than thrilled to take home the Writer's Guild weekly scale pay of just under two thousand dollars.

On Thursday afternoon, David Larkin asked Bill to see him following the day's shooting. He wanted to discuss the funeral arrangements for Randy. Larkin intended on keeping his promise to Benton and Jennifer Stein by holding the open house after the burial on Saturday. With the police breathing down his back, he was really in no mood to do it, and he needed Bill's help to coordinate information with the staff.

Coordinating Randy Stein's wake was not a task Bill accepted without protest. In the end, Bill knew that this was no time to enlist any moral imperatives. There was no right and wrong to discuss. It was too late in Randy's case, and besides, Larkin was under too much pressure.

Bill took over for D.L. and made the announcement to cast and crew inviting those who cared to attend Randy's funeral and the open house that would follow.

"What about Chris?" asked one of the girls in the wardrobe department. "When's his funeral?" Bill didn't know what to say. He realized that he hadn't even asked D.L. if he knew whether the police had contacted Chris's family in Illinois.

"The arrangements haven't been made yet with his family. But the open house at David Larkin's will be for both of them." Bill satisfied the girl and the rest of the crew of Chris's friends, who really didn't know, or care much about Randy Stein.

Bill turned Larkin's reception for Randy into one for Chris Reynolds as well without clearing the matter with Larkin. He would explain later. Meanwhile, Moran had called another meeting and Bill was late.

• • •

Laurie asked Bill to escort her to the funeral at Forest Lawn on Saturday morning. He picked her up at her West Hollywood apartment by 9:00 a.m., an hour early, in order to get to the cemetery before the throngs of press and public gathered at the front gate seeking a glimpse of despair in the faces of the famous. Laurie's giant black-framed dark glasses hid most of her face, and her feelings. The rest was obliterated by the thick blonde hair that had become her trademark.

To avoid the paparazzi at Forest Lawn, Bill and Laurie would have had to have arrived by dawn. Being an hour early was, in fact, useless. Bill inadvertently drove Laurie right into a hornets' nest of reporters in his old blue Mustang.

The service was called for 11:00 a.m. in the chapel, with internment to follow in the Hartman family crypt. By 10:30 the police were called in to control the crowd which had grown to over two thousand people. Every agent, lawyer, manager, studio and network executive, publicist, producer, and star turned out to say goodbye to Randy Stein, and to say hello to Benton. The Country Club crowd was there too, as were most of the southland's captains of industry and government.

A very solemn and short service was provided by Jennifer's family minister, the Reverend Arthur Wolcott Emerson, who had presided over most of the major events in her life, including her only son's christening some twenty-two years earlier. Reverend Emerson delivered the eulogy as well as the prayers. There were no other speakers.

Benton Stein watched from the private family pew and cried silently for his lost boy. He had tried to come to terms with Randy's death, but it was impossible for him. His actions had killed his son, he believed, and he couldn't shake his immense guilt. Praying to God, any God that would listen, any God that would hear him the God of his Jewish roots or the God of his Christian wife he begged for forgiveness, for guidance, for some vision to help him cope with this loss for which he harbored full responsibility.

Laurie Dalton desperately wanted to run to her grieving lover's side and tell him how much she cared, but it was impossible. Bill did his best to comfort her, still unaware that her tears flowed more for the loss of the father than for the loss of the son. They stayed in the background as best they could, joined by David Larkin and his ever-loyal assistant, Marie O'Neil.

The mourners left the chapel and the pallbearers carried Randy's coffin to its final resting place. The Reverend Emerson recited the Lord's Prayer and the coffin was placed in the family crypt, next to Jennifer's parents.

• • •

Back at the Larkin estate in Bel Air, a young woman had arrived from Philadelphia. Jodi Winkler had flown into LA the night before, spending Friday night alone at the Westwood Marquis Hotel, choosing not to call Bill. She had debated going to Randy's funeral, deciding against it at the last minute, preferring to wait and meet Bill at Larkin's house for Randy's wake.

Her presence shocked Bill as he arrived with Laurie. Jodi's hair was different. She'd cut it shorter. Dressed in a suit of elegant black wool cashmere, collared and cuffed in black suede, the former love of his life and the woman he thought he'd never see again, looked very beautiful standing in Larkin's grand entrance hall. Crossing one leg in front of the other like a ballerina ready to plie, Jodi looked more at peace than he had ever seen her look before.

Leaving Laurie at the door, Bill ran to Jodi, throwing his arms around her, thrilled to see her again. Bill believed that she had come back to him, and he was very excited that out of this tragedy might come a new beginning for both of them. This time things would work out better. After all, he was on his way now, the career was happening. They could move into a better apartment, Jodi could pick anything she liked. Two thousand a week would go a long, long way.

"God, it's good to see you. You've never looked more beautiful." Bill was practically in tears. He stood back after their initial embrace and stared at her. She smiled warmly and generously at him.

"I'm so happy to see you again, too. I wish it were under different circumstances. I know how much you're hurting over Chris, I've thought about him so much this past week."

"It was real decent of you to come, even brave," Bill added.

"Not really. I needed to face the whole thing one last time, and I needed to see you. Can we go somewhere quiet and talk?" Bill came closer to her, taking her hand and leading her outside into Larkin's garden.

The reflecting pool leading from the foyer to the rear yard had been emptied, cleaned, the tile polished, then refilled with water. Like everything else in the house after the police had made their marks, Larkin had ordered his residence cleaned short of fumigation, and the work had been done round the clock all week.

As the spotless water rippled over the marble tiles, Jodi leaned down and ran her hand along the edge. "This water feels like a mountain river," she said, taking her hand out of the cold waters.

"I can't believe you're really here. You're a vision, that's what you are, a present from God! When did you get here?"

"I got in yesterday and spent last night in a hotel room... with room service, and I watched your show. I thought it was really good."

Bill looked perplexed.

"Why didn't you call? I would have met you at the airport. We could have had that much more time together. I don't get it."

Jodi spotted an iron bench in the yard, got up from the fountain, and asked Bill to join her. "I wanted to see you again in person to tell you something important," she said.

Bill jumped in immediately before she could say another word. "I'll never ask you to be my work partner again, I promise. I swear we'll move out of downtown tonight after we leave here, you can rent any place you like, we'll stay at the Hotel Bel Air again until we find the right place." Jodi's presence neutralized so many of Bill's bad feelings, the emptiness caused by Chris's death, the anger over Randy. He felt that Jodi was medicine for his soul, for his heart.

"This is going to be a lot harder than I ever thought," Jodi offered quietly as she took Bill's hand. "Seeing you again in person makes me less confident of what I have to say." She took a long pause and then found the courage to say, "I'm in love...with a guy I met right after Christmas at home. He's a doctor... He asked me to marry him last week and I said yes."

Nothing in life ever was what it appeared to be. Reality wore such brilliant disguises. Bill had no idea what to say. He was devastated. Suddenly overwhelmed with grief, he'd lost his best friend and now the girl he'd loved had come to tell him she was getting married. Jodi tried to help him understand her feelings and decisions with more explanation, but the more she said the worse he felt, and the less he understood.

Jodi got up from the iron bench, gently releasing Bill's hand. She began to walk out of his life through the growing crowd of mourners that had overflowed from the house into the sculpture garden.

Bill snapped out of his glum stupor to realize that Jodi had flown three-thousand miles just to say good-bye. He began to feel a desperate need to see her one last time. Maybe he could win her back. Maybe there still was a chance. As he lost sight of her in the crowd, she reached the front door of Larkin's house. Just as she was about to walk through it, Bill came up behind her.

"You know, doctors have to go out at all hours of the night to work," he said, smiling.

"Writers and producers don't bother to even come home at all," she replied in a soft voice.

"Doctors are faced with so much life and death tension it can take its toll on their emotional stability," Bill added. "Producers live or die with each project, each meeting, one phone call," Jodi said, once again taking Bill's hand.

"All those nurses. Doctors are always around all those, those seductive nurses. You know what they say about nurses," Bill laughed a little at his own absurdity.

"And all those little blonde sainted actresses, every one raised in a convent by nuns!" Jodi had all the answers.

"Well, there you go. It's all really just the same, whether you go back to Philadelphia and marry the doctor, or stay in California and marry the producer. At least if you stay here, well, you'll save the airfare back. And besides, you're here already anyway, and you are the most beautiful woman I've ever seen… and I love you so much… I'll never get over you if you leave again, never." He moved closer to Jodi with those last words and kissed her. They remained in an embrace for a time as mourners circled around them. Bill and Jodi held each other, undisturbed, practically invisible.

As they slowly parted, she quietly whispered, "I'll always love you... but it's time to say good-bye. My flight leaves in a couple of hours and I've got to get back to the hotel first. Wish me luck, okay? I'm going to be very happy and so are you. I know you will, you'll see. Don't be so hard on yourself. God, you're whole life is ahead of you and you know what?"

"What?" Bill asked.

"You really are special. You're a real person in an unreal town. Don't forget that."

Bill said nothing, he just kissed Jodi again for the last time, a final kiss.

"Okay, Jodi. I'll do that." Bill held back his tears. "Chris always told me that you'd come back, that we'd be together again. I guess he was only half right."

"Yes, I guess so." Jodi squeezed Bill's hand, then turned and walked through the open door, past the continuing flow of entering well-wishers and obligated drop-ins. She didn't look back.

"Excuse me. Pardon me, I'm looking for David Larkin. Can you tell me where I can find Mr. Larkin?" The deep, booming voice of a large man sounded out amidst the latest entering throng. The man was looking about in all directions. Bill was still standing in the same spot where Jodi had left him seconds earlier. He saw the man coming towards him.

"Excuse me, have you seen David Larkin? Can you tell me where I might find him?" the large man asked Bill. A waiter stopped and offered them champagne or wine off his silver tray. Bill accepted a glass of wine, the other man refused.

"I'm sorry, I haven't seen him at all since I arrived. Why don't you check with Mr. Lee, his houseman. I saw Lee go towards the living room over there." Bill pointed the large man in Lee's direction and then took a large gulp of the wine. The man went in search of Mr. Lee, followed by three others. Bill didn't recognize any of them.

Mr. Lee was supervising the caterer in the living room. The entourage of strangers approached him as he was rearranging trays of food set out for the guests.

"Excuse me, Mr. Lee, can you direct me to your boss, Mr. Larkin?"

"Detective Arnold. What you doing here today?" Lee replied, upset to see the policeman in David Larkin's house.

"I need to see Mr. Larkin. Where can I find him?" Arnold repeated.

"He upstairs in his room. I take you." Lee left the trays and moved quickly out of the living room followed by Arnold and his men. The unlikely assemblage ascended the formidable stairs to the second floor.

Mr. Lee knocked loudly on David Larkin's closed bedroom doors. Larkin came to the door and opened it.

"Mr. Larkin, Detective Arnold is here to see you," Lee said dutifully, with a horrified look on his face.

"I can see that, Mr. Lee. Thank you. You may go. I'm sure the gathering downstairs needs your supervision." Lee nodded and walked away with the same intensity and speed of his arrival.

"What do you want, gentlemen?" Larkin opened his door only part way for Arnold and his men to enter. Arnold said nothing as they entered. The last man shut Larkin's door behind him.

Larkin turned to face Arnold. For a moment there was an awkward silence in the dimly-lit bedroom suite. Then, taking a deep, full breath, Arnold began, "Mr. Larkin, I'm here to arrest you for the murder of Peter Barker. You have the right to remain silent, the right to..." Arnold's speech of rights was surreal to Larkin. He'd written it so many times for characters in his movies and TV shows.

Two of Detective Arnold's men placed handcuffs on the suspect, following the recital of the Mirandas.

"You'll have to come with us now, Mr. Larkin," Arnold said.

"I didn't think I had a choice," D.L. replied. "Do you know how absurd this is, Detective? I didn't kill Peter Barker. I can't believe you have a case it's just too impossible to believe..."

The men led a handcuffed David Larkin out of his master suite and back down his stairs into the crowd. Suddenly, all eyes were on the police procession. Larkin stood tall and was silent, as Detective Arnold held his arm and guided him through the crowd. Bill rushed up to Larkin to see if he could help.

"David, what's this all about?" Larkin said nothing. Detective Arnold was quick to answer for him.

"Mr. Larkin has been arrested for the murder of Peter Barker. Now, if you'll excuse us please?" Arnold was a conquering general enjoying victory. This was his finest hour, announcing the arrest to all of Hollywood, conveniently gathered under the roof of the accused man.

Larkin looked like a political prisoner, defeated, confused by his arrest, wanting to scream out his innocence to the masses of wondering comrades all around him. But he did nothing and said nothing, his dignity intact. Arnold and his men escorted him out to the waiting police cars.

John Moran grabbed Bill while he was watching Larkin disappear into a patrol car. Moran was shaking.

"Bill, I want you to meet me at the studio, in my office in one hour. You got that? One hour." Moran ran off without any response from Bill, gathering loyal troops around the room, issuing orders, and then rushing out the door.

• • •

The studio was a ghost town on Saturday afternoon, with or without half of the employees at a funeral. Bill walked down the long dark hallway on the top floor of the executive building towards John Moran's office. The door was open, he entered finding the executive behind his desk writing. Moran looked up and saw Bill standing before him, silent, at the edge of his desk.

"Sit down, Parker. I'll be done with this memo in two seconds." Moran continued to scribble a mass of wordage on his yellow legal pad, and Bill waited. Upon finishing his missive, Moran spoke, at first without looking up at Bill at all.

"Larkin's arrest complicates life around here," he said. "I am going to step in temporarily as the executive producer on the show. I want you to be the producer and head writer under me."

Bill said nothing, Moran went on, patting himself on the back, the Lone Ranger to the rescue.

"It's going to be tough for me to cover both sides of the fence, wear two hats so to speak, but I have no choice. Where are you with the next few weeks of scripts?"

Bill stared at him. The silence was so uncomfortable, Moran repeated his question to Bill about the scripts. Bill finally answered.

"They're in fair shape. Outlines are solid, no dialogue yet."

"Did Larkin make particular writing assignments on any of them?" Moran continued his questioning.

"No. Not yet. He was set to get going on Monday."

"That'll be difficult from the county jail," Moran said smugly.

"How do you know that he won't be out on bail and back to work on Monday?" Bill said sharply.

"Because Larkin's being held without bail. At least for now. The studio lawyers have already checked."

"Boy, you guys really do have all the bases covered." Bill was caustic.

"Look Parker, we didn't kill Peter Barker. We've got a business to run here."

"Do you really think Larkin did?" Bill replied.

"How the hell do I know?" Moran said.

"Well, you've known Larkin for years. Don't you have a feeling for the man, whether he's capable of murder?" Bill kept after Moran, just as he had grilled Larkin over Chris's death a week before. He was desperately looking for a hint of humanity in him.

"I told you, I don't know," was all Moran offered.

"God, I can't believe what's happening!" Bill put his head in his hands.

Moran stood up behind his desk and shouted, "Are you in, or are you out, Parker? I need an answer now. Will you produce and write this show with me, at least for an interim period, until we straighten things out around here?"

Bill raised his head and faced Moran. "Yes. I'll do it. I'm not here for an interim period, I'm here for the duration." Larkin's harsh words of warning about the backstabbing nature of the business haunted Bill as he made his deal with John Moran. The "almighty's" prophecy had indeed come true. The proverbial understudy was replacing the star, hauled off in a police car.

CHAPTER 31

Beverly Hills
Five Years Later, September, 1980

I t was time for Bill Parker to go before an internationally televised tribunal of his peers at the Emmy Awards. The joy of being nominated as a producer for the "Best Dramatic Series" had been drained out of him over the fear of losing. Winning had been a wonderful fantasy. Now it was an absolute necessity. An Emmy tonight would put Bill's name on a contract tomorrow. After all, everybody loves a winner. And what's a Future Hollywood Mogul without an Emmy?

For a time, Bill thought the best move was to remain aloof, to avoid the ceremony altogether. Wrong, said his new agent. He had to go. Aloof was for Howard Hughes. Even his good pal-turned-superstar, Laurie Dalton, said it was career suicide to avoid the Emmy's. Besides, she told him, it was good luck that she was asked to present the final award of the night which just happened to be — Best Dramatic Series.

The former star of Bill's former TV series was now the hottest female movie ticket in town. Laurie Dalton was a bankable movie star with television in her past.

Laurie left "The Reilly's of San Marino" following a fifth year contract dispute. Her exit created a Hollywood shuffle that ultimately wiped out her friend and champion producer, Bill Parker. He took all the heat for losing her. The studio and network bosses screamed for blood, and when the ratings went on a downward dive as a result of her absence, Bill's best writing wasn't enough for them.

The cause of his problem was now his date for the Emmys. Bill loved Laurie. Actually, they were both in love with each other, but they had never slept together. In the world of show business, both of them were survivors, and they were still just in their twenties. Their talents and brain power and looks matched. But their hearts just never collided. Too many others had come in-between. Grand schemes and goals had united them and kept them apart. Nothing poetic, no Romeo and Juliet, just another bizarre Hollywood love story without a familiar ending.

Bill often thought about loving Laurie. Then he thought about Benton Stein. Years after Randy's death, she still was involved with Benton on occasion. And there were a lot of other rich and powerful men in and out of her life. Bill didn't fit. But, he was her date for the evening, so he straightened the bow tie and cummerbund of his tuxedo. He was late, and the limo was outside, waiting in his driveway.

The National Emmy Awards telecast began at 5:00 p.m. in Los Angeles. All the Hollywood players were expected by 4:00 for the arrival circus and the obligatory "How does it feel to be nominated?" interviews. How odd it was, Bill thought, to be dressed in a tux at four o'clock in the afternoon, especially in the near one-hundred-degree heat of Indian Summer in Los Angeles. Bill wiped the sweat from his neck, and took another look in the mirror. Approving his image one final time, he left the security of his home, got into the rented limo and was off to pick up Laurie for the telecast.

A procession of black and blue limousines crowded all of the easterly arteries of The City of Angels. Several thousand people, two-by-two, in black tie and glitter, all bound for Mecca. Laurie and Bill begged the driver to crank up the air conditioning. Their formally attired flesh was sticking to the formally upholstered blue velour seats in the rear of the stretch limousine that the studio had sent for them. It was no use, the driver replied. He had turned the air up all the way. The traffic jam wasn't helping, either. The car was beginning to overheat.

The limo made the rest of the journey downtown with the rear windows lowered. Bill kept the ice water flowing from the stocked limo bar. Laurie raised the crystal glass to toast her friend.

"To the only straight man I've ever loved and never fucked. May you return home tonight with another lady in this car called 'Emmy'." Laurie smashed her glass of ice water into Bill's. The force sent water spilling over the front of his tuxedo. "You're all wet," Laurie laughed, trying to brush the water off his jacket.

"Washed up. That's what I heard," he answered, smiling.

"That'll all change tomorrow. You'll see." Laurie was confident that Bill was going to win.

"Hey, let's skip this circus, hijack the limo, and head for Tijuana." Bill put his arm around her.

"You want to make love to me in Tijuana?"

"It crossed my mind. Especially since I'm the only straight man you've never fucked."

"That's not what I said — and you know it!"

"Tijuana or the Emmy's?" Bill asked.

"Boy, that's some choice. How could a girl refuse a proposition so romantic?"

The driver hit the gas, propelling the limousine up the 3rd Street hill in downtown Los Angeles. The Dorothy Chandler Pavilion was over the crest, the final destination of the over-heated journey. With the windows down, they could now hear the fans screaming with each star-studded arrival in front of the massive complex. Their turn was coming. Tijuana was now just another dashed fantasy for Bill Parker.

As they arrived, the driver put the windows back up, and the air back on, what there was of it. Fans lined the street ten-deep, arms outstretched, desperate to touch the passing fame.

"This is it," the driver warned them. "We're here."

The rear door was opened by a TV network usher wearing a red jacket and black bow tie. Red velvet stanchions were supposed to keep the adoring throngs back, but with each door that opened, the sea of fans furiously lapped over the ropes.

Bill, who was sitting next to the door facing the crowd, blocked Laurie from the fans who were saying, "Who's that?" "I don't see anybody," "It's nobody," until Bill Parker stepped out of the car revealing The Star in full glory.

"Oh, my God, it's HER," one woman screamed out before Laurie had stepped out of the automobile. With that, the pushing began and the velvet barrier truly became the useless symbol of separation that it indeed was. Security guards and ushers appeared like Marines from out of nowhere. When it was safe, Bill reached out for Laurie as she stepped out of the limo into a lightning storm of photographic flashing.

The screams were deafening. Aphrodite had arrived at the Temple of Zeus. Hollywood chronicler of the famous, Army Archerd, introduced her to the crowd, and to the audience at home glued to their TV sets. "You're here tonight as both a nominee for Best Actress in a Dramatic Series, and also as a presenter, I'm told."

"That's right, Mr. Archerd," Laurie cooed.

"Please, call me Army," he replied, taking her by the hand and offering his microphone for more.

"I was lucky enough to win last year, Army. Two years in a row would be too much to hope for."

Bill stood behind her in the shadows. Suddenly, Laurie reached behind her, grabbing Bill and pulling him forward.

"Army, this is Bill Parker. He's up for Best Producer/Best Dramatic Series, tonight. And my bet is that he's got it in the bag!"

"Mr. Parker, a pleasure to meet you," said Army into the microphone. "Ladies and gentlemen, meet Bill Parker, the producer of 'The Reilly's of San Marino'. We wish you both the best of luck, tonight. Laurie, before you go, tell me what's next for you?"

"I'll be starting a new movie in a month or so. It's a thriller, set in Europe on the Riviera. Bill's going to be with me, too." Laurie reached behind Bill, who was standing close to her, and pinched him on his backside.

"He'll be producing the film?" Army asked.

"Sorry, Army, we've got to go... love you, Army. Thanks!"

Bill and Laurie were then thrust down the tunnel of fame into the Dorothy Chandler Pavilion as the crowd and the press landed the next big limo fish. As the pair walked down the center aisle towards their seats, heads turned like dominos falling as they went by. Bill held Laurie close. He was her friend, date, and bodyguard.

"What movie, and what am I doing?" Bill spoke in a hushed tone, while nodding and helloing everyone as they walked by.

Laurie smiled, leaned down, and kissed a man sitting on the aisle.

"Who was that?" Bill asked.

"Some guy on the aisle," she replied.

"Oh, I see."

Bill took Laurie's arm and proceeded down the pushily carpeted runway behind the usher. Just as another one of Laurie's admirers sitting in an aisle seat reached out to congratulate the star, Bill saw a man that he recognized instantly. He froze.

The man now had a full head of grey hair, and his ramrod posture had given in to age and harder times. But it was him. He still wore those oversized, black horn-rimmed dark signature glasses, and the impeccable tailored tux that fit like he'd been born wearing the silk-trimmed gabardine.

As Laurie turned toward Bill to see why he'd stopped so suddenly, she saw the man, too. "Oh, my God, it's David," she gasped, clutching Bill's arm tightly. The usher tried in vain to get the star-crossed couple to follow him to their V.I.P. seats. It was no use.

David Larkin was walking up the aisle, right at them. Despite his dark glasses, Bill knew that the almighty's pupils were fixed on him.

"I heard that he was back in town a few weeks ago," Laurie whispered to Bill, still smiling and waving to the crowd, her image intact. Bill said nothing. His mind whirled. He could feel his heart pounding in his chest. Droplets of sweat formed on his brow.

David Larkin had spent the better part of two years of his life, along with the better part of his once formidable bank balance, defending himself against the charges of murder in the Peter Barker case. The media blitz surrounding the civic circus had, at one time, been the national buzz.

In the end, Larkin was a free man. A hung jury sent Larkin back to Hollywood in spite of protests from the District Attorney and case Detective Hector Arnold. There would be no rank promotion for Arnold, and, as Larkin soon discovered, there would be no open doors in Hollywood for him. He was now considered to be a living pariah.

To cool off, David Larkin took what money remained and made the South of France his pre-destined Hollywood exile. Larkin did not live in the grand regency environs of Cap di Antibes of Monte Carlo. Instead, he made his home in a small, rented, stone farm house in the hills of Provence. The next three yeas he would write, write, and write some more.

Now he was back in Hollywood, with grey hair and a well-guarded film script that he expected would set tinsel town ablaze.

"What shall we say to him?" Laurie asked Bill as Larkin drew closer.

"He must hate me," replied Bill. "My testimony at his trial did not help him at all."

"You told the truth. It's not your fault that the DA twisted it all. At one point I really thought David was guilty," added Laurie in a feeble attempt to boost Bill's confidence.

"No. It was wrong. I should have done more. The lie was preferred to the truth. This man gave me my start, warned me that Hollywood was a ruthless, stab-you-in-the-back kind of town, and I ended up inadvertently doing just that to him." Bill was so full of remorse he choked on his last words to Laurie as Larkin faced them not one step away.

"Laurie, you look very beautiful. It's good to see you again," Larkin spoke in a subdued yet sincere tone as he reached out for Laurie's hand. She instantly threw her arms around him. They kissed. More than the Hollywood air kiss, less than the real thing.

"It's been so long, David. I'm so sorry about everything, but it's good to see you back," gushed the star as they parted lips. Bill was silent.

"It's good to be back," were Larkin's final words as he left Laurie's side. He was about to pass by Bill without saying a word, continuing to walk up the aisle in the opposite direction. Instead, he stopped right in front of him. They were inches apart.

"Bill, will you call me? I'm in town at the Beverly Hills Hotel, Bungalow 8, for the next week. I want to discuss my project with you."

Bill remained speechless. He remembered that 8 had always been Larkin's lucky number. An awkward moment of silence was finally broken as Bill replied, "David, I'll call. How about tomorrow?"

"That would be just fine — the sooner the better," David answered, walking past them, up the aisle, greeting his comrades along the way as if the five years in exile had been a summer sojourn.

Finally, the now frantic usher was able to escort the golden couple to their privileged perspective. Two seats awaited them, front row center. Surrounded by the most famous faces in the world, Bill and Laurie took their places. For Bill, the Hollywood experience had just reached new heights of absurdity. Alone, near penniless from months of forced unemployment, and living in Beverly Hills, Bill Parker sat in the front row of the internationally televised Emmy Awards, himself nominated as the producer for Best Dramatic Series, his world famous date nominated as Best Actress. His former boss, mentor, friend, whose career he'd literally snatched right from under him through the force of circumstances, had just asked Bill to call regarding a new project. Parker had expected a right hook to his jaw.

Once they were seated, Laurie turned toward Bill. "I want you to come with me on location."

"What? Come on, what would I do?"

"For starters, it would be a great break for you. Six weeks in Europe, the best time of the year. We could travel together... I think it would just be the best, the absolute best." Laurie put her arms around Bill's neck, pulling him close to her and kissing him behind the ear.

"I think every guy in this place would like to be in my shoes right now, but how could I go with you? You'll be working night and day and I'll look like a gigolo along for a ride. It's not my thing."

"So, we'll get you a job on the movie. You'll rewrite my dialogue or something."

Bill didn't have a chance to give Laurie his one word, two letter response. He was interrupted by the opening announcer for the 1980 Emmy Awards. The network director, on an open microphone, began to guide his glittered crowd through the paces before them. Winning an Emmy was no walk in the park. There were rules to follow, although practically nobody ever did. Even the public was aware of that while watching the shows. But the director tried to order the chaotic crowd of two thousand other directors, regardless.

"Please, listen carefully," the director repeated in vain three or four times before the volume began to subside. "All winners are to go to the stage as soon as possible following their announcement. Please, only use the stairs on either stage left or right. My main man — Harry is down there — wave, Harry. There he is, okay. Harry is our first stage manager and he'll get you on stage to accept your award. Okay..."

The director went on for what seemed like an eternity with the rules. Before long, the crowd was at its loudest and the director compensated by turning up the volume on his public address house microphone.

Bill held Laurie's hand, and the two sat in silence, allowing the frenzy around them to hypnotize them into an unexplainable calm. It was as if no one else at all was in that vast hall.

Music began to fill the room, an overture, at last. The lights went to dim, then to dark. And finally, the director wished his cast of thousands good luck.

Laurie gave Bill a kiss on the mouth. "Good luck, my friend. I love you," she said.

He kissed her back and held the moment for as long as he could, giving in to the invisible pressure of the staring all around them. They had barely parted lips before the host, Johnny Carson, finished his opening monologue, and the names of the first nominees were echoing through the Chandler Pavilion.

"…And the final nominee for Best Actress in a Dramatic Series is Miss Laurie Dalton for 'The Reilly's of San Marino'." Camera Two rushed in for a close-up of Laurie in the audience. Bill was in half of the shot until the cameraman moved in on a close-up of her face. For a moment, her eyes were closed and her head bowed in a sort of prayer formation. Fifty-million viewers at home prayed with Laurie.

The usual envelope fumbling, the delay of a joke or two to make the nominees want to kill their presenter, and, finally, relief.

"And the winner is — Laurie Dalton!"

Laurie screamed, literally screamed, hearing her name. She stood up, waiting a moment, again closing her eyes, a quick prayer of thanks. Then, as if all the energy in the universe had gathered in her being, Laurie shook her entire body, hair flying backward, arms outstretched, embracing the stage ahead of her. She was a jet on the runway preparing for take-off.

Laurie's landing on stage was perfection. She'd milked every step along the way. The jaded crowd was in love with her. They watched a legend in the making. Fifty years forward they would remember that walk to the stage. That walk.

Laurie accepted her Emmy and held it against her bosom. The golden world held by the winged character of the statuette indented her flesh at the top of her cleavage. It was the ultimate jewel. Standing at the podium for a television eternity while the crowd cheered her with a standing ovation, Laurie cried.

The show director pounded the control console begging the crowd to stop. His shouting was only audible to the crew interfaced with headsets. "A successful Emmy telecast is an on-time telecast. TV is the medium of the moment. Seconds count," he screamed.

The frenzy was replaced by silence. A total pin-drop kind of silence. Laurie looked forward, straight ahead. A tear ran down her face. She smiled, her eyes flashing, still clutching the Emmy at her bosom.

"This is for Chris," was all she said. Then she walked off the stage with tremendous grace. No rush, no waving, a regal kind of exit is what she gave her crowd. The applause was deafening.

"Who's Chris?" was whispered a thousand times throughout the crowd. Bill knew. Larkin knew. They were probably the only ones that did. So many years had passed. Of all the people in her life to honor. Bill was proud of her.

The two hours between the first award and the last were painful. For Bill, it was filled with a meaningless stream of gushing sycophants clutching their golden gooses. Of course, in part, they were meaningless because they didn't belong to him. Jealousy, frustration, boredom, cynicism, all such monsters in check.

"And, now, ladies and gentlemen, to present the Best Dramatic Series award for 1979, is none other than our Best Actress winner, Miss Laurie Dalton."

Laurie took the podium, the stage, the whole show. Napoleon conquering Europe.

"And the nominees are:

"Peter Elson and Michael Villeneuve for 'The Time of Our Lives'; Peter Seeley for 'Seven Saturdays'; Steven Heller and Gary Grimes for 'Ann and Marty'; and Bill Parker for 'The Reilly's of San Marino'."

The customary, obligatory quad screen-split flashed across the faces and logos of the four nominated shows in front of the millions of fans rooting for their favorite. "The Reilly's" was a definite favorite. The ratings this last season Created by Administrator had never been greater.

Laurie tore open the secret envelope, and peeled out the winning card for her eyes only. "Yes," she screeched, "Bill Parker — for 'The Reilly's of San Marino!'"

The card read, "Peter Seeley — 'Seven Saturdays.'"

THE END

ABOUT THE AUTHOR

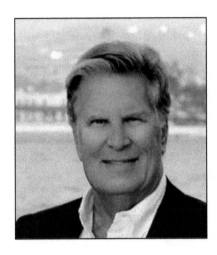

Graduating from USC in 1974, Bruce Cook set out to make it in television. His first real job, following a year of knocking on doors and being turned away, was passing out tickets to "The Mary Tyler Moore Show" for the CBS Television network. He was paid $180 per week, before taxes, and worked out of a six by eight cement windowless bunker in the basement of Television City, Hollywood. He thought he had landed on the moon.

It was the start of a twenty year career that would lead to writing and producing credits including: "The Redd Foxx Show" on ABC where Cook was the youngest producer on a network show in the business at the time, "The Dick Van Dyke Show", "The Lola Faiana Show", "The Marie Osmond Show", "The Diahann Carroll Show", and sitcoms such as "Too Close For Comfort", "Three's Company", and the new "Lassie".

In 1980 he was summoned to Paramount to join a team that would create a ground-breaking concept covering celebrity news. The three-minute sound bite interview was born with the launching of

"Entertainment Tonight" where Cook served as one of the producers for four years garnering two national Emmy nominations. From there he helped to create the iconic "Lifestyles Of The Rich And Famous" followed by "The Late Show Starring Joan Rivers" for FOX, and also worked for the studio of the late and legendary Aaron Spelling in a development capacity.

Today Bruce Cook pens a column for The Daily Pilot/Los Angeles Times. He is also heard on Southern California radio hosting "Bruce Cook Live Sunday Night" on Angels Radio AM830 KLAA. In the genre of sports broadcasting Cook was an original production executive on the team launching the CBS-TV sports division, followed by serving as entertainment producer for the 1984 Olympics in Los Angeles, and then working with the NFL as Super Bowl halftime producer instrumental in transforming the show into its worldwide celebrity phenomenon.

The author of six books, Cook is presently working on a new "coming of age" novel set on the California Riviera. Married with three adult children and four grandchildren, he resides in Newport Beach, California.

Connect with Me Online:

Smashwords:
http://www.smashwords.com/profile/view/mainlinemedia

CPSIA information can be obtained
at www.ICGtesting.com
Printed in the USA
FSHW021747090220
66813FS